Custody

NANCY THAYER

St. Martin's Paperbacks

This novel is a work of fiction. Any inaccuracies about the Probate and Family Court system in the Commonwealth of Massachusetts are my own.

CUSTODY

Copyright © 2001 by Nancy Thayer.

Library of Congress Catalog Card Number: 2001041980

ISBN: 0-312-98498-7

Printed in the United States of America

St. Martin's Press hardcover edition / November 2001
St. Martin's Paperbacks edition / January 2003

St. Martin's Paperbacks are published by St. Martin's Press, 175 Fifth Avenue, New York, NY 10010.

10 9 8 7 6 5 4 3 2 1

More . . .

AN ACT OF LOVE

"I just couldn't put it down . . . I couldn't guess who was telling the truth."

—*Good Housekeeping*

"Anyone who wants to get inside the skin of a contemporary woman simply has to open Nancy Thayer and start reading."

—Elizabeth Forsythe Hailey

"Thayer [creates] a moving chronicle of one family's pain."
—*Publishers Weekly*

"A brilliant novel . . . The four main characters and the support cast come across as genuine, real people struggling to deal with the cataclysm that has left them all raw and in near ruin. In the hands of a magician like Nancy Thayer, the story line is less soap and more genuine, turning this into a classic reading experience that should not be missed by fans of relationship novels."

—Harriet Klausner, *Painted Rock Reviews*

ST. MARTIN'S PAPERBACKS TITLES BY NANCY THAYER

Between Husbands & Friends

An Act of Love

Three Women at the Water's Edge

Belonging

FOR MY LOVELY MOTHER,
JANE FINDLY WRIGHT PATTON,
AND FOR MY LOVELY MOTHER-IN-LAW,
MARTHA JOHNSON WALTERS

ACKNOWLEDGMENTS

I COULDN'T HAVE WRITTEN this book without the assistance of many informed and generous people.

My deepest gratitude and most profound admiration to: the Honorable Sheila E. McGovern, First Justice of the Middlesex County Probate and Family Court; the Honorable Beverly W. Boorstein, Associate Justice of the Middlesex County Probate and Family Court; the Honorable Angela Maria Ordonez, First Justice of the Nantucket County Probate and Family Court; and the Honorable Paula Marie Carey, Associate Justice of the Middlesex County Probate and Family Court.

I am tremendously indebted to Sylvia Howard, Register of Probate, Nantucket County Probate and Family Court, for her kindness, knowledge, inspiration, and assistance.

Enormous thanks go to Jennifer Maggiacomo, Assistant Register of Probate, and Maria Nannini-Dunn, Assistant Register of Probate, Middlesex County Probate and Family Court.

Many thanks to Sophia C. O'Brien, M.Ed., Chief Probation Officer, and Kevin Coughlin, M.A., Assistant Chief Probation Officer, Middlesex County Probate and Family Court.

Also to Barbara B. Hauser, LICSW, Director, Family Service Clinic, Sherry B. Moss, M.A., clinical social worker, and Adam Rosen, J.D., Ph.D., licensed clinical psychologist.

Thanks also to Al Moses, Assistant Chief Court Officer, and Joe Barbati, Court Officer, Middlesex County Probate and Family Court.

Much appreciation to Massachusetts State Representative James Marzilli.

On Nantucket, my thanks to Kevin Dale, attorney. Also, to Tim Howard, Court Officer; Michelle Cranston, First Assistant Register; and Susan D. Beamish, Deputy Assistant Register of the Nantucket County Probate and Family Court.

I send my thanks to Dr. Elizabeth Panke, Director, Genetica DNA Laboratories.

Many thanks to librarian Susan Pitard, for her help in understanding twelve-year-old girls.

Thanks to the multi-talented Buzz Williams and the beautiful Min Adinolfi, and to George Hull.

Many thanks to my editor, Jennifer Weis, and my agent, Emma Sweeney.

And as always, much love and continuing gratitude to Josh Thayer, Sam Wilde, Dionis Gauvin, Jill Hunter Wickes, Pam Pindell, Martha Foshee, and my husband, Charley Walters.

Custody: n.
1. a guarding or keeping safe; care; protection; guardianship
2. detention; imprisonment

Webster's New World Dictionary, College Edition, 1968

PROLOGUE

September 5, 2000

SOME DAYS, KELLY THOUGHT, ARE more important than others. Some days you wake with your heart pounding and your hopes higher than the sky. Some days you know you are exactly where you are meant to be.

Today, the first Tuesday in September, Kelly drove, in the early morning sunshine, down Cambridge Street, feeling like a well-read traveler entering a foreign country for the first time.

This was a day she would remember all her life. This was the day she began the work she had dreamed of, sacrificed for, and worked toward steadily and without rest for thirteen years.

During the past month she had become slightly accustomed to wearing the black robe and accepting the deferential greeting of "Judge." But for the past month she had been sitting on cases with other judges, moving through various courtrooms in the Commonwealth, as she went through the standard month of training that all Massachusetts Probate and Family Court judges receive before they sit alone.

Today she would sit alone. Leaving the heavy traffic, she turned off onto Thorndike Street, entered a lot, and parked her silver Subaru in a space reserved with her name. She stepped out of her car, clicked it locked, and looked up at the stately back of the century-old, four-story, redbrick courthouse.

Here she would render justice. Here she would listen to, evaluate, and then—using all her wisdom, knowledge, logic, and fierce intellectual skill—decide, entirely by herself, the fates of the people who stood before her.

She was only thirty-five years old, but she was competent. She was ready. She knew, better than anyone else, how hard she had worked for this.

With her own key, she let herself in through the back entrance of the courthouse. Inside, she nodded at the security guard as she shouldered through the throngs crowding the central lobby and side halls. So early in the morning, the noise of whispers and coughs, shoes clicking across corridors, briefcases snapping shut swirled up through the balconied floors toward the blue and gold dome. Too impatient for the ancient elevator, Kelly hurried up the smooth, wide steps, their marble worn into silky troughs. The crowded hallways buzzed with whispered consultations, arguments, greetings and laughter, filling her with a calm exultation as she hurried to her chambers.

Her chambers!

Printed in gold on the glass door were the words:

> JUDGE KELLY MACLEOD
> PRIVATE
> DO NOT ENTER

With a shiver of anticipation and a blissful sense of entitlement, she opened the door. She entered.

"Good morning, Judge." Her secretary, an Asian woman in a plaid suit, was already at her desk, up to her elbows in cases and folders.

"Good morning, Luanne."

"Good morning, Judge."

Kelly smiled at the court officer, a tall, bald, stately African-American, in his navy blue uniform. "Good morning, Ed."

"Good morning, Judge." Dignified in her beige silk suit and pearls, Sally Beale, Kelly's clerk, was the key to a smooth transition into this court. Sally had been here for a dozen years. Sally knew everything.

"Great suit," Kelly told her.

"Thank you, Judge." She was reserved, treating Kelly with respect, and Kelly was grateful. Sally had known Kelly as a law student, a fledgling lawyer, a pro bono activist, and a judicial applicant. If anyone had an idea of how far Kelly had come, it was Sally.

"What have we got today?" Kelly asked, looking toward the door to the courtroom. That door was all that stood between this place of quiet and the storm of human lives.

Sally handed her the trial list. "First, a quick and easy divorce. Then a child custody case. That won't be short, and it won't be sweet."

"Then we'd better begin."

"Right. See you out there." Sally slid through the door into the churning whispers of the courtroom.

Kelly took her black robe off the hanger, pulled it on over her gray pantsuit, adjusted the shoulders and collar. Some of the older women judges wore beautiful scarves at the neckline, but Kelly wanted to keep her image severe for now. Quickly she scanned her reflection in the mirror hanging on the closet door. She'd subdued her blond hair in a twist at the back of her head, and not a hair had dared escape. Fine. She looked fine. No reason to hesitate. She nodded to Officer Harris.

He asked, "Ready, Judge?"

"Ready."

He opened the door.

Kelly walked into the courtroom.

Her courtroom.

She'd been in this room before, many times, as a lawyer representing one side or another in a divorce or child custody case. The enormous room was brightened by many windows, its walls painted a peaceful pale blue trimmed with cream. The ceilings were perhaps twenty feet high. The wood of the railings, witness stand, conference tables, clerk's and judge's bar, officer of the court's station, was golden oak, darkened by the years, glowing with the patina from the touch of generations of petitioners, lawyers, registers, and judges.

It was a lovely room.

Behind her, his voice rich and solemn, Officer Harris announced, "Hear ye, Hear ye, Hear ye. Court, all rise. The Middlesex Probate and Family Court is now in session, the Honorable Judge Kelly MacLeod presiding. God save the Commonwealth of Massachusetts."

The Honorable Judge Kelly MacLeod settled in her chair behind the high bench, her black robe resting at her ankles. She nodded good morning to the court stenographer, then looked out, with confidence, at the courtroom.

She saw, as she knew she would, clusters of people seated in the gallery. She saw a couple, well-dressed, elegant, and miserable, sulking next to their attorneys at the lawyers' table. Their divorce. Her first case.

Beyond the railing, she saw a lovely, slender, blond woman, the female plaintiff in the child custody case, with her lawyer.

She saw another lawyer speaking to the male defendant in the child custody case.

And she saw, with a terrible thrill, that this was the man whom, over the past few months, she had secretly known, secretly met, and secretly come, desperately, to love.

ONE

August 3, 2000

AT FOUR O'CLOCK ON THE first Thursday in August, a small, elite group gathered in the waiting room of the Governor's executive suite in the gold-domed State House in Boston, Massachusetts. Some of the most powerful and respected officials in the Commonwealth were there: the Governor, the Chief Justice of the Probate and Family Court Department, three judges, and several attorneys.

They were all there because of Kelly MacLeod.

This afternoon she would be administered the oath of office as Associate Justice of the Middlesex County Probate and Family Court.

At thirty-five, Kelly MacLeod was the youngest woman ever to become a Massachusetts judge.

And at this moment, she certainly felt young.

From the far end of the hall came the hum and rustle of nearly eight hundred people gathering for the ceremony in the state legislative chambers. Kelly's mouth was dry. Her knees were weak. Her mind was blank.

Her fiancé, Jason, strode toward her through the crowded room. The scion of a wealthy Boston family, the son of a lawyer, a lawyer himself, Jason drew admiring looks as he passed. Now he put his hands on Kelly's shoulders in a steadying way and said, "You look beautiful."

Dutifully she replied, "Thank you." The truth was, she didn't want to look *beautiful*, whatever that meant. She wanted to look intelligent and dignified, and perhaps—she was six feet tall, she could achieve this—*imposing*.

She'd better settle for beautiful. She'd better settle for *conscious*. Here she stood, about to realize her life's grandest dream, and she thought she might faint. Her lungs seemed paralyzed. She put one hand on her chest. Her throat was closing. She was drowning in the air.

"I'm going out to join Mother," Jason told Kelly.

She nodded.

"You'll do fine," he said. He planted a kiss on her hair, right next to her cheek.

Had he mussed her hair? She'd worked fiendishly to subdue it in a French twist.

Judge Colburn, Kelly's role model and mentor for the past few years, appeared at her side. She had gray hair, solemn black eyes, a wise and wrinkled face, and an ability to read minds.

"Your hair is perfect. Everything's perfect, Kelly. This is your day. We're all so proud of you."

Judge Linda Steinberg approached her, slowly, limping slightly. "It's time," she said.

Kelly nodded. Here it was, the moment for which she'd been striving all her adult life, and she was on the verge of blacking out.

"Deep breaths," Judge Colburn said. "Look at me, Kelly. Deep breaths." She demonstrated, putting her hand on her diaphragm and breathing in slowly.

"Deep breaths," the nurse had coached Kelly. "Look at me, Kelly. Deep breaths. . . ."

Looking into Judge Colburn's eyes, Kelly put her hand on her own diaphragm. She pulled sweet air into her lungs.

The sergeant-at-arms, complete with top hat and staff, approached. "Ready?"

Judge Steinberg looked at Kelly. "Ready?"

Kelly smiled. "Ready."

Judge Steinberg turned to the others in the room.

"All right, everyone," she said. "Show time."

They fell into line: the Governor, the judges, the attorneys, and Kelly. They walked down the majestic marble halls.

When they came to the wide center doors, the deputy clerk pounded the gavel three times. The sound reverberated through the air, hushing the crowd.

"Oyez. Oyez. Oyez. All rise," the deputy clerk called out. "The Honorable Governor of the Commonwealth of Massachusetts, accompanied by Judge Designate Kelly MacLeod. Please rise."

Kelly broke out in goose bumps from head to toe.

Eight hundred people stood to watch the group filing in.

The sergeant-at-arms led them in stately ceremonial step into the magnificent House Chamber. They entered through the center doors and walked single file down the aisle, over the bright blue rug with its gold fleurs-de-lis to the front of the room.

Three massive chairs of black leather and ornately carved wood waited at the dais between the flag of the United States and the flag of the Commonwealth. Governor Hamilton took a chair, the Chief Justice of the Probate and Family Court Department, Judge Steinberg, took a chair, and Kelly took one. The other judges sat in the first row, where family members would ordinarily sit.

Kelly smoothed her cream silk pants and suit jacket, aware that hundreds of people were smiling at her: friends, colleagues, former clients. It had taken her long hours into the night to compile her list and address the invitations she'd had printed. Now she was glad she'd made the effort. It was wonderful that so many people had come.

It almost made up for the fact that no one she could call family was here.

Ironic, really, since she was about to become a family court judge.

"Good afternoon," Judge Steinberg greeted the assembly.

The hum of voices quieted. People settled in their seats. The room was still.

"We are gathered here today to witness our good friend Kelly MacLeod receive the oath of office as Associate Justice of the Middlesex County Probate and Family Court," Judge Steinberg announced. "This is an honor and a charge of great magnitude. In all of the Commonwealth of Massachusetts there are only forty-nine justices in the Probate and Family Court, and they are appointed to serve until the age of seventy. We put our trust for today and for the future into the hands of our justices, and we give our trust to Kelly MacLeod with great elation."

Kelly looked out at the audience. She spotted Professor Hammond, one of her first law professors, in his sagging tweed and bow tie. In a dress of flowered silk, Sally Beale, the woman who as a register of the probate court had taught her so much of the real work of justice. Donna Krebs, her best friend and colleague, buttoned up tight in a navy blue suit, trying to look solemn, but grinning like an idiot while tears sparkled in her eyes. Stout Fred Dunlap and lean Wallace Reed, senior partners in the firm where for seven years Kelly had had her professional home. Scattered throughout the crowd, other lawyers and clerks and secretaries. Some policemen. Some members of the Probation Department and the Family Service Clinic. She saw her fiancé, Jason, his face flushed with pride, and his mother, Eloise, sitting next to him, turning the diamonds on her fingers, looking completely bored.

There had been only one time in all her life when she had missed—when she had needed—her own mother more.

Judge Steinberg was saying, "Everyone here today knows Kelly MacLeod. We have studied with her, worked with her, built cases with her, heard her argue cases before us. We have fought with her. In many cases we have fought against her. And always, we have admired her. Perhaps we think we know her. Today we have invited three different people to tell us about the Kelly MacLeod they know."

"First, we would like to introduce Bettina Florez."

A plump young woman approached the podium. No one would ever have called her pretty, because all the lines of her face were too extreme: her jaw protruded in a triangular wedge, her enormous nose featured nostrils that were larger than her small black eyes, and her tight bush of black hair could not conceal her elephantine ears. But she carried her head high, and though her hands trembled as she lifted the pages of her speech, her eyes burned with pride as she looked out at the crowd—and as she looked at Kelly, they softened with love.

"My name is Bettina Florez," the woman said. "I first met Kelly MacLeod twelve years ago through the Big Sister program. She was just beginning her first year of law school, she was living in a two-bedroom apartment in Somerville with three other women, and she drove a fifteen-year-old Chevy with one hundred and sixty-five thousand miles on it. I do believe that car was in the shop more than it was on the road."

Bettina smiled then, and the audience smiled with her, for her smile was a lovely sight.

"Kelly was working weekends and nights as well as attending law school, but she always found a way to spend time with me at least two days a week, and she never once canceled a date. I was fifteen years old then, living in Roxbury with my mother and my three brothers and sisters. I was smart, but I was starting to do drugs, mostly just to have a crowd to hang with. I was never a very popular girl, and I was very lonely. I think it's fair to say that I also wasn't the most charming of children."

Kelly smiled to herself, thinking, *That's an understatement.* For their first few months together, Bettina either refused to talk or muttered profanities.

"Kelly had hardly any money herself, but she took me to museums and lectures and concerts. She brought me to her apartment and showed me how someone with very little money could still have a decent life and, more important, have hope. Kelly loves to read and she started a reading program with me, introducing me to the works of Toni Morrison and Maya Angelou and Julia Alvarez. She couldn't afford a bicycle, so she taught me to jog. I had become accustomed to despising myself because I'm so big, but Kelly MacLeod, who is, you might have noticed, six feet tall, taught me to carry myself with pride and dignity.

"I will tell you honestly that my mother gave up on me. My teachers gave up on me. But Kelly MacLeod never gave up on me, not even when I gave her cause—and a great deal of it—to do so. Because of Kelly MacLeod's belief in me and the help she gave me, I not only finished high school, I also attended Bunker Hill Community College. Even when I turned twenty-one and was no longer eligible for the Big Sister program, Kelly continued seeing me at least once a month, even though she was then also working with another Little Sister. She saw me on Christmas Day, and she took me out on my birthday." Bettina smiled at Kelly. "I hope she always will.

"As my life changed, so did hers. She got her law degree, passed the bar exam, and began working for a law firm. She was able to get rid of that old Chevy—which by that time had a rejected sticker on it—and to buy a newer used car. She was able to move into an apartment all her own.

"She was able to loan me money to buy my schoolbooks.

"When all others, including my own mother, saw only a fat, ugly, impoverished, and worthless individual, Kelly MacLeod saw a human being with potential. With her help, I graduated last year from the University of Massachusetts and I have been admitted to the Suffolk Law School, where I will begin my studies this fall with the aim of becoming a paralegal.

"As I look out at this audience, I see the faces of four other women who have been Kelly MacLeod's Little Sisters, and who have become admirable women because of her help. Kelly MacLeod honored me through so many years with her respect and her belief in my potential. I cannot tell you how proud I am to be here today when we honor her.

"One last thing. I know that Kelly asked me to speak today not to praise her, but to tell you all about the Big Sister program, and so I ask a few more moments of your time."

Of course, I believe in reaching out to those who are not connected by family, Kelly thought. If Professor Hammond had not reached out to her, who knows where she might be now? Certainly not here. At a time when she was lost, he had pointed her toward her future. He had made all the difference in her life.

In her junior year at U. Mass, Kelly took Professor Hammond's course on law and society. One day he called her into his office to tell her how impressed he was by her papers and her class participation. She had a quick and incisive mind. Had she considered a career in law?

It was when he asked the question that Kelly knew, in a flash as powerful as true love, what she wanted to do with her life.

Professor Hammond became her mentor. He helped her change her major from political science to pre-law. He suggested books she should read. He told her he'd write such a brilliant recommendation for her that no law school would turn her down.

And when her grandparents died and everything changed, he hadn't given up on her. The assistance he offered her was so extraordinary that no one but a handful of people knew about it.

As was fitting, it had been perfectly legal.

"Sometimes," Bettina Florez was saying, "sometimes your own family, no matter how much they love you, just can't help you, no matter how much they might want to. Sometimes we all need the insight, good will, and sheer hard work of strangers to take us by the hand, *by the hand*, to touch us, to help us see that there is a good path open to us, and to help us onto that good path. To stop us from being the worst person we ever could be, to guide us toward becoming the very best person we could possibly be. To help us dream, and to help us make those dreams come true. That's what Big Sisters can do for their Little Sisters. That's what Kelly MacLeod did for me." She looked right at Kelly. "Kelly, I love you."

"I love you, too," Kelly mouthed back. Today was Bettina's triumph as much as Kelly's.

After the applause died down, Judge Steinberg returned to the podium. "Our next speaker," she announced, "is a woman many of us know and have had the pleasure of working with, Daria Wittington."

The next speaker could not have looked more different from Bettina if she tried. Petite, blond, a symphony of caramel from her frosted pale hair to her tennis-tanned skin clad in fawn silk, Daria radiated wealth and privilege.

"Good afternoon," she said, in the perfectly modulated tones of one quite accustomed to public speaking. "I want to thank Kelly MacLeod for asking me to speak here today because in doing so she allows me the opportunity to tell you about my work, the work for which Kelly has for eight years now volunteered innumerable hours and inestimable expertise. I am the head of MASCC, the Massachusetts Adoption of Special Children Center. We specialize in the placement of children eight years and older who have received, through the misfortunes of fate, extreme mental or physical challenges. Many of these children were born to mothers who were permanent drug users or who were HIV-positive. To be blunt, these are the children no one wants. No one even wants to see them. We don't like to know that they exist. But they *do* exist, and they are human beings just like the rest of us, with the deep, human need to be loved, treasured, nurtured, taught, and valued.

"All of these children have been raised in foster homes with less than optimal conditions. There is never enough money to help these children. We have a small committee of generous patrons who financially support us so that we're able to have an office with a paid secretary. Everyone else who works for MASCC is a volunteer. For eight years now, Kelly MacLeod has spent at least two nights a week helping with the legalities of running a non-profit organization and preparing the necessary adoption papers."

Adoption.

In November of her senior year, Kelly had been summoned to Professor Hammond's office.

He had actually growled. "You haven't applied to law school!"

"No."

"Would you be kind enough to tell me why?"

"I can't afford it."

"So apply for a fellowship. Get a loan."

"Professor Hammond, I wish I could, but I'm already deeply in debt. There have been some . . . changes . . . in my situation." How, Kelly wondered, could the white-haired gentleman sitting before her in his beautiful, ancient tweeds, behind the magnificent desk he'd inherited from his father, comprehend her situation?

She needed to be clear. "I've had to get a loan to finish my senior year. I'm working every night as a waitress at Michael's. I clean houses on weekends. And I can still barely pay the rent on my apartment and buy food and car insurance and gas and health insurance. Oh, yes, and I owe an oral surgeon over a thousand dollars for removing my wisdom teeth!"

"I see." The professor leaned back in his chair, stee-

pled his fingers, and thought. "Can your family help you, perhaps?"

She flinched. "No."

"Well. This is a difficult state of affairs, but not an impossible one. Not unique."

"It's unique for me."

"I wish you'd apply, anyway, Kelly," Professor Hammond urged. "Don't give up."

"I have given up," she told him.

More applause, appreciative murmurs, and the stirring of the assembly brought Kelly back to the present. Daria Wittington returned to her seat. Judge Steinberg introduced the third and final speaker: Professor George Hammond.

He made his way to the podium slowly, hampered by his age—he was in his seventies now—and by the crippling effect of Parkinson's disease. When he began to speak, Judge Steinberg moved to the podium to adjust the microphone for him, for he had trouble projecting his words. Yet when he spoke, the room went still.

"I knew Kelly MacLeod before she helped Daria Wittington with her organization. I knew Kelly before she met Bettina. I knew her when she was only a junior in college, and I would like to say that way back then I was so insightful I knew that Kelly would one day be standing here before us, about to become a judge for the Middlesex County Probate and Family Court.

"But I didn't know that. I didn't have that kind of foresight. What I saw, all those years ago, was only a young woman with a mind both quick and profound. A young woman with a skill for words, a talent for judicious reasoning, and a fierce hunger for knowledge.

"I pride myself on being the person to suggest she choose law for a career. But I could not know, as no one can know, that Kelly MacLeod would have the pure, dogged persistence to make it through the yards of reviews, the miles of legal texts, the mountains of difficult casework, past the traps of vanity and pretension, the siren lure of wealth, and especially the abyss of cynicism and downright exhausted despair to this day.

"But here she is. My pride in her is boundless. My hopes for her are infinite. And this is what I want to say here to her now:

"The Massachusetts court system is the envy of the world. People come from every other country on this planet to study our courts, because in spite of all its faults, and there are many, it comes as close as humanly possible to rendering justice on this earth. What we do here effects not only the parties directly involved in each legal case. Its reverberations extend throughout the Commonwealth, the nation, and the world. The responsibilities of judges are awesome. The consequences are illimitable.

"Those who must come to court do so in the darkest hours of their lives. They cannot see their futures, and their pasts have been shattered like broken mirrors. There is light in their future, but it is the black robe of the judge which, like the expanse of night sky, makes the stars of hope visible. Take away that robe, and the light disappears. Take away that robe, and there is no way to see the dawn of the new day."

Professor Hammond cleared his throat. He took a sip of water. Then he continued.

"I thank you all for bearing with me as I waxed poetic. I have done so in the hope that Kelly MacLeod will carry with her, into her future, the thought of the night sky, and its vastness, which is like the vastness of the responsibilities of the mantle she is about to don."

The crowd applauded slowly, steadily, and then, one by one and in groups, they rose to give the man a standing ovation.

He was probably the most revered man in this room, Kelly thought, and he knew everything about Kelly: *everything*. If anyone could judge her now, as she stood before her peers, it would be Professor Hammond. *He* had judged her, and he approved. He understood, more than any other person alive, what she had sacrificed to her passion for the law.

Judge Steinberg was continuing. "I now am honored," she said, "to introduce to you the Governor of the Commonwealth of Massachusetts, Richard Hamilton."

Blood drummed so loudly in Kelly's ears that she couldn't really hear what the Governor was saying. Then he turned to her and smiled.

So she rose and stepped forward, suddenly and serenely triumphant, and raising her right hand, she began to take her oath of office.

TWO

August 6, 2000

SUNDAY MORNING KELLY SAT CROSS-LEGGED next to her mother's grave. Because the days and nights just after her ceremony passed in a blur of celebration and a scattered attempt at organizing her desk, her calendar, and her life, Kelly appreciated even more than usual the tranquillity of the cemetery today, when the summer air lay lush and heavy against her skin and the traffic of the surrounding city was muted. Only the occasional singing bird broke the silence.

Just when she was wondering whether or not the man would come, as he had every Sunday she'd been here, she saw him walking up the paved lane, a sheaf of lilies in his hand.

Kelly had noticed the man before, and liked the look of him, although she chastised herself for having such thoughts in a cemetery—especially since she was engaged.

But she couldn't help observing that he was there when she arrived each Sunday morning, or appeared soon after, walking up Magnolia Path, carrying fresh flowers—pale yellow roses, white lilies, and once, tulips of a breathtaking coral—in his hands. She admired him for bringing perishable flowers rather than a more durable plant—for wasn't that why we grieve, because what had once been living and beautiful had vanished from the earth forever? She wondered if the grave was his wife's.

In May, even in June, the man had worn a suit and tie, and Kelly had admired that, too: the respect suggested by his attire and the attitude—could you call it optimism?—implied that an invisible spirit was aware of this, the person for whom he mourned, or perhaps God. Or perhaps he dressed so formally only for his own awareness, in which case she admired him more.

He was a tall, broad-shouldered, massive man with a head of silver-blond hair. She'd never been close enough to see the color of his eyes, but she'd bet they were bright blue, Viking eyes, the color of the oceans his ancestors once sailed to fight with bronze spear and shield, conquering countries and earning names such as Fergus the Brave or Ivan the Stouthearted.

She knew she spent too much time thinking about this man.

But how could she help it? Every Sunday morning Kelly visited her mother's grave.

She had done this since her mother's death two months ago, and she thought she might very well continue to do this every week for the rest of her life, because the moment she passed through the Gothic gates of Forest Hills Cemetery, she felt lighter and peaceful. She could be herself here; she could think whatever she wanted to think, or not think at all and simply sit listening to the birds sing. She could catch her breath.

By nature energetic and decisive, by profession critical,

Kelly lived according to more rules, standards, and goals than most people did. In addition was the irrevocable, irreducible fact of her height, a physical reality with psychological consequences. She was six feet tall, and had been the tallest in her class and tortured for it ever since kindergarten, when Donny Ramos, in a burst of creativity, invented the taunt: "Kelly makes me laugh! She's tall as a giraffe!" A fierce kind of pride had forced her then as well as now to stand erect, *never* to stoop, to keep her head high and her shoulders back even if it did, as she grew into her teens, accentuate the shelf of bosom that the toughest sports bra could not conceal.

In the cemetery her height didn't matter, nor did the size of her bosom, the gravity of her profession, the magnitude of her goals, the pettiness of her vanities. Here she was just herself, with many talents and good qualities, and, she supposed, as many flaws as any normal person on this earth.

This morning in the very middle of July steamed with heat. She had parked her car behind the chapel, waved hello to the groundskeeper, and headed up past the Bell Tower along Mulberry Avenue. She wore a short blue sundress and for the sake of coolness had pulled her pale hair up into a careless clump on top of her head and fastened it with a clip. As she walked, long tendrils escaped, curling down around her ears, tickling her skin. Absentmindedly she tucked them back up, and a few minutes later they fell out all over again. She didn't notice, really, or care. Six days of the week her hair was immaculately tamed. This morning, she was free.

She had strolled along Sweet Briar Path, Magnolia Path, Cowslip Path—she loved these names—past Lake Hibiscus, up Fountain Avenue and Tulip Path, until she came to Lilac Path. Here rested not a soaring marble angle or a sober gray tombstone but a small sturdy boulder of granite glistening with pink quartz.

The stone marked Kelly's mother's grave. Next to it

lay the modest flat plaques marking the graves of Ingrid's first husband, Otto, and his mother and father. Interesting, Kelly thought bitterly, that Ingrid chose to be buried here, that her second husband didn't object. But why would he object? The plot had been bought years and years ago when Ingrid and Otto married. It had been waiting for her. It saved René Lambrousco from having to pay for a plot.

Kelly had folded her long legs and sunk cross-legged onto the grass. Closing her eyes, she urged bitterness from her heart and said a prayer. Then she merely sat, letting the worries of the past week seep out of her into the warm silence of the air around her, until she was calm. She talked then, quietly, to her mother. Sometimes she stayed there for as long as an hour.

She'd lost so much time. For years she hadn't spoken to her mother. Hadn't seen her mother. *For years.* She had meant to punish her mother, but now she knew she had punished herself, as well.

She hated feeling grateful to her mother's husband, but she had to be. If René hadn't phoned her, she'd never have known they'd moved back to Boston. Fifteen years of silence stood between Kelly and her mother, a stone wall of silence, thick with hours and days. When Kelly finally reunited with her mother, there had not been enough time left in Ingrid's life for Kelly to lift away, word by word, stone by stone, that barricade. And Kelly had always been aware that her mother was dying. She did not, *could* not, burden her mother with her own sorrows or ask her mother for what she no longer had the strength to give.

While Ingrid was dying, Kelly had been at her bedside as often as possible, but her mother usually slept, and in the latter days Kelly had no idea how much her mother understood of what she told her. There had been a moment, in the middle of one April afternoon, after the doctors and nurses had done what they could for Ingrid MacLeod Lambrousco's suffering body, and before Kelly's stepfather came in from work to spend the evening with his wife, when Ingrid had suddenly opened her eyes and spoken.

"Kelly." Her voice was a low rasp.

Kelly had been proofing an article she'd written for the *Massachusetts Law Journal*. Sun filled the room, glancing off the chrome on all the machines and the bars of the bed, and the air-conditioning hummed, so it seemed they were in the private cabin of a small, steadily traveling boat.

Kelly dropped her papers. "I'm here, Mom."

Ingrid's pale blue eyes shone with a light that had been missing over the past weeks. For a moment she seemed free of pain and also of the drug-induced fog that had dimmed her gaze.

Kelly took her mother's hand in both of hers. Ingrid's skin was dry, papery, hollow-feeling, like a petal past its prime—weightless.

"I love you, Kelly," her mother said.

Kelly's eyes, as pale a blue as her mother's, had filled with tears. "I love you, too, Mommy," she whispered.

Ingrid had smiled. "I know, darling. I've always known. Every single day."

How Kelly had longed then to let it all pour out, to tell her mother everything—about all the decisions she'd made and the sacrifices she'd undertaken during those confusing, amazing, mysterious years when by law she became an adult, yet in her heart was little more than a child, when more than ever she had needed her mother's guidance, but had been prevented from seeking it by her own anger and pride. Kelly wanted her mother to know her as she was now, tempered and forged by the kiln of experience. She wanted her mother to laugh and cry with her, to praise her, to mourn for her—she wanted her mother to say, "I understand. And what you did was right."

But her mother's eyelids had fluttered, and she'd made a tiny coughing noise deep in her throat that alarmed Kelly, who'd risen from her chair, wondering whether she should ring for a nurse. But Ingrid had taken a shuddering breath and said, "Darling, I must sleep."

That was the last real exchange between the two women. Ingrid had not known that Kelly had applied for a judicial position. She had not been alive when the grand news came to Kelly that she had won the appointment. She had not been alive when Kelly took her oath of office. She had not been alive to rejoice or advise.

Kelly still had much to say. She still needed to be with her mother. Somehow she felt she really *was* with her mother in this cemetery where only life and death and love mattered, far away from the laws of man. So she came here every Sunday.

And every Sunday the man came, too.

Today she'd been sitting by the stone for almost an hour when she saw him arrive, clad, in concession to the heat, only in khakis, a blue shirt with the sleeves rolled up, and a tie. Today he looked less like a warrior and more like someone who had once played college football. He strode up Lilac Path, a level below Kelly's mother's grave, and right within her line of view—she didn't have to go out of her way to see him. She couldn't help seeing him.

Still, when he knelt at the foot of the grave, Kelly, out of respect and the wish to give him privacy, rose and quietly moved away. She would walk. She always walked around the cemetery after visiting her mother.

The MacLeod plot lay along Lilac Path, just before the land dropped down to Chrysanthemum Path. Kelly took the higher road to avoid interrupting the man in his devotions, and strolled along Cherry Avenue. She paused for a moment by the modest granite slab marking e. e. cummings's grave. Cummings had written: "if most people were born twice, they'd improbably call it dying."

Wandering past stone and marble monuments, mausoleums with stained glass and wrought-iron portals, past statues of winged angels and fallen soldiers, Kelly wondered, not idly, whether or not cummings was right. Might her mother be alive somewhere, on another plane of existence about which mortals could only dream?

If so, then Kelly's father and *his* parents were alive there as well, in which case Kelly doubted very much that that particular corner of heaven was all sweetness and light.

"How could you!" Kelly's grandparents would demand. "We trusted you. You betrayed us, and you betrayed your daughter as well."

Maybe that would happen. Could happen. Maybe not. Everything Kelly had read or heard on the matter made it seem that once humans left this earthly realm they left behind the woes and worries that had plagued their lives.

Which meant that if there would ever be justice, it had to happen here and now in the world we know. Kelly believed fiercely that one individual could make a difference, that what people do in their lives could tip some kind of invisible scale toward good or evil. She was determined to do what she could to weigh in on the side of good.

Preoccupied by the vague and immaterial thoughts she allowed herself on Sunday mornings, Kelly wandered beneath a bent, witchlike tree, its branches already bearing the hard green knots that would, one day, be apples. The lane curved, forked, and led down to Lake Hibiscus. The sun gleamed on the still surface of the water. Blinking, she reached into her pocket for her sunglasses, overlooked a fallen branch on the path, tripped, and tumbled down, falling flat.

She wasn't hurt, but she felt like an idiot. She sat up, brushing leaves from her hands.

"Are you all right?"

The man came along a path toward her.

For the first time she saw his face directly. He was handsome in a brawny, healthy way, and Kelly felt herself blush. She'd gone down fast, breaking the fall with her hands, but still skinning one of her knees.

"I'm fine. What a dope. I must have been a funny sight." Several locks of her hair had come loose and hung in her eyes. She yanked off the barrette so that all her hair tumbled down around her shoulders, an incorrigible mass that went wild in humidity. She captured it all in her hands and fastened it up on the back of her head.

He grinned. "More startling than funny. I thought an angel had toppled off her pedestal." He offered his hand to help her up.

Reluctantly, because she always felt too tall with most men, she placed her hand in his. With ease he pulled her up, his grip firm. He was strong.

"Thanks."

"You're quite welcome."

She took her hand back, but their gazes held. His eyes were blue, patriot blue. His face was rugged, but not tense with the nerves of a warrior: he looked intelligent and tired and very slightly overweight, and kind. Flushing, she bent to brush imaginary grass from her dress then looked up at him again. She couldn't *stop* looking at him.

She said, "I've seen you here before."

He nodded. "My mother."

"My mother, too."

His mother, not his wife. So he was undoubtedly married; how could he not be married with that fine open-hearted face, like a blond Ernest Hemingway, broad and tanned and generous and masculine, and eyes as clear as goodness.

She cleared her throat. "Recently?"

"Three months."

"Ah. Two months."

They looked down through the trees at the lake. The still water reflected the lush dappling of shadow and sun.

"It's silly, perhaps," Kelly confessed, "but I've gotten into the habit of coming here to talk things over with my mother."

"Not silly. I do the same with mine." He paused. "Although if I'm honest, I often find it a relief that she can't talk back."

Kelly laughed. "I know what you mean."

"Shall we walk?"

"Sure." She fell into step next to him. He was taller than she was, which was unusual. Their strides matched easily. He was older than she'd thought: at least forty, though she couldn't be sure. Something weighed on him. Grief, perhaps. She sensed him studying her face. "I like walking here. Somehow, I can *think* here. It's so peaceful, so quiet."

"And it doesn't matter who you are."

She glanced up at him. "Exactly."

His voice was low and steady. "Well, what better place to reflect upon our lives than here? Wealth doesn't matter here or prestige. We're faced with fundamental truths here. We have to look at life more honestly."

They rounded a bend thick with ancient willows, the thousands of delicate leaves on their bowed branches cascading like a green waterfall.

"And you feel you need to do that?" she asked. "Look at life more clearly?"

Bending, he picked up a pebble and held it in his hand, turning it with long, dexterous fingers, as if it were a talisman. He sighed. He looked at Kelly, out at the lake, down at the small gray rock.

"Well. As a matter of fact, yes. Yes, I have come to a time in my life when I must do a lot of serious thinking. I've thought of seeing a therapist about certain problems—" He smiled at her—he had very straight, white teeth. "Normal problems, I mean. I wouldn't want you to think you're out here alone with a psychopath."

"I don't think that."

"Good. But I don't believe I need a therapist. I just need to slow down and *reflect*."

"Are you at a transitional point in your life?" Kelly asked.

He raised an eyebrow. "Are *you* a therapist?"

She laughed. "No. I'm—"

He held up his hand. "Don't tell me who you are or what you do, and I won't tell you."

"Oh, dear. You *are* a psychopath." Kelly couldn't understand it, but she was happy. It was so easy to talk with this man. It was as if they'd been having conversations all their lives.

"Only my wife thinks so."

"Ah. You're married."

"Separated. In the process of getting divorced. It's a damnably confusing and painful process." He tossed the pebble into the water. It splashed. Concentric rings rippled outward like visual echoes in the clear water. "One that makes me relish all the jokes about lawyers."

"So I've heard."

"And you?"

She hesitated; then she held out her left hand. "I'm engaged."

"Beautiful ring."

"That's true."

"When's the wedding?"

They came to *Ascending Spirit*, the rather contemporary white marble woman sculpted by Thomas Gould. "This is one of my favorites," she said.

"Mine, too." Then he waited.

Now Kelly was the one to sigh. "I don't know. I'm not sure I want to marry Jason."

"Yet you're engaged to him."

She bit her lip, twisting the engagement ring on her hand. When it faced inward, it dug into her palm when her hand was closed, and sometimes she liked the feeling, the little bite of pain.

"When my mother was dying, she wanted so terribly to know that I would be safe, which to her meant being married. She needed to know that someone would love me and take care of me. She liked Jason. Well, I *like* Jason. It made her happy to know we were planning to marry."

"The road to hell is paved with good intentions."

"Oh, Jason wouldn't be *hell*. He's a very nice man."

"My wife is a very nice woman. But I can assure you that marriage to someone you don't really love is a mistake."

"Do you have children?"

"A daughter. Whom we both love. Who will be happier when we're divorced, of that I'm sure."

They began to walk again, ascending a small hill in silence until they reached the summit and saw the lush green tops of trees along the Jamaicaway and the traffic, just bright dots blurring along.

"Perspective," the man said. "That's another thing I like about being here, the way it distances me from the pressing problems of my life. Provides space."

Kelly nodded in agreement. "Jason thinks it's odd that I come here. He's more efficient than I. And competitive."

"With you?"

"With everyone. I think his right eye competes with his left to see farther. He's even ambidextrous."

The man laughed. It was a rich, deep sound, the laugh of someone with a zest for life. "Competition, aggression. They aren't necessarily bad. They can indicate a kind of optimism."

"Yes, I suppose." Kelly considered this as they fell into step, walking back down the hill. "Still, the more Jason pushes at me to name a date, the more resistance I feel. This isn't some kind of contest, I keep telling him. He won't *win* if he forces me to marry him when I'm uncertain. We'll both lose."

"Do you love him?"

Kelly stumbled. The man put his hand on her arm to steady her. She looked at his hand—broad and firm, with clean, blunt nails—and then up into his blue eyes. "Have we met before?"

"I don't think so. I wish we had."

A blush rose from her chest up her neck. The connection between them was so intense, she had to look away.

After a long moment, they began to walk again, past mausoleums with intricate iron doors, brass doors, marble friezes.

"I'm always surprised that more people don't come here," she said, testing the steadiness of her voice. "Some of the most beautiful artwork in the world is here."

He nodded in response.

"Jason hasn't offered to visit the cemetery with me. Well, he came to the funeral, of course. But now—*Every week?* he asked. Isn't that a little *morbid*? It helps me clear my mind, I tell him. It helps me remember what really matters. I think Jason sees his life as a kind of track event, with hurdles he's eager to cross as soon as possible. He's already achieved sufficient status professionally. Now he wants the other stuff: marriage, a great house, a vacation home, some children. He's itching for a reason to buy a Mercedes four-wheel drive." Kelly shook her head. "I apologize for going on like this. I can't imagine what's gotten into me."

"I like listening to you," the man said. Laugh lines around his mouth and eyes engraved pale streaks in the tan of his face. "It makes me realize how most of my conversations are just small talk."

They continued along a path planted with high, leafy rhododendrons. A squirrel dashed across the lane, stopping to fix them with an indignant stare.

"Hi," Kelly said to the squirrel.

It flicked its tail and raced off into the bushes.

"Tell me some good things about Jason."

"All right. Let's see. He's very smart. And basically kind. My mother liked him."

"Your father?"

"My father's dead. My 'stepfather'—" Kelly paused. The spell snapped. She looked at her watch. "Damn. I've got to go. I've got an appointment."

They had arrived at the lane leading to the chapel, office, and parking lot. They stood on Snowflake Path, in the middle of July.

The man held out his hand. "It was nice talking with you."

Kelly placed her hand in his, meaning to shake it as she would shake the hand of any other acquaintance. Instead they both looked at their hands, palm to palm, and he seemed as bemused as she was by the flush of lust that bloomed there like an orchid with an open throat.

"Well," she said, after a moment, when she could get her breath.

"I'll be here next week," the man told her.

"Good. It will be your turn to talk."

"All right." He still held her hand.

"Shall we exchange names?"

"I don't think so. I rather like the anonymity."

"Me, too. If you call this anonymity. I mean, I don't even know your name, but I feel as if I know you. Certainly I'm telling you things I don't tell anyone."

He looked solemn. "Perhaps this is something we both need."

With a little laugh, she pulled her hand away. "Normally I'm a very rational person. A *responsible* citizen, with a discerning mind—" She smiled. "I've even been considered judicious."

"I'm sure that's true. But sometimes—" He gazed up at the Bell Tower. "Sometimes we devote so much to the perfection of our professional, public selves, that we forget to honor our messy, greedy, irrational, private selves. We— we lose our souls."

She studied his profile. His nose was long and high, a patrician nose marred by a slight bump that made his face, from this angle, resemble George Washington's. "That's very serious."

"It is." Suddenly, turning and pinning her with the bright blue beam of his eyes, he said in a rush, "I've tried very hard to be a good person. To do the right thing. These days I feel beset by devils. From within myself as well as from without. I mean the divorce. I once loved my wife. I still admire her. I don't want to hurt her."

He ran his hands through his thick hair. When he was done, his hair stood out every which way, an oddly endearing sight. All at once he seemed young, a confused but eager boy.

"She's a public person, my wife. In a way, the burden of her celebrity's imposed on me. There's no one I can talk to about her, or about our daughter, or any of it. But you—" He stared at Kelly. "You're a good person, I can tell. And for some inexplicable reason, I feel I can talk to you." Reaching out, he took Kelly's hands in both of his own. He could not, it seemed, keep himself from touching her any more than she could stop herself from wanting that touch. "Let's make a pact. When we meet one another here, let's tell one another only the truth. And whatever we say to one another will remain just between the two of us."

Kelly couldn't speak.

"Oh, dear. Now you think I'm a psychopath again."

"No." She cleared her throat. "Not at all. I'll make that pact with you."

"Good. Then I'll see you next week."

"Good."

They stood another moment looking at one another, holding hands, and then he said, "If you didn't have that appointment, I'd suggest we go somewhere for coffee. To continue the conversation."

"I'd like that. But I do have this appointment."

"Well, then."

"Yes." She nodded toward the chapel. "My car's down there."

He nodded in the opposite direction. "My car's over there."

"Good-bye, then. See you next Sunday."

"I look forward to it."

Still they stood.

"One of us has to move, you know," she told him.

"Let's do it together. On the count of three."

She laughed. "All right."

"One . . . two . . . three."

They broke away. Kelly hurried toward her car, looking, she realized, far too happy for someone in a cemetery. When she glanced back, she saw him walking rapidly away. He turned and waved. She waved. Then he went around a corner and was enveloped by the trees.

THREE

TESSA MADISON SPILLED OUT THE passenger door of the silver BMW before her mother had even turned off the engine. She raced across the raked white pebble drive, heaved back the heavy oak door, clattered into the house and across the front hall and up the stairs, yanking the pink ribbon off the long French braid that pulled her pale blond hair away from her face. By the time she'd reached her bedroom, she had the braid undone, and she shook her head wildly like a dog coming out of the water, so that her hair flew all around her face.

Limbs spinning, she managed to unzip her pink linen dress and at the same time kick off her white dress shoes so hard they flew into the wall with a satisfying thud.

"Tessa."

She turned to see her mother standing in the doorway.

"What." Looking away, Tessa peeled off her dress, letting it fall to the floor. She hated her mother seeing her in her underwear, but she hated wearing that stupid dress more.

"I thought we had an agreement."

"We do. And I kept my part, didn't I?" She pulled on her black jeans and the man's navy cotton shirt she'd bought from the thrift shop. Her mother didn't know Tessa had gotten it there; she'd freak if she knew. Tessa had told her that Tracy had given it to her, and still Tessa's mother had put it through the wash five or six times, on hot, before telling Tessa she was permitted to wear it. It was very soft now, comfortable to the touch.

"I don't understand why you're so upset."

Tessa looked at her mother. *You don't understand anything,* she wanted to yell, *O Great Queen of Perfect Control.*

"I told you. Because it's embarrassing. Because the dress is dorky. *Because I'm twelve years old!* Because no one my age dresses like that."

Anne Madison sighed. Her suit was the same pink of Tessa's dress—she coordinated the clothing they wore when they were together in public, remembering that one of her advisers had said that since a picture is worth a thousand words, the sight—the snapped shot—of her and her daughter in similar colors was worth gold in what it conveyed.

Anne's suit was not wrinkled. Anne's clothing, subject to the mysterious laws that governed her life, never wrinkled. Her blond hair was pulled back in its neat French coil, and pearl earrings—not too large, not too small—gleamed from the lobes of her ears, the same size and sheen as the pearls at her neck.

"Darling." Crossing the room, she sat down on the lavender velvet bench at the foot of Tessa's bed. "We've talked about this. You care about my winning the election as much as I do. I know you do. All the issues I'm fighting for will directly affect your life. I think it's a small sacrifice to make, to wear a beautiful dress to church, knowing that that will help me get elected and will help all women have better lives."

Tessa stared at her mother. Sometimes she thought

that, beneath the perfect pink dress, beneath the silk slip, on her mother's slender back, beneath her bra strap, lay a plastic button and a small plastic door where the batteries were inserted.

"I miss Dad." Tessa hadn't meant to say that; it just came out. Her life was a mess right now, her brain was scrambled, she said things without meaning to. Sometimes she wondered if she had a disease.

Anne took a deep breath. With infinite gentleness she began to rub at a spot on her dress. "Yes, well, I miss your father also. Why don't you tell him the next time you see him that I'll let you skip church completely if he'll return home just until after the election."

"Mom," Tessa said, "he's not coming back."

Anne's head snapped up. Two roses bloomed in her cheeks, as if she'd been struck hard, twice. She stood and stalked away—then she stopped at the doorway to glare at her daughter. "For that cruel remark, little miss, you're grounded today."

"That's not fair!" Tessa protested.

Anne raised her chin. "And you're restricted to your room."

"Mom! What about lunch?"

"I'll bring you something. Although it wouldn't hurt you to miss lunch for once." She left the room, then came back in. "I've got an appointment. We're going to make the videotape for my television ads." She paused. "Want to come along?"

"No, thanks." Tessa was always surprised how bad it made her feel to disappoint her mother, even though her mother had just been *totally* unfair.

Anne waited. "You know it's Carmen's day off."

"Duh, *yes*."

"You'll be fine here alone."

"I know."

"The taping might be fun." The silence stretched. "Very well, then." Anne went away.

Grubbing through the junk on her desk, Tessa found her Discman, clapped the headphones on, and threw herself onto her bed.

Tessa hated her mother for being so mean. She hated herself for hating her mother. She hated herself for becoming such a retard.

Sometimes she consoled herself with a fantasy: she'd boot up one of her friend's computers, click on to her mother's Web site, and send a letter to the world: The *truth* about Anne Madison, candidate for the State Legislature, Arlington and Medford Districts, Massachusetts.

But her mother really wanted to win that campaign, and as much as she hated her mother, Tessa loved her, too. And winning that position might make her mother happy in a way she'd never been before.

And then maybe her mother would let her have a cat. Cats weren't as bad as dogs. Andrea's Siamese had kittens, tiny chocolate creatures with eyes like huge blue jewels. But her mother didn't want pets in the house—they were too much work. How could they be too much work when her mother had a housekeeper? Tessa had asked, but her mother had snapped, "Don't get fresh with me, Tessa."

If she had a kitten, she'd treat it so gently. She'd give it lots of cream and salmon and scrambled eggs. She'd let it sleep in bed with her. When Tessa was an adult, she'd have lots of cats and let them all sleep in bed with her.

When she was an adult, she'd *have* to have cats sleep in bed with her; she was too ugly ever to get a man.

Although Chad had said hey to her when he saw her at the orientation for Camp Moxie on Friday. Chad's parents were as wealthy as Tessa's, and totally as bizarre.

Tessa's stomach rumbled. She was hungry again. She was always hungry. It was so easy, her mother said, to gain weight, weight crept up on women like a kind of fog, you didn't even see it coming and the next thing you knew, it had glommed onto your body, lying just beneath your skin like slabs of yellow cheese. Her mother was already worried about how fat Tessa's thighs were.

For breakfast, Anne had black coffee, a small glass of orange juice, and one Ry-Krisp cracker. She let Tessa have a bowl of Cheerios, but only a small one, and watched her eat it with a look of disgust on her face, as if Tessa were spooning mud into her mouth. Since her father had left, her mother was even more vigilant about the food she allowed in the house.

Tessa curled on her bed, staring at the wall. She didn't really mind being grounded. She was too tired, really, to go anywhere. And here in her bed was really the best place. She could close her eyes and be in a world of her own.

Kelly slammed her Subaru to a shuddering halt, threw herself from the car, and raced up the stairs to her apartment on the second floor of the handsome stone building on Memorial Drive.

Donna was waiting in the hall, leaning against Kelly's door, reading. "You're late," Donna said.

"Sorry. I'll hurry." Kelly unzipped her dress as she walked into her bedroom, dropped it on the floor, yanked on a severely cut blue linen sheath, fastened her grandmother's pearls around her neck, stabbed pearl studs into her ears, dabbed her skin with perfume, and grabbed her purse. "Ta-da," she sang out, returning to the living room. "Ready."

Donna shook her head. "A miracle." She squinted her eyes. "But maybe your hair . . ."

"It's too hot to wear it down."

"Put it in a chignon."

"Not enough time. Come on. We'll be late."

"You get away with a lot because you're tall and slender," Donna sighed, following her down the steps.

"But you get all the men because you're a short little bitty girly-girl."

This was an old argument, one that had started years

ago when they joined the same law firm, where they camouflaged their femininity beneath stiff mannish suits and
competed with one another in cold severity, until finally
they got into a fight that ended up in an all-night laughing/
crying true-confessions session and their eventual best-
friendship.

Donna slid into the passenger seat. Only five foot two,
and as full of curves as a bag of apples, her usual expression was a fierce scowl, the only way she could get most
people to take her seriously. "May I remind you, Your
Honor, you're the one who's engaged."

"You've had how many men propose?"

"True." Donna giggled. "While we're on that subject—"

"Yes?"

"I want you and Jason to meet Eric."

"This sounds very serious."

"I like him a lot, Kelly. We can talk law, or just be
together. When I curl up next to him, I feel so content—"

"How lovely for you, Donna."

Donna hugged herself smugly. "Lovely. Yes."

"Donna . . ."

"Mmm?"

"I met a nice man today."

"A *nice man*? Isn't Jason a nice man?"

"Jason is a handsome, brilliant, ambitious pain in the
butt. The guy I met was a nice man."

"Define *nice*." They were almost at the house. Donna
pulled the sun visor down and checked her reflection in the
mirror.

"I don't know, Donna, there was just something about
him. He was so easy to talk to. Sort of like what you're
saying about Eric. I didn't have to perform for him, and I
don't think he was performing for me. He seemed . . . honest. Real."

"You met him in the cemetery?"

"I'd seen him there before. His mother died recently."

Carefully Donna touched up her mascara. "How old?"

"Maybe forty."

"Then he's married."

"Getting a divorce, actually."

"Did you tell him you're engaged?"

"Yup. I also told him I wasn't sure I was doing the right thing."

"You met this guy this morning and told him about Jason?"

"Donna, I can't explain it. I felt like I knew the man. I felt like . . . like we were old friends." The thought of his face, the entire healthy sense of the man flashed through her. "More than friends."

"What's his name?"

"I don't know."

Donna slapped the visor up and slam-dunked her mascara wand into the open Kenya bag resting on the floor by her feet. "Okay, you know how strange this sounds? You met him this morning, you feel like old friends, but you don't know his name."

"But you liked Eric all at once!"

"Yeah, well, we also exchanged names and other appropriate information like whether or not we were on the Most Wanted List."

"I'm not explaining it well. We *agreed* not to give our names to each other. We're going to meet again next Sunday, and we wanted the freedom to be able to talk then as openly as we did this morning. You'd have to be there, I guess, to understand. The whole atmosphere of the place is so otherworldly—"

"To say the least," Donna interposed wryly.

"It was as if we were in our own universe. We could talk about what really mattered. We could say anything."

"Good grief. You're glowing."

"Really?" Kelly tilted the rearview mirror so she could look at herself. "Yeah, I am." She was silent a moment as they sat waiting for a light to change. "If I didn't think it sounded so absolutely impossibly insane, Donna, I'd think I'd fallen in love."

"Aren't you in love with Jason?"

"Not like this. I've never felt like this before."

Because the forty-five thousand citizens of Arlington, Massachusetts, are, in general, neither disgustingly wealthy nor painfully impoverished, Anne Madison lived in Arlington and wanted to represent that district.

Also, twelve years ago, she'd fallen in love with a house.

She'd often thought—secretly, of course—that she loved the house more than she loved her husband. And the house did seem to respond to her needs more perfectly than Randall ever had.

Something about the French Provincial house on Elm Street—its flawless proportions, high ceilings, spacious rooms—was calming to Anne, who loved, who *needed* order. Its placid cream stucco walls, square-cornered and symmetrical, provided a refuge for her, and the steep pitch of the dark green hip roof offered the illusion of a kind of convent to which she could retreat from the pressures of the cruel world. Her home was a haven in which she was the queen bee, safe at the center.

Some days it was more difficult than others to force herself from that sanctuary. She disliked leaving Tessa alone. She hated leaving her when things were unsettled between the two of them, but increasingly as Tessa grew older and more independent, things were more often than not unsettled.

Today Anne *had* to go out. The Democratic state primary election was Tuesday, September 19, and that was the election that mattered, since no Republican had won a position in Arlington for years. Anne was running against an incumbent, Marshall O'Leary, a well-loved and venerable septuagenarian who had done much good for his district and state, but who was, it was generally agreed, running out of steam. Marshall's concerns were limited to making Arlington more pedestrian-friendly and developing bike paths; he just didn't have the energy these days to fight for broader issues more crucial to the Commonwealth, such as an increase in the minimum wage, or to wade into the muddy, complicated waters of health care issues.

Anne had the energy for that. She was nearly incandescent with ideas regarding health care reform, and she needed to let the constituency of Arlington know this, and soon.

Anne's assistant, Rebecca Prentiss, had persuaded Mick Aitkins, a brilliant young videographer, to put together her campaign video, but she had to do it when he was available. Mick only yesterday informed Rebecca that he had to go off to the Cape on Monday morning to tape a series of weddings. So Rebecca had grabbed this Sunday noon appointment, even though Anne was already scheduled to attend a PR brunch at Eleanor Marks's. Unfortunate, but it couldn't be helped. Anne had asked Eleanor to express her regrets, and Lillian Doolittle, her campaign manager, promised to cover for her.

Mick Aitkins worked out of his home on the top floor of a two-family house on Edward Avenue. A rather bizarre-looking young man with a shaved head and a sparse goatee, Mick was slightly manic as he arranged Anne in a chair and played with the lights.

"White shirt. Not good," he muttered.

"We're trying to convey the idea of *nurse*," Rebecca reminded him.

"Okay, I see, but, we'll just . . ." Mumbling to himself, he adjusted this and that. Then he approached Anne. "Just here on your shirt," he said.

"The microphone," Rebecca interpreted.

Anne sat docilely as Mick clipped the tiny mike to her collar and ran the wire—another strand in his spider's web of cords, wires, and cables—to the videocamera set up on a tripod.

Rebecca squatted next to Anne. "Just some powder, here." She dabbed a sponge on Anne's nose.

"Rouge. Cheeks." Mick instructed.

"Got it." Rebecca brushed blush on Anne's face. Generally Anne disliked makeup, the film it cast over her skin, the way it seemed to be a kind of integument, available to all dust and germs floating through the air, but she understood the necessity of makeup for television ads.

"Ready," Mick barked.

Anne leaned forward. Rebecca stood at Mick's side, holding up cue cards, but Anne knew by heart what she wanted to say.

"Are you concerned about the health—?"

"Don't lean forward," Mick said.

Anne nodded and forced herself to press her spine against her chair. She began again. "Are you concerned about the health of your parents, your children, your community, yourself? Are you tired of struggling through the indecipherable red tape of HMOs? Are you concerned about the financial health of your family? Do you care about the needs of the elderly, the health of our public schools, the lives of those unable to take care of themselves? I know I do.

"I'm Anne Madison. I am a certified registered nurse with three years' experience at Brigham and Women's Hospital. I have a twelve-year-old daughter, and six years' experience on the Arlington School Committee. I serve on the Massachusetts Council Task Force on poverty, health, and nutrition.

"I'm asking you to vote for me for State Representative in the September Democratic primary. We already have a good representative, but I want to be better than good. I want to fight. I want to change things. And I will. Remember, a vote for me is a vote for health."

"Cut," Mick said. "That was okay, except your slogan's pretty lame, Anne."

"I disagree. Health is an issue—"

"Vote for Anne Madison, for the health of it," Mick said. "That's what you should say."

Anne flinched. "I don't think—"

"I do!" Rebecca exclaimed. She clapped her hands. "Mick, that's brilliant. Anne, come on, think about it. It's very catchy. It's memorable."

"It's slightly inappropriate."

"Not at all."

"You don't think it's a bit . . . vulgar?"

"No, Anne, it's brilliant. Trust me."

"Very well." Anne leaned back in her chair. "Do you want me to say the entire thing again?"

"No. Just the last bit. I'll splice it."

"Start with *Remember*," Rebecca coached.

Anne nodded. "Remember, vote for Anne Madison, for the health of it."

"Cut," Mick said. "Anne. You look like you're sucking limes. *Health* is not a bad word. *Hell* isn't going to offend anyone. Smile when you say your last line."

"He's right, Anne. You need to look friendly."

Anne nodded. "Ready?" She took a deep breath. "Remember," she said, and smiled—

"Teeth," Mick called.

"What?"

"Let's see your teeth when you smile!" Rebecca added. "Think of something pleasant, something that makes you happy."

Anne swallowed. She used to smile at the thought of Tessa with her hair in braids tied in ribbon, rushing up to hug Anne after school, presenting her with another painting for the refrigerator. She used to smile at the thought of Randall, when they were newly married, volunteering with her to help campaign for whatever Democrat was running for president, governor, or senator, meeting for dinner to plot strategy with other like-minded people.

These days, however, the thought of her child and her estranged husband only made her heart feel heavy.

For God's sake! Rubbing at a spot on her skirt, she thought desperately. Couldn't anything make her smile? Rebecca and Mick waited impatiently.

Looking down, she forced herself to still her hand. *What*, she thought. *What?*

Like a floodgate opening, the image came to her, and she felt the tension release her shoulders, free the rigidity of her jaw.

She imagined her study at home, at the back of her deep white house. Her desk, orderly and serene. The calendar, the clock, the letter opener, the blotter. Everything lined up precisely, perfect, obedient, attending.

She said, "Remember, vote for Anne Madison, for the health of it." And she smiled as she spoke.

Driving home, Anne considered the week ahead of her. Every morning except Sunday she rose at five-fifteen, exercised in her basement work-out room, showered; then woke Tessa and had her breakfast of green tea and a Ry-Krisp cracker while Tessa ate her cereal.

Tomorrow morning she had a general strategy conference at seven-thirty with Rebecca and Lillian. Carmen would arrive at six-thirty to organize breakfast for the three women in the morning room. Tea, croissants, pastries. Anne would have only tea, but the other two women were always delighted to find a tray of delicacies awaiting them. They worked better that way. Carmen could also get Tessa dressed, fed, and off to her day camp while Anne showered and dressed. Thank God for Carmen.

At ten a young man was arriving to teach Anne how to build and use a computer database to list all pertinent information about her constituents. At noon, she had to leave for lunch at the Ritz to join several members of the Democratic Party in a discussion about the upcoming presidential and senatorial elections. At three, she had—something—she couldn't quite remember, some meeting, and then at four, she was having tea with the board she was chairing on the Working Family Agenda—

She remembered, with a jolt, what the three o'clock meeting was.

It was with the guardian *ad litem* the judge had appointed two weeks ago at the pre-trial conference. A psychiatrist. Dr. Martin Lawrence.

The supposed function of a guardian *ad litem* was to represent the best interests of the child in a custody battle.

This set Anne's teeth on edge. How could any stranger, any man, a psychiatrist to boot, with his erudite knowledge of bizarre human eccentricities, his undoubted professional penchant for interpreting the mildest of frailties as perverted or sick, possibly interview members of a family two or three times and then make a logical, useful recommendation?

It made her ill to think of it. And it made her furious.

And worst of all was the realization that she was helpless to change anything. It was ordered by the court. It was part of the hideous process Randall was imposing on her with this senseless divorce.

She reminded herself that Addison Bemish, her lawyer, had assured her she would do just fine. Last Thursday they'd spent two hours discussing every question the psychiatrist would want to ask. And she could be charming when she needed to be. So she would be flawlessly charming.

It helped that she was not the only one forced to see him. Randall had to, and Tessa, and others in their immediate sphere: Carmen, whom Anne could count on to speak favorably about Anne, and Mont, Randall's father, who, of course, would be on Randall's side.

Tessa's appointment wasn't until next week. After Anne met this Martin Lawrence, she'd know how to approach Tessa about him, how to coach her to respond to his intrusive probing. All Tessa had to say, surely, was that she wanted to remain with her mother. And Tessa would say that, wouldn't she? Addison had assured her that in ninety-five percent of all cases, custody was given to the mother.

Still, it was too bad all this had to happen now, when she wanted to focus on her campaign!

The brunch was being given by Eleanor Marks in the Markses' glass-and-wood postmodern mansion hidden behind a high cedar fence on Brattle Street. Cars lined the street for blocks in all directions; they had to park on Oak and hoof it to Brattle to follow the group of women hurrying up the walk.

A woman in a maid's uniform stood at the gate. "Just through there," she said, gesturing toward the open front door.

Kelly and Donna joined the crowd streaming through the maze of huge sheets of glass, white plaster walls, Ionic columns, and a freestanding bronze staircase. African masks scowled down at them while bulbous fertility idols gleamed from behind glass cases. Heading toward the sound of voices, they found themselves in a jungle-green atrium around a free-form pool where clusters of women chatted, munching on the canapés served to them on silver platters.

"You're here!" Adelaide Stein swept up to encompass them in hugs and emanations of Joy. "Amazing, isn't it?"

Before Kelly could answer, a tiny, thin, leather-skinned female tottered up to them on four-inch heels. Her head seemed disproportionately large for her body, and it was a wonder that she could stand, let alone move, so laden was she with heavy gold jewelry.

"*Judge* MacLeod! My dear!" She seized Kelly's hand. "May I congratulate you. We're all *so* proud of you! We've watched your career with such interest and we're so excited to see, if you will, justice"—she interrupted herself to trill a laugh. "—being done!"

Kelly murmured, "Thank you." She hated being targeted for attention like this, so quickly she turned toward Donna. "I don't know whether or not you've met my friend Donna Krebs."

"Hello." Eleanor lasered her calculating eyes on short, voluptuous Donna.

"Donna's an attorney with Dunlap and Reed, where I worked."

Eleanor's smile deepened. "We *are* pleased to meet you. We can't tell you how exciting it is for an old hen like me to see you lovely young chicks working right alongside the big boys."

"It's pretty exciting for us, as well," Donna replied.

"Mrs. Marks."

When her personal secretary tapped her arm, Eleanor turned on a dime. Frowning, she listened to the message, then flashed Kelly and Donna a smile.

"We must take a call. We'll be in touch, Kelly. So glad to meet you, Donna."

She whirled away.

"Where does she get her energy?" Donna murmured. "And what's with the royal *we*?"

Kelly snatched two mimosas in frosted flutes from a passing tray and handed one to Donna. "You can dis her, but you've got to remember her age. She's eighty-one."

"No way."

"Way."

"That explains the high heels and stiff hair."

"And the face-lift and the jewelry, yes, but still, she's been fighting for women's issues since before we were born. I wouldn't be surprised to find a pair of jeans in her closet—"

"I would be."

"—but no matter what she looks like, her values are solid. Her heart's in the right place. If she'd been born forty years later, she'd be the one running for office, and not the state seat, either."

Donna scanned the room. "This is an impressive

crowd. All right. You've sold me. Although I find it hard to like anyone with this much money. And I hate parties like this with only women."

"That's because you're indoctrinated to think that a group of only women is a second-rate assembly. The only thing women get together for is to talk about cosmetics or Tupperware, right? Just think of all the power conferences in smoky rooms men and only men have taken part in over the past few decades—hell, centuries. This is just the female version, and about time."

Something like a loud bronze gong sounded, followed by the staccato of a knife tapped on glass. The loud chatter in the room dimmed to a buzz as everyone turned to face the raised platform where Eleanor Marks stood in front of a microphone.

"Hello, everyone. Thank you so much for coming. I'm Eleanor Marks, by the way, your hostess, and I can't tell you how exciting it is to see so many friends gathered here together.

"I've just received a phone call from our guest of honor, Anne Madison. Her assistant, Rebecca Prentiss, scheduled her for two meetings in this time slot—we all know how easily that can happen, don't we? Most of us know Anne already, and are eager to help her win this election, but I'd like her campaign manager, Lillian Doolittle, to speak just a few moments, just to remind us why we need to support Anne Madison."

Applause fluttered lightly over the room as Lillian Doolittle stepped up to the microphone. Lillian was as chubby as Eleanor was thin, but she radiated the same kind of optimistic vitality. Unlike Eleanor, Lillian wore trousers, a loose tunic that hid her bulk, and no jewelry. Her shoes were flat-heeled and her hair a short, dry thatch. But her eyes gleamed, and energy glowed from her.

"First, I want to thank Eleanor for hosting this little get-together. If you look around the room, you'll see that we've got a powerhouse of political possibility gathered here. Just stop and think for a moment: if everyone here joined forces, who could possibly stop us?"

Again, scattered applause broke out over the room.

Lillian continued. "Let me tell you about the woman you came here to meet. As you can see from the brochures we've left on just about every table here—Please take one. Take several and hand them out!—Anne Madison is the people's candidate. All her life, Anne has fought for women's rights and for the rights of the poor, the endangered, and the ill.

"Anne grew up in Concord and Nantucket, attended Concord Academy, Wellesley, and B.U., where she received her R.N. Her father was a surgeon, and Anne always knew she wanted to work in the health field. She worked at Brigham and Women's Hospital before marrying and deciding to stay home full-time to take care of her daughter, Tessa, who is now twelve. Anne remained active in the health care field, as a lobbyist, volunteer, and activist. She organized research into the home health field, initiated a program for the public schools to teach students about contraception, AIDS, STDs, and drugs. She's currently working as an activist to make insurance companies and HMOs more responsible and more personal. She's on the board of the commission for Better Care for the Elderly. She's been elected to School Committee twice and has served as a delegate to the Democratic State Convention in ninety-two, ninety-four, ninety-six, and ninety-eight."

Lillian paused for a sip of water. "We're here today to ask you to help Anne Madison win the Democratic primary election for the state senate this fall. You are all influential women, and we ask you to use your power in spreading the word about Anne. She's running against—I can say it right out in this room—a 'good old boy' who will be hard to beat because he's so well known. We implore you for any financial assistance you might be able to give. Television and radio spots and newspaper ads are expensive, and we want to blitz the region. We want to be sure Anne gets elected by a landslide. So please, help us. We're here, if you have any questions, suggestions, or comments."

After another round of applause, the questions started.

"They didn't say anything about her husband," Donna remarked.

"Why should they?" Kelly asked. "Is he relevant?" She looked at her watch. "Let's go."

"So soon?"

Kelly put her flute on a nearby table. "Anne Madison sounds great to me. I've heard all I need to, and I don't want to be here when they discuss fund-raising."

"Already avoiding the appearance of impropriety?"

"You bet your ass. Besides, I have a ton of things to do."

They pressed through the crowd, around a bronze statue of what appeared to be a giant Slinky, and out the door.

"Are you seeing Jason today?"

"We're going Rollerblading. Want to join us?"

Donna groaned. "No, thanks. Will you be in the office tomorrow?"

"I will. I've got to clean out my desk and instruct Clara on my cases . . . she'll be taking over most of them."

"I'm going to miss you like crazy," Donna said.

"We'll still see each other. Just not every day."

"Are you excited?"

Kelly smiled. "I can't wait."

Tessa's private phone rang. Even through her headphones, she heard it, and dived for it.

"Princess," her father said.

"Dad!" Her spirits soared, while a violin string of guilt thrummed inside her heart. Her mother hated her father calling her Princess, insisting that it perpetuated the image of the young female as lazy, helpless, spoiled, and useless.

"What are you doing on this bright sunny day?"

"Well . . . we went to church."

"And this afternoon?"

". . . Mom's being videotaped. I don't know about later."

"Want to drive out to see Grandpops with me?"

"Yes!" The word jumped out of her mouth before she could think.

"I'll be by in fifteen minutes."

"Cool."

With trembling hands, Tessa plaited her hair into two braids, just in case Dad let her ride one of Grandpops' horses.

Randall leaned on the split-rail fence, watching his daughter and father ride off across the pasture. The horses pranced and shook their manes, happy to be out beneath the sun on a fine hot day. Tessa looked tiny on Blue Boy's enormous back—this sight would terrify Anne—but Blue Boy, although larger than Frisk, was easygoing, a big, softhearted, lazy baby who wouldn't know how to run away with anyone.

His father looked good on Frisk, looked almost like the man he used to be, before his seventy-seven years and a knock-out punch of grief started dulling his mind.

Today Randall and Tessa arrived to find Montgomery Madison clean-shaven and pretty much dressed, except that he'd forgotten to take off his pajama top and wore it like a striped shirt tucked into his trousers, which happened to be corduroy . . . perhaps, Randall thought, giving him the benefit of the doubt, because he felt cold. A lot of older people did feel cold all the time.

Randall couldn't tell whether or not Tessa realized her grandfather was wearing his pajama top. She ran into his arms happily, hugging him, and when he proposed going for a ride, Tessa probably wouldn't have cared if her grandfather had been wearing a swimming suit and parka.

Randall wished he could be with them, but over the years his father had had to sell off some horses, or not replace them when they died. He really couldn't take care of more than these two. Randall had had his daughter's company during the drive out and would have it on the way back, so he let the two of them go off together. When they went over the hill, he turned back to inspect his father's house.

Right now this house held more memories of the past than dreams of the future, Randall thought.

He'd grown up here, luckier than probably any one human being on the planet had a right to be, the son of a physician father and an artistic mother, baby brother to his adoring and fascinating older sister Evangeline. He'd learned to ride a horse before he learned to ride a bike, he'd swung from a rope into the pond at the foot of the meadow, he'd had friends spend the night in his room when he was six, in the barn loft when he was ten, and in sleeping bags out in the woods when he was twelve, all of them involved in fantasy adventure games, pretending to be Lewis and Clark discovering the Northwest Passage.

When Tessa was born, Randall had envisioned her spending long weekends and summer days at her grandparents', riding, swimming, reading mysteries on rainy days. But Anne found just about everything about the farm too dangerous for a little girl: disease-carrying ticks could hide in the tall grass, not to mention snakes, and horses threw people, breaking their necks, and God knew what lurked in the black mud at the bottom of the murky pond.

And these days, Anne wouldn't let Tessa spend any time alone with Randall's father. He was too forgetful, she insisted, and she was right. Some days Mont Madison's mind was as clear as a bell, but other days it seemed fogged over, scratched deep.

Randall studied the outside of the house. White clapboard with dark green trim, it was in pretty good shape; Randall had seen to that. He paid a carpenter to keep the gutters, roof, storm windows, and stone steps in good repair.

Now he entered the house, as everyone did, through the mudroom leading into the kitchen. When his mother had been alive, this room had been green with potted African violets and scented with geraniums growing in both windows, but after Madeline died two months ago, Mont kept forgetting to water the plants, so Randall had had to throw them out. That had been oddly difficult, as painful as burying a beloved pet, for the geraniums were ancient, huge twisted survivors with fragrant fuzzy leaves and stems thicker than his thumbs.

Dog leashes had hung here, too, and were here no longer. When Rover died, Mont had refused to get a new dog, no matter how Randall persisted in his suggestions. There was a cat, which they simply called The Cat, a permanently exasperated creature who deigned to enter the kitchen for food and warmth on the coldest winter days but preferred to sleep in the barn or slink around outside waiting for moles or mice.

The kitchen, Randall saw with relief, was basically clean. He had a standing arrangement with Dorothy Olson, one of the women from the nearby town, to keep the kitchen and the bathrooms acceptably hygienic. Now and then when Mont let her, she ran the vacuum through the rest of the house, but that wasn't often. As Mont grew older, he'd accumulated more stuff, mostly paper, newspaper articles about medicine, and medical journals, of course, and books of crossword puzzles and word games, and he had always kept his beloved *National Geographic*s. Recently he'd begun to pull files from the cabinets holding all the old information on patients in his medical practice, and now the files leaned in manila-colored towers on top of the television, on the back of the toilet tank, in the middle of the dining room table, on the front stairs. When Randall asked his father about it, Mont told him he was thinking of writing a book.

On the windowsill two tomatoes from the garden ripened in the sun, and in the middle of the table sat a clear

Mason jar of roses, just as if Randall's mother were still here. Randall checked in the refrigerator: red grapes, grapefruit, a small filet of beef, a pitcher of lemonade. So his father was eating well. Except for the pajama top, he was showing no signs of senility. Of course, he forgot words now and then, but so did Randall.

Randall walked through the rest of the downstairs, reading his past in every nick in the woodwork. The walls were covered with his mother's paintings, portraits of her children, pets, and friends, still lifes of flowers and fruit, some landscapes. She had been, if not a famous painter, an accomplished one, with an eye that saw the harmony in diverse and ordinary objects.

As Randall paused before a still life of a ceramic mixing bowl, a muddy pair of gardening gloves, an open book, and a tangle of turquoise beads, he was transported back to the moment when his mother came in from church, checked to see that the bread was rising, took off her necklace and earrings so she wouldn't lose them in the garden, and rushed outside. The open book was there because there were open books everywhere in the house.

He wished his mother were still alive, for Tessa's sake. Walking through this house, with its worn Oriental rugs, rump-sprung armchairs, sofas with faded slipcovers, and its shelves of books on almost every wall, Randall contemplated not for the first time the possibility of moving here. Was it odd—was it *sad* somehow, a grown man dreaming of living in the home where he'd been a child?

The thing was that Tessa loved animals and was wild for the outdoors. She adored her grandfather and worshiped Brooke Burchardt, a thirteen-year-old horse-crazy girl who lived across the road with her three younger siblings, a father who taught elementary school, and a plump, jovial, stay-at-home mother.

Certainly Randall was eager to move out of the temporary quarters he'd established when he left Anne, hygienic but stark rooms in a block of expensive modern apartments on Mass Ave. The only good thing about his present lodging was that it was close to Tessa. True, if he moved out here, he'd have a long commute every day to and from the hospital. But he never had felt at home anywhere like he did here.

It had been Anne who loved the French Provincial house he had so gladly left. He just couldn't get comfortable there. It was too formal, too artificial, like the rooms of a posh hotel. You could admire the high windows with the swagged draperies, the chandeliers, the marble floor in the foyer, but you couldn't relax there. Randall had felt like a kind of visiting diplomat in those gilt and rose rooms.

Anne had wanted that house as much as she ever wanted anything in her life, and so they bought it fifteen years ago. Cool and elegant, it was a civilized environment that let nothing affect it. So in its way, it provided a contrast for Anne, a haven. You couldn't imagine anyone being sick in those rooms, or crying out in the extremity of pain or fear or grief. The rooms smelled of flowers and perfume, not of antiseptic, gangrenous flesh, and death. The mutations of the weak and mortal body were held at bay there, had no place there, in that stiff patrician edifice.

Years ago, when he met Anne, she was a nurse at Brigham & Women's. He was just beginning his practice, and he came to admire and love her for the way she handled medical exigencies, remaining rational when others were screaming, her movements sure and deft and sober. Over the years of their marriage, Anne had decided she wanted to save not just lives but the world, or her portion of it, and she had the self-confidence, the necessary arrogance, and the skill to do just that.

He wished her well. But he was not the only person affected by the way Anne's chilly self-control carried over into the most private parts of her life. Tessa was affected, too.

And as Randall walked through this old house that smelled of fruit and new-mown grass and hearth rugs still exuding the odor of dog, he thought that this very place might provide the perfect balance for his daughter's life.

For the first time in a long time, he realized that he was happy. He was *looking forward*. It had something to do, he was certain, with the woman he'd met in the cemetery. She'd made him feel something he had forgotten still existed—*hope*.

After the brunch, Kelly dropped Donna at the Harvard Square T stop, zipped through the maze of streets to the parking lot behind her apartment, jumped out, locked her car, raced up to unlock the back entrance of the building, and went through to the foyer.

"Hey." Jason stood by the elevator, Rollerblades slung over his shoulder. In his white shorts and red polo shirt he looked as healthy as a glass of milk. "Perfect timing."

Perfect timing, she thought, what is that? When you meet at the time you said you would? That's just *expected*. Perfect timings surely must be when two people meet accidentally, without forethought or planning. As she had met that man this morning.

Guilt made her peck a kiss onto Jason's cheek.

The ornate bronze doors of the elevator slid open. They stepped inside. Jason pressed Kelly into a corner, resting his forehead on hers. He was very tan and smelled like sun and lemonade. "Sure you want to go out?"

"I'm sure." The handrail bit into her back. She'd started this with her kiss, but he was making her feel trapped. She pushed him away. "Don't, Jason."

The elevator pinged. The doors slid open. Always the gentleman, Jason moved away to let Kelly exit first. She led him down the carpeted hallway, fit her key neatly into her door, and opened it. She could feel him right behind her, the heat of his body coming toward her.

He put his hand on her waist.

She moved away. "Give me just a minute to change."

In her bedroom, she stripped off her dress and pearls.

The third change of the day, she realized as she tugged on black-and-fuchsia spandex bike shorts and a sleeveless turquoise tee, and not the last one, either, for she and Jason were having dinner that night at his mother's.

She came out of her bedroom to find Jason lounging on her sofa, remote control in his hand, rapidly switching channels. Unconsciously he tapped a foot on the floor—Jason was always moving. He was like a young stallion, charged with energy, impatient, eager, restless. Black Beauty, she thought, looking at his gleaming black hair.

When he saw her, he sprang to his feet, clicked off the television, and tossed the remote control on the coffee table. "You look colorful."

"I *feel* colorful," she replied. He came toward her, smiling. She opened the closet door and ducked inside to grab her Rollerblades. "Let's go."

They sat on the apartment steps to lace up their skates, dropped their shoes in the vestibule, and headed for the long stretch of Memorial Drive closed off on Sundays for roller skaters and bikers. It was a hot day, bright with light bouncing off the Charles River paralleling their path. When they coasted under the graceful shady leaves of the ancient sycamores, it was like swimming through cool pools of air.

Jason was lean and muscular, but he was just a fraction of an inch shorter than Kelly, so she had to alter her stride a bit to match his as they went along, weaving in and out among the crowd. Still, they looked great together, Kelly so fair, Jason so dramatically dark.

Jason had known they would, the moment he saw her during a pre-trial conference where they represented opponents in a divorce case.

Jason was a junior lawyer for a prestigious Beacon Hill firm of which his deceased father had once been a partner. The very best of private education had honed his natural intelligence into a diamond-sharp dazzle. Quick-witted and shrewd, his mind flashed like a fencer's foil, and there was nothing he loved like a good opponent, which made him a formidable attorney—and a tireless suitor.

When they met, only months before, Kelly was still a lawyer for a small but growing firm based in Cambridge, but her hopes were high. She'd applied for a judicial position and just received a summons for an interview with the Eastern Regional Committee of the Massachusetts Judicial Nominating Council.

The law was her life. She loved what she was doing and dreamed not of walking down an aisle in a flowing white bridal gown, but entering a courtroom in a somber black robe. At thirty-four she'd never succumbed to that state of helpless dementia people called love, and that was fine with her. She had no time for love. No interest in it. As far as she was concerned, it was a conscious, deliberate choice people made to let themselves act like idiots. Absolutely *not* for her.

She *had* had several brief sexual liaisons of varying degrees of satisfaction. Sex was very nice, she realized, but god, it caused so many problems! She'd never seen a Venus's-flytrap, but she imagined love was like that: sensuous, alluring, so that people leaned forward to smell the fragrance, feel the satin petals—then *snap*! All at once there they were, eaten alive. You couldn't be a family court lawyer without developing some cynicism about what was called love. As well, there was her own past.

That first day, the moment she entered the conference room and set eyes on Jason, her entire body had bristled. Even now she wasn't sure whether it was hostility or desire that caused that frisson. Perhaps both.

At one end of the long black conference table, Jason had been standing next to his client, leaning over her shoulder to point out something in a pile of papers. His gray suit clung to his lean body as only something tailor-made could do; Kelly was glad she'd worn her new black Calvin Klein. A thin gold Chopard watch gleamed against Jason's left wrist; on the little finger of his right hand he wore a discreet gold signet ring stamped with his family crest. His lush black hair shone like polished onyx; his profile was sharp, bold, aristocratic. He might as well have worn a badge stating: OLD MONEY AND LOTS OF IT.

Kelly hated him on sight.

And on principle. She had no time for guys like this, born entitled, chauffeured along the paths of their lives in gleaming limousines. They had no clue about suffering, and suffering was what opened a person to the realization of the problems of others, Kelly believed. Suffering brought compassion. Men like Jason, privileged by birth—and stunningly handsome as well—thought they were above the world. Well, they *were* above the world. They had more than they deserved.

She knew the moment she looked at him that she'd be damned if she'd let him win this case.

At the same time, with astounding irrationality, she was glad she'd worn her red lace Victoria Secret bra and garter belt.

They were brilliant adversaries that day. Afterward, like actors after a play, they were both high on performance. The moment Jason was alone with his cell phone, he called to invite Kelly to meet him for a drink.

Amazed at herself, she accepted.

"I have to warn you," Kelly told him that night, "I don't have time for dating."

"You'll find time for me," he assured her.

She had liked his cockiness, but she'd spoken the truth. In addition to her duties at the law firm, which paid her salary—and, unlike Jason, she needed her salary—she did *pro bono* work, sat on several committees, and was writing an article on improving the court's assistance to *pro se* representation in divorce. When she wasn't working, she had to take her clothes to the dry cleaners, buy her own groceries, clean her own apartment. *She* didn't have a housekeeper.

So she had declined his next few invitations. Jason

wasn't used to rejection. The more Kelly refused him, the more determined he became to win her.

First, he treated her friends and colleagues to dinners at posh restaurants where he questioned them thoroughly about Kelly. What kind of flowers did she like? What perfume? What music?

Next, bouquets of irises arrived at her door, CDs by Aerosmith and Wagner, glittering bottles of White Shoulders and Passion, with never a note or return address. Kelly couldn't prove they were from Jason, but she knew they were, and she couldn't help but enjoy this kind of courtship and admire his persistence.

Then a season ticket to the opera arrived in the mail. Kelly was mad for opera, but she never could have afforded such a marvelous seat, so she went, and was not surprised to find Jason in the seat next to hers.

It would have been churlish and silly not to talk to him. He invited her to the Federalist for a late supper after the opera, and she accepted. During the meal he was charming, and she couldn't deny that he was handsome, and entertaining, and clever.

Still, over the next few months, she remained evasive. She wasn't playing a game—she was just focused as she had always been on her work.

And deep inside, where she told herself the truth, lay the suspicion that it was only the challenge that kept Jason pursuing her; if he ever caught her, he'd lose interest in her. She didn't need that kind of insult and injury.

Then René phoned to tell her that he and Ingrid had moved back to Boston because her mother was dying of cancer and needed to be hospitalized.

The world closed in on Kelly. She dropped almost everything but work to make time to visit her mother at the hospital. She became emotionally vulnerable in a way she hadn't been for years. She'd kept herself so closed off for so long she'd almost forgotten how much she could hurt, but now sorrow pierced her again. It made her weak.

All she would tell Jason was that there had been a rift between her and her mother fifteen years ago. She did still love her mother, but she disliked her mother's husband. Someday she would tell him the rest, she promised, thinking that that day would never come.

For the next few months, Jason accompanied her often when she went to visit her mother in the hospital. In spite of herself, Kelly became fond of Jason. He was the one who brought a small CD player with earphones and classical CDs for Ingrid, for the few rare times she felt well enough to listen. He showed an exquisite instinct for leaving Kelly alone with her mother when necessary, almost before Kelly wished it herself. He brought expensive, fragrant flowers. When he took Kelly home afterward, he often found ways to amuse her, even to make her laugh. Perhaps this was all a kind of game for him, another kind of adversarial event, Kelly thought, one grand challenge: *Jason Gray* vs. *The Grim Reaper*.

Still, she was grateful, and in gratitude and a kind of exhaustion, she finally gave in and went to bed with Jason. She enjoyed it, and didn't feel guilty for the pleasure she took. She knew that the presence of death sharpened all the appetites of the living. She knew she was forcing back the sights and smells of the sickroom with those of the bedroom. She was not the first person to use the heat of sex as an antidote to the looming chill of the grave.

She'd assumed that was all it meant to Jason, too. She assumed she was a conquest for him or that he stayed around out of courtesy.

When Jason proposed marriage to her at her mother's bedside, Kelly accepted with genuine gratitude for the smile this brought to her mother's face. What a brilliant theatrical move, she thought! What a star he was!

She hadn't actually believed he meant it, even when he brought, from his jacket pocket, a small turquoise Tiffany box, and inside it a small black velvet box, and inside that, a rather enormous diamond ring.

She said, "Yes, I'll marry you," but she nearly said, *"Well done!"*

After her mother's death, Kelly offered to return the ring to him. Jason was horrified. He'd *meant* it, he insisted. He wanted to marry her. Didn't she want to marry him?

The truth was that she really didn't know. She told him so. Things were all coming at her far too fast—her mother's sudden return to her life and then, as suddenly and so finally, her departure. On the heels of the funeral, the nomination for the judicial position and all that entailed.

"Anyway," she said to Jason, speaking as honestly as she could, "I don't understand why you want to marry me."

"Why, because you're beautiful, and you're intelligent, and you take the law seriously, and you laugh at my jokes," he told her.

"But I'm not—how can I put this? I'm not part of your world, Jason." Her frankness exposed her insecurities. "I didn't go to private schools. I only recently learned to play tennis. I don't know how to sail."

"I realize that, but it doesn't matter. Or rather, it does— it makes you rather glamorous."

"Glamorous?"

"Yes. Mysterious. An unknown quantity. You didn't see me stumble over my feet at dancing class or vomit when I was learning how to hold my liquor. You didn't go wild at any of the painfully memorable house parties of my college years."

"Ah," Kelly said. "You mean I haven't slept with any of your friends."

Jason waggled his eyebrows. "Well, yes. There's that, too."

Now Jason continually pushed her to choose a date for the wedding. Kelly kept putting it off.

She couldn't put a word to the cause of her reluctance. This afternoon, rushing through the bright air, she didn't want to try. She was full of energy. "Slow down!" Jason ordered, more than once, but she *couldn't*, somehow; she needed to *move,* so she circled around him, nipping at his heels like a puppy, shrieking with laughter.

"You're in good spirits," Jason remarked.

"Yes, I am," she agreed, darting away from him in a burst of speed and then zipping back. Jason thought her good mood resulted from her recent appointment to the Massachusetts judiciary—and it did, really. Mostly. She was proud of the appointment and excited about it; it was the most important thing in her life, something she had dreamed of achieving. But it was a *serious* thing, and *right now,* for some reason, she was simply buoyant with a kind of *giddy* happiness.

She thought of falling that morning in the cemetery and of the man who'd offered his hand, so easily helping her up. "I thought an angel had fallen off her pedestal," he'd said.

The taping had been exhilarating for Anne, but as she drove home her mind moved relentlessly to thoughts of the week ahead. There was *so much* good needing done in the world, and right when she should be focusing on that, she had the meeting with the psychiatrist to consider. All because of Randall, *damn* him, and his stupid, selfish insistence on ruining Anne's life.

By the time she brought her BMW to a stop in the circle drive of her house she was shaking. Thank God, she thought as she stepped from the heat into the cool front hall, for this pale palace that rose around her like a medieval cloister. Shutting the front door firmly behind her, taking solace in the determined click of the lock, she leaned against it, taking deep breaths.

The entrance hall always calmed her, its floor a cool streaked rose-and-green Italian marble, the newel post of the winding staircase a marble basket of flowers, perfect immutable flowers greeting her every time. Her grandparents looked down on her imperiously from the heavily framed age-darkened oil portraits hanging above the refectory table. She liked having these portraits here, where anyone entering the house knew at once from what kind of stock she descended.

Thank you, Grandmother, she prayed. *Thank you, Grandfather.* They had had the foresight to leave her a trust her own parents could not break to squander on their beloved immigrants. True, Randall had paid for half the house, as well he should have, but quite probably he wouldn't have agreed to buy such a place—he found it ostentatious, undoubtedly because it wasn't shabby and smelling like wet dog like his parents' home—if he hadn't known that Anne could pay cash for the property herself, and would have done so, if necessary. Now Randall was gone, and she was even more glad to have a beautiful, *serene,* home for a haven. It made such a difference in her life.

On the long refectory table against the wall rested two antique silver and marble epergnes, and between them a chased silver bowl. Over the years the family had gotten into the habit of dropping the mail here, and all messages. There was a note torn from his prescription pad, written in Randall's distinct, direct, block writing—unusual for a doctor, but Randall was an unusual man—for Anne.

Randall had taken Tessa off with him for the afternoon.

Legally, it was within his rights to do so. It was understood when Randall left that Tessa would remain in this, Anne's, house. She and Randall would discuss, day by day, in a cooperative manner, Tessa's care, even though they were battling fiercely, each one of them, for sole legal custody.

Anne had been so sure Randall's departure was temporary. But the divorce, like an inexorable shredding machine, was grinding on, and Randall was driving it. She could not believe he was fighting her for custody of Tessa.

A kind of trembling moved over her. This day was too much. First Rebecca making that stupid scheduling conflict so that she had to miss her own fund-raiser. Then Tessa making such a violent scene about having to wear a truly beautiful dress! Now Randall taking Tessa off to his filthy farm without her consent.

Anne hurried up the stairs and into the safety of her own bedroom. Tearing off her clothes, she dropped them in the hamper in her pristine white bathroom and stepped into the shower. Using pHisoHex, the soap they used in hospitals, she scrubbed her limbs and torso, ten times, and shampooed her hair. Afterward, her skin was bright red, nearly raw.

And still she did not feel clean enough. She did not feel purged.

Randall had taken Tessa to visit her grandfather. On the farm. That *filthy* farm. Horseshit lay everywhere, and the cat was allowed to wander in and out of the house, catching rats, then with the same mouth and paws padding through the kitchen, licking Tessa's hands. Anne hated the farm, hated it when Tessa went there. Hated it when Tessa came home, carrying into the house God only knew what sorts of germs and foul matter. When Tessa returned home, Anne would personally bathe Tessa herself, and shampoo her hair vigorously.

How Randall, a physician, could allow Tessa to be exposed to such a plethora of germs, Anne just couldn't understand. Anyone who had ever worked in a hospital, who had ever seen the wounded human flesh, would know vigilance was necessary in this world. Cleanliness was essential.

Of course, it was a losing battle. Anne was aware of that. She was not a fool. As she pulled on clean, crisp clothes she admitted to herself that she was more intelligent than most people, and blessed with abundant energy and a keen perception. She intended to do her part to change the world for the better, but she would not let down her standards on the home front in the process.

She would not be like Randall, who had promised to

love and honor her, who vowed to change the world with
her and then betrayed her.

Who continued to betray her. Over and over again.

Fortunate Tessa, *spoiled* Tessa, fussing because she
had to wear a two-hundred-dollar dress when children all
over the city were hungry, illiterate, ill clad. Tessa, whom
she had *ordered* to stay in her room, gone. With Randall.
To the farm. Leaving Anne only a note lying face-up in the
silver bowl on the front hall table. (What if Anne hadn't
seen the note? She would be frantic with worry by now!)

Anne stormed into Tessa's room. Carmen had Sunday
afternoons off, so it was up to Tessa to keep her room neat.
Just for part of one day. Surely not too much to ask of a
twelve-year-old.

And Tessa *had* hung up the lovely, expensive,
painstakingly sewn dress she'd worn to church and then so
recklessly stripped off at noon. Her shoes were neatly
tucked away into the shoe bag hanging on the inside of her
closet door.

With trembling hands, Anne opened one of the drawers
of Tessa's gilt-trimmed white bureau . . .

. . . And found chaos, T-shirts and sweaters and sweat-
shirts, crumpled inside out, crammed and jumbled together
like rags.

How many times had she told Tessa to take proper care
of her clothing? How often had she shown Tessa how her
clothing must be folded when put away: face-down, divided
into thirds lengthwise, the arms folded back and smoothed,
then the shirt top lifted and brought back over the lower
half, the collar arranged to lie just so, and all of it smoothed
again. But no, Tessa had to just *toss* her things in any which
way, as if they weren't the best, most expensive clothes
money could buy, while all around her thousands of poor
girls wore hideous cast-offs, and ailing babies and old people in grave pain went without medicine.

Oh, Anne was angry. Still, she set to work. As a nurse
she knew that the slightest disorder could breed disaster, a

milligram of medication, a moment without oxygen, could bring tragedy down upon one's life.

Tessa's brush, silver-backed, part of a set Anne had bought for her daughter one year at Harrod's in London, lay on the bureau next to the matching mirror. Long strands of blond hair gleamed, caught in the bristles. Anne shuddered as if those hairs were threaded in her throat. She hated hair. It was so unruly, pervasive, drifting everywhere, swirling like evil, just one hair making a web to catch dust and dirt.

Dust, which bred germs, which bred illness, which bred death.

She wasn't able to bring herself to remove the hair from the brush. She'd tell Tessa to do it when she returned home.

She felt more than heard the front door open.

She flew down the stairs.

"Tessa! Tessa, are you all right? How could you go off? Randall, how could you take her? Without my permission! Without even phoning first."

Randall stood with his hand resting on Tessa's shoulder. They were both wearing jeans; both smelled of sunshine and sweet grass. "I did phone first. Tessa answered. You were gone. Even Carmen was gone."

Anne clutched Tessa by her shoulders. "Are you all right? Did you ride? Tell me the truth, did your father put you on a horse?" Without waiting for a reply, she spun toward Randall. "I have asked you—I have *begged* you— to keep her away from those horses. She could be injured. She could fall, have a concussion, break her spine, snap her neck—"

"Anne, look at her. She's here. She's just fine."

He sounded so reasonable. How she hated him for this, for making her look irrational by contrast. And he was so very handsome, even though his shirt was rumpled and he needed a haircut and barn dust covered his boots.

Randall. His clear blue eyes, his massive shoulders, his

calm, bull-like confidence. Why couldn't he continue to love her? She knew she got carried away sometimes. She knew she wasn't easy to live with. But if she'd been a man, her wife would not only have dealt with her eccentricities, but also would have revered them as part of what made her unique.

"You look tired, Anne," Randall said.

She sagged. "Yes. I am."

They were all still standing in the front hall. "Let's go in the kitchen and have some tea," Randall suggested.

Her heart thumped. Perhaps he wanted to talk. He sounded friendly, conciliatory—"Yes. All right."

The routine movements of making tea soothed Anne. Boiling the water, warming the pot, setting out the flowered china cups and saucers. Here, in this room of scrubbed pine and polished chrome, Anne could relax. Carmen kept this room in perfect order.

"How was the taping, Mom?" Tessa's nose and cheeks were pink from the sun.

Anne looked at her daughter. Her beautiful, healthy, fortunate child, gleaming with a body fed with the best substances, cleaned, groomed, loved, and educated.

"It went well. My new slogan seems to be, 'Vote for Anne Madison, for the health of it.'"

Randall laughed. "That's great, Anne. Catchy."

He sat at the place he'd always had when he still lived here, wearing clothes Anne knew as well as her own. The blue shirt with the sleeves rolled up, those khakis—his socks didn't match. They were both white and both cotton, but not a pair. She thought of his rented apartment, his clothes neatly folded away in cheap new furniture, and shuddered.

"I like it, too, Mom."

Anne poured the tea. "Good."

Randall rose and dug in the cupboard for the sugar. Anne eyed him disdainfully as he spooned it into his tea. "Tessa?" He nodded toward the sugar.

"She doesn't need it," Anne snapped.

Randall stirred his tea, sipped it, then said, in a companionable sort of way, as if he were discussing something minor, "Anne, you remember about the GAL appointment this week, don't you?"

She felt her mouth tighten. "Of course I *remember*. It's not likely I'll forget something as important as that."

"I'm only trying to be helpful. I know you've got a full schedule with your campaign."

Placated, Anne agreed. "True." She brightened. "Let me try an idea out on you two. The videotaping gave me an idea: What if we could produce a television show, something fun and engrossing, like a sitcom, but incorporate into the plot all the simple things we're trying to teach? Not drinking during pregnancy. Taking medication daily. Proper diet. That sort of thing."

"That's a really cool idea, Mom!" Some of Tessa's hair had come free from the braids and curled in the heat over her ears.

"It *is* a good idea, Anne. You should pursue it." Randall's voice was warm.

"Yes. Yes, I will." Anne rose. "I need to get a pad and make some notes." As she left the room, she looked back. "Randall, give Tessa some dinner if you haven't already, will you? She can have a salad—there are lettuce and a cucumber in the refrigerator. Be sure to use the fat-free dressing; the other is Carmen's. And a banana for dessert."

Randall's voice cut through her instructions. "Anne. Tessa's too thin—"

"I'm *not* going to argue about this!" Anne snapped. "I am her mother." She turned to Tessa. "*Nothing else. I mean that, Tessa*. And Tessa, if you've been at your grandfather's farm, you must shower and shampoo your hair before you do anything else. Certainly before you eat. And use pHisoHex."

Tessa stood staring down at the floor.

"Well?" Anne demanded.

"Yes, Mom," Tessa said.

"That's better." Anne left them, hurrying over the plush pale ecru wall-to-wall carpet that sank like butter beneath her heels down the hall into the rose-and-cream room she claimed for her own. Here her antique white-and-gold desk awaited her, everything on it belonging there, everything dusted and ordered.

Sinking into her leather chair, she folded her hands and took a deep breath. She touched, in ritual order, her white telephone, the small caller ID box, the thick Rolodex, and delicately moved her daily calendar a fraction of an inch, so that it was exactly in the center of her desk. She touched her tape dispenser, her stapler, the malachite box where she kept her stamps. She touched the pastel Lucite in and out boxes. Last, she set both hands on the silver-and-amethyst tray where her pens lay.

Her blotter was centered perfectly on her desk. Everything gleamed. She thought how much she loved marble and other veined stones whose fissures and stains were incorporated to make an even more beautiful whole, the way a streak first caused by a virus gave new breeds of tulips stripes and speckles and flaws that were considered assets.

She drew a yellow legal pad toward her and took up a pen. Her fingernails were glossy with a pale pink polish, nothing chipped. She would write a letter to her friend Natalie Henderson, who was in charge of public relations at the local PBS station.

Taking a deep breath, Anne began to work. Here, in the familiar order of her study, she could begin to change the world.

Tessa looked at her father across the pine table. "So you aren't going to talk to her today? About me living with you?"

"Sweetie . . ."

"Dad, you *promised*. And you said you'd make her let

me have a computer!" She blinked back angry tears. "Everyone breaks their promises."

Her father gave her a level look. "Would you like me to go talk with her right now?"

Exasperated, Tessa bonked her head right down on the tabletop and tugged at her hair. She knew the worst thing to do was to interrupt her mother when she was working in her study. If her dad went to her mother's study now there'd be a fight, and Tessa hated it when they fought.

She gave the table leg a good solid kick. "Okay, *fine*."

"Tessa, remember what I told you on the way to the farm?"

"What."

"Your mother and you and I are all going to speak with a man, a wise man, a psychiatrist, who knows all about families like ours, families involved in a divorce. He's going to help us decide what's best for you. The judge we saw told us we have to see this man, because it's the best thing for you. After that, the judge will decide where you will live. Until then, it's best for you to stay here."

"But that's crazy. Come on, Dad—" Tessa squirmed. "Can't you just *make* Mom let me live with you? I don't want to talk to strangers about it. Mom would go crazy if she thought I'd told strangers—" She kicked the table leg again, frustrated with the convolutions of her own thinking. What she wanted was to be magically transported out of her mother's house without her mother knowing that that was what Tessa wanted, so that it wouldn't be Tessa who hurt her mother's feelings.

Did this make her a *monster*, that she wanted to leave her mother? Or a *coward*, that she couldn't tell her? *Something* was wrong with Tessa, she knew. Sometimes she felt so angry and sad she thought she'd explode right out of her skin.

"Oh, Tessa, I know this all seems complicated and difficult right now. But it will get straightened out soon. It really will." He stood up. His hair fell over his forehead and was shaggy around his ears. His clothes were rumpled and a thread dangled from the hem of his shirt collar. "Honey, I've got to go. We'll talk about this another time."

"Sure." She stared down at the table.

He came behind her and put his hands on her shoulders. "At least," he said, bending down to whisper, "at least I took you to McDonald's."

There were days when this would make her smile, days when she treasured the conspiracy between her and her father, because her mother would freak out if she knew Tessa had eaten there. McDonald's, Dunkin' Donuts, any of those fast-food places were the spawn of the devil as far as her mother was concerned. Not only would they make Tessa accumulate fat, it also would be a peculiar blobby fat that comes with empty calories, and it would make her face all zitty, too, from the grease.

But today Tessa thought: So then why did her father, who was a doctor, take her there? It couldn't be only, as her mother said, that he did it to spite her, to try to be the Disney parent, while she was left to enforce the standards of good health by herself.

"Tessa," her father said. "Honey."

"I want to meet my birth parents," Tessa blurted out.

He was standing behind her, so she couldn't see his face, but she heard him inhale sharply and she felt him tense up. He came around to face her, pulling up a chair. He took her hands in his.

"Why?"

He looked so kind and worried, her dad, and all at once he looked tired and about three hundred years old. He'd given her such a perfect day.

Her father had enough worries on his mind, she knew. A physician specializing in geriatrics, he saw lawyers, professors, and brilliant doctors he'd once studied under transformed by Alzheimer's, Parkinson's, cancer. He worked too many hours at the hospital and the clinic, and added to those hours by visiting his patients at their retirement homes, checking in on them. Sometimes he took Tessa with him, and usually she liked it. The old people were so nice, with skin as soft as her sheets and bright bird eyes. Sometimes they creeped her out, though—the ones who cried or tried to touch her.

"Tessa?" her father prompted.

She looked away. She couldn't see his earnest worried face and talk about it. "We're studying DNA at school. Inherited characteristics." She pulled her hands away from his.

"Ah." He leaned back in his chair. He folded his arms over his chest. He sighed. "Have you told your mother this?"

Tessa snorted.

Calmly, her father said, "It's not the best of times to drop it on her, do you think?"

"Why does it always have to be about *her*?"

"That's not fair, Tessa, and you know it. It isn't always about her. This is just a difficult year for her, a *complicated* one. Our divorce. Her campaign for the state legislature—"

"I don't care!" Tessa burst out. She brought her fists up against her mouth to hold everything else back.

"You should care. Your mother loves you very much. Your happiness is her first priority. And you're not a child anymore, Tessa. You're twelve." His voice was level but firm. He wasn't shouting at Tessa, but Tessa felt like he was shouting. "You need to cut your mother some slack, Tessa." His voice dropped. "Look. Let's make a deal. The minute the election's over, we'll start the search."

She was so full of emotions it was like trying to contain a tornado inside her skin. She wanted to throw a tantrum like Brooke's little brother did, flinging himself on the floor, kicking and wailing. Why, when everyone said she was getting older, more mature, did she feel so childish?

"Fine," she muttered.

Her father stared at her without speaking.

"I said *fine*."

Her father heaved a gusty sigh. "Want me to fix you a salad?"

She shook her head.

"How about a banana?"

"I'm not hungry." Her poor dad. He hated leaving when she was sad. He'd blunder around forever trying to find something or say something to make her smile. *Then* he could leave. "I'm okay, Dad, really. I'm stuffed from McDonald's."

"Sure?"

"I'm sure."

"You've got camp tomorrow, right?"

"Right."

"What will you do?"

"Tennis. Swim. Maybe do beadwork."

"Did you make that?" He nodded at a beaded bracelet around her wrist.

"No."

"Well, it's cool."

"Want me to make you one?"

"Well, yeah. Yeah, that would be great. Only no pink, okay?"

The thought of her dad with a pink beaded bracelet on his wide hairy wrist brought a helpless smile to her face. "Let me measure your wrist."

She found the measuring tape from the miscellanea drawer—one good thing about her mother being such a neat freak, you could always find whatever you needed, unlike her grandfather's house where everything was cluttered together. Her father's wrist was eight inches around. Hers was barely five.

"If it rains," she told him, "I might get it done in one day. If it's sunny, we'll probably be out all day."

"I'll call you tomorrow night."

"Okay."

He stared down at her. "I love you, Tessa."

"I know, Dad. I love you, too."

"Eat a banana, for goodness' sake. For *my* sake. So I won't feel too guilty about McDonald's."

She smiled. He left.

Tessa waited until the front door shut. She took a banana from the fruit bowl and went out to stand in the hall. Her mother's office door was closed.

She didn't really want a banana. But her mother would interrogate her about what she ate, so Tessa carried it up to her bathroom, stripped off the skin, broke it in little pieces, and dropped it into the toilet. She was afraid the skin would plug up the toilet if she put it in all in one piece, so she found her scissors in her desk and cut the skin into segments, then put those in the toilet, too, then flushed the toilet. Everything went down.

She was a horrible person. People just a few miles away were malnourished, people would be glad to have had that banana that she'd just wasted. There was nothing her mother could say to chastise her that Tessa wasn't already saying to herself. And her mother didn't even have a clue about the horrible feelings that swarmed inside her belly and heart like a pack of Stephen King monsters.

Tessa was pretty sure her birth mother was a criminal in prison.

Tessa often thought about her birth mother. She'd be fat, with cold dead eyes and a frightening hideous temper. Probably she'd killed someone, or more than one person.

Or maybe her birth mother was crazy. Maybe she was in one of those special security prisons for the criminally insane. Maybe she paced back and forth, back and forth, in her cell, muttering swears to herself, laughing maniacally, tearing at her flesh with dirty fingernails.

Maybe sometimes she screamed, kicked the walls and screamed until her throat was raw. Tessa felt like doing that, a lot. She felt like doing that right now.

Instead, she curled up on top of her bed, still wearing

her clothes. Closing her eyes, she held on to her stomach and sank into one of her favorite memories: the animated movie *Anastasia*. Anastasia had lost her parents, her brothers and sisters, her whole world. When she was Tessa's age, she'd lived in a terrible orphanage run by a cruel hag. But that was only the *beginning* of her story.

Tessa assured herself that she was only at the beginning of her own.

She was, wasn't she?

Which is worse, Kelly wondered, as she and Jason sat unlacing their Rollerblades on the steps of her apartment building: refusing to make love with your finacé, or making love with him, while imagining, the entire time, another man?

The heavens smiled down on her, delivering her from the choice—the Red Sox had an afternoon game. When they walked into the living room, the first thing Jason did was to turn on the television set.

She took her time showering and then dressed in a severe beige sheath with, once again, her grandmother's pearls. She put her hair up in a French twist. Jason trotted down to his car for the clothes he'd stashed in the trunk, and after his shower, pulled on summer-weight flannels, white shirt, blue blazer, red tie. Sunday evening dinners at his mother's were not casual.

It was a brief ride from Cambridge across the river to Boston, but in many ways it was a voyage to a different country. They parked in the garage beneath the Public Gardens, walked up Beacon Street to the redbrick buildings sternly lining the streets, buzzed themselves in, and took the elevator to the fourth floor.

"Jason, dear. And Kelly. How lovely."

Eloise Gray stood before them, poised and cool, in a Lilly Pulitzer silk shirtwaist she'd probably worn thirty years ago. Certainly she hadn't gained or lost a pound in all those years. And pearls. And heels. With, on this hot summer day, hose. Of course, the apartment was air-conditioned and humidity-controlled for the art and books.

Briefly, Eloise held her cheek out to be kissed.

They went into her living room, which glowed with ancient Oriental rugs, heirloom vases and furniture, and oil portraits of her ancestors. Above the fireplace hung a painting of Eloise at eighteen, when she was a debutante. She'd possessed the exquisite dramatic beauty her son had inherited, black hair straight and heavy as wood, piercing dark blue eyes beneath straight black brows, and skin as pale as snow. It was no wonder she'd had her choice of suitors.

"Kelly, my dear," Eloise said now, "I am so proud of you. The ceremony was most impressive. I thought we should have some champagne."

"Champagne would be wonderful, Eloise."

"In that case, Jason, will you do the honors?" Eloise nodded toward the silver bucket where a bottle of Perrier-Jouët waited on ice.

At first Kelly had been uncomfortable with the stilted conversation, the formality, the stretches of silence in Eloise's presence, and she knew from Jason that more than one woman had been so daunted by his mother's disdain that they'd broken off with him.

If *she* broke off with Jason, she would be damned if it would be because she couldn't rise to his mother's provocations. Deep in her character ran a rod of pride that made her face down any dare. So she had kept any negative thoughts about Eloise to herself.

When Jason had asked, "Don't you find my mother cold?" Kelly had replied, "Not at all. I like someone who doesn't gush."

When Jason had asked, "Do you feel like my mother ignores you during dinner?" Kelly had responded, "I enjoy watching the two of you talk."

When Jason had asked, "Don't you find my mother rather forbidding?" she had answered, "Jason, don't be silly. I really like your mother."

Then, one day, she realized that what she said was true, because Eloise reminded her of her grandparents, her father's parents, whom she had fiercely loved.

When she was only eighteen, Kelly's mother, Ingrid, had come from Sweden to work as an au pair. Within a year she'd met Otto, within two years she'd married him, and less than a year after that she was a widowed mother. Kelly's father, Otto MacLeod, was killed in Vietnam in 1965, the same year she was born. He was an officer and a hero, but that was not much consolation to his parents, for he was their only child.

Ingrid MacLeod considered moving back to Sweden, but only her father was alive there, a dour, pessimistic fisherman drinking himself to death in a wind-blasted village.

Besides, Otto's parents begged her not to return to Sweden. Move in with them, they implored.

The older MacLeods had a large house on a tree-lined avenue in Arlington, and no one to share it with. If she lived with them, they would take care of her while she took care of Kelly, and she could have time to decide what else she wanted to do with her life, perhaps attend college. Ingrid agreed.

The MacLeods owned a handsome fabric store on Mass Ave where they carried the best of material, wools imported from Scotland, England, and Ireland, silks from Japan and China, accessories from Italy and France. Their home on Flora Street, within walking distance of the shop, furnished in sharp-cornered angular teak, reflected their stern sense of economy. They had only the necessary furnishings, and those were spartan and clean. Like Jason's mother, their favorite adage seemed to be: "Use it up, wear it out, make it do, or do without." They could make a chicken last a week, and even at their most prosperous chose to have soup made from old bones and leftover vegetables rather than throw anything out.

Hardworking Presbyterians, they frowned on drinking,

dancing, and card playing. Because they did not easily touch, kiss, or compliment, Kelly was always shy around her grandparents, but as the years went on, she came to appreciate their sensible reliability and the tranquil orderliness of their days, the logic by which they lived their lives.

For Ingrid it was different. For the first few years her relationship with her daughter sufficed, but she was a young and beautiful woman who could not help yearning for more adult embraces.

When she finally did fall in love, she changed everything in Kelly's life. She betrayed Kelly. She ruined Kelly's life. She broke Kelly's heart.

In a way, Kelly thought, her grandparents were returned to her, through Eloise. The same self-restraint, the same cool facade hiding a steady heart.

On Sundays Eloise's housekeeper had the entire day off, so Eloise prepared the meal, set the table, and served the dinner: lamb chops, wild rice, asparagus.

"Will you pour the wine?" Eloise asked her son.

"May I help?" Kelly offered, as always—and as always, Eloise refused.

A bowl of roses sat between the candles in their twisted silver sticks. The silverware was luxuriously heavy. Eloise sat at the head of the table, her posture magnificently straight. Conversation passed among them with the measured solemnity of a pavane.

"I attended the Symphony Friday night," Eloise told them. "They performed Ned Rorem's new song cycle, *Evidence of Things Not Seen.*"

Jason cut into his chop, chewed a piece, swallowed. "Did you like it?"

"Very much."

After enjoying chocolate eclairs from a bakery, they rose, leaving everything for the housekeeper to deal with the next day, to take coffee in the living room.

"I've agreed to chair the committee for the renovations at the Sadler Museum," Eloise told them, stirring cream into her cup with a heavy silver spoon. "I wonder, Kelly, if you would be kind enough to serve on the committee."

Kelly hesitated. "I won't have much free time, with my new duties—"

"I wouldn't expect you to do much," Eloise countered.

Kelly paused. The Sadler was established to collect and display portraits by lesser-known Boston painters of the Boston aristocracy during the past three centuries.

"Come on," Jason urged. "It's an honor to be asked to serve on anything to do with the Sadler. It's prestigious."

I don't care about prestige, Kelly thought. And I'm not even slightly interested in the Sadler. I want to spend my time on serious causes. She fastened her gaze on Jason, hoping he would read her mind. You ought to know that much about me by now, she thought.

Kelly turned to Eloise. "May I have some time to think about it? I don't know what my schedule will be like yet, how much free time I'll have."

"Of course, dear. I understand." Eloise turned to her son. "Are you going to the Holmes girl's wedding on the Vineyard this Saturday?"

"Absolutely," Jason replied.

"And Kelly?"

"I'm afraid I can't come. I've got so much to do . . ." Kelly had met Muffy Holmes and her fiancé, Buster Bendigen. They were a yacht club, sailing, tennis, skiing, martini-swilling couple just like their parents, without even the pretense of half a social conscience between them. They had buckets of money, it would be an amazing occasion, and Jason felt he had to go; he'd gone to private elementary and boarding school with Buster.

"In that case, Jason, would you be my escort?" Eloise inquired.

"Sure."

"Lovely. We'll stay with the Worths." Eloise smiled at Kelly. "I'll make certain he behaves at the reception and doesn't spend too much time with any of the bridesmaids."

FOUR

MONDAY MORNING MONT MADISON STEPPED out of the shower, toweled his arthritic grizzled old body dry, and, spotting the robe hanging from the hook on the back of the door, pulled it on.

It was Madeline's. He knew that. Of course he did. He wasn't senile enough quite yet to think this robe of pink terry cloth with white piping and white flowers embroidered on the pockets was a man's robe.

The thing was, it was so damned comfortable. Once, by accident, in the days just after Madeline's death, he'd accidentally pulled it on after a shower, not discovering his mistake until afternoon, and even then he hadn't taken it off because it brought Madeline back to him so forcefully.

"I'd be glad to pack up Mrs. Madison's clothes and take them to the church thrift sale for you," their cleaning lady, Dorothy, had offered, more than once.

Mont knew she was well intentioned, but he found her infuriating and intrusive. For God's sake! Why would he want to get rid of Madeline's things? They still held her scent, and a life full of memories surrounded him whenever he entered their bedroom and saw them, through the open closet door, hanging in the same colorful disarray in which Madeline, in her later years, had lived her life.

Now Mont shuffled down the stairs and into the

kitchen for his standard breakfast of orange juice and Grape-Nuts. Without Madeline around, it wasn't worth brewing a pot of coffee, and he couldn't stomach the instant stuff, so he did without. He tripped going over the threshold into the kitchen because he was wearing Madeline's slippers. One thing about Madeline, she had had big feet for a woman. She'd hated their size, but Mont had always found them oddly attractive, sexual, generous, like the rest of Madeline's body, and bold, like her spirit.

He stood in front of the sink, spooning cereal into his mouth, staring at the yard—the grass needed cutting again—thinking how much he wanted to die.

Not in any sentimental, mawkish, searching-for-attention, crying-for-help bullshit way. But just plain honest die.

He couldn't tell his son this because it would distress Randall so much, when, in fact, the truth of it was the very opposite of distressing.

How many people could say they'd had a marriage like his? He and Madeline had been together for over fifty years, and loved each other passionately, even in the midst of savage disagreements, every second of every one of those decades of days. Volcanic in their early lusty years, life and its pressures had pressed them together so firmly they were, finally, one single thing, bedrock lined with a deep gleaming vein of gold. With Madeline gone, Mont was not even less than half of something. He was only the shape of something, the substance vanished.

Sure, he loved his son. That love was what drove him to pretend he was working on a book. Randall, dutiful enough for two since his sister Evangeline moved out to the West Coast, was clearly relieved by any signs that Mont was pursuing something intellectually, that he was in any way at all going forward.

Neither one of his children could comprehend the kind of marriage Mont and Madeline had. Mont loved his daughter, and was admiring of and slightly amused by the way she lived her life, unmarried, bisexual, weaving tapestries

and shawls from the hair of animals—goats, sheep, dogs—
on an island off Puget Sound. Evangeline was always too
adventurous, too fickle in every way, to settle down to just
one person. And Randall, well, now, he was a sweet lad,
deep down. Mont was sad that Randall's marriage hadn't
worked out. Divorce was always sad, but secretly Mont was
glad for his son, for he had always thought Anne was one
frigid, neurotic, cantankerous harpy. Mont was glad Randall had another chance at finding happiness.

Mont loved his granddaughter best. Tessa was a joy.
Always had been. The only reason he didn't write a farewell note and ingest several dozen tablets was that he felt
he needed to do what he could to help Tessa, who, as she
grew into a young woman, was being poorly served by
Anne with her nerves, phobias, and tics. Mont had seen
many things in his long life, and nothing about Anne had
ever pleased him, but more and more about Anne just plain
frightened him. How Randall, a *physician*, could not see
that his daughter was clearly undernourished, troubled
Mont. The thinness, of course, was only a symptom, the
tip of a particularly sinister iceberg.

Madeline had always been able to counterweigh any
damage Anne did to the child. Madeline had simply swept
blindingly clean, thin, tidy Tessa up into her plump, energetic arms and hustled her off into her studio where she
clad the child in one of her own smocks and let her loose
with finger paints. And how many nights had Madeline sat
with Tessa in the barn, watching cats or dogs give birth?
Madeline had read to Tessa, had sung to and danced with
Tessa, had taught Tessa to ride bareback, had taken Tessa
skinny-dipping in the stream behind the house. Had taught
Tessa to make jams from berries they picked, and cookies
and pies and cakes, and Tessa had been so caught up in the
sheer exuberance of Madeline's pleasure in life that she'd
eaten heartily without a thought.

Now Madeline was gone, and much of the lust of living had disappeared from all their lives. Mont could never

hope to do for Tessa what Madeline did, but Madeline would expect Mont to do, at the least, what he could to keep the child safe and happy.

So for Madeline's sake—and for Tessa's—Mont finished his cereal, then climbed to his bedroom to dress and begin his day.

Anne was pleased that the psychiatrist was male. Often females reacted to their first meeting with Anne with a subdued, instinctive hostility. There were many reasons. Anne understood them all. She was thin, in a culture where thinness was admired above all other qualities, the kind of thinness that few females could achieve without deprivation and grueling discipline.

She was also wealthy, and her ancestors had been wealthy and those ancestors had been wealthy, and so much inherited wealth shone from her like an aura. She could not dim it. It was as much a part of her as the way she moved across the room. She left her jewelry at home, she wore the plainest white shirt and gray skirt, and she still looked exactly like what she was: an American aristocrat.

Still, because he was male, he would tend to like her. Most men did, especially if she went to the trouble to smile and put them at ease. Later, when both men and women got to know her, they came to admire her. Perhaps not to enjoy her company, or to want to share secrets, or to light up when they saw her. Seldom that. But to respect her, yes. They always came to respect her.

Anne had just seated herself on the green leather sofa when the secretary peered over her eyeglasses, produced a professional smile, and announced, "Mrs. Madison? Dr. Lawrence will see you now."

Anne knew how to enter a room, and she'd given a great deal of thought to the way she should approach this meeting. She must be calm and firm and sympathetic, but resolute. She'd thought of appearing nervous—letting the psychiatrist feel his power—but decided against it. She wasn't nervous. She was angry, really. Indignant. But prepared to be polite.

It was not, she saw at once, the office of a wealthy man. The furniture, desk and chairs, were traditional inexpensive "executive" pieces one could buy at any office-supply store. A bookcase along one wall held books, framed family photos, toys and games.

The psychiatrist came out from behind his desk to shake her hand. With surprise she saw that he was rather attractive, not what she'd expected. No eyeglasses, no bushy brows, no hair in his ears. Instead, he was tanned and fit. In gray summer flannels and a long-sleeved black cotton (perhaps silk!) T-shirt, his dark hair clipped close to his skull, he looked youthful, urban, and contemporary.

"Mrs. Madison? I'm Dr. Lawrence. Thank you for coming in." He gestured to a chair.

"Please call me Anne," she requested, sitting, smoothing her skirt over her knees, crossing her legs at the ankles and slipping them to one side. She hung her purse by its strap over the back of the chair.

"Anne." He settled behind the desk. "Would you like some coffee, Anne? Or tea?"

She hesitated.

"How about some iced tea," he suggested. "I'll have some, too."

"That would be lovely."

He tapped his intercom. "Carrie? Would you be kind enough to bring in some iced tea for the two of us?"

He rummaged around on a desk piled with folders and notebooks. It needed, Anne thought, a good dusting. She let her hands lie at ease in her lap as she waited. He opened a folder, glanced at it, opened a desk drawer, brought out a pen, laid it next to the folder, and finally looked up at Anne.

"All right, now. I see we're here about your daughter, Tessa."

She nodded.

"You and Mr. Madison, um, Dr. Madison—he's a physician, right?"

She nodded again.

"You're divorcing, and you both want to have full custody of your daughter." He looked at Anne expectantly.

"That's correct."

"You understand that I, as court-appointed guardian *ad litem*, will be talking with you and Tessa and her father."

"I understand that."

He looked at his notes. "In fact, over the next month, I'll be seeing quite a lot of you and your daughter. The appointments are scheduled very close together. Is there a reason for the rush?"

"Is there a reason *not* to rush?" she countered coolly. "Tessa starts school in September. She'll be busy all day, and she'll have extracurricular activities. In my opinion, it would be best for everyone to get this settled. Tessa needs to know where she's going to be living for the school year."

He cleared his throat. "Often the expense of so many sessions close together is too difficult for people to deal with all at once."

"That's not a problem. For either of us. Randall and I have no issues about money. I have—and always will have—a comfortable living from a trust fund from my grandparents."

"All right, then. Well, first, why don't you tell me something about your marriage and the reasons for your divorce?"

She cleared her throat. It was, after all, harder than she'd thought it would be. A welling of emotion conflicted with her need to control this meeting.

"Randall and I have been married for fourteen years. We met fifteen years ago, when he was a resident at Brigham and Women's and I was a nurse. We were both idealistic. We both intended, in all naiveté, to save the world. And I suppose, in our own ways, we're still working toward that."

Dr. Lawrence smiled. "A difficult task, saving the world."

"True. And, of course, we both know we can't really do that. But we have to try. *Someone*, after all, has to try."

"An admirable thought." He paused a beat and, when she did not continue, said, "And so you married."

"And so we married. We wanted children—" She dropped her eyes. It's all right, she assured herself, anyone would expect her to find this difficult. Anyone would feel sympathy. She raised her head and looked right at him. "During our first year of marriage, I became pregnant twice. And both times—" She clasped her hands together. "Both times I had an ectopic pregnancy. Do you know what that is?"

"I'd be grateful if you'd refresh my memory."

"An ectopic pregnancy takes place when the egg is fertilized somewhere other than in the uterus. In my case, in the ovary. As the embryo grows, it quickly becomes too large for the ovary and the ovary bursts. The result is that the woman no longer has ovaries or eggs."

"How very sad."

"Yes. Very sad. And painful. Very painful. I mean physically, not just emotionally." She looked away.

A tap came at the door, and the secretary entered carrying a tray with two glasses of iced tea, the ice tinkling musically.

"Just put them here." Dr. Lawrence nodded to the corner of his desk. "Thanks, Carrie."

"Is that your sailboat?" Anne asked, looking at a photograph on the wall behind him.

"Yes. It is. Sugar in your tea?"

"No, thank you." She picked up her glass and took a small sip. She heard the door close behind her, shutting Carrie out, and felt her shoulders relax.

"So it was a tough time for you then, the first year of your marriage."

"Indeed." She felt anger flush through her. "I believed,

and I always shall believe, that it was Randall's fault."

Dr. Lawrence looked slightly startled. "Oh?"

"Randall is sexually rapacious. I'm sure that if he had not insisted on having sex so often, I wouldn't have had the physical problems that I had."

"Is there any statistical evidence to back up this theory?"

"I wouldn't know. I don't read medical journals. Besides, it might be purely psychological, I mean the cause and effect. I don't care about *statistics*, anyway. They wouldn't change things for me. They wouldn't make me capable of bearing children."

Dr. Lawrence stirred a packet of Sweet'N Low into his tea. Sweet'N Low was a woman's thing, Anne thought, watching. Still the action of his stirring, the domesticity of it, soothed her.

"And so we decided to adopt," Anne continued. "But we both knew, from working at the hospital, how crucial those first few hours, days, and weeks are for an infant. Things can happen then that can impact a child's character forever. You must, as a psychiatrist, be aware of that."

He nodded.

"In addition, I also felt strongly that I would like to have a child who looked rather more like us than less. Not just to prevent awkward explanations with other people. I thought I would relate more strongly to a child who looked like us."

"Perfectly understandable."

"So we decided to use a surrogate mother, a woman with my coloring and so on, who would be artificially inseminated with Randall's semen." She cleared her throat. She was a nurse, yet saying those words—*semen, inseminate*—brought a flush to her face.

"We arranged it through a friend of Randall's. He found a willing surrogate mother for us, a blond woman, young, healthy, and—perhaps we should not have cared about this, but we did—of high intelligence. So Tessa was born—"

"Were you there for the birth?"

Anne flinched. "Heavens, no. We never met the woman. We insisted on retaining our anonymity." She waited for him to respond. He only nodded. "So—Tessa was born. A hired nurse brought her to us within hours of her birth." Anne smiled at the memory. "She was a lovely baby. A lovely little girl. I'd been secretly hoping for a girl. She has one flaw, a birthmark on her neck, rather ugly, but otherwise she's beautiful, and she looks like us. People are always saying to us that they can't decide who she looks like more, Randall or me."

"A fortunate little girl."

Anne smiled at the compliment. "I stopped working when Tessa was born. I thought it best if I stayed home with the baby. I have nothing against mothers who work—I want to make that clear. I think children can be just as happy and well adjusted if they spend part of their early years with caregivers. That just wasn't what I wanted for our daughter." She stopped to sip some tea.

Dr. Lawrence waited calmly for her to resume her narrative.

"I did find, after the first blush wore off, that I was a bit bored, just staying home, and after a while I got into the habit of volunteer work. The more I volunteered, the more I wanted to work. My parents had raised me to be altruistic. As the years passed and Tessa was in school, I became more involved. I initiated a hands-on educational program for teaching high school students about contraception, AIDS, STDs, and drugs. I've sat on, and sit still, on several boards. As you might know, I'm campaigning for the Democratic slot for state representative from the Arlington district. I believe I have a fairly good chance of winning the election. I have quite a few supporters—"

"Is it a problem with your husband? Your social commitments?"

The interruption annoyed Anne, threw her off track. She sipped tea once more, trying to regain her poise. She considered his question.

"No. No, that's no problem for Randall. He has always supported me in my work."

Dr. Lawrence continued to look at her.

"Oh, I see." Anne threw him a smile. "You want me to focus on why Randall and I are divorcing."

"I'd like to know about that, yes."

How to put it in the most flattering light? She knew if she were vitriolic about Randall (which certainly she deserved to be), it would somehow reflect badly on her.

"Randall and I—have grown apart over the years. I suppose many people say that, but in our case it's true. He works perhaps sixty hours a week, and in addition sits on boards, and with my schedule—well, I'm sure you know how it is."

"You've discussed the possibility of his cutting back?"

Anne flicked a piece of lint off her skirt. "No, because that's not really the problem." She saw a stain on her skirt, just slightly darker than the rest of the linen, and rubbed at it. Lifting her head, she forced herself to say it. "Randall is promiscuous. He has been for years. I find it insulting, degrading, and disgusting."

"You've talked about this with him?"

"Of course I've confronted him! It does no good. You have to understand, Dr. Lawrence, the physical side of marriage has never been important to me. Randall *knew* that when we married. I thought he had accepted it and would adjust himself accordingly. His life is full, after all. He has his work, Tessa, me, his parents and their farm. He's not an adolescent any longer." She leaned forward, impassioned. "This is why it's crucial that I have custody of Tessa. Tessa's at a delicate age now. She's *twelve*. She hasn't started to menstruate yet, but when she does, it's her mother she'll need to turn to, not her father. Randall's attitude toward sexual matters is so . . . so *reckless* that it can only harm her."

"Do you mean he might behave sexually toward her?"

"What?" Anne blinked and then flushed deeply. "Good God, of course I don't mean that. Randall would never—" She shuddered. "I would never accuse Randall of anything so abhorrent."

"That's good, then. We've got that out in the air and out of the way."

"Randall is a good man, for the most part. But just because he's basically good doesn't mean that Tessa should live with him. He works too many hours, and he spends too much time with his father on that filthy farm, and he takes far too many different women into his bed . . . that would have to have a deleterious effect on Tessa. If we had a boy, I'd agree the child should live with Randall. But Tessa's a girl. She needs her mother."

"Tell me about Tessa."

"Gladly." Anne leaned back in her chair and gathered her thoughts. "She's beautiful. Really beautiful. Slender, with long blond hair. I work hard, encouraging her to remain slender—children eat so much junk these days—but I believe her hair will stay blond as she gets older. I think her birth mother must have been Scandinavian. She's got that look about her. I have a picture in my purse. Would you like to see it?"

"I'll be meeting with her soon. I'd rather hear you talk about her."

"All right. Well—she was a good baby. A happy baby. Indeed, I think she's a naturally happy child. She's extremely bright. She might be gifted, but I've never wanted to have her tested. It's not necessary. She's receiving an excellent education at a private school."

"What about friends?"

"What about them?" Anne realized her tone had been hostile. She made herself smile. "Tessa has friends. She sees children her age at school, of course, and this summer she's attending a day camp. There is one point of contention between Randall and me. I might as well go ahead and mention it. He's certain to bring it up: I don't allow Tessa to visit other girls' homes very often."

"Oh? Why is that?"

"I feel very strongly about the negative aspects of computers, television, and music. There's simply too much sex, too much violence. I see this as an insidious evil in our culture."

"I'm afraid you're right."

"Well, then, you'll understand. How can I allow Tessa to go to someone else's house? I can't control what they see or do there. Other parents aren't as vigilant as I. Even the things they're exposed to on HBO . . ." Again she rubbed at the stain on her skirt.

"And yet children need to be with friends."

"Tessa is with friends. At school. That's most of the day, five days a week. Or, as now, at camp. She sometimes attends birthday parties or goes to the movies with a friend."

"What about boys?"

"Boys?"

"Does she have a boyfriend?"

"Absolutely not! She's twelve years old."

Dr. Lawrence nodded. "Okay. Let's talk about something else. Tell me what you and Tessa like to do together."

Anne reflected a moment. "I have to think about that," she admitted. "If you'd asked me this a year ago, or two years . . . we were closer then. You must realize that as girls grow up, they want to spend less time with their parents. And I've had to spend so much time lately, campaigning. Well, for one thing, Tessa and I used to go shopping together all the time. I loved buying her clothes, and even when she was five or six, she was capable of helping me select my clothing." She smiled. " 'Mom,' she'd say, '*no ruffles.*' Tessa has never liked ruffles.

"But now—she's almost a teenager. She's swayed by

the opinions of the girls in her class, who in turn are brain-washed by ridiculous television ads. Everyone looks so *sloppy* these days. Baggy jeans. Oversized shirts. Children wearing slacks so low on their hips they walk on the hems, intentionally."

Anne picked up her glass and found it empty.

"Would you like more tea?"

"No, I'm fine. I just—" She threw him one of her most charming smiles. "I suppose I was just trying to give myself time to think. I feel I'm taking a test. I want to get the answers right."

"There are no right or wrong answers."

"Of course there are. You're going to base your recommendation to the judge about the custody of my daughter on my answers! If I tell you, for example, that I used to do a lot with Tessa, such as reading, I always read to her, every night, when she was small, but of course now she reads to herself and doesn't want me reading to her, so it seems I don't do as much with her—but you have to understand—" She brought her hands to her face, pressing the tips of her fingers against the bridge of her nose. She'd lost her train of thought, she'd lost her self-control.

"Please don't be upset," Dr. Lawrence urged. "I know this sort of session is difficult. But you're doing just fine."

She looked up. "Then you'll recommend that I have custody?"

"We're just starting the process, Anne. I need to speak with Randall, and with Tessa, probably twice for each of you. And perhaps some other people as well." He flipped through a pad. "I have a list here. Carmen, your house-keeper. Randall's father, Montgomery."

"The minister of our church, Reverend Christopher."

"Yes, perhaps. His name is here. In any case, our time is up for today."

"I just want you to know," Anne said, her voice low but urgent, "I consider it essential to my daughter's psychological welfare that she live with me. I know I seem controlling. I *am* controlling. Randall, on the other hand, is capricious, promiscuous, unpredictable, messy, and indulgent. Not the qualities of a monster, I realize, but combined with the fact that he's a man and Tessa's a girl, add up to the unbelievably simple fact that Tessa should be with me."

"You seem quite passionate about that."

"I am." Anne rose. She knew a good exit line. "I am not passionate about much, Dr. Lawrence, but I am passionate about that."

When Kelly awakened Monday morning she lay for a few moments, indulging herself in the pure animal sensations of good health and happiness. Sun filtered through the breeze-stirred summer leaves, making their shadows dip and flutter on the floor. The classical radio station that her alarm clicked on sent something like Mahler into the air. *Mahler,* Kelly thought. *Ugh.* Reaching out, she punched the seek button to the classic rock station.

"Good golly, Miss Molly!" Little Richard shrieked.

This is more like it, Kelly thought, jumping out of bed. She had a million things to do. She showered, sipped her coffee while dressing in a pale cream linen dress and comfortable flats—she'd be doing a lot of walking today—twisted her hair into a chignon, grabbed her briefcase, and headed out the door.

Dunlap and Reed was housed in an ugly aluminum-sided duplex on Cambridge Street. They kept it purposefully unpretentious: its humble appearance made it seem hospitable to people who might feel shy around lawyers, and provided their opposition with a false view of their strength.

"Good morning, Your Honor," Jackie Cortez greeted her from her receptionist desk. "You're looking mighty fine today."

"Feeling mighty fine, Jackie," Kelly said. "How did Emanuel's game go?" Jackie's thirteen-year-old son, the

youngest of five children and the only boy, played on a
Little League team.

"Lord, he hit a home run!"

After hearing a detailed description of Saturday's
game, Kelly headed to her office at the back, in the room
that had once been the kitchen and still had its linoleum
floor. Three walls were lined with inexpensive pine shelv-
ing stacked with Massachusetts Law Statutes, law reviews,
ancient legal volumes, and piles of current advance sheets
on changes in the law. Her desk, a valiant metal veteran,
squatted beneath the weight of a computer, printer, phone,
answering machine, and towers of files, papers, and folders.

Sinking into her chair, she checked her e-mail and
flipped through snail mail. Then she turned to the contents
of her drawers. Behind her, on either side of a window,
stood file cabinets once so full she could scarcely close
them. Since she'd been notified of her appointment, she'd
begun the complicated effort of cleaning them out, and it
was almost sad, how empty they looked.

Dragging a cardboard storage box from the pile in the
corner, Kelly settled in to finish the job. Half the files at
the back were so old they'd been there when she arrived.

She'd left her door open in case any of the other lawyers wanted to wander in for a chat. She was just hefting
an armload of files into the box when she heard a knock
on the door.

"Come in!" she called. "Oof!" She dropped the files,
brushed her hands, and turned.

René Lambrousco stood there, grinning.

Kelly had seen him at her mother's funeral, so she
knew that by now, nearly sixty, René had lost much of his
startling sexual appeal. However, René was not yet aware
of this. He struck a pose in her doorway, absolutely lounging against the door, clad in black jeans, black motorcycle
boots, and a black silk shirt open to reveal several gold
chains. His style, Kelly thought, had definitely deteriorated
over the years. He wore his hair pulled back in a ponytail

and a thick salt-and-pepper beard camouflaged his sagging jowls. An unlit cigarette hung indolently from his full lips.

"Smoking's not allowed in here," Kelly said peevishly.

"And I'm delighted to see you, too, dear stepdaughter," René retorted, his voice oily with false pleasure. He put the cigarette in the breast pocket of his shirt.

"You're not my stepfather," Kelly snapped. "What do you want?"

"I'm not allowed to stop by? To say hello? To offer my congratulations?"

"René," Kelly said, very calmly, "go away."

Instead the man advanced into the room, draped his body in the chair facing her desk, and swung one leg over the armrest. "Imagine my surprise when we read about you in the paper. A judge. Most impressive."

Kelly stared at him.

"Please remember"—René pouted—"when your mother was dying, I went to the trouble to search you out."

"Don't tell me it was difficult. You had only to look in a Boston phone book."

"Even so. I made the effort. Without me, you would not have seen your mother ever again."

Kelly shut her office door. She didn't need her personal life aired to everyone. Sinking into her desk chair, she said quietly, "Yes, René, what you say is true. I am grateful. And I know, and you know, that Ingrid was grateful. But she's gone now, and she was the only connection between us."

René's eyes narrowed. "You think you're so much better than the rest of us because you're a judge, don't you?"

"No, René, I don't. I only think I worked harder. I only think that when my birthright was taken away from me, I had to find a way to fend for myself, and I know that you have *no idea* what kind of sacrifices I made. And you never will know."

"Whatever your sacrifices," René countered smoothly,

"here you are. You're going to be a judge. You should be happy with yourself. Proud."

"I am proud. I am happy."

"Then why not be friends?"

"I have enough friends.

"Ah, what a pity. You've become *hard*."

"Probably."

"Don't you ever think about Felicity?"

A vision of Felicity flashed through Kelly's mind: a teenager, too thin, sullen, astoundingly gorgeous with her pale skin and cascading black hair, standing at the graveyard while their mother's coffin was lowered into the ground. Felicity had exhibited no interest in Kelly. Hiding her eyes the entire time behind dark glasses, she'd seemed foreign and forbidding. "So that's it. What do you need? Money for her?"

"She's fifteen. She's your half sister. She'll be wanting to go to college soon."

"René, I have seen your daughter exactly twice in my life, once in the hospital when mother was dying, and again at the funeral. I feel no connection to her whatsoever."

"You should."

"I *should*? How can you, of all people, tell me what I should feel?" Kelly felt her face flush with anger.

"My dear Kelly, I've never made excuses for what I am, for how I live my life. I'm not here now to ask for anything for myself. I'm here, quite humbly, to congratulate you, and to ask you to consider thinking of your half sister."

"Very well," Kelly said. "You've come. You've spoken. Now go."

René's face darkened. "How can you be a family court judge when you don't even communicate with your own family?"

"You're not my family. You never have been."

René sighed and shrugged. "Ah, well," he said. "What a pity. Felicity is a marvelous girl. But quite bowled over by her mother's death. She needs someone feminine in her life. I was hoping that you—"

Kelly kept her face blank.

René rose. "Then I'll leave you."

"Please do," Kelly said.

"It is your loss, you know," René told her.

She didn't respond. René would try to trump any comment she made, and besides, in her heart she thought that very probably he was right. It was undoubtedly a loss that she did not know the young woman who shared her blood, but it was a loss that Kelly chose, and that made it tolerable.

Sarah Franklin picked up the ringing telephone, heard her daughter's voice, and immediately overcome with weariness, collapsed into a chair.

"How are you, Mother?" Anne asked.

"Ugh!" Sarah gasped. "Sorry, dear, Brownie jumped right up on my stomach. Knocked the air out of me. Fine, darling. How are you?"

"Good."

"Busy?" Keeping her arm around Brownie, their newest pet, an abandoned husky–pit bull mix MSPCA adoptee, Sarah reached under her to pull out the object poking her thigh. It was a shoe. A man's shoe. Stroking Brownie's head as she settled deeply into her lap, she observed how much her head was shaped like the shoe, wide between the ears, narrowing steadily toward the nose.

"Very. Eleanor Marks gave me a PR brunch last Sunday, but Rebecca, the imbecile, had scheduled me for two different events at the same time and I had to have a videotape made, because the videographer offered to make a campaign tape for nothing, but it had to be done then."

Thomas came, slumping, into the room. "There is something I am missing."

"Actually, it looks as if it will be a great tape. Mick Aitkins—he's the videographer—helped me come up with a rather clever slogan. 'Vote for Anne Madison, for the health of it!' "

Sarah made an encouraging, ambiguous *mmmm* sound, indicating, she hoped, to both Thomas and her daughter her utter, fascinated attention.

Smiling, she waved the shoe at the willowy man in his green Stop & Shop shirt. Thomas, from Russia, lived rent-free in their attic with three of his friends, the newest members of the New World program Sarah and her husband and like-minded families throughout New England had started thirty years ago. Project New World found jobs with local businesses for the immigrants, an easy enough task when Nantucket's tourism was booming and the merchants desperate. In addition, the Franklins provided free lodging for the men. This way the immigrants could save most of their salaries for the pursuit of education or investment in a business or airfare to bring their families to the States. Over the years Sarah and Herbert had personally helped perhaps a hundred people in this way. At Christmas their mail carrier came staggering to the door, weighted down with cards and photos and expressions of continual gratitude from a complete United Nations of recipients of their generosity.

Sarah had enjoyed them all—some, of course, more than others—but she couldn't recall anyone quite as handsome, in a gloomy way, as Thomas. Of course, he *would* be melancholy, with his wife and little boy left behind with his parents and brother and sister in a crowded cottage without electricity in an impoverished rural village. Heartbreaking, and truly shocking, the way some people were forced to live. All their lives Sarah and Herbert, children of rather disgustingly wealthy families, had tried their best to balance, in their own small ways, the scales.

"Mother? Are you there?"

"Yes, darling, hanging on your every word. Just a second . . . Is this what you're looking for, Thomas?"

He came toward her, smelling of Zest, Brylcreem, and

Listerine—he kept himself flawlessly clean. "I do not know how this shoe came to be in this room."

"Brownie, I think. She seems to think shoes are her children. It's rather sweet, isn't it?"

Thomas held his shoe up, inspecting it carefully. "Here it is moist."

"Yes, the leather is a bit soggy, but it will dry. Brownie was very gentle. No bite marks anywhere."

"Mother!"

"Sorry, Anne, but Brownie seems to have adopted poor Thomas's shoe. She brought it all the way down here from the attic." Laughing, Sarah fondly stroked Brownie's pointed head.

Silence.

"Darling, I *was* listening to you. I am. Go on. Video thingy, wasn't it?"

"Oh, never mind!"

"Thank you," Thomas said, taking the shoe. "I go to work now."

"Remember to smile, Thomas!" Sarah instructed. "They like you better if you smile. Come on. You can do it."

Slowly Thomas widened his mouth, exposing horrible teeth. Maybe it would be best not to encourage him to smile.

"Mother?"

"All right, Anne, so sorry. Thomas just left. You have my entire attention."

"I don't want to bore you."

"Come on, you never bore me," Sarah lied, silently asking the fates how she and Herbert had ever managed to raise a child as deadly serious as Anne. Anne's intentions were without fault, but the grim resolution with which she pursued them, exhausting.

"I've come up with a great idea for a local access television show. Something like a sitcom that would be fun for children to watch but would teach them, *subtly*, about issues like not drinking alcohol during pregnancy and the necessity of proper diets for mothers—"

Oh, this was going to be a long conversation. Sarah lifted Brownie onto the floor, hefted herself out of the armchair, lumbered into the kitchen, and cut herself a large slice of chocolate cake. Opening the cupboard, she discovered there were no clean plates. She'd forgotten to run the dishwasher, which was overflowing. Clamping the phone to her ear with her shoulder, she filled the detergent tray and switched the machine on; then she sat down at the table to eat the cake right off its plate. Sarah's mother would have had apoplexy. For that matter, so would Anne. That was it, of course: Sarah's mother's anal compulsions had skipped Sarah and landed in Anne, like one of those genetic diseases she'd read about. Appropriate, then, that the majority of Sarah's mother's estate had gone to Anne.

Sarah hadn't minded. Sarah's mother had had maids, lots of them, scurrying around their huge Chestnut Hill mansion with brooms, dustpans, cloths, vacuum cleaners, like something absolutely out of Dickens. Her mother had snipped and snapped at those women, who in response nodded meekly, nearly prostrating themselves with expressions of servility. As a child, Sarah had cringed at the injustice of it and vowed she would never cause another person to be her servant.

She'd kept that vow. Unfortunately, no one had ever taught her how to attack in orderly fashion the running of a house. It had taken her a very long time to learn the simplest things, like the good sense of the dustpan living with the broom. To this day, when she and Herbert were in their sixties, their home—they had now, only the one, this summer home on Nantucket they'd had insulated and renovated for year-round use—displayed not so much messiness and dirt as a simple lack of organization and systematic routine care.

When she turned fifty, Sarah had finally hired a girl to come in twice a week to see to the basic things like scrubbing the kitchen floor and the bathrooms, but Sarah had never learned to bond with furnishings. Because she always found the lives of the cleaning girls much more interesting than whether or not the freezer was defrosted or the bathtubs scrubbed, Sarah continually invited them to sit down with a cup of coffee and a muffin for a good long talk about their gloriously dramatic lives. She paid the cleaning girls for eight hours, knew they barely worked three hours, and didn't care. What, after all, was money for?

"—don't you think?" Anne concluded.

"Muphg," Sarah responded, her mouth full of cake.

"What are you eating?" Anne demanded.

Sarah sighed, scattering cake crumbs on the bosom of her turquoise summer shift. One of the reasons Sarah and Herbert had decided to give up their winter home in Boston and move full-time to Nantucket was this maddening watch-dog attitude of Anne's. "Chocolate cake," Sarah admitted, knowing she might as well tell her daughter she was eating live babies.

"Mother, think of your cholesterol."

"I'd rather not. How's Tessa?"

"Oh, I don't know, honestly I don't. She's so volatile."

"Did you send her to camp?"

"Yes. She's there now."

"Does she enjoy it?"

"I suppose. Listen, Mother, I need to ask you a favor."

"Oh? Well, go on. Out with it."

"You know Randall and I are having a battle about who should get custody of Tessa."

"Yes, you want him to take her and he wants you to have her?" Sarah laughed heartily.

"This isn't a joke."

"I know it's not. I apologize. But wait a few years, until Tessa reaches full-scale gale force adolescence. You might understand better then."

"Mother. Concentrate. Please."

"Yes, dear," Sarah said dutifully.

"Randall and Tessa and I have to meet with the guardian *ad litem*. It's ordered by the court. I told you this at the beginning of July, just after the fourth, remember?" She didn't wait for her mother's reply. "I've already met with him. Dr. Lawrence. He seems intelligent and fair. I'd like you to come talk with him. Help me convince him that Tessa should be with me."

"Oh, Anne, you know how I hate leaving the island."

"I do know that. But this is urgent, Mother. You must understand. I could lose custody of Tessa."

"I don't actually see why that would be so bad, Anne." At the explosive sputtering from the other end of the line, Sarah cried, "Wait a minute, would you please? Hear me out! I'm thinking of *you*, Anne. I know you think I'm dotty, but I'm not really, and I do love you in my own way, and what's more, Anne, I *know* you, probably better than anyone else does. Probably better than you do. I know what you were like as a little girl. I know how much you hate disorder. I know—"

"Mother. I have Carmen."

"I'm not talking about keeping the house clean! I'm talking about relationships. I'm talking about dealing with a young woman! Adolescence is fraught with tensions, animosities, hormonal explosions. This is when daughters start rebelling against their mothers. They can't help it. It's like the course of the seasons. They *pull away*."

"Tessa and I—"

"Read the literature, Anne. Please. As a favor to me. There will be all sorts of hell breaking loose in the next few years, Oedipal stuff, Electra stuff. Tessa won't be a little sweetheart anymore. She'll be hostile and secretive and emotional. You'll try to help and she'll shut you out. It will be very hard on you."

"Other mothers survive it. I'm sure I can. Anyway, I can always—"

"Always what? Take more Valium?"

"I don't take Valium."

"Xanax, then. Or something. Be honest. Don't you take tranquilizers?"

"My work is very demanding, Mother. I get nervous, and with the election coming up I get anxious."

"Then you should let Tessa live with Randall."

"I can't *believe* you said that to me! I can't believe you feel that way! What kind of mother are you?"

"One who loves you, Anne." Sarah gripped the phone. She could feel her daughter listening. "One who loves you and admires you *enormously*. And sees you clearly. Anne, I wish you'd think about why you want Tessa living with you. Your gifts are many. You have the chance to make vast, significant changes that will better the lives of thousands of people. Why tie your hands with the responsibility for one adolescent?"

"I can't—"

"Please hear me out. It's not as if Randall is vindictive. You know that if Tessa lives with him, he'll let you see Tessa any time. Let *him* deal with the exhausting daily stuff. Then you'd be free to travel—what was that conference you were asked to speak at last spring? In San Francisco? About public transportation and working parents?"

Interesting, Sarah thought, how something as ineffable as a telephone connection—was it actually bouncing off a satellite in space?—could convey so much anger and despair in nothing but silence.

"Anne? Darling?"

Her daughter's voice was flat. "So I can't tell the guardian *ad litem* that you'll speak with him."

"Right. It won't matter, I'm sure. Just tell him we live on an island and seldom see you or Tessa. That's the truth."

"Fine. I've got to go. I won't say it's been a pleasure talking to you."

"Oh, my dear."

"Good-bye, Mother."

Sarah clicked off the phone. Looking down, she saw

Brownie sitting at her feet, adoration and gluttony in her eyes.

"They say chocolate's bad for dogs," she told her.

She wagged her tail hopefully.

"Although I've always fed my dogs chocolate with no ill effect."

Brownie shivered all over in ecstatic expectancy.

Why couldn't people be more like dogs? Sarah wondered. Bending, she fed Brownie just the tiniest sliver of cake. Mostly white icing, really.

Anne stood in her shower, weeping. What an *awful* day today was! Rejected and insulted by her own mother!

She soaped herself all over, for the tenth time. The water sluiced over her, swirling down the drain, and still she felt unclean.

Sarah had always liked Randall best, right from the moment Anne brought him home to meet her parents. They were so much alike, warm, openly, even flamboyantly affectionate, humorous, given to spells of silliness. They behaved almost flirtatiously with each other. Sometimes when they were together, they made Anne feel like *she* was *their* parent. Randall didn't mind the chaos of the Franklin household. He even seemed comfortable in it. Of course, he would.

Still, Sarah was Anne's mother, not Randall's!

No use torturing herself. She hadn't counted on her mother. Long ago she'd learned not to do that. She still had Carmen to support her at the psychiatrist's and, of course, Reverend Christopher. Still, she hated it that she had to demean herself by asking them to speak to Dr. Lawrence. How could her mother chastise her for using the occasional tranquilizer? It was a wonder Anne wasn't using more, what with the election coming up at the same time as her divorce, and Randall, once her husband, suddenly her enemy. And it didn't help *at all* that Tessa's personality was changing. Randall said it was normal, and Anne supposed it was. Tessa wasn't a child anymore. She was almost a teenager. God, she'd probably start her period any day now, poor child. She'd be even more difficult to deal with then. The subject of boys would arise—it was all too disgusting to dwell on.

"Mom?" Tessa's voice broke into her thoughts, startling Anne so that she dropped the soap on her foot.

"What?"

"Carmen's going to drive me to camp now."

Anne turned off the water, grabbed a thick white bath sheet from the heated drying rack and wrapped it around her. When she opened the door, steam billowed out around her into the bedroom.

Tessa stood there in her white shorts and navy T-shirt, her backpack slung over one shoulder, her long blond hair neatly plaited and tied with a plaid grosgrain ribbon. Lovely innocent child, Anne thought, smiling, although over the past few weeks as Tessa had grown taller, it appeared that her waist was thinning and her chest developing, making the sight of her bittersweet.

"Have fun, then," Anne said. "I'll be here when you get back this afternoon."

"Okay. Bye, Mom." Tessa skipped from the room and down the stairs. The front door slammed.

Anne dressed in an empire-waisted dress of violet linen and slipped a matching headband on to hold her blond hair away from her face.

The house as she walked down the stairs and through the hall to her office hummed steadfastly around her: air conditioner, refrigerator, clocks, computer—all the machines that so reliably, more reliably than human beings, attended to her needs.

Carmen had dusted and vacuumed her office while Anne showered, and now it waited in immaculate serenity for Anne's presence. Anne's assistant, Rebecca, had today off. Anne would be blissfully alone while she worked at her desk, making phone calls, dictating letters into her tape recorder, catching up on her mail.

Anne seated herself at her desk. Folding her hands, she took a deep breath: then with the tips of her perfectly manicured fingernails, touched her white telephone, the small caller ID box, the thick Rolodex, and delicately moved her daily calendar a fraction of an inch, so that it was exactly in the center of her desk. She touched her tape dispenser, her stapler, the malachite box where she kept her stamps. She touched the pastel Lucite in and out boxes. Last, she set both hands on the silver and amethyst tray where her pens lay. Her blotter was centered perfectly on her desk.

She opened her appointment book and began to work.

After taking the oath of office, all new judges spent a month in training at four different courts around the state. Tuesday morning Kelly began hers at the Middlesex County Courthouse—the largest court in the state, serving over one and a half million people—the courthouse where at the end of the month she would preside.

Today she sat with Judge Marjorie Spriggs, a wiry, tiny African-American woman in her fifties. Kelly had argued cases before Judge Spriggs before and had been impressed by the woman's astuteness and compassion, a dynamite mixture.

When Kelly entered Judge Spriggs's chambers at 8:45 on Tuesday morning, she found the office already bustling.

"Good morning, Kelly," Judge Spriggs called from behind her desk, barely looking up from the piles of folders she was plowing through. "Welcome to the madhouse."

"Good morning."

"Arlene, meet Kelly. Kelly, Arlene."

Judge Spriggs's secretary rose briefly to shake Kelly's hand before diving back into the papers on her desk. "We can't find a file. We have to manually file all our cases, and it's time-consuming and confusing. We need to be computerized."

"We need a whole new courthouse," Judge Spriggs barked.

"But it's a beautiful building," Kelly protested.

"Beautiful, schmutiful—this place is a dump. Found it!" Yanking a folder out, Judge Spriggs flipped through it, scribbling her signature on various documents, talking to Kelly as she worked. "It's unsafe and impossible to organize. The staff has to run all over the place to get anything done. Ask the probation officers about 'beauty.' Hah! Judges and registers and staff have to ride the same elevator as the people we've just ordered to give their wives their life savings. Security's impossible here. You'll be getting your own key for the back entrance of the courthouse. Don't lose it. You can ask a court officer to escort you from your car and back, and you ought to do it. Don't forget that attorney, what's his name—"

"Barton," Arlene said.

"Barton—a few years ago, leaving the courthouse with the woman he'd represented in a divorce, the ex-husband shot and killed both the woman and the lawyer. Don't forget you're dealing with people in states of terrible emotional distress. Men hate letting someone else tell them what to do. I predict in the next few years we're going to see our court officers carrying guns. And I need another cup of coffee. Where's my mug? Arlene, have you seen my mug?"

"Here you are, Judge. Would you like some, Judge MacLeod?"

"No, thanks." Kelly felt she was absorbing all the adrenaline she could handle just by being in the same room with Judge Spriggs.

Judge Spriggs's register opened the door from the courtroom. "Ready, Judge."

"Come in here a minute. Judge MacLeod, this is Merry Wickes, my register. The registers are our guard dogs— remember that. Merry's bright and thorough. You need anything, ask her. Okay, let's go."

Merry went out. Judge Spriggs chugged down her coffee like a frat boy draining a bottle of beer, grabbed her robe from the closet, nodded to Kelly to don a robe as well, and announced, "Show time."

Judge Spriggs led the way into the courtroom and up behind the judge's bench. The court officer had already brought up another chair for Kelly, placed next to Spriggs's. In a baritone voice that would part waters, he announced, "Hear ye, Hear ye, Hear ye. All rise. Court's in session. The Honorable Marjorie Spriggs presiding. God save the Commonwealth of Massachusetts. Turn off your cell phones and pagers."

Kelly sat looking out at the courtroom, for the first time behind the judge's bench rather than before it. The large, beautiful room with its high ceilings, brass lamps, blue and gold walls, was packed.

"Good morning," Judge Spriggs greeted the courtroom. "We've got a new judge with us this morning. Judge MacLeod. She'll be helping me out, so you'll get double your money. Let's go. Who's up first?"

The clerk reached up to hand Judge Spriggs a folder and then read the docket number, the name of the case: *Hodges* vs. *Hodges*, and the cause of action: contempt.

"They're both *pro se*, Your Honor," the clerk said.

"Okay, come up here," Judge Spriggs directed, waving her hands toward her chest.

The couple who approached the witness stand made Kelly think of the old nursery rhyme about Jack Sprat who could eat no fat and his wife who could eat no lean. The moon-faced woman covered her nearly three hundred pounds with a shapeless gray garment. Her ex-husband creaked up on toothpick legs encased in worn but clean jeans and a short-sleeved white shirt from which his thin arms protruded like twigs.

Register Wickes swore them in.

"Okay," Judge Spriggs said. "What's going on?"

"Your Honor, when my wife and I were divorced two

months ago, I was given weekly visitation rights so I could see our son. Well, it's been two months, and I haven't been able to have him over at my place yet. That's not right."

The judge peered down at the woman. "Mrs. Hodges?"

The young woman wrung her hands together. "Judge, Keanu is just a little baby. He's too young to be away from his mother."

Judge Spriggs flipped through the papers in her folder. "How old is this child?"

"He's eighteen months old, Your Honor," Mr. Hodges replied. "He's walking."

"Tell me about your home situation, Mr. Hodges."

"I work five days a week at the Mobil station, but I get weekends off, and I could take care of my little boy in my house then. I've got a room set up for him, his own little bed. New sheets. Toys and everything. Also, I've got a girlfriend now, and she could help me with Keanu."

At the mention of the girlfriend, Mrs. Hodges burst into tears. "Don't take my baby away from me, Judge! He shouldn't be separated from his mother!"

Judge Spriggs looked down at Mrs. Hodges. "Tell me about your situation, Mrs. Hodges."

"I live with my mother and father. I don't work because I want to take care of my little boy twenty-four/seven. I told Harry if he wants to come see Keanu he can come to my house."

"Well, Mrs. Hodges, it does say here in the divorce papers that Mr. Hodges gets twenty-four hours a week to have his son at his house. That's only fair."

"But Keanu is only a little baby!"

"No, he's a toddler, and he needs to spend some time with his father. And you know what, Mrs. Hodges?" Judge Spriggs lowered her voice seductively. "You need some time off. If you've been taking care of your baby twenty-four/seven for eighteen months, you've got to be exhausted. You need some time for yourself. You can go out and see a movie, go shopping with a friend, or just use the time to kick back and relax. It would be good for all of you."

Mrs. Hodges sniffled.

"Now Mr. Hodges is way behind in his time with this child, so I'm going to order that he have the child every Wednesday night for the next month. Does that suit you, Mr. Hodges?"

"That's fine, Your Honor."

Mrs. Hodges wailed.

"Mrs. Hodges," Judge Spriggs said, "I hope you understand how lucky you are to have the father interested in your little boy. I can't tell you how many cases I see where the child has a father who won't pay child support or even see the child. I want you to think about something: Do you hate your ex-husband more than you love your child?"

Mrs. Hodges swayed on her tiny feet as she contemplated the question. It seemed almost beyond her comprehension. At last she whimpered tentatively, "No?"

"That's the right answer." Judge Spriggs looked over at the scrawny father. "Mr. Hodges, I hope you will be as helpful as possible in making this situation comfortable for Mother."

"Yes, Your Honor, I will."

"Mrs. Hodges," Judge Spriggs said, steel entering her voice, "I don't want to see the two of you back in my courtroom because you haven't let your husband have access to his son. I don't want to have to fine you or put you in jail for contempt of court. You understand?"

Pouting, the woman nodded.

"All right," Judge Spriggs said. "Now I hope the two of you can go off and cooperate. You've got the best interest of your little boy to keep in the forefront of your thoughts. Okay, good luck."

As the couple went off, Judge Spriggs leaned over to Kelly. "If they come back, they'll have to go to the court clinic. But sometimes they really need to hear it from a judge. No matter how trivial or tiresome it might seem, especially at the end of a long day, each case has to be heard as if it's the most important one around."

Kelly nodded.

"Okay," Judge Spriggs snapped. "What's next?"

The day ripped past. They dealt with matters of motions to compel production of documents, motions for temporary orders, and uncontested divorces which, as "amicable" as divorces could be, still aroused powerful emotions. One woman stood before the bench in taut, fiercely controlled dignity, while tears streamed down her ashen face. Another time, the husband standing before them seemed to age years within minutes as he acknowledged in a strained voice that yes, their marriage was irretrievably broken. His face turned gray, his lips blue, and his shoulders slumped forward— his entire body seemed to cave in as his married life crumbled and officially, legally, dissolved.

This was not a new sight to Kelly, but it was always hard. Sitting on the bench provided her with quite a different picture of the proceedings than representing a client on a case had done. She could witness a defendant blushing, or cringing; she could see a plaintiff drop his eyes, bite his nails, or attempt to hide all traces of emotion, only to give it away by the muscle that clenched and unclenched along his jaw.

After one day on the bench she realized that even the wisest, most sympathetic person couldn't solve all the problems that came before them. An impoverished mother, divorced, with three small children, came to ask the court to give custody of those children to her ex-husband, their father, because she was ill with cancer and would not have the energy, with various treatments, to care for the children. But the father was a drug addict and an alcoholic, barely capable of taking care of himself. He pleaded with the court not to be given custody; he was afraid the stress of having to care for three small children in his straitened circumstances, in his small apartment over a sporting-goods store, would drive him back to drink and drugs. Neither party had parents or siblings who could help out. "Let's ease into this with baby steps," Judge Spriggs decided, ordering the father to take care of the children two days and one night a week for the next month, after which they'd review the situation again. Kelly didn't think she could have come up with a wiser ruling.

By eight o'clock on Wednesday morning, Randall was in the elevator at Mt. Auburn Hospital, on his way down. He'd just finished his rounds and was wondering whether or not to stop somewhere for a decent breakfast. Right now, he was running on caffeine and sugar, and he had a full schedule ahead at his office. His stomach rumbled and burned. Crankily he ruminated on the knowledge that he was no longer a young man who could go all day on coffee fumes and last night's lonely microwaved "man-size" prepackaged meal.

He really was going to have to change his life. Find more time for Tessa. More time for himself. Stop burying himself in his work and rushing through whatever it was that he called his private life.

The elevator dinged, stopped, and the doors slid open. One woman waited, the crisp lines of her white nurse's uniform unable to disguise her generous curves.

When she saw Randall, her dark eyes went wide.

"Randall." She started to step inside the elevator and then hesitated, biting her lip.

"Lacey. Hello." Randall was almost as unnerved to see her as she was to see him. "Going down?"

"Um." Her hand went to her throat. She laughed uneasily. "Yes." Taking a deep breath, Lacey Corriea stepped into the elevator. The automatic doors slammed against her arms, then popped back, wide open, leaving Randall and Lacey together, side by side, staring out at the empty hallway. For what Randall thought must surely be the only time in the hospital's history no one else was racing to catch the elevator, no orderly with a stretcher or wheelchair, no doctor, nurse, visiting relative. The elevator floor shuddered slightly beneath them, its cables humming. They might have been alone on the moon. Or in a private room.

It seemed like an eternity before the doors slid shut and the elevator clunked, shuddered, and organized itself to descend.

Randall smiled at Lacey, who was sweet and young and beautiful. He couldn't help but remember with gratitude the nights he'd spent burrowing into her generous warmth. He had not enjoyed his year of lonely, celibate nights. "So. How have you been?"

"Fine." She cleared her throat. "You?"

"All right."

"How do you like surgery?" It had been twelve months since he had ended their affair, and Lacey, heartbroken, unable to face him every day, had moved from the geriatric floor.

"It's pediatrics, Randall," she corrected.

"Ah, right." He could tell by her expression that it hurt her that he hadn't remembered where she'd transferred. He hated it that anything he said or did still had the power to wound her. She'd changed her hair since he'd last seen her. The flyaway curls were gone, in their place a severe bell. "I like your haircut," he offered.

"Oh." She blinked and touched her hair with her hand. "Thanks."

The elevator stopped on the second level. The doors slid open. No one was there. Damn, Randall thought silently, this was way too intimate. He was uncomfortably aware of her body beneath the uniform. Proximity sparked an image: luscious Lacey, naked, a fragrant, giving cushion a man could sink into forever.

He remembered Lacey's bedroom. Like her entire apartment, it was decorated in pastels and inhabited by what seemed like a million baby dolls and stuffed animals. Lacey wanted children, lots of children. She was proud of her full breasts and deep hips. They were perfect, she said, for babies.

"How about a drink some time?" Lacey asked brightly.

He smiled gently, looking at her mouth, not wanting to meet her eyes. "I don't think that would be a good idea, really."

She laughed. "Oh, come on. It's just a drink."

He shook his head. "I'm straight out."

"What about Friday night?"

"I'm busy, Lacey."

"Come on." She laughed, and her laugh was the way he remembered, as intoxicating as a good burgundy wine. "Let me prove I know how to be grown up. Just a drink between friends. Aren't you curious about what I've been up to the past year?"

He hesitated.

"Saturday night?"

"I can't."

"Why don't I call you next week and see if you've got anything free?"

The elevator rumbled to a halt. The doors opened. It would be easier to refuse her on the phone. "Well, maybe."

"Great." Lacey stepped off, tossing him a little smile over her shoulder. She hurried down the hall, and Randall knew that extra sway in her hips was for him.

In a changing room of the girls' locker room of Camp Moxie, Tessa huddled in perfect misery, slipping out of her tennis clothes and into her bathing suit.

The thing Tessa liked the most about camp was the boys, and the thing Tessa hated the worst about camp was the boys.

They had tennis first. Sharing two courts, all morning they marched up to the net, one after the other, to practice forehand, backhand, serve, lob, volley, blah blah blah; then they were free to swim for an hour before lunch.

Until this year Tessa had loved swimming. She'd created an elaborate, terribly private fantasy about being a mermaid. One of her very best fantasies, gorgeously detailed, it was also impromptu enough to incorporate the shrieking interruptions of her girlfriends as they dived into the water next to her and even the serene, rather whale-like (although she'd die before she'd let him know she thought that) figure of her father as he floated majestically on his back past her or churned, blowing and spewing, through the water doing laps.

Her mother did not swim. She enjoyed swimming, she told Tessa, because it provided excellent exercise, burning off calories and slimming the torso. She was just always so busy, or if they were on vacation, she had so much she needed to read.

Really, Tessa knew, having overheard her mother confide this to her father two years ago, the thought of putting her body into water polluted with the sweat, urine, mucus, and general oils of other human bodies was repellent to her. She had taken Tessa to Water Baby classes at their private club three years in a row, she was willing to sit watching her daughter swim, if necessary she would dive in to save Tessa's life, but unless that was called for, she was not entering any pool, lake, or ocean again in her life.

Tessa didn't mind other people's stuff. She had no sense of it around her as she slid through the fluid turquoise or lay on her back, kicking the liquid aquamarine into spatters of diamonds. She liked the weightlessness of her body, the way things blurred underwater, the way noises became mysterious and indistinct, like signals from outer space.

Or rather, she had liked all that, and she had *loved* her mermaid fantasy. When she was a kid she would swim for hours, lost in a make-believe world. She'd been so *free* then, splashing and gliding around in happiness, oblivious of her appearance, so lost in pleasure and dreams she scarcely thought of her body as a body at all. She'd played pool Frisbee with her friends and raced them the length of the pool in a passionate churning frenzy that made her chest heave as she gasped for air.

This year, suddenly, everything changed. The locker room was full of giggling and whispering girls, painfully, nearly paralytically, conscious of their bodies. Clarissa Donovan, not even the oldest, had left to go home in the middle of tennis because her period started. Thinking of this, a thrill of terror shot down Tessa's tummy from her belly button to her thighs.

"Come on!" Tracy yelled now.

Reluctantly, Tessa left the safety of the dressing room and joined the humiliating cluster of girls who, bumping elbows, hiding brace-bracketed mouths with their hands, stumbled out into the fierce, unforgiving sunlight.

The boys were already in the pool or diving off the board, or shoving each other, laughing donkey laughs, into the water.

Tessa and her friends dawdled over to the shallow end to sit dabbling their toes in the cool water, talking about television shows, pretending not to notice the boys. It was as if an evil sci-fi scientist had zapped their brains so that they had, as a group, forgotten what a swimming pool was for.

Of Tessa's clique, Tessa was the tallest, but only Tracy and Kristen had developed bosoms and hips. *They* didn't join the pathetic huddle but with breathtaking self-possession sauntered over the burning cement to spread out their towels on pool lounges, where they reclined, slathering themselves with sunblock.

Chad wasn't anywhere—then his sleek dark head surfaced in the deep end. He saw her looking at him, and Tessa's whole body went hot.

Cynthia, Beryl, and Shiobian giggled like a pack of brainless morons, and suddenly Tessa couldn't stand it any longer. She dived right into the water. Everyone else was tan, but she was white as a fish belly; her mother didn't want her to get skin cancer when she was forty.

She thought maybe Chad liked her. He smiled at her a lot, and once he said hi. Tessa had never had anybody like her at the same time she liked them. But, then, mostly her crushes were on guys like Leonardo DiCaprio or Ricky Martin, so she'd felt safe getting all moony; they couldn't see her back.

She knew she was retarded about sex. Part of it was her mother's fault—Anne strictly censored all television, so the only time Tessa could see *Buffy the Vampire Slayer* or *Sabrina* was at her friends' houses, and sometimes even chubby, bug-face Beryl, who was always so thrilled to have Tessa hang out with her that Tessa got to dictate what they did, got fed up with Tessa's hunger for TV.

Girls grew up too quickly these days, Tessa's mom insisted. They looked trashy so young, wearing makeup and fingernail polish, getting their ears pierced. Tessa's mom wouldn't even let her buy a two-piece bathing suit, but for once Tessa didn't mind her mother's rules, because her belly was a soft, pale, wobbly embarrassment Tessa wanted to keep hidden. No way would Tessa ever wear a belly button ring! Except for Tracy and Kristen, who wore bikinis, Tessa's clique and a lot of the others wore Speedo tanks. Tessa's was dark blue with red stripes up the side. The top rose high enough to cover the pathetic swellings, like hard-boiled eggs, that passed for breasts on her body.

The water was cool and dreamy. Surfacing, Tessa lay on her back and just floated, letting the sun bake her face and the tips of her feet as she fluttered them gently. Her mermaid fantasy drifted out of her brain in a blue haze, surrounding her in a blue-green dream. Tessa could almost feel glittering scales, like sequins, sprout on her legs.

"Yaaaah!"

With a yell like an ax murderer, someone grabbed her ankle, jerking her sideways and under. Unprepared, Tessa swallowed water and choked. Kicking, flailing, she fought her way to the top. A bunch of her hair came free from its braid, plastering her face, blinding her. Her feet couldn't touch bottom and she couldn't see which way the deep end was, so she just treaded water as she swiped her hair out of her eyes. Snorting, she blew water out her nose. *So attractive.*

Her vision cleared enough for her to see Cynthia, Beryl, and Shiobian at the shallow end of the pool, all of them latched to the side with their elbows, kicking their legs out lazily. Tessa swam over to them.

"Did you see who pulled me under?"

Shiobian said, "Chad." Then they burst into laughter like a trio of idiots.

"Did he, or are you guys teasing?" Tessa demanded.

"Did he, or are you guys teasing?" Beryl echoed.

"Retards," Tessa muttered, pulling herself up onto the pool side. When she sat, her thighs spread out forever, like a couple of pale pink baby pigs, and from the leg of her suit blond pubic hair, new this summer, curled like bean sprouts. She adjusted her suit, trying surreptitiously to shove them back in.

Tracy came strolling toward her. She was so cool, so sexy. A thin gold chain glittered around her narrow waist. Tessa and Tracy had been in the same private schools since first grade, but Tessa couldn't believe Tracy would spend any time with her now.

"Hey." Tracy lowered her beautiful body next to Tessa's. Every move she made seemed fluid, enticing. "I saw Chad pull you under."

Tessa shrugged. Beneath her suit her heart thumped.

"I think he likes you."

"I'm so sure."

Tracy dabbled her toes, flicking little pearls of pool water into the air. "Tessa. He does."

"Yeah, me and Beryl are his dream dates."

"You're sick." Tracy placed her hands behind her and leaned back, lifting her face to the sun.

"I'm fat."

"Jesus, Tessa! How many times do I have to tell you?

You're thin. You're too thin." Ruthlessly she added, "You'll never have breasts if you don't gain some weight."

"I don't *want* breasts," Tessa said in a fierce whisper. She knew Tracy was trying to be nice, but this whole conversation made her angry. Breasts, pubic hair, sex, the way Chad made her feel, babies . . . all that slimed her mind, making her think things she shouldn't think and feel things she shouldn't feel. If her mother knew what went on in Tessa's head, she'd be horrified, she'd wish she'd never adopted her.

"Your birth mother was a lovely, intelligent young woman," her parents had told her, but Tessa knew better. Where else would she get such indecent thoughts, such images flashing through her mind, if not from her birth mother's genes?

Sometimes when Tessa looked at Chad, such a rush of prickly heat flashed through her that she was surprised not to see a rash, red and bumpy, spread over her skin. Sometimes she felt absolutely demented, a real sicko. She wished she could talk to someone about this, but who? Not her father—this was way too yucky to discuss with a *man*. Not with her mother, so perfect, so pristine—she wouldn't have a clue.

"He's looking at you right now." Tracy's voice was half whisper, half squeal.

"Cut it out!" Tessa snapped, and dived deep into the cool obscuring water, wishing she could come up five years old, or not come up at all.

Late Wednesday afternoon, after a grueling day in court, Judge Spriggs took Kelly out to dinner. They walked from the courthouse over to the Galleria Mall, breathing in the fresh summer air and talking idly of summer plans, but once they settled into a booth at the Cheesecake Factory, Judge Spriggs said, "Good. It's noisy here. No one will be able to overhear us." Then she ordered a Scotch for herself, insisted that Kelly have something alcoholic—she chose a margarita—planted her elbows on the table, and got down to business.

"So. Two days behind the bench. Whadda ya think?"

Kelly ran her finger around the rim of her glass and licked the salt as she considered her words. "When I was a lawyer, I always felt triumph when I won, disappointment when I lost. Now, seeing divorces from the bench, I can tell how little triumph there is in any of it."

Judge Spriggs nodded. "Good point. I always tell my parties that if they both walk away dissatisfied, then I've done a good job." She knocked back her drink and signaled the waitress for another. "You're coming from private practice. You're used to thinking that the amount of money you've gotten awarded for your client or the amount you've saved him or her translates into success or failure. Forget that. Here's what you think about now: What are the best interests of the child? Here we think of the child first."

"The couple we just saw. You said you'd take the case under advisement and send them your findings."

"Right. Sometimes it's best to do that, even if you already know your decision. Gives them time to separate, cool off. Court's stressful enough. Emotions are high. Let them have a day or so to get over it. Send your decision to their lawyer. They know their lawyer is their advocate; he breaks the news to them privately. Keeps them from wanting to kill each other in the courtroom."

The waitress set their food before them: a filet mignon for Judge Spriggs, pasta primavera for Kelly. She nearly inhaled her food.

"Gives you an appetite, doesn't it?" Judge Spriggs noted, chewing. "You've gotta have fuel for this job."

When she'd finished the greater portion of her meal, Judge Spriggs took a pen from her purse and grabbed the paper napkin from beneath her drink. "Okay. You asked about the last case. Here's one trick I have that helps."

She folded the paper four times, lengthwise, then drew a line down the middle, making four columns. On one side of the paper she wrote FATHER, on the other half, MOTHER; beneath those words she wrote STRENGTH and WEAKNESS.

"For the couple we just saw, Father's strengths are obvious. He's a hard worker, a good provider, well respected in the community, devoted to his kids. But he's a salesman, often traveling for weeks at a time. Also, he's been involved with a series of women, which has got to be confusing for his kids. At first glance, Mother looks great, but she's so hung up on revenge she's hurting her kids. For example, Father planned a big birthday picnic for one of the kids last month; just before he came to pick them up, Mother treated them to enormous ice cream sundaes so they weren't interested in the hot dogs he'd grilled or the cake he'd bought. Mother undermined Father's success at her children's expense. If Father's two minutes late picking the kids up for his time with them, Mother whisks them into her car, drives them somewhere he can't find them. She's depriving them of access to their father and blaming it on the father. Not a good habit. If you add all this up, you get a pattern."

Kelly nodded. "So custody goes to the father?"

"I also watch for what I call 'Red Lights.' Kicking the dog, for example. Heavy drinking. Bringing a new girlfriend to each school event, just to drive the ex-wife crazy. It's easy, of course, if there's one obvious flaw, but in most cases you've got to pay attention to every little bit. In this case, the father doesn't have one single glaring fault. So it's like putting a jigsaw puzzle together. In most divorces, the parents aren't thinking of their children. They're all wrapped up in their own misery or revenge. It's our job to consider the children. We always have to rule in the best interest of the child."

"So how will you rule in this case?"

"I usually award custody to the mother unless she's a monster. For this case, joint legal custody, with sole physical custody to the mother. The kids are still young. They've got to have stability—someone to cook their oat-

meal and pick them up after school—and the father just
can't do that if he's out traveling for two weeks at a time.
He'll have liberal visitation rights and a say in matters of
education, medical care, religious and moral development,
and so on. If he settles down, marries again, establishes a
permanent, stable home environment, he can always come
back to court to get the arrangements changed. And I'll tell
him so."

When the waitress returned, Judge Spriggs ordered a
double espresso. "I've got to go back to my office for an
hour or so. I'm behind in my cases."

"Is there any way I can help?"

"Thanks, but no." She downed her espresso, scribbled
her signature on the charge form, snatched up her credit
card, and stashed it in her purse. "Let's go."

As they walked back toward the courthouse, Judge
Spriggs said, "You've got to remember, this is the most
human of courts. Criminals know the ramifications of going
to jail. People who come to probate, both sides, probably
feel like they've just been hit by a ten-ton truck. My motto:
Power should be used to ease the pain of others. See you
tomorrow, kid."

"Yes," Kelly replied, breathless. "Tomorrow."

"Dr. Madison. Hello. Thank you for coming in."

Randall shook the shrink's hand, sizing up the other
man, as he knew Lawrence was doing to him. Lawrence
was smaller than Randall—most men were—and younger.
But he had the eyes of an old soul. Randall had noticed in
med school that he could almost always peg the ones going
into psychiatry, either by their hyperactive chatter or the
alternate—their sense of nearly fatal calm and those old-
soul eyes.

"You'll have to forgive my appearance," Randall said,
sinking into the chair the shrink had indicated. "I was up
most of the night. A patient died of asphyxiation—from a
rope around his neck."

"A young person?"

"No, an elderly man. Friend of my father's, actually. Everyone loved him, the nurses are just demented with grief and blaming themselves, it's a real sad sight out there." He rubbed his hands over his face, feeling his beard bristle against his palms, and up through his hair. Then he stared at Lawrence.

"Would you like a cup of coffee?"

"No, thanks. I've had enough to float a ferry. With the nurses. They called me at four, when Amy discovered him. He'd hung himself by the sash of his robe from the light fixture. Pat knew he had Parkinson's, and his wife was dead, and all his kids had predeceased him. He'd just moved himself into the retirement home. But he seemed to be making friends. He joked with the nurses. I drove my dad out to visit him just last week. Dad thought Pat was going to do all right. He was only seventy-three." Randall shuddered. "Jesus, I'm sorry. Going on like this. I apologize."

"No need to apologize. It sounds like a tough night. Did you have to tell your father?"

"Yes." Randall shook his head. "He took it hard. My mother died just three months ago."

The psychiatrist was quiet, in respect.

Randall roused himself. "But you want me to talk about Tessa."

"Yes."

"What would you like to know?"

"Anything. Everything. Tell me about her."

"Have you met her yet?"

"Not yet."

Randall smiled. "You've got a treat in store. She's bright and witty, and she's got an amazing mind. I mean more than intelligence. She's creative. Thoughtful. One day when she was about six, she asked me, did trees talk to telephone poles? Have you ever heard of anything like that?"

Smiling, Dr. Lawrence shook his head.

"Well, that's what she's like. Surprising. Clever. She makes me think of that Wordsworth poem, you know, trailing clouds of glory, the child being father to the man—I mean, she's *wise*. And she's so incredibly open. She loves animals. Loves to ride. Loves everything, really."

"It sounds as though you and your wife have done a good job with her so far."

Randall pondered this. "To be honest, it's been more Anne than me who gets the credit. She stayed home until Tessa went to kindergarten; she did all the diapering, feeding her organic food, that kind of thing. Oh, I suppose I walked her sometimes at night when she was crying, but Anne did the major work."

"And yet you don't want Anne to have custody of Tessa."

Randall leaned forward, elbows on knees, hands clasped between them. "That's right. I believe Tessa would be better off with me, and I'll fight for that."

"Why?"

"I think I can provide Tessa with a wider world, for one thing. Anne doesn't like sports, swimming, horses, that kind of stuff, and Tessa does, and I think she needs that. I'd let her have a computer, too, and I'd let her watch television—Anne is afraid, and she does have reason, that the popular culture is too violent for Tessa. But we can't keep her in a china cabinet. We just need to keep talking to Tessa about stuff, not hiding it from her."

Dr. Lawrence looked down at his notes. "What about the whole issue of sexuality?"

"What about it?"

"Well, for one thing, Mrs. Madison says you're promiscuous."

Randall slumped back in his chair, looking infinitely weary. "Anne has reason to say that. For years I *was* promiscuous. I don't deny that. But for the past year, ever since

I served Anne with divorce papers, I've been abstentious. Completely."

"Because?"

"Because I don't want to give Anne any ammunition, of course," Randall shot back.

Dr. Lawrence nodded. "How do you see your future?"

Randall straightened. He looked the GAL in the eye. "I want to have a woman in my life. A real flesh-and-blood woman I can love. I want to get married again. I want to have more children. I want Tessa to have brothers and sisters. I want her to have a dog and a cat that shed so much our black coats turn white. I want her to see me kiss someone and hear her say, 'Eeeu, gross,' and know she feels secretly happy. I want to provide a role model for her of a normal loving family, and I think that can happen if she lives with me and I don't think there's a chance in hell of that happening with Anne."

"Okay." The shrink looked down at his notes. "It seems you work a lot. Can you tell me your weekly schedule?"

"I'm on the staff of Mt. Auburn. I make rounds there about six in the morning—"

"Which means you're up and out of the house around five?"

"Right. Rounds from six till eight-thirty. Over to my office in Cambridge from nine till twelve. I'm on the consulting staff of Shady Dale's retirement home—where Pat was. I try to get over there from twelve to two. Back to the office from two to five. Over to Shady Dale from five to seven or so."

Dr. Lawrence scribbled something on his pad. He looked over at Randall. "So you've got a thirteen-hour workday."

"I guess I do. Or have had."

"Saturdays?"

"Then, too, unless I have Tessa."

"You're on some boards? American Academy of Geriatrics? And you also write and deliver papers—"

"I've already resigned from the boards. I'm easing out of my hours at the retirement home. Look, Dr. Lawrence, whether or not I get custody of Tessa, I'm curtailing my schedule drastically. I'm limiting my work. If I get custody of Tessa, I absolutely will put her first. I'll attend every cheerleading practice or Girl Scout ceremony or baseball game, whatever draws her passion. I'll drive her to school and pick her up. I'll get her a new horse. She loves to ride, and my father's horses aren't much sport."

Lawrence looked up at the ceiling a minute, considering, and then said, "Mrs. Madison feels that since Tessa's female, she'd be better off with her mother. That's not an unreasonable thought. What do you say?"

"I say Tessa would be better off with me. You've met Anne. She's a paragon of virtue. She's determined to do good in the world, but what she demands in return is that everything in her life, every single thing, be clean, and tidy, and immaculate. No nasty hungers for booze or chocolate or sex. No music too loud, no emotion too powerful."

"For example?"

"For example, it's crucial to Anne that Tessa be thin. The result is, Tessa is almost malnourished. Wait until you meet her—you'll see for yourself. Of course, she wants to please her mother, but the cost is just too high. I want Tessa to be able to eat junk food. Now and then. Not every day. It can just be part of normal life. That's what I want for Tessa, a normal life."

"What about the issue of sexuality? Tessa's twelve—"

"Well, for one thing, Tessa learned about the whole reproductive business from my mother, on the farm. Tessa saw horses mate, and dogs, and chickens. She saw puppies born. Tessa knows a lot, and she's comfortable with it."

"But there's a difference between farm animals and a young girl."

"Oh, yes, I realize that. There's also a difference between a young girl and a porcelain doll. I can assure you that what Anne tells her is going to need an opposing side to balance it out. Somewhere along the way Anne got the idea that sex is dirty, that normal human desire is bad. I don't want my daughter turned into a breakable porcelain doll, and if my wife gets custody of her, that's exactly what's going to happen."

"You sound angry with Mrs. Madison."

"*Angry?*" Randall considered this. "Yes. I suppose I am." He sighed deeply. "Anne can deal with her own standards. But she's the only one who can. Tessa should be with me."

Lawrence wrote something on his pad. "Okay. Our time's almost up. I'll be seeing Tessa this week, and let's see—" He scanned his list. "I'll be interviewing Carmen, the housekeeper, and your father. Oh, yes, and Mrs. Madison asked me to speak with Reverend Christopher. On your way out, why don't you make an appointment for another interview with me in about ten days."

"Fine." Randall rose and extended his hand. "You've got a difficult job."

Dr. Lawrence shook Randall's huge paw. "Not so difficult this time around. I mean," he hastened to add, "Tessa is fortunate to have two capable parents who love her and want her. Not every child who comes in here has that. Often the courts have to decide between two evils. In this case, it's been two goods."

"That's heartening." Randall said, and went out the door to make his appointment with the secretary.

Friday it rained. The gray skies and plummeting temperatures echoed the mood of Judge Spriggs's court as one long and contested battle began between a couple fighting over every possible issue: division of property, alimony, child support, custody of the children. The couple was rancorous and bitter, the lawyers oddly also antagonistic, and each litigant had brought a cluster of friends and relatives who sat at the back, on opposing sides of the courtroom, smiling, snorting, scoffing, and rolling their eyes to indicate their scorn of their adversaries' words.

Finally the wife's lawyer said, "Your Honor, my client is being intimidated by Mr. Herbert's relatives. His sister and brother, especially, are laughing every time she speaks."

Judge Spriggs sighed. "All right, counselor." She peered out into the courtroom. "Mr. Herbert and, uh, what's your name—?"

Register Wickes supplied the name. "Mrs. Anders."

"Mrs. Anders. Would the two of you please do me a favor and separate? Mr. Herbert, you go sit on the left side of the pew, and Mrs. Anders, the right."

Curling their lips, the pair did as they were asked, almost.

"Mrs. Anders." Judge Spriggs shook her head. "You're to sit on the opposite side from your brother."

Tossing her head, the woman rose and walked to the middle of the bench.

Judge Spriggs wagged her head to the far end. "Little further. Little further. Oh, come on, Mrs. Anders."

"I'm just trying to follow your instructions. I'll sit anywhere you tell me. I'll sit on the witness stand if you tell me to."

"Right there will be just fine, Mrs. Anders."

Kelly made a note on her pad, a question she'd ask the judge later.

The case went on and on. Rain slid down the windows. Kelly's bottom went numb. Mrs. Herbert didn't want Mr. Herbert's girlfriend to pick up the children from school on Mr. Herbert's day to have the children. Mr. Herbert didn't want Mrs. Herbert to take the children to Disney World because he couldn't afford to because he had to pay child support, so why should she? Mrs. Herbert didn't like Mr. Herbert giving their daughter his mother's emerald bracelet. She was only ten, and she'd lose it, and then everyone would be mad, and besides, it was just a bribe.

"Look!" Judge Spriggs snapped, her eyes flashing. "You should be able to settle these matters out of court. This is costing you both tens of thousands of dollars in legal fees, as well as taking up much of the court's valuable time. Quite frankly, I'm so displeased by your inability to reach agreement on the slightest matter that if I didn't have the best interests of your children to consider, I'd make the two of you remain married! Honestly, now, how are you going to provide a tranquil and pleasant environment for your children if you can't compromise on any one issue right now?" Sighing, she looked down at the enormous stack of papers in front of her. "I want the two of you to see the court clinic."

"Your Honor," one of the lawyers said, "they've already done that."

"Then do it again! I want the children interviewed, and I want a report on how these children are doing." She glared at the estranged couple. "Would you *please* consider your children? I'm worried about them. If you two can't find some way to compromise, it's your children who will suffer." She rubbed her eyes. "All right. That's all."

In the judge's chamber, as Kelly and Judge Spriggs removed their robes, Kelly said, "Judge Spriggs. You seemed awfully patient with all those relatives. I'm surprised you didn't cite Mrs. Anders for contempt. She spoke so rudely to you."

Judge Spriggs yawned. "She did. You're right. But this is a tough enough case. These people are like a pack of rottweilers. If I'd reprimanded the sister, they would have said—if I ruled at all in favor of the mother—that I was prejudiced against the husband and his family. They'd appeal my rulings. Hell, they probably will, anyway."

The judge sat on the edge of her desk, removed one of her pumps, and rubbed her foot. "I am always struck by the sight of a couple standing before me for their divorce. *Press rewind,* I think, and there they are ten or twenty years ago, standing together before a judge or minister, being married. Even the words they say—I do, I will—are similar."

"You look tired," Kelly remarked.

"I am. I'm beat. You've got to learn to pick your battles in court, Kelly. You've got to sniff out what you can do and what you can't. What will work and what won't. Your instincts will sharpen after a while, and you'll need to follow them as much as the rule of law."

The register and secretary were shutting desk drawers, flicking off computers.

"Do you still believe in marriage?" Kelly asked as she gathered up her briefcase and purse.

"Sure do. I believe in divorce, too." And, she said, smiling, "On Friday nights I believe in a pizza and a video with my husband!"

Ribbons were wound around all the poles supporting the sugary white tent shading the flower-strewn tables laden with carved meats, cheese, breads, salads, and fruits. The sun rolled through the bright blue evening, casting drifting light on the drinks table, making the champagne and liquor bottles so deftly handled by the bartenders in their crisp white jackets gleam and sparkle.

The wedding had been splendid—the reception, flawless. Muffy Holmes was now a rather disheveled and flushed Muffy Bendigen. Toasts had been made, the six-tiered wedding cake cut and devoured, the band had played, everyone had danced, and the reception was not over yet, for as soon as dark fell there would be fireworks.

Jason had a headache. Horrible changes took place in one's thirties, he was beginning to realize: at Buster's bachelor party and today as well his body had clearly informed him that he couldn't consume the amplitude of alcohol he'd imbibed in his twenties and get away with it. At the drinks table he asked for two Perriers with ice and lime, which he carried over to the far table where his mother sat with

Bud and Alyssa Worth and a number of other parental types.

"Darling. How did you know?" Eloise took her glass gratefully. She looked peerless in a lavender silk dress and a creamy straw hat adorned with a cluster of silk lilacs. "Sit with me a while."

She didn't have to ask twice. Even in his summer-weight blazer, he was hot, and his headache made him so cranky he didn't trust himself to talk to anyone but his mother just now.

"Great wedding!" Bud Worth announced heartily across the table to Jason.

"Right, sir. Great wedding."

"Lovely couple," Alyssa Worth added. "Just lovely."

They'd said exactly these words at least seven times before, Jason thought muzzily, and each time the slurring of their words grew more pronounced. It occurred to him that perhaps his words were slurred, as well. Or perhaps the Worths' words weren't slurred but his hearing was! The thought made him bark with laughter.

"What?" his mother inquired.

"Nothing," he told her, adding, "I think I'm a bit tipsy."

The band had advertised that it played a broad spectrum of music, from big band all the way to pop rock, and it was true they performed a variety of songs, but since they sugar-coated every note and set it to a Lawrence Welk beat, everything sounded pretty much the same. Still, when the twist began, Bud Worth hauled himself up from his chair and led his wife to the dance floor where he clasped her to his bosom and steered her around the floor in a jaunty two-step.

Across the table several of the older people were engrossed in a heated debate over Hillary Clinton. Caleb Livingston, a widower and old chum of Eloise, sat by himself at the foot of the table, watching the dancers, drinking steadily, his nose turning redder with each swallow.

Sotto voce, Eloise said to her son, "And to think I once had thoughts of seeing that man, after Helen died."

"Really!" Jason was shocked, not at what Eloise said but that she said it at all. She must be a bit tipsy herself, he decided, to tell him something so personal.

"You seemed to be having rather a good time with the Hudson girl," Eloise remarked.

"Mother," Jason said warningly.

"Well, Jason, she *is* beautiful, and refined, and well educated, and sweet. I can't help but think what a lovely wife she'd make."

"Yes, for someone else. I'm not attracted to her, Mother."

"Well, you should be. Look at her."

Jason looked at her. Bobbie Hudson, in bridesmaid peach silk, was at the moment being transported around the dance floor by her father. She'd tossed off her hat hours ago so that her brown hair curled around her face, floating seamlessly over her extremely tanned and slightly bulky shoulders—Bobbie was a jock.

"Mother. Perhaps you've forgotten. I'm engaged to marry Kelly."

"Engagements can be broken."

"And why would I want to do that?" Jason had known this was coming for a long time and decided it might as well be now, while he was fairly well anesthetized by alcohol, and so that tomorrow his mother could forget what she'd said—or claim to have said it because she wasn't thinking clearly.

"Because Kelly is not the right woman for you."

"Go on."

"What worries me most is the matter of children. She's already thirty-five. You haven't even set a date for your wedding yet. By the time you two are actually married, she may not even be able to conceive."

Unwittingly—or perhaps wittingly, for Eloise *was* his

mother, after all—Eloise had hit upon a real concern for Jason. "I thought you liked Kelly."

"Well, I don't. I find her opinionated, aggressive, argumentative, and *hard*."

Jason ran his hand over his forehead. "Kelly likes *you*. She thinks you're fond of her."

"Then Kelly is not very perceptive and will make a mediocre judge."

Jason shook his head. "I'm getting another drink. One with booze in it."

Jason rose and headed toward the drinks table. Bobbie Hudson was already there, and when she saw him coming, she gave him a great big smile.

FIVE

SUNDAY MORNING, THUNDERCLOUDS ROLLED OVERHEAD, muttering threats, darkening the sky, and as Kelly drove through the sleeping streets of Cambridge toward the cemetery, fat raindrops began to drop, one at a time, then slid with a kind of languor, slowly, down her windshield.

Probably he would not come today. A storm was predicted. It wouldn't be sensible to come today.

She wanted to see him so much she could scarcely breathe. All week she'd thought about him, his massive gentle size, his honest face, his laughter, the way he listened to her and then was quiet, thinking, before responding.

All during this past week, even in the midst of all its new challenges, she thought of him. She didn't even have to close her eyes; it took only the brush of fabric across her palm or the scent of flowers to transport her instantly, helplessly, back to the moment when she stood in the sunshine saying good-bye to the man, when a flower of heat blossomed between their hands. Every night as she lay in bed, waiting for sleep, his face would appear before her, the aura of his presence would surround her, and she would have to pull a pillow against her and squeeze it hard.

By the time she arrived at the cemetery the wind was rising, dancing through the trees, then vanishing. She parked behind the chapel and walked up Mulberry Avenue past the Bell Tower and around until she reached Lilac Path and her mother's quartz-and-granite rock.

She looked down the slope toward Magnolia Path. No one was there.

"Oh," she said aloud, disappointed.

She sank down onto the grass, folding her legs sideways beneath her so that she leaned a little, in a companionable way, on her mother's stone. She tugged at the hem of her short dress, smoothing the lime-colored cotton over her lap, noticing with a little sigh how pale, right in the middle of the summer, her legs were.

It felt lovely, really, simply to sit. To have the time to think about something as insignificant as a tan.

She was glad her first week of training was over. It had been exhilarating and frustrating. The more she saw of custody and divorce cases, the more she saw of negligent and even harmful parents, the more she realized how fortunate she'd been as a child.

So now she folded her hands, bowed her head, and said a prayer, beginning her own ritual. Occasionally she'd wished she had some rules to follow, some established ceremony. Most times she was comfortable simply talking to her mother, aloud or silently, in a casual, spontaneous way, as if she were speaking with her on the phone over a very long distance satellite connection that she wasn't sure really worked. Odd, perhaps, but still somehow satisfying.

Here, where only her mother and God were witness to her thoughts, she felt both free to be truthful and obligated to do so. Certainly her mother of all people would understand this powerful, irrational attraction Kelly felt for a man. Would her mother help her think through to some solution?

"Mom," she said now, "I'm confused."

A gust of wind tossed a spatter of raindrops at the trees around her, making brisk popping sounds. One drop splatted, a quick shock, against her bare arm.

A man called out: "You're here!"

At the sound of his voice, her heart lifted. Was his arrival, at this exact moment, some kind of answer to her question? Certainly her confusion had evaporated, replaced by utter joy.

He came walking up the hill toward her, wearing khakis and a pink button-down shirt with the sleeves rolled up. Around his neck hung a red-and-blue-striped tie with the knot tugged down. He looked weary, his hair more silver than she'd remembered, and completely wonderful.

"You're here, too," she remarked idiotically.

He sat down on the other side of the rock, crossing his legs Indian style, resting his arms on his ankles, and peered across the two feet of ground separating them. "I'm very glad to see you."

"I'm very glad to see you."

They smiled at one another, pleased.

"I thought about you all week," he said. "And I had an idea."

"Oh, yes?" She felt positively radioactive with happiness.

"I like it that we can talk to one another the way we do, without the kinds of limitations normal conversations hold, but I can't keep thinking of you as"—he lowered his voice into a humorous portentous bass—"the Woman at the Cemetery."

She laughed.

"So I think we should give one another names."

"You mean tell our own names?"

"No, I mean I name you and you name me. Whatever seems right."

She looked at him. "Okay." She decided at once: *"Ernest."*

He groaned. "That's awful. It sounds like a shy little boy who studies too hard."

She laughed. "Not at all. It makes me think of Ernest Hemingway, who was big and bearlike, and full of sincerity and integrity, and genuineness."

"You're sure I couldn't be a Fabio or Lance?"

"Quite sure. Now what would you call me?"

"I was thinking of Buffy."

She stared at him, appalled.

Throwing back his head, he laughed. "Serves you right for Ernest. No, I've been calling you Morgan in my mind. After the enchantress Morgan le Fay."

An enchantress! "Well. But wait a minute. Isn't she evil?"

"I don't remember, to be honest. I could look it up. It's the only enchantress I can think of other than Samantha on *Bewitched*, and I thought Morgan would impress you more."

"All right," she agreed. "Morgan and Ernest."

"An unlikely pair. Sure you wouldn't go for Lancelot? Or even Arthur?"

She shook her head. I'm sitting in a cemetery, she thought, talking to a man I don't know but have just named Ernest, and I don't know that I've ever been happier in my life.

She asked, "How was your week?"

"Slow. I wanted it to be Sunday right away."

His honesty made her hands tremble. She folded them together in her lap and looked down at them. The wind passed through, whispering the leaves against each other.

He continued: "I couldn't wait to see you again. I kept talking to you in my mind. I want to tell you about myself. I want you to know me. Not the persona I've constructed so carefully over the years, but the real me."

"Then tell me."

"And you'll tell me about you? In exchange? The real you?"

"All right." She met his eyes. They were very blue, pure, clear blue like a bottle you'd set in a window to catch the sun. And he looked as if he'd spent time in the sun this week: his nose was peeling on the very tip, and his arms were dark brown, the hair on them bleached pale. His eyebrows were a shaggy mix of brown and blond and silver and gold.

He asked, "Could we walk?"

"Sure."

They stood and headed down the hill toward the pond. The wind was rising, making the trees shiver around them. The water danced, tossing specks of light.

"I spent a lot of time with my father this week," the man she called Ernest said. "Since my mother's death, he's deteriorated rapidly. He seems to wander through his life, as if he's lost without my mother."

"I'm sorry."

"I am, too, and yet"—his voice deepened—"and yet, I'm jealous. To love someone so much, to be so much a part of someone's life, to really be like *that*"—he gestured toward a statue of a tree cleaved asunder—"to be joined so completely with another person that you're broken, mind and body, when they've gone—" He caught his breath. "I envy him."

His intensity stirred her. "Do you have any brothers or sisters?"

"An older sister. Evangeline. She lives in the Northwest now. Growing up, she was a wild tomboy who thought I hung the moon." He smiled down at Kelly. "I was a terribly spoiled little boy, I'm afraid. Perhaps nothing can be as good as the love you get when you're a child."

The wind lifted his tie, fluttering it against his shirt. Strands of Kelly's hair tickled her neck.

"I can't believe that," she said. "I don't want to believe it. Surely your father wouldn't."

He looked at her. "And what do you believe?"

A long roll of thunder broke through the sky, and lightning streaked downward, a shaft of brilliance piercing the dark air. Rain spilled down on them, a sudden torrent, the cool wetness delicious on her warm skin.

She turned to face him. He was smiling, as she was, both of them smiling as the rain made coins of moisture blossom on their clothes. It was like being touched quickly, gently, all over.

She gave his question serious thought. "I've always believed in the power of the mind. Logic. I think that now—*now*—I believe in good luck."

He reached out to brush a curl away from her forehead. She stood very still. He brought his hand down to cradle her chin; then he leaned forward and very slowly, very softly, kissed her mouth.

"You're cold," he said, because she was trembling. "We're getting soaked. Let's go get some coffee."

"All right."

"My car's just over there."

He took her hand, and they ran through the rain, down Magnolia Path, along Primrose Avenue. It felt good to run in the rain—peculiar, something her body seemed to remember. It was like being a child again, and like being an animal, freed of the constraints of rules and words, and also like being a spirit, part of the wind and rain.

He brought her to a huge black-green Jeep shining with rain. Opening the passenger door, he helped her step up and in. Then he hurried around to his side, slamming the door with an agreeable solid thud. She watched him as he slid the key into the ignition, making the big engine roar into life, and deftly turned all the dials so that soft warm air blew around them and the windshield wipers sprang to life, clicking back and forth. His hands were massive but oddly elegant, and smooth, unscarred.

"Have you had breakfast?"

"Just a cup of coffee."

"There's a small café not far from here. We'll go there, and then I'll bring you back to your car afterward."

"Lovely."

As he steered the Jeep through the high stone gates and out into the real world, Kelly dug around in her bag, found some tissue, and dried her hands and face, as careful as an adolescent not to touch her mouth, as if his kiss still lingered there.

"Are you a surgeon?" she asked.

He looked at her, surprised.

"Your license plate," she explained.

"Of course. No, I'm not a surgeon." The streets shone in the rain, and trees bowed and dipped in the wind. "I'm a geriatricist."

"Why that specialty?"

He turned off onto Morton Street. "I don't really know. I've always liked older people. I've always thought our society doesn't pay enough respect to its elders. We put far too much value on looking young, being young. We let our children learn about the world from the television set rather than from talking to their aging relatives."

He pulled the Jeep into the parking lot of Pearl and Joe's Diner. The low aluminum-sided building was small and slightly shabby, but the parking lot was full. They hurried through the rain to the front door, which he pushed open—what a treat it was for Kelly to be with a man who could effortlessly reach past her—and entered the café. The air was warm and steamy, smelling of coffee and bacon, buzzing with conversation and the clink of forks against sturdy white plates.

Ernest led her to a booth at the far end, the only spot open except for one round stool at the counter. A young waitress with pink hair and black lipstick sauntered by with a platter of scrambled eggs and fried potatoes for the booth next to them.

With infinite boredom, she muttered, "Be right there."

Kelly leaned back against the booth. At one corner its red vinyl was ripped and mended with electrician's tape, but the back was high, giving them a sense of privacy.

"Now," she said. "Go on. About geriatrics."

He ran his hand through his hair, took some paper napkins from the aluminum holder, and dried his hands. "I'm afraid I was beginning to lecture. I'd rather talk about you."

She smiled. "And I'd rather talk about you."

"Our first argument."

They sat grinning at one another, smug.

"Coffee?" Their waitress also had a nose stud. Her name tag said STAR.

"Please," Ernest said.

"Pretty name," Kelly told the young woman as she filled two thick white mugs.

Star shrugged. "It's so seventies," she sighed. She took their order and wobbled away on platform shoes with heels a good six inches high.

"I wouldn't be her age again for anything," Kelly said.

"Me, either. Although I wish I had her energy."

They both watched Star clop lethargically down the aisle.

"Well," Ernest corrected himself, "maybe not *her* energy." He reached into his pocket and placed a quarter on the table. "Here's what we'll do. Flip a coin. The loser has to talk first."

"Okay." Kelly sipped her coffee, which was fresh, strong, and fragrant. "Heads."

She watched his dexterous, elegant hands as they deftly flipped the coin.

"Heads, it is. Okay, what do you want to know?"

Kelly thought. She knew so much already—that he was separated, had one daughter, was a physician. That he seemed kind. "Last week you said you feel beset by devils. Tell me about that."

He stirred sugar and milk into his coffee. "Ah. Very

well. Where do I begin?" His forehead wrinkled, and he nodded to himself, as if deciding upon something. "I'm concerned about my daughter. Let's call her—let's call her Grace. My wife—I'll call her Joan—is a nurse. Very involved in good works—schools, free clinics, AIDS research. She's driven, intelligent, ambitious."

In spite of herself, Kelly realized she and Joan shared similar traits. "She sounds admirable."

"She *is* admirable. And she lives her life according to certain puritanical principles, but like all things, once they get carried past the point of moderation, they become, well, not *vices* exactly, but no longer virtues. She's developed certain eccentricities that might harm Grace."

Kelly sat very still.

He registered this reaction. "Please, I don't mean anything evil, or sexual, or perverse. Not at all. But serious, I think. Quite serious. She, Joan, has a real phobia about weight gain, for one thing. I'm afraid she's turning Grace into a borderline anorectic."

"All women and girls worry about their weight," Kelly pointed out.

"True, but this is extreme. Also there's the matter of the whole sexuality business." He paused to consider his words. "Over the years, perhaps because she's seen what the worst of sex can do to the body—AIDS, babies born deformed because of drugs, that sort of thing—Joan has come to see all sex as something defiling. Degrading." His face filled with shadows. "This is what I'm afraid she's passing on to our daughter, and it makes me very sad and worried for her."

"A difficult situation."

"Yes. Joan would counter, to be completely frank, that I've erred at the opposite extreme. I mean"—he looked steadily at Kelly—"over the past few years, I've had quite a few affairs. I'm not proud of it, but it always seemed the best thing to do, to keep myself from going quite demented from frustration while at the same time not imposing my needs on my wife."

His words created the oddest sensation in Kelly's stomach, a mixture of jealousy and desire. "Your wife knew about these affairs?"

He nodded. "Most of them. The first time she was very angry. She felt betrayed, understandably. But when I pointed out to her how little interest she had in sex, when I said that I'd be willing to go to counseling, or take a vacation in Hawaii, or anything, whatever would help—she shuddered. She was repulsed." He looked as if he were going to weep.

Kelly was silent, unsure what to say.

He put his fingertips on her wrist. "Listen. When I decided to divorce Joan, I stopped sleeping around. I haven't been with anyone for a year. I want you to know that."

"Oh." She cleared her throat. "Good."

He smiled crookedly. "It hasn't been out of some kind of spiritual decision. It's because of the damn lawyers. They can twist anything, find a way to make anything dirty, and I don't want it to hurt my chances of getting custody."

Star strolled back with their breakfasts, setting Ernest's order, an enormous mound of eggs, bacon, fries, sausage, and biscuits in front of Kelly, and giving Kelly's order of a small stack of blueberry pancakes to him.

"Thank you," he said to Star, and when she'd gone away, he traded plates with Kelly.

For a while they ate—or Ernest did. Kelly's stomach was too full of butterflies. She busied herself buttering her pancakes and cutting them into little bits.

"How's your breakfast?" he asked.

"Delicious," she replied, and ate several bites to prove it.

He spread a triangle of toast with jam. "I've decided in my long life that we're each of us given certain gifts, and certain faults."

"By our genes?"

He shrugged. "Perhaps. Perhaps by fate. The point is that no one is perfect, and sometimes it seems that the more extreme a person's goodness is, the more extreme her weaknesses. I've thought about this a lot, trying to find a way to talk to our daughter about the divorce."

Star strolled by to refill their coffee cups.

"Is Grace living with her mother?"

"Yes. For now. We agreed to separate this spring. Grace was still in school, so I took an apartment near my hospital. It's cramped and sterile, but I had to find something fast once Joan and I separated. Then my mother had her stroke, and was in the hospital, and then died, and everything became complicated. I'm only now sorting it out."

"Tell me about your mother."

"Gladly." He wiped his mouth, shoved his empty plate to the side, and set his elbows on the table. "She was an artist, a good one. She and my father had a kind of gentleman's farm—my father still lives there. My father's a physician. I love and admire him greatly, but my mother had a rare talent for enjoying each day. She loved everything: cooking, painting, she even loved cleaning the house. I know that sounds odd, but she was just that way, she'd put an opera on the stereo and storm around the house singing at the top of her lungs, scrubbing at the bathtub, sweeping the floors." His face softened at the memory.

"I can see why you miss her."

"Yes, selfishly for myself, but more than that, for Grace. As long as my mother was alive, she provided a kind of antidote to Joan."

Star lounged up to them. "More coffee?"

Ernest said, "No, thanks."

She tore off a piece of paper and dropped it on the table. "Check. You pay at the counter."

"I believe there's quite a crowd waiting for tables," Ernest said.

"Oh." Kelly looked over her shoulder at the door. "You're right." Reluctantly, she said, "I suppose we should go."

"Let's get some coffee to go. We can finish it in the car."

"All right."

They paid at the register, picked up their paper cups, passed through the crowd at the door, and raced to the Jeep. Ernest set his cup in a holder on the dash; Kelly held hers in her hands for warmth. The rain was still steadily falling, the streets hissing with water.

Randall continued as if there'd been no interruption. "I'm thinking of moving back to my parents' farm. The public school system in Concord is excellent, and I think Grace would be happy there. She loves the farm, the horses, my father."

"What about your work?"

"Yes, that. Well, I've got to make some changes. My schedule's too full. I do daily rounds at Mt. Auburn, as well as my own private practice and at Shady Dale Retirement Home. I've also, in the past few years, written a lot of papers and served on several boards." His smile was slightly grim. "There's nothing like an unhappy marriage to make a man a workaholic. I've already dropped the boards and the writing. I'm phasing out the retirement home. If I get custody of Grace, I'll want to be sure I have plenty of time to give her. To attend ballet recitals or school plays, or just to hang out."

"You sound like a wonderful father."

"I do? I'm not. Or, rather, I haven't been. I've let myself get too absorbed in my work. And I let Joan have too much of the responsibility for Grace, partly out of the simple desire for a peaceful home. It's just been easier to let Joan have her way."

He paused to concentrate on the Sunday traffic. Kelly liked the way he drove, with the same calm deliberateness that seemed to infuse all his movements.

"The thing is, Grace's told me she wants to live with me. Grace loves her mother and doesn't want to hurt her, so I've got to find some way to get custody of her without hurting Joan even more."

He turned onto the winding road leading to Forest Hills. They drove beneath the stone gates. He parked next to her car, but left the engine running.

Turning sideways, he leaned against the door. "But I think I've talked enough about me for today. It's your turn."

Taking his cup from the holder, he popped open the white plastic lid. The rich aroma of coffee filled the interior of the Jeep.

The constant rain, the comforting hum of the engine, the regular sweep of the windshield wipers acted like a drug on her. She felt safe and enormously content. Unfastening her seat belt, she drew her legs up and tucked them under her, settling so that she faced him. "What shall I talk about?"

"*Your* mother."

"Wouldn't you rather find out about my work? My hobbies? What movies and books I like?"

"Nope. Our mothers brought us together, in a way, after all. Besides, I have a hunch I'll find out a lot about you if you tell me about your mother."

She looked down at the white coffee cup in her hands and tried to gather her thoughts.

"Is it hard to talk about her?"

"It is, actually."

"Hey." Reaching over, he touched her hand. "I'm sorry. I shouldn't push you. Talk about something else instead. Whatever you want."

"No. That's all right. I just—I've never talked about her much. I did love her. As much as you loved yours, I'm sure. But—she betrayed me, enormously, unforgivably. For much of my adult life I hated her more than I loved her, or at least as much. I was *so angry*. And I was right to be angry. I'm angry still."

"What happened?"

"It's a long story." She hesitated. "I've never told anyone about this."

"We've got time."

All around them the rain fell steadily.

"I have to leave at noon."

"It's just after eleven."

"All right, then." But she didn't know how to begin.

He prompted her: "What was your mother like?"

Kelly sipped her coffee. "She was very lovely. She came here from Sweden when she was a girl to work as an au pair, and she met my father and married him. She loved him. I never saw them together, but she told me that she loved him, and I know she did. His name was Otto MacLeod. He was killed in Vietnam in 1965, the same year I was born. I never met him."

"I'm sorry."

"Yes. I would have liked to have a father. Still, my father's parents, my grandparents, remained very much a part of my life, and my mother's. When my father went into the army, she moved in with them, and when I was born, I was brought to their home in Arlington. My grandparents were a hardworking, rather somber couple. Otto was their only son. They loved me, and they loved my mother, but my mother was young, only twenty, when I was born, when her husband died. A baby and a pair of frugal in-laws can't replace a living man."

"No."

"For a long time Mother saw no one; she just stayed home and took care of me. Then when I started kindergarten, she began to date. She saw quite a few different men. I met some of them. I liked some and didn't care for others, but I was glad she was having fun. She seemed more alive. More herself. She was never *serious*, though, not about anyone. Then she met René Lambrousco."

Kelly thought of René's dramatic arrival in their lives. The child of a French mother and an Italian father, René was blindingly handsome, with flashing black eyes and feminine torrents of black curls which he constantly tossed dramatically away from his face.

Pictures of Kelly's father showed Otto with his light brown hair in a stern crew cut, straight shoulders, a proud chin lifted high. Otto would have joined his parents in their business, eventually inheriting it. René had no interest in business. He considered himself an actor, and indeed he did perform often, in local theater. To support himself, he worked as a waiter while he waited to be discovered.

She said, "René was an actor. He was dashingly handsome, with great charm and magnetism. He could make my mother laugh with an abandon I'd never seen before, and for a year or so I adored him almost as much as she did, because he made her so happy." She looked down into her coffee, as dark as the memory.

"And then?"

It was still painful, no matter how many years had passed, no matter how far she had brought herself away from that time.

"One evening at the end of my junior year of high school, my grandparents sat me and my mother down at the dining room table for a kind of summit conference. They wanted to assure me that they'd saved enough money to pay my college tuition. Also, they told my mother that when they died, they wanted their estate, in its entirety, to go to me. When I was small, they'd already made a will naming my mother as executor and heir. They saw no reason to rush to change it.

"During my junior year of college, both my grandparents suddenly died. They didn't leave a huge amount of money, partly because in their old-fashioned way they never felt comfortable investing their savings in stocks or mutual funds, afraid that they would somehow lose it all. But, with the sale of their house, they left a sufficient sum—" Kelly caught her breath, for it would never fail to wound her. "My grandparents never bothered to change their wills when I turned eighteen. They trusted my mother to take care of me. Of course they did! When they died, according to their will, their estate went to my mother. My mother married René Lambrousco. René persuaded her to give all the money to him."

"Wow."

"René convinced her it was a kind of investment. They moved to New York, where he was certain he would be discovered as an actor, and, he assured her, he'd make a fortune, pay her back, with interest. From his point of view, he was in the process of making me rich."

"Did it work out that way?"

Kelly snorted. "No. Oh, they moved to New York. He took acting lessons, paid for with my grandparents' money. I think perhaps he had two or three off-Broadway parts. Other than that, he didn't work. He didn't have to."

"Christ. You must have been furious."

"I was. More than that, I was—*lost*. I was twenty years old. My grandparents had died. My mother married and moved away. I had no money. I had no guidance. I didn't have anyone to turn to. So I did something that seemed right at the time. Now I regret it. Every day of my life I regret it."

"What did you do?"

Kelly shifted in her seat. She wanted to tell him the truth, all of it. Yet something held her back—her awareness of his enormous love for his child.

She settled for a smaller truth. "I made a terrible scene. I screamed horrible things at my mother. The entire time René just stood there, watching me. When my mother looked at him, he furrowed his forehead in concern—he was an actor. But he was so creepy, so manipulative—when Mother looked at me, he smiled at me over her shoulder. He *gloated*. He looked so *triumphant*."

"He sounds evil."

"He was. He is."

"And then?"

"I packed up my things and stormed from the house. I told my mother I never wanted to see her again."

"What did she say?"

"Nothing. She just wept. My last sight was of René coming forward, wrapping his arms around her, patting her back, comforting her, and looking at me with his lip curled. He had her and my money. He had won."

"You must have hated him."

"Yes. Her, too. For fifteen years, I never saw my mother."

"Did you phone? Write?"

"They moved a lot. So did I. She did track me down occasionally—I'm in the directory. She'd call to talk. She had a child, a daughter, almost immediately. She wanted me to be happy for her. I just felt—abandoned. Stupid, perhaps, but that's how I felt."

"But you saw her recently. When she was in the hospital."

"Yes. They moved back to Boston when Mother was sick. There was a cemetery plot already paid for, waiting for my mother, here with the MacLeods, and that was fine with René, saved him money. But I'll give him this much credit, he did phone to tell me they'd moved back here, that Mother was in the hospital."

"You reconciled then?"

"Yes. Although, because she was dying, she was always so tired—"

"Did you meet your sister?"

"Half sister. Yes. Briefly. She looks very much like René. She's fifteen, has that bored adolescent look." Her chin came up. She flashed an angry look at Ernest. "Don't suggest that *she* can replace my mother. Nothing can replace her."

"I don't think that."

"I lost so much when I lost her. But I didn't know how to forgive her."

"No. No, of course you didn't." He put his hands on her shoulders, steadying her.

She could tell he must be a very good doctor. He must have seen so much sorrow, so many people in pain, distress, or fear. He was big enough, physically, emotionally, to handle it all, she realized, and all at once, to her surprise and dismay, she found herself on the verge of tears.

"Hey," he said. "Do you know what I'd like to do?"

She shook her head, not certain she could speak.

He took her cup from her hands and settled it into the dashboard cup holder. Then he put his arms around her, drawing her to him. His warmth and gentleness seemed infinitely familiar. He smelled of sunshine and starch and, just faintly, a medicinal hint like rubbing alcohol. His mouth moved against hers in a long, warm, sexual swoon of a kiss. When finally it ended, they looked at one another, stunned, and Kelly saw how his blue eyes had become heavy-lidded with desire. She knew hers were, as well.

He drew away, nodding toward the clock on the dashboard. "You have an appointment."

Reluctantly, she agreed. "Yes." She pulled away from him, smoothing her hair.

"When can I see you again?"

It was hard to focus. "I've got a busy week ahead."

"Then next Sunday morning? Here?"

"Yes. Then. Here."

The rain was letting up, the sun winking out. It was nearly twelve. She sighed. "I really must go."

"I'll see you Sunday?"

"Next Sunday." She stepped out of his Jeep. He waved and drove away. Once inside her car, she leaned her head back against the seat, eyes closed, and put her fingers on her lips, where his mouth had been.

SIX

MONDAY EVENING RANDALL ARRIVED AT the Harvard Club early. He was already ensconced in one of the big leather club chairs when Anne walked in.

He rose as she came toward him. Heads turned, as they always did, when she walked by, slender, regal, blond, beautiful. She wore a plain black linen dress and her hair was held back by a black velvet headband.

Her perfection made him aware, as always, of the general rumpledness of his own appearance. Today, like all days, had been crowded with appointments, and there'd been an emergency during which one of his patients, a ninety-two-year-old man recovering from an operation, died, so everything was backed up. He didn't get to his final appointment until almost six o'clock, when he spoke with the son and daughter-in-law of Gifford Clifton, once one of Boston's finest gynecologists, now a victim of Alzheimer's, whose rantings, heavily laced with scatological and perverse sexual references, disrupted his family's household and frightened his grandchildren. In cases like this, where Randall knew the family, there was no way to rush through a discussion. It took time for the children of Alzheimer's patients to come to terms with the devastation the disease wreaked upon their formerly brilliant, loving, admirable parents.

So Randall hadn't had time to change but had rushed straight to the club from his office.

He saw Anne register his appearance. Her lips tightened and thinned, her gaze grew chilly, but still, because they were in public, she forced a smile and kissed the air next to Randall's cheek in a display of warmth that only she and Randall knew was false.

"You look beautiful, Anne," Randall said as they sat. And she did. She always did.

"Thank you."

The waiter arrived to take their drink order.

"Our reservation's at eight-thirty," Randall said.

"That's fine." She smoothed her dress over her lap, touched the pearl earring on her right ear, on her left, then the pearls at her throat.

"How's Tessa? I haven't had a chance to phone her yet today."

"She's well. Carmen's with her."

"She seems to like camp."

"Yes. Though she returns home terribly grubby. I can't imagine what they do there."

Randall smiled gently. "It's a *camp*, Anne. They're supposed to get grubby. That's the *point* of camp—tennis, swimming, baseball, hiking. Seeing the great outdoors."

"I've always considered camp more of a boys' thing."

"Yes, I know you have. And I'm grateful that you allowed Tessa to go to camp this summer."

"I thought our agreement was that I would allow Tessa to attend camp if you kept her off your father's horses."

"That's what *you* said, Anne. I never promised that."

She went silent, turning her head away, as the waiter brought their drinks, a Scotch for him, a martini for her.

As Anne took a delicate sip, she saw a spot on her skirt and rubbed at it with her thumb. "We need to talk about Tessa."

"All right."

She took another sip of the icy liquor and aimed a level gaze at Randall. "I don't want you to fight me for custody."

"Of course you don't, Anne. I know that."

She leaned forward. "You don't understand. I'm *serious*."

"And so am I. I believe Tessa would be better off living with me, and I'm going to fight for that."

"You're trying to destroy my political career."

"This has nothing to do with your political career, except that I believe it will take up more of your time, as it should, and that will affect Tessa."

"Think, Randall. Just *think*, will you? How will people regard me when they find out I'm divorced and don't even have custody of my daughter? You know what will happen." Angry tears glittered in her eyes. "I can't believe you would be so vindictive."

Randall waited while Anne finished her martini. He ordered another for her and sat in silence while she composed herself. She looked down, away from him, at her skirt, where the spot still tugged at her thumb.

"I'm not sure we should get into all this here," he said at last.

She glared at him. "Are you suggesting I have something to hide?"

"No, Anne. No, I'm not." He tried to keep his voice civil. "Anne, please understand. I *want* you to win this election. I think you would be an excellent representative, and I wouldn't be surprised if you spent the rest of your life in public government. You're good at it. You're genuinely concerned, hardworking, judicious—I only wish there were more people like you."

"Thank you." Her hand trembled as she lifted her martini to her mouth.

"But the personal qualities that make for a fine government official aren't necessarily the same qualities that make for a good mother."

"How dare you imply—!"

"Stop it, Anne." He kept his voice low but firm. "I'm not *implying* anything. I have no wish to insult you in any way, but I'm worried about Tessa. Very worried, if you want to know."

"Tessa is just fine."

"No, she is not. She's terribly thin, and she's becoming more and more withdrawn and secretive."

Anne snorted. "She's a teenager."

"She's twelve years old—"

Anne leaned forward, indignant. "How dare you correct me! Don't you think I know to the minute the child's age?"

"Anne—"

"The point is that she's *emotionally* a teenager. Of course she's going to withdraw and be secretive. It would be odd if she didn't."

"Very well, then. With whom is she *not* withdrawn? In whom is she confiding? Not you, not me. Certainly not Carmen, who is your confidante. Does she talk with other kids on the phone? Go to other kids' houses? To movies with them? Shopping at malls?"

"Yes, of course she does."

"Really? How often? Once a week? Twice?"

"She sees plenty of peers at camp."

"What about her friends from school?"

"She knows she can invite them to our house."

"Does she go to their houses?"

Anne shrugged and finished her drink. The spot on her skirt was making her wild; she rubbed and rubbed at it.

"When was the last time Tessa went to a friend's house?"

Anne straightened. Leveling a vexed gaze at Randall, she said, "I refuse to be interrogated like this."

"I'm asking you a simple question about our daughter."

Anne looked at her glass. It was empty. She rubbed the spot on her dress. "You know how I feel about Tessa going to other people's houses. They let her eat rubbish there, all kinds of disgusting junk food, and they watch the very worst television shows. Have you ever seen *The Simpsons*? Or some of the videos on MTV?" Her voice took on the quality of righteousness that served her well as a politician. "That's not even taking into account the kinds of movies her friends are allowed to watch, or the magazines they're allowed to bring into their homes. Some of them have older brothers, so older boys hang around, with God only knows what in mind for innocent girls like Tessa. Saying who knows what to her. *Touching* her. There's so much filth in homes these days, Randall, you know that. When I think of Tessa having to use the toilet in a home where teenage boys are allowed—" With enormous self-control, she brought herself to a halt.

"My dear Anne," Randall said sadly. "You promised me you would see someone."

Coldly, she retorted: "I changed my mind. I don't need a therapist, and it would be the kiss of death if my constituents knew I was seeing one. Besides, I don't agree with you. I don't need any kind of psychological help. Perhaps I'm more strict a mother than others, but that's hardly a sign of mental instability."

"Anne," Randall said very quietly. "Look at your hand."

Her eyes flashed to her lap where she was rubbing, *rubbing* at the invisible spot. She clutched her right hand with her left, halting its frenetic action.

"If I am exhibiting symptoms of anxiety, Randall," Anne stated very decisively, "it is completely understandable. You are leaving me, divorcing me, and now you want to take my child away as well. Of course I'm anxious."

"Anne—"

"And you *know* how to help me. You can stop telling me how to mother Tessa. And you could come home. I've told you I'm willing to try to work things out."

Randall studied the beautiful woman sitting across from him. "Are you willing to try making love?"

She shuddered. She could not help it or hide it, she shuddered with revulsion. "All this isn't about Tessa. It's just about sex. About you and your sexual needs."

Randall leaned forward. "Anne. Please, for God's sake, see a psychiatrist."

"This is getting us nowhere," Anne announced. She rose.

"Anne, please don't walk out."

"I have nothing more to say to you."

Randall rose as well. "Then we'll have to leave it all to our lawyers."

Her gaze whipped his face. "Don't threaten me."

"I'm not threatening. I'm merely stating a fact. If we can't come to some kind of—"

"Anne, darling! And Randall!"

A grand dame dripping with pearls swayed across the room, her portly husband in her wake. She embraced both the Madisons, who put appropriate social expressions on their faces and made the necessary small talk until the couple sailed away toward the dining room.

"Stay for dinner," Randall urged Anne as the couple walked away. "We have a reservation."

"I have nothing more to say to you, Randall," Anne said, and walked away, back straight, head high.

Kelly's second week of training took place in Berkshire County, in the western Massachusetts town of Pittsfield. Sunday night she made the three-hour drive across the state to set up quarters for the week in a Holiday Inn. Monday morning she arrived early at the courthouse in the middle of the town's business district.

The probate judge here was a man, as different from Judge Spriggs as night from day: Judge Samuel Flynn, a colorful American flag of a character with blue eyes, a red nose, and a white beard.

"Good morning, Judge MacLeod!" he boomed when she entered his chambers.

"Good morning, Judge."

Jovial and energetic, Judge Flynn introduced her to the clerks, the secretaries, and as he held her robe for her to slip her arms into, told her, "Don't worry yourself about what you're going to have to do today. You'll be a bit like a body at an Irish wake. We need you to have the party, but we don't expect you to say much."

Laughing himself into a coughing fit, he wiped his whiskers with a starched handkerchief and, without further ado, clapped his hands together loudly.

"All right! Let's go, darlin'. Out to the Boulevard of Broken Dreams."

Opening the door, he led her into his courtroom. They settled in their chairs. His clerk handed him some papers. Like many judges with a backlog, he managed to sign the papers his clerk put in front of him and at the same time converse about something completely different.

Finally he put down his pen, blew into his whiskers, and looked out at the courtroom. "Okay, counselors. I see we've got a complaint for contempt. Mary Berrie and Douglas Berrie. Come on up."

The Berries approached, each with a lawyer, the lawyers standing in the middle forming a barricade between the two people. All four gathered up near the witness stand.

"What's going on?" Flynn asked.

"Good morning, Judge. I'm Marshall Merrill, representing Mrs. Berrie. She and Mr. Berrie were granted a divorce six months ago. Since then we've had to come back to court twice, first to have the court issue a restraining order, and next to ask the court to remind Mr. Berrie that he must obey this order."

The judge glared at the ex-husband, a mild little man with illusions of a mustache. "Okay, Mr. Berrie, tell me about it."

"It was a birthday card, Your Honor! That's all! I only sent her a birthday card!"

"Yeah, well, look at it, Judge!" Mrs. Berrie, short, fat, pale, and not particularly clean, trembled with indignation. She thrust something toward the judge. The clerk took it from her, looked at it, and handed it to Flynn. Flynn looked at it and passed it to Kelly.

"She got no sense of humor," Mr. Berrie said.

On the front of the card was the grim reaper, wringing his hands in anticipation. Inside, the greeting read, "Another year closer. Happy Birthday." It was signed, "With my enduring thoughts, Dougie." Kelly shivered. The subtext was definitely threatening.

Judge Flynn blew through his snowy white whiskers. "Mrs. Berrie, if you get any more mail from your ex-husband, don't read it, just tear up it and toss it in the trash, okay? And Mr. Berrie, don't send any more mail to your ex-wife. No birthday cards, no Christmas cards, no get-well wishes, nothing—do I make myself clear?"

Mrs. Berrie's lawyer spoke up. "Judge, this is the second time Mr. Berrie has violated the restraining order. We were hoping for a more forceful action, perhaps some jail time or a fine—"

"Forget it. You're not going to get it. Okay, what's next?"

The couple walked off. Judge Flynn devoted his attention to another stack of papers. Kelly had no idea how he did it, but while his eyes were on a file, he saw, at the back of the courtroom, Mr. Berrie approach Mrs. Berrie with an object in his hand.

"Hey!" Judge Flynn yelled. "Mr. Berrie! What are you doing?"

The little man jumped a foot. "I, uh, I'm just giving her a present."

"Get back up here," Judge Flynn ordered.

The two Berries and their lawyers once more approached the bench.

"Do you want to go to jail?" Judge Flynn asked Mr. Berrie.

"Your Honor, it's a piece of jewelry. It's a charm. You see, every time we come to court, I give her a charm for her bracelet."

"I don't want his charms!" Mrs. Berrie said. "I want to start my life over without him!"

Judge Flynn blew through his whiskers. "Mr. Berrie. I

don't want to put you in jail. So would you please listen to me? I want you to keep away from Mrs. Berrie. I don't want you to send her something, or give her anything, or phone her or mail anything to her. I want you to wait in the courtroom today until Mrs. Berrie leaves. If you're shopping in the grocery store and you see her coming down the aisle, I want you to go in the other direction. Are you getting the picture?"

"Yes, Your Honor," Mr. Berrie said eagerly, like a good schoolboy.

"Counselor," Judge Flynn said to Mr. Berrie's lawyer. "Will you please spend some time explaining all the ramifications of a restraining order?"

"Yes, sir."

"All right, for God's sake." Judge Flynn waved them away.

"Can I give her the charm now?" the little man asked.

Camp Moxie, where Tessa spent five days a week, took place on the grounds and outbuildings of the Hawthorne School, a small nine-month private school for the select few gifted young adolescents whose parents could afford the tuition. During the summer months, the main buildings were closed, except for the administration building, where the Hawthorne secretaries and headmaster worked; the cafeteria, where the camp participants had lunch; and the gymnasium, where indoor activities were held if the weather made it impossible for them to swim, play tennis, or hike through the two hundred wooded acres of Hawthorne property.

Wednesday it rained all day, forcing the entire camp to stay in the barn where the counselors broke them up into groups of six or eight, working on various crafts. Tessa wanted to join the beadwork table—she'd promised her father she'd make him a bracelet. She'd begun it, choosing beads in earth colors so it would be masculine, and she enjoyed doing it so much—it was a private, soothing sort of job—that she thought she'd make her mother a bracelet, too. That would be a good idea anyway, so her mother wouldn't be jealous.

Beryl and Cynthia had chosen needlepoint, Shiobian was with the group learning to sketch and paint, and in the far corner of the barn, some of the guys, on mats, were working on elementary martial arts while others engaged in frenzied Ping-Pong games.

Tracy, clad in a batik blouse that came only to her midriff and tight bell-bottom jeans that hung from her hip bones, sauntered over to Tessa and, looping her arm through Tessa's, whispered, "Come join the photography group."

Tessa shook her head. "Photography bores me."

"Chad's in the group," Tracy teased in a singsong voice.

A good reason, Tessa thought, to stay away from photography. If she were around Chad, she'd become a nervous geeky wreck, she'd drop the cameras, ruin the film, and make a general fool of herself. "I don't like photography."

"You are so retarded," Tracy sighed. "Who cares if you like it or not? We're the only group that gets to leave the barn."

"Why would we want to leave the barn! It's pouring out."

"We'll be taking nature shots. Raindrops on leaves, that sort of thing. It'll be fun." She yanked Tessa's arm. "Besides, Youssif's cute."

"Youssif's *old*," Tessa said, but she allowed Tracy to pull her over to the photography group.

Four kids stood around a table, a girl named Ellen and three guys. One of the guys was Chad.

"Hey," he said to Tessa. He smiled at her with a glittering mouth.

Since the last camp session he'd gotten braces. He looked really goofy now, and way younger than he was—

vulnerable—and all at once Tessa's heart expanded, as if a fresh new chamber had just opened up.

"Hey," she replied.

Their counselor was a terrifyingly handsome eighteen-year-old named Youssif. His mother was Egyptian; his father, the CEO of some major corporation. Tracy had a major crush on him, *as if* she had a chance with someone in college.

"Okay, group, grab a camera," Youssif said. "And a roll of film."

"I've got a better camera than this," Benjamin, a fourteen-year-old with a bad case of acne, sneered.

"The technology doesn't matter if you don't have a good eye," Youssif told him. "This summer we're going to work on your eye. What do you see that others don't? Can you make us look at something ordinary and see something mysterious? Play with your camera. Play with your mind. At the end of each week you'll have photos to take home, and at the end of the summer we'll have an exhibition your parents can attend. We'll give out some awards."

The campers crowded around the table where ten sleek black Nikons waited next to a pile of film. Youssif led them through the process of loading the film into the cameras and locating the zoom button, the lens cap, and the light meter.

"We know this already," Ellen protested, but Youssif said, "Have a little patience, my friend. You need patience if you're going to be a photographer. Patience for details."

Mrs. Allison, the co-director of the camp, rushed over with a list. One of the counselors had left early with a stomach flu she prayed was not contagious. Another counselor had simply not shown up. Much of her gray hair had escaped from its bun and frizzled humidly around her anxious face.

"I just need to check off your names," she told them breathlessly. "Must be sure everyone's somewhere."

"We're going out for a nature walk," Youssif told her.

"In the rain?" Behind her glasses, her eyes bugged out of her head.

"The light's too monotonous inside," Youssif told her. "The conditions will provide the students a chance to experiment with a variety of light and shadow."

"Well, then, how nice." Mrs. Allison pottered off, clearly overwhelmed.

Outside the rain drummed down steadily, monotonously, like static on a TV set, but the air smelled sweet. At first Tessa shivered, ducking her head, but Tracy held her arms up and twirled, catching the rain with her tongue. The rain was warm against her skin. Her heart opened in the expanse of fresh air.

Youssif led them past the tennis courts, past the storage sheds and the woods where the canopy of leaves provided cover. Near a small shallow stream a clearing opened like a bright private room. Youssif climbed up on a boulder and looked around.

"Okay," he said. "You've each got twenty-four shots. You've got light, shadow, movement"—he nodded toward the flowing water—"stillness, and all kinds of texture. I want you to choose an area, do a study. Close-ups. Unusual angles. Play with the light. Get some shots that will confuse us. Surprise us. See things in a new way."

The campers splintered, wading through the tall grass, claiming their territory: a dead tree, a pile of rocks, the stream itself. Two guys went downstream to pee, cackling like idiots. Chad looked at Tessa, then wandered around by himself, pointing his camera at things.

Tessa squatted in front of a clump of ferns, their green heads bowed as if in prayer. Next to her, Tracy aimed her camera at the sky. Youssif walked by.

"I wish I had a cigarette," Tracy sighed.

"Smoking's bad for you," Youssif said, and stepped across the stream to tell Chad something.

Tessa lay on her back, trying to get a shot of the underside of the ferns. The ground beneath her was moist but not wet, and smelled like herbal tea.

"Tessa!" Chad called.

She looked across the stream at him.

"Smile!" he ordered.

She smiled.

He clicked his camera several times. "Cool. Thanks."

Tracy sat on a nearby boulder, idly clicking one shot right after the other. "See," she whispered to Tessa. "I told you he likes you."

"Tracy!" Chad called. "Smile!"

Tracy just stared. Chad clicked off a shot, then turned to focus on the boys wading in the stream.

"I guess he likes you, too," Tessa said.

"Trace!" Chad yelled. "Get in the frame with Tessa."

Tracy knelt next to Tessa who lay on her side facing the camera, head on elbow, ferns fanning around her head. Chad clicked a shot; then he waded across the stream.

"Let me get one of you and Tes," Tracy said, rising.

Tessa started to sit up but Chad sank to his knees and began to tickle her stomach. She laughed helplessly. Tracy clicked shots until Tessa cried out, "Enough!"

Chad rose, grabbed Tessa's hands and started to yank her up, but Tessa said, "Wait. I have an idea." She framed a shot of Chad's legs, just below the knee, next to a pair of young birches. Then she clicked a shot of Tracy's shins. She'd do a study of legs, she decided, then see if everyone could identify themselves by just that section of legs. It might be fun—it might even be difficult, especially when the legs were blended in next to trees.

Chad went off downstream to take photos of the other campers. Tracy hung around Youssif, asking questions. The rain stopped and watery shadows played across the rocks and stream. As Tessa looked around, she realized that twenty-four shots weren't nearly enough—when you looked closely, there was so much in the world to see.

• • •

Anne's day was packed with meetings. Late in the afternoon she sat at her desk, making notes, when she heard the front door open. Rising, she hurried out into the hall to greet her daughter.

Tessa stood just inside the front door, pulling her backpack off, her clothes disheveled and dirty, her hair hanging in sodden braids from which her hair escaped in wild strands, her sneakers absolutely black with mud.

"My God, Tessa! What have you been doing?"

"Lots of cool things, Mom. We took nature photographs in the rain—"

"What do they think they were doing? Letting you go out in the rain! You could catch pneumonia."

"No, Mom, it was really cool." Tessa laughed. "I mean it was really warm. The air was warm. The rain was warm. I mean it was cool taking photographs in the rain."

Tessa headed down the hall toward the kitchen, leaving a trail of mud behind her.

"Where do you think you're going?" Anne demanded.

Tessa looked surprised. "To clean out my backpack."

"I'll take that," Anne ordered, lifting the backpack away from her daughter with a delicate pinch of two fingers, as if it were a bomb. "Before you do anything in this house, you're going to take a shower and clean yourself up."

"Fine." Tessa turned and plodded upstairs, her mouth grim.

Dropping the backpack on the floor, Anne followed her daughter up the stairs and through Tessa's bedroom into her bathroom. Tessa was beginning to lift off her T-shirt. To Anne's surprise, Tessa turned and glared at her.

"I don't want you in here now."

"I don't care what you want," Anne snapped, brushing past her daughter to turn on the shower faucets.

"I'm not taking a shower until you leave."

Anne stared at her daughter, appalled. "How dare you speak to me that way!"

Tessa stood before her in her mud- and rain-stained clothes, her fists clenched at her side.

"Mom, I'm twelve years old."

"I'm perfectly aware of that, and as far as I'm concerned, you're still not capable of taking a decent bath. You're covered with filth and it's my responsibility as a mother to be certain that you get yourself clean."

"Mom, I know how to bathe. I know how to shampoo my hair. I know what you want me to do. I know how to make myself clean."

It was the patient tone of barely disguised superiority that infuriated Anne.

"Oh, do you really think so? You want me to be satisfied with your standards of hygiene when you enter the house dripping *muck*?"

"Mom," Tessa choked out, "I want you to leave me alone from now on *forever* when I bathe."

Anne stared at her daughter.

"Otherwise, it's just too weird!"

Anne raised her arm and brought it down with the stinging slap on Tessa's face. "How dare you call me weird!"

Tears spilled down Tessa's face. "I didn't call you weird," she whispered. "I meant the *situation* is weird."

Anne stared at the red mark on her daughter's cheek. It wasn't the first time she had slapped Tessa, and like all the other times, Anne couldn't believe she had done it. It was a horrible thing to do, Anne knew that, a horrible thing. A violent shaking raced over her body. She hugged herself with her arms.

"I'm so sorry, Tessa. I'm so sorry."

"It's all right, Mom. I'm okay."

Frantically, Anne looked around the room. All at once it seemed strange to her. She felt dizzy. She felt lost. "I don't know, Tessa—" She was becoming agitated, anxious, and no matter how hard she held herself, she was afraid she was going to fly apart. "Oh, Tessa—"

"Come on, Mom. Let's go to your study."

A warning bell rang in Anne's mind. Vaguely registering the sorrow and distaste with which her daughter crossed the room to put a guiding hand on her arm, Anne hated herself so fiercely it made her nauseated.

But more than anything else, even more than the gratitude Anne felt at this moment toward her daughter, was the anxiety pumping itself through Anne's blood. With Tessa guiding her, Anne nearly ran down the stairs, along the long hallway, and into the sanctuary of her study.

She sank into her chair. Leaning forward, Anne touched her white telephone, the small caller ID box, her Rolodex. Carefully she positioned her daily calendar so that it was aligned exactly in the center of her desk. Delicately she touched the tip of her fingers to her tape dispenser, her stapler, the malachite box full of stamps, her pastel in and out trays.

She was calming down. She could catch her breath now. The hideous anxiety receded. She put both hands on her silver and amethyst pen tray.

She was aware of Tessa standing there. As the anxiety retreated, shame washed through her.

"I'm okay now, Tessa." She was too humiliated to look at her daughter.

Tessa cleared her throat. It sounded as if she was crying when she said, "Good, Mom. That's good. So I'm going to go take my bath now, all right?"

Anne nodded her head. She was so exhausted she could hardly think straight.

"I'll do it exactly as you've taught me," Tessa reassured her. "I'll shampoo my hair four times. I'll rub the soap over me and rinse six times. Okay?"

"Okay. Thank you."

She felt Tessa's hand on her shoulder. She knew Tessa was trying to comfort her, she knew her daughter meant to be affectionate, but it took every bit of her strength not to cringe away from Tessa, still covered as she was with grime and filth from the camp.

"I'm okay," Anne said again. "Go on now. Get cleaned up."

Tessa left the room. Anne heard her steps on the stairs. Because she needed to, she went through her touching ritual again, starting with her telephone, ending with her pen tray. Ten items. Ten was such a beautiful, complete, organized number.

Still, when Anne heard Tessa's bathroom door close and the rush of the water through the pipes, she put her face in her hands and wept.

As Tessa sat with her mother in Dr. Lawrence's waiting room, Anne flipped through an old copy of *People*. She kept leaning over to Tessa, wanting Tessa to *oooh* with her over a picture of Celine Dion's stupid outfit or a man who had survived a plane crash. Tessa knew what her mother wanted her to do, she wanted her to act like they were best buddies. She wanted to put on the *Wonderful Anne and Her Adoring Daughter Show* for the receptionist.

A door opened. A man came out. He looked really cool in loose flannels, a white T-shirt, and a black cashmere vest. This wasn't how she'd thought a psychiatrist would look.

Anne nudged Tessa, who rose obediently.

"Hello, Anne," the man said. Briefly he shook Tessa's hand. "I'm Dr. Lawrence, Tessa. Nice to meet you." To Anne, he said, "She'll be out in about an hour. If you have some errands to do—"

"You won't be needing me?"

"Not this session."

"Very well, then. I'll be back in an hour, Tessa." She pecked her daughter on the top of her head and, reluctantly, took her leave.

Dr. Lawrence held the door open for Tessa, and she entered his inner sanctum. It looked, she thought, just like any other office. She was glad when he shut the door firmly behind her. With his hand he indicated the chair she was to take.

He sat behind the desk. A *Lion King* frame enclosed a snapshot of a little girl.

Following her gaze, he said, "That's my daughter, Stephie. She loves *The Lion King*."

Tessa smiled shyly. "Me, too."

"Comfortable in that chair, Tessa?"

She nodded. Now that she faced him, she could tell that Dr. Lawrence was an old guy with a young look, like a lot of teachers at her private school. Funny, because there were also lots of teachers who were very young but dressed like they were old.

"Want something to drink?"

"No, thank you."

"Do you know why you're here?"

"I guess."

"Can you tell me?"

She shrugged. "My parents are getting divorced. You're going to help the judge decide who I should live with."

"Good. That's good. I'm glad you understand." Leaning back, he folded his hands over his flat abdomen. "How are things at home?"

She shrugged again. "Fine."

"I've met your mother and your father both. At separate times. They're both great people. Fascinating, capable."

Tessa looked at him warily.

"But that doesn't mean they're perfect parents. No one's perfect. No child is perfect, or all bad, and no parent's perfect, or all bad."

"I guess."

"What's it like, living with your mother?"

"Okay." Tessa smoothed her blue skirt against her legs. She thought she saw, in the bright sunlight streaming through the window behind Dr. Lawrence, a spot on her skirt.

"Is she strict?"

Tessa looked up. How could he tell? Of all the things to ask, how could he know about that?

She nodded. "She's really strict."

"In what ways?"

Tessa rubbed her thumb over her skirt, then brought it up and chewed her thumbnail. "She's really strict about being clean. She's a nurse and all, so I guess she's more aware of all the germs everywhere than most people. She's trying to protect me, I know that. Still—"

"Still—?"

She chewed on the inside of her mouth.

"I'm not going to tell everyone else what you tell me, Tessa. Part of my job is knowing what to keep quiet about. You and your mother are going to meet with me together, you know—you and your father, too. Maybe you can tell me some things you'd like to talk about, the three of us. Sometimes it helps to have a mediator. Someone outside to sort of hear both sides."

Tessa squirmed uncomfortably. "They're so different, my parents. I love my dad's farm. I love Grandpops' horses." She paused. "I really miss my grandmother. She was awesome." Brightening, she added, "But I've got a friend—Brooke Burchardt—who lives across the road from the farm. She's a year older than I am. She's an awesome rider. She let me ride her horse Go-Cart once." The memory swept over her, her fear of the powerful animal, the ecstasy of the smooth, deep canter, the pride she felt afterward.

"But?" Dr. Lawrence prompted.

"But—Mom hates it when I go there. She's afraid I'll get hurt, or sick."

"When you have time with your dad, do you usually go to your grandfather's?"

"Yeah. 'Cause Dad's moved into an efficiency apartment. There's nothing to do there. Sometimes Dad will take me out to eat. Sometimes he lets me bring a friend and we go to a movie."

"Do you feel safe with your father?"

"Sure. He wouldn't let me ride if he thought the horses were dangerous." She thought of Go-Cart and grimaced.

"What was that thought about?"

"That thought?"

"You got a funny look on your face."

Tessa squinted at him. "Dad doesn't know I rode Go-Cart. Grandpops doesn't, either. Only Brooke knows."

"Go-Cart's a dangerous horse?"

"I don't know. Maybe. A little. He's younger than my grandfather's horses, and he's bigger, but Brooke pampers him like a baby." She flashed on his height, his strength. "He's an awesome horse."

"A stallion?"

"Good grief, no! Not even Brooke would have a stallion around. He's a gelding. Spirited, and he can really run. Grandfather's horses just sort of creak along, sighing and shaking their bridles."

"You'd like a horse more like Go-Cart?"

"Well, yeah, but it's not like that's ever going to happen."

"Why not?"

"My mom would have a fit."

"You understand where she's coming from?"

"I guess." Tessa studied the man, wondering how much she could tell him. Wondering if he could ever help her. Wondering what *help* would be. "I know my mom loves me. I know she wants to keep me safe. But she's so queer sometimes. Like yesterday? I came home from camp? It had been raining, and a bunch of us went out with our counselor to shoot pictures in the rain. So when I got home I was, like, muddy all over. And Mom freaked. Totally."

"She got really mad at you."

Tessa looked at the shrink's desk, but saw the way her mother's face had contorted when she slapped Tessa. Anger and pity flushed through her, and stronger than that, a sense of helplessness—"Mom really *really* hates dirt and stuff," she whispered.

"Did she hit you?"

Tessa stared at him, shocked at his guess, then dropped her eyes to her lap. Could he freaking *mind-read*? This was getting way too scary. She had to get him off that track, fast. It would break her mother's heart if Tessa told him that.

Guilt leapt through her. "You know that movie *Anastasia*?" She was trying to guide him onto a safer path, but at the same time, here was something she really wanted to say to him.

"The Disney cartoon version?"

"Yeah. That one. You know after she leaves the orphanage? She's out in the woods in the snow, and she sees a sign, and the mean old crone at the orphanage told her to go left, but she wonders what would happen if she goes right? Then she looks up at the sky and says, 'Give me a sign!' And *right away* a cute puppy appears, grabs her muffler, and prances off toward the right. So she chases after him, and there's Saint Petersburg all spread out before her. She finds her real grandmother, and Paris and wealth, and true love and everything!" Her smile fell away from her face. She was happy, remembering the story. But really, she was here, in this psychiatrist's office.

"One of the hard parts of growing up is dealing with the fact that life isn't like a Disney movie."

"I know. Still—"

"Still, you wish you had a *deus ex machina* to arrive to show you the way?"

"A what?"

"*Deus ex machina.* A god in the machine. It's a theatrical device. Suddenly, at the crisis point, a god floats down from the clouds to help end the conflict. Or comes down to earth to solve the problem, show you the way, so you don't have to do it all by yourself."

"Like in the Mary-Kate and Ashley movie, um, *It Takes Two*, when the helicopter came down?"

Dr. Lawrence nodded.

Tessa grinned. "Yeah. I could use one of those."

"It's gotta be hard, choosing between parents. Being in the middle."

Tessa said softly, "They're not my real parents."

"Oh?"

"I'm adopted."

"Right. I knew that. You have birth parents and adopted parents. 'Cause they're all *real*, aren't they?"

"I don't know. I'd like to meet them. My mother, especially."

"Have you talked this over with your parents?"

"Dad says Mom would die if I told her I wanted to meet my birth mother."

"Do you think she'd die?"

Tessa squirmed uncomfortably. "Not *die*. It would upset her a lot, though. It would be too hard on her, especially with the election."

"You think you could ask her about it after the election?"

"Yeah," Tessa said, brightening. "If she wins, I could."

"What if she loses?"

"Oh, *please*," Tessa begged, but with a smile, "let's not even go there. Let's not even *contemplate* the possibility that Mom could lose!"

"That would be bad?" the shrink asked lightly.

"That would be very bad," Tessa told him. Staunchly she added, "But I think Mom will win. She should win. She's really smart, and she's got a ton of great ideas."

Dr. Lawrence leaned back in his chair, crossed his arms behind his head, and stared at the ceiling. "So——" he said. "Let's say your mom does win. That would be in September, right? What else would you ask for? Other than to find out about your birth parents?"

Tessa didn't have to think long. "A computer. And my

own TV. At least the chance to watch more TV."

"Oh, yeah?"

"Yeah! I'm the only girl in the *world* who can't do the moves to the Britney Spears songs! Mom won't even let me hear her music on the radio! She won't let me watch MTV, and she won't let me watch the Britney Spears specials!"

Dr. Lawrence looked thoughtful. "Well, that would be a problem, I know. Even Stephie likes Britney Spears."

Encouraged, Tessa went on: "And I'd get my ears pierced. Everyone else has her ears pierced. Tracy even has her belly button pierced!"

"Would you like to have your belly button pierced?"

"Eeeugh, *no*. I just want—maybe—like, to paint my fingernails black or blue. Or to wear those removable stencil tattoos. A lot of girls have these like star and moon stick-on tattoos. They're really pretty. Mom won't let me have one."

"What would your father say about having your ears pierced?"

Tessa deflated against the chair. "I guess he wouldn't like that, either. He wants me to wait awhile. But he would let me watch more TV. And he would let me have a computer. He thinks I should have one."

"Let's say we talk to your parents, and your mom agrees to let you watch more TV and have a computer. Would it be okay then for you to stay there with her, living with her?"

Tessa said slowly, "I don't know."

"Well, think about that question, why don't you? I'm going to be talking to some other people this week, and next week we'll have you in to talk with me with your mother, the two of you together. Maybe we can broach some of these subjects then. Okay?"

She nodded.

"You're a bright girl, Tessa, you know? And you're a good girl, too. Don't beat yourself up too much because you think you might hurt your parents' feelings, okay? Give yourself a chance to feel what you really feel. Your parents are both strong. They can take it." He rose. "Our time's up. I'll bet your mother's out there waiting for you."

Tessa stood up, too. "I'm sure she is."

Mont Madison parked his ancient beloved woody station wagon carefully in the garage. No longer confident about his driving, he only brought it out on special occasions, and the funeral of one of Concord's old-timers was quite certainly a special occasion.

He hadn't cared for Franklin Sparks much, and they'd always been on opposite sides of the political spectrum, but he'd known Franklin since childhood, which caused its own kind of affiliation. And Jeanette Sparks was a lovely woman, and kind, and when she'd asked him to speak a few words at the memorial service for Frank, how could Mont refuse?

So he'd spoken. And he'd done fine, almost.

Mont went through the kitchen from the garage, and up the back stairs to his bedroom. His good gray suit was loose on him—he'd had to wear suspenders to keep his trousers up. Probably, he thought as he carefully hung it in the closet, it wouldn't be worn again until the time he was buried in it.

Which, if he was lucky, would be soon.

He was a useless old man. And he was becoming a forgetful old man. It was funny, in an ironic kind of way, that during his eulogy he'd forgotten the name of the disease that took Frank's life: Alzheimer's.

What wasn't so funny was that this morning he'd forgotten to turn the burner off under Madeline's treasured teakettle. Got up to look like a cat, the tail its handle, the kettle had a plastic bird in its spout that whistled when the water boiled. Mont hated that damned whistle. It was just too shrill. So he'd removed it, long ago.

This morning, rushing a bit to get organized for the

funeral, Mont had decided he'd better have a cup of coffee to jump-start his system. Disliking instant but needing the boost of caffeine, he'd stirred the crystals in boiling water, then tottered back up the stairs to shave and dress.

It was sheer luck that he'd decided to drive the woody instead of the Jeep. He'd had to return to the kitchen to fetch his other keys off the hook by the door, and it was then that he smelled something burning. There on the stove was that blasted kettle, boiled dry and kind of rocking on the glowing red burner.

He'd turned off the heat, then fortunately had the sense to grab a dish towel to protect his hand, tried to lift the dry kettle off, but it was welded to the burner.

For a long moment he was nauseated with shame. If Randall found out . . . Poor Randall had enough on his hands without the knowledge that his senile father had nearly burned the house down.

He waited until the burner was cool, then lifted it away and set it in the sink. Paint flaked off the bottom.

Enough, he told himself, one thing at a time. Funeral first. So he went, and spoke, and said the appropriate things to Jeanette and her three children, and now here he was sitting on the end of his bed with his shoes in his hands, staring off into space.

He roused himself. He slipped on his disreputable old loafers, which he sloped around in with the heels bent down beneath his foot. Madeline wasn't here any longer to chide him about that.

Madeline wasn't here any longer. That was the problem in a nutshell.

"I just don't want to go on," Jeanette had told Mont after the service, weeping.

"I know," he'd replied. And he did know. But he made the expected protest: "But you've got to think of your children."

Jeanette had smiled through her tears. "Cindy's having another baby. This time they hope it's a girl."

Mont rambled down the stairs and into his study. He'd eaten a huge amount of food at the Sparkses' home, and he was drowsy in the heat of the early afternoon. He checked himself over—buttons buttoned, fly zipped—just in case someone dropped by—then settled into his recliner. Taking up a copy of *Yankee* magazine, he opened it, laid it in his lap, rested his head back against the chair, and fell asleep.

When he woke, it was twilight. He'd slept the day away. He sat there a moment, orienting himself, cogitating. He couldn't conquer a sense of embarrassment, a deep shame, each time he woke after a nap during daylight hours. It reminded him how unnecessary he was. The greatest pain of aging wasn't the aches of joints or the indignities of the guts and bladder, although those could be cruel. The worst thing was the sheer simple uselessness, the sense that you were only taking up space and air, and contributing nothing.

He missed his friend Patrick. He'd been furious at him for committing suicide, but with each passing day, Mont understood the impulse that drove his friend to end his life.

And so, he prodded himself, what should he do about it? Hang on desperately until some kind of illness claimed him, in the meantime risking the chance of burning down the house he intended to leave to his children?

He'd never been a passive man. No reason he should be one now. As a physician, he had any number of painless pills he could drink down with a glass of fine single-malt Scotch. He wasn't afraid of death. He doubted that there was an afterlife, but whatever awaited him there wasn't half as difficult as facing a future full of empty days, dwindling faculties, and loneliness.

Slowly he stirred his creaky old joints and dragged his dreary old self into the kitchen, where he stood staring into the refrigerator as if expecting by magic something tasty to appear there.

Perhaps just some cheese, he was thinking, when he

heard the car and a few moments later Randall came in. His suit was wrinkled, his tie loose and twisted, and his silver-blond hair sticking out in all directions like some kind of punk rocker's. Still, the sight of him delighted Mont. No doubt about it, even rumpled, Randall was a good-looking man.

"Hey, Dad." He set a flat cardboard box on the kitchen table. "Pizza."

Mont slapped his forehead. "Was I expecting you for dinner?"

"No. I just had the urge to come out. If you've already eaten, we can freeze some of this for another day."

"No, no. I haven't eaten. Smells good."

"Mushrooms, sausage, anchovies, double onion, the works." Randall took two plates from the cupboard and set them on the table.

Mont lifted an eyebrow. "Am I being bribed?"

"I brought beer, too." Randall dug through the utensil drawer, found the church key, and popped the lid off a bottle. "It's still cold." He handed a Heineken to Mont.

"Aren't you supposed to be at your office?"

"I've moved a lot of my patients to other physicians. I'm cutting down. Almost in half."

"You're kidding."

"No, I'm not. This divorce business—well, it's made me realize how little time I was giving to Tessa. I can't do everything and still find time for her."

Mont deliberated. "Yes, you're right about that."

His stomach grumbled as Randall lifted the lid, slid a spatula under a triangle of pizza, and hefted it onto Mont's plate. He took a bite. "Good pizza."

Randall nodded. They ate in companionable silence. When he was lifting his second piece from the box, Randall announced, "I had another idea, about Tessa and me."

"Oh?"

"Yes. About Tessa, me, and you, actually. I want to move back here. I want this to be my primary residence. I want Tessa to go to school in Concord. What do you think?"

"Well!" Mont scratched his ear, pretending to think about it, trying not to explode with joy.

"The thing is, Dad, if I get full custody of Tessa, or even joint custody, I want a stable home for her, someplace she's comfortable in, someplace she'd like to bring friends home to. No rented apartment I can find can ever compete with this place in Tessa's heart. And something else, I think it would make a big difference in getting custody if there were two adults here looking out for Tessa. Certainly it would make my life simpler and Tessa's happier, if she knew you were always here. That way if I got called away on an emergency or was going to be late some evening, I wouldn't have to worry, and Tessa would feel safe. Plus, she likes being with you. She wouldn't be lonely. And her friend, Brooke, lives right across the road. It seems perfect."

Mont's heart swelled up so full it pushed tears into his eyes. Hiding them, he coughed into a napkin. "Something in my throat," he croaked.

"Take a sip of beer. So what do you think, Dad?"

Mont took a sip of beer, and when he could trust himself to speak, he said, "I think it's a great idea."

Every evening after court adjourned for the day, Judge Flynn and his wife treated Kelly to dinner and an evening of music at Tanglewood and once to the theater in Stockbridge and another night to the theater in Williamstown.

"This is what you've got to learn, too," Judge Flynn assured her. "You can't live with the law every minute of every day. You'll burn yourself out too fast if you do. Yes, you do need to keep up on your reading, the statutes, the changes in the law, but you wouldn't be a judge if you weren't already a Type A, driven, compulsive, heart-attack contender in the making. You have to get out of your house, or you'll start drinking too much or eating too much and brooding on the terrible state of the world. You've got to force yourself to go off and get entertained. It's good for you. It's like mental vitamins. Without something amusing, distracting, you'll get sick."

Friday night after the last case was finished, Judge Flynn asked Kelly, "Millie and I are going out to dinner at the 1886 House. Want to join us?"

"Thanks, but I've got to get back to Boston."

"You all packed and ready to roll?"

"I am."

"All right, then." He shook her hand, patting the top of it with avuncular affection. "I've enjoyed your company this week. You've got a good head on your shoulders. You're diligent, thorough, and patient. For what it's worth, I think you'll make a helluva judge."

"Thank you, Your Honor."

Kelly grabbed the suitcase she'd stashed in the judge's chambers and headed out to her car. She stopped at a gas station, filled the tank, and, fortified with a twenty-ounce Diet Coke and a bag of M&M's, blasted down Route 7 to the Mass Pike and then east for three hours.

As she drove, her mind reeled from thought to thought. She had wanted to be a judge; she'd secretly wanted to be a judge for years, but only now was she realizing that along with the power came a staggering weight. It was one thing to be a lawyer, representing clients with the best scholarship, mental agility, and hard work possible. Quite another to be a judge, whose decisions were final, who looked out at so many couples who had once ("Press rewind") gazed upon each other with loving eyes—eager to promise one another the moon—and granted that couple a divorce.

It forced her to think seriously about her own life. She was engaged to one man and in love, or at least infatuated, with another. What the hell was she going to do? What would Judge Spriggs do?

Mentally she divided a paper into fourths, with Jason on one side and Ernest on the other.

Jason was handsome, kind, wealthy, intelligent, and also a lawyer, a real plus, because he and Kelly would always be able to share their work.

Ernest on the other hand was not even yet divorced. He was a father. With just those two facts the complications for difficulties multiplied enormously.

Jason had no children yet, but wanted them with Kelly. Jason didn't consider Kelly a statue on a pedestal: he'd seen her angry, and grieving, and grumbling around in sweat-pants during a period, and he still loved her. His mother loved her. They had friends in common.

And yet she'd never been able to tell Jason about her own background, about René and the way he'd stolen Kelly's inheritance. Why had she been able to talk about it with a man whose real name she didn't even know? How was it that she felt she could be more truly herself with Ernest than with her own fiancé? Something was lacking in her feelings for Jason. She'd always known this, and shied away from the knowledge, unwilling to examine it, telling herself to be grateful that a man as clever and sexy and bright as Jason thought he loved her.

But Ernest—just the *thought* of Ernest made her *shiver*. The sight of him made her heart leap with joy, and simply sitting with him, hearing his voice, looking at him, satisfied her deeply. He woke up her body. He woke up her spirit. When she was around him, her whole being reso-nated with a childish satisfaction laced with adult desire. And kissing him had been—such a *surprise*—as if some-thing enormous sleeping within her had awakened. As if magic really did exist.

For Jason, she had well-articulated arguments, clear-cut lists of facts supporting his appeal to her. *Words*.

The arguments for Ernest came not with words but with the fluency of the senses. She didn't so much *think* of him as remember him with all her body. And it was Ernest she wanted to remember, not Jason. Flicking the SEEK button on the radio, caught on the hook of love songs, it was Ernest whom she, helplessly, happily, thought of.

So, Kelly, *Judge MacLeod*, she declared, where is all this taking you? In the privacy of her car, as the summer darkness slowly fell, staining the sky with endless variations of blue, she let herself dream. No one would be hurt by her dreams, after all. No one would ever know.

What if she broke her engagement with Jason? He would be hurt, but he'd recover. Jason was a survivor, always. Handsome, wealthy, clever. He'd be surrounded by women in a flash. He wouldn't suffer long.

And then—and then Ernest would divorce his wife. He and Kelly would—this was only a fantasy, after all—marry.

No. She was going too far, too fast. She had to slow down. She'd think simply of *seeing* Ernest again, only that.

And only that was enough to make her smile and stretch herself all up and down, her body luxuriating in the memory of his kiss like a cat curling up in the warmth of the sun.

Carmen Cruiz entered Dr. Lawrence's office with her head held high. A small woman in her forties, wiry and thin, she wore a navy blue suit and no ornaments except a gold cross around her neck. She settled into her chair and glared at the psychiatrist, communicating with every bit of body language she possessed that she was not even slightly amused to be here.

"Thank you for coming in, Mrs. Cruiz," Dr. Lawrence said. "We're all grateful for your help. Would you like some tea or coffee?"

"No, thank you." Her feet were planted flat on the floor, her pocketbook gripped tightly on her lap with both hands, as if she suspected he might try to snatch it from her.

"I assume Mrs. Madison has explained to you why we've asked you to speak with me."

"You are trying to take her daughter away."

"Oh, no, that's not the case at all, Mrs. Cruiz. What I'm supposed to do is to find out what would be best for *Tessa*. I am to investigate Tessa's situation and find out what her best interests are."

"Tessa's best interests are to be with her mother."

Lawrence leaned back in his chair. "You are fond of Mrs. Madison?"

"Very."

"You've worked for her"—he looked at his notes—"for ten years?"

Carmen nodded.

"And for Dr. Madison, too, of course."

She shrugged.

"What can you tell me about Dr. Madison?"

She curled her lip. "He is a man. What else do you need to know?"

"Well, what I'd *like* to know is how Dr. Madison is as a father."

Carmen shrugged. "Not good."

"Not good?"

"Not good! How can he be *good*? He is leaving his wife! Mrs. Madison cries all the time. Tessa worries. No. He is not good."

Dr. Lawrence picked up a pencil and studied it, as if trying to gauge its length. "Any other reasons?"

"That is enough."

With great deliberation, he lay the pencil down. Folding his hands on his blotter, he leaned toward Carmen, fixing her with a stare. "You have an unusual position in this matter, Mrs. Cruiz. You have known this family for many years. You work right in the heart of the house. You have seen Tessa grow up. You've seen and heard many private things."

"That is true."

"Your opinion will be of great help to me. That's why you must be fair and honest."

Steadily she met his eyes. "This is what I know: Mrs. Madison is a saint. A *saint*. She works very hard. She keeps her house very clean, her clothes very clean. She loves her daughter, Tessa. She is a good mother to her. You should not take her daughter from her."

"Dr. Madison loves his daughter, too, doesn't he?"

Carmen didn't reply.

"You think he doesn't love Tessa?"

Carmen sniffed.

"What makes you think he doesn't love Tessa?"

"If he loved Tessa, he wouldn't leave Mrs. Madison."

Dr. Lawrence stifled a sigh. "But do you have any other reasons? Have you ever seen, for example, Dr. Madison hit Tessa?"

Carmen studied her shoes. "No."

Dr. Lawrence looked at his notes. "All right. Tell me about Tessa."

"What about her?"

"Well, what is she like?"

"She's a good girl. She obeys her mother."

"Do you have children, Mrs. Cruiz?"

"No." She polished the snap on her purse with her thumb. "I was married. My husband drank. When I was pregnant, my husband hit me. I lost the child. Mrs. Madison came to the hospital. She took me into her own house until I recovered. She helped me find a new place to live. She helped bring my sister here from Mexico to live with me. She found a job for my sister."

"You live with your sister now?"

"Yes."

"So you're divorced?"

"No. I do not believe in divorce. I'm a good Catholic."

"I see. Your husband—"

She shrugged. "He moved away."

"When did you last see him?"

"Maybe five years ago."

"Well, Mrs. Cruiz, I think that's about all. You've been most helpful. Thanks for coming in." Dr. Lawrence rose.

Carmen Cruiz rose, too, but stood her ground, facing the psychiatrist. "Dr. Lawrence. Please. Please do not take Tessa from her mother. It would not be right."

"It's not my decision to make, you understand, Mrs. Cruiz? I'm only one person, speaking in the interests of a child."

"The best interests of Tessa are to remain with her mother." Leaning forward, Carmen Cruiz declared vehemently, "A daughter must be with her mother."

Dr. Lawrence smiled a professional smile. "I understand your concern, and I appreciate the time you've taken to speak with me."

Mrs. Cruiz turned sharply on her heel and left the room, muttering as she went.

Randall sat in his office, trying to decide what to do with what was left of this beautiful summer day. His last patient had come and gone, he'd taken care of ordering prescriptions, and from the reception area he heard Pam shutting and locking up the file cabinets, humming as she went.

As he slipped off his white lab coat and pulled on his jacket, he heard the office door open and then Pam's cry of delight. Almost immediately came the scent of lemon. Groaning, Randall quickly pulled on his lab coat, settled at his desk, and got busy at the computer.

It was Lacey, he knew. It had to be. Pam adored Lacey, who always found time to talk with her, who remembered her children's names and ages and habits as well. Laughter floated from the front room. Then a knock came at his door and Lacey peered in.

"Randall?" She wore a tight flowered summer dress. "Pam told me it was all right to come on in."

"Of course," he replied. "I'm just finishing up some paperwork." He rose, staying behind the desk.

In her hands Lacey held a magnificent lemon meringue pie, its peaks a whirl of glossy white. She set it gently on his desk. "I had the day off," she said, looking up at him girlishly through her eyelashes, "and I felt like baking, and I remembered how much you like lemon meringue pies—"

"That's kind of you, Lacey, thank you." He tried to be polite but restrained.

"You know I love to cook, Randall." She smiled seductively. "In fact, I've got a leg of lamb in the oven right now."

"I'm afraid I'm buried with work. I've got to visit my father this evening," Randall told her.

She didn't blink. "Well, then," she responded cheerfully, "you'll have someone to share the pie with."

He stared at her with admiration and irritation, searching for the perfect words that would make her leave without hurting her feelings.

She actually laughed. "It's only a *pie,* Randall. Don't look so grumpy!" She went out the door and then looked back in, her luscious pink lips glistening with a smile. "I'll call you next week. Maybe then you'll have time for that drink."

Saturday evening Kelly slipped into the passenger seat of Jason's red Saab convertible. "Hi." Leaning over, she kissed his cheek. "Hey. Look at you. What a great tan!"

"Unlike some people I could name who can't find time to step outside on a gorgeous summer day."

"Jason, come on," Kelly cajoled. "I've been away from home all week. Today I had to do some basic maintenance. Don't sulk. Wouldn't you prefer it if I wore clean underwear?"

He waggled his eyebrows. "I'd *prefer* it if you wore *no* underwear."

Gunning the engine, he shot them out into the flow of traffic. It was seven o'clock, the evening warm and bright, a lovely night to be in a convertible. Kelly leaned her head back against the seat.

Tomorrow, she thought dreamily, *is Sunday.*

"Must be a pretty sweet fantasy," Jason said.

Her eyes flew open. "What?"

"What were you thinking of just then?"

Guilt made her stutter. "Sun—sun. Sunshine. Peace and quiet."

"Tough week?"

"Tough but good. I'm learning a lot. But it's always wrenching, seeing families torn apart."

"So forget about all that. Go back to your fantasy." Jason patted her knee.

I am a terrible person, Kelly reproached herself.

Lying back in the seat, she gazed at Jason. No doubt about it, he was just plain gorgeous. His teeth were brilliant white against the even tan of his face. The red collar of his polo shirt lay against his navy linen blazer, accentuating the dramatic darkness of his eyes and hair.

Feeling her studying him, Jason turned. He held her eyes with his. "You're beautiful."

She looked away. "Can't compare with you," she said lightly. His desire came toward her like a missile—and she felt nothing in return. In remorse, she amplified her compliment. "You look like a movie star. Truly. How did you get such a great tan in just a week?" She put her hand on the back of his neck, stroking it lightly.

He relaxed into her touch. "Tennis. Three afternoons this week and again this afternoon. And yesterday I took off, went down to the Cape, and spent the day sailing with Buster and the gang."

"Well, I got to see some great theater. Stockbridge one night. Williamstown the next. Frank Langella. Blythe Danner. Plus hear Seiji Ozawa at Tanglewood."

"Oh, hey. Buster and Muffy invited us for Labor Day weekend. They're having a great smash of a house party at his parents' place on the Vineyard."

"Oh. Well—great!" She forced herself to speak with enthusiasm. After all, tonight they were on their way to have dinner with Donna and the new love of her life, and while Jason didn't dislike Donna, he didn't consider her one of his set. Donna was too argumentative, he'd complained to Kelly, who'd retorted, "You just think that because she doesn't agree with you."

Turning off Mass Ave, Jason pulled into the parking lot of Marino's and switched off the ignition. Kelly flipped the visor down to check her hair in the mirror.

"Don't worry," Jason assured her. "You look good." Leaning over, he nuzzled her neck. "Good enough to eat," he murmured, and nibbled on her ear.

His touch irritated her like a mosquito's whine. She caught her breath, stunned by her reaction.

Jason misinterpreted her gasp. "Let's make this a short night, okay? I want to take you to bed, Kelly."

"Mmm." She met her own eyes in the mirror of the visor. *Liar,* she accused herself. *Fool.*

She didn't want him to spend the night. She *really* didn't want him to go to the cemetery with her in the morning.

She pulled away from him. "Sure, but not too short, okay? I mean, this is a big deal for Donna, Jason. This is the first guy she's been really serious about in a long time. We can't eat and run."

Jason stroked her cheek. "Whatever you want, swee-tie."

The restaurant was crowded. Donna and her new beau were already there, at a table in a far corner. As Kelly crossed the noisy room, her hand in Jason's, she was aware, as always, of the way people looked up at them and then looked again. She could feel the admiration. The envy. It was like a spotlight on them; she felt highlighted, on stage. Few people became lawyers or judges who didn't enjoy this sensation. Jason *loved* it, she knew. And they did look like such a perfect pair—tall, lean Jason, dark like a prince, Kelly floating next to him, pale as a swan.

Donna rose to kiss Kelly. Her dark hair tumbled down to her shoulders, which supported two tiny red straps that in turn supported a dangerously stressed, plunging, skintight red silk top. "Hi, you guys! Jason, this is Eric."

"Eric." Jason shook hands with the other man.

Eric rose. He was short, with the kind of meticulous grooming that made his beard and the hair on his head equally short and bristling with urban chic. This did not quite offset the fact that he was short and portly, with the gentle brown eyes of a cow set in a round cherub's face. He was as plump as Donna—they looked, in fact, like brother and sister. What *round* babies they would have, Kelly thought.

"You look fabulous," she whispered to Donna.

"I *feel* fabulous," Donna giggled.

The four settled around the table, adjusting their chairs, flapping open their napkins, making small talk while the waitress took their orders. Eric was a lawyer specializing, like Jason, in tax law and inheritance, so the two spoke a common language and were quickly involved in a heated discussion.

Donna leaned close to Kelly. "So? What do you think?"

"We just got here! But he seems nice."

"He's terribly brilliant."

"You're smitten."

"Oh, Kelly, I am!" Donna glanced over and, seeing that Eric's attention was fully on his conversation with Jason, confided, "He's an amazing lover!"

Kelly looked at Eric. In spite of his bristle cut, she could see that he had a receding hairline and a bald spot at the top of his head. His cheeks were actually rosy. He looked as innocent as the Pillsbury Doughboy.

Donna was flushed. "It's not just sex, Kelly. I think it's love. *The real thing.*"

A wave of wistfulness moved through Kelly. She wanted to reach over and stroke her friend's face. "Oh, honey. How great. I'm so glad for you."

"Well, don't look so sad. You're engaged, for heaven's sake."

"I know. Believe me, I know."

Both women did a quick surveillance of the men.

"—Dewar's for every day, but to celebrate, I like a good single-malt Scotch," Eric said.

Jason topped him. "Have you tried Glenrothes? Sixty-five bucks a bottle."

Donna looked at Kelly. "What's going on?" Donna asked. Then, pouncing: "You've met that man again!"

Kelly moved close to Donna. "Last Sunday. Donna—all you're saying about you and Eric? That's how I feel about this man."

Donna's eyes went wide. "Have you *slept* with him?"

"No. But I want to."

"Oh, jeez, Kelly, that's getting into dangerous territory."

"I know."

Donna put her hand on Kelly's. "Hon, think about it. You don't want to lose Jason just to sleep with some stranger. Have you even found out his name?"

The waitress set their first courses before them. Kelly got very busy with her salad.

"Well, have you?" Donna demanded.

Kelly laid her fork down. "I don't know his name. He doesn't know mine."

"And you want to have sex with him."

"It's kind of a game we're playing."

"A game."

"Look, he's a doctor, I know that much. And he's a father. He's got a little girl he's crazy about, and he's involved in a custody battle."

"And you want to have sex with him."

"More than that. Oh, I don't know how to explain it, Donna. I just feel—*at home* with him."

"And you *don't* feel at home with Jason?"

"Not like this." Guiltily, Kelly looked over at Jason.

He caught her look and smiled. "How's your salad?"

"Delicious. Yours?"

Eric leaned forward. "Donna tells me you're a new probate court judge. Congratulations." His smile curved up, a perfect half moon.

"Thank you."

"You were in training this week?"

"Yes. My second week." Kelly was glad to have her interrogation by Donna derailed. "I was in Berkshire County this week."

"Lucky you. Beautiful out there. What kinds of cases did you have, Kelly?" Eric inquired.

"Some divorces. Child custody. One adoption. That was pretty nice. The happier side of probate law."

Donna speared a tomato. "Have you been following the fight in Oregon? About their new law? Measure fifty-eight, Adoptee Rights. It gives adopted children legal access to birth certificates, and thus to their birth parents. At least to their birth mother."

"It's an understandable wish, to know who your birth parents are," Kelly said. "So many people are searching, and I can understand it. It's like looking for a part of yourself. I've worked occasionally with a group called Bastard Nation, a national organization devoted to the opening of birth records to adopted children."

"Remind me of the law here in Massachusetts," Eric requested.

Kelly knew this by heart. "Identifying information will be released to a twenty-one-year-old adult adoptee, *if* there's written permission from both the adoptee and the birth parent."

"That makes sense to me," Eric said. "Provides some protection for the mother."

Jason gestured with a bread stick. "I don't know. Out in Oregon, the opponents of Measure fifty-eight are claiming that release of the birth mother's name, the appearance of a child in the woman's life, could cause humiliation and all sorts of terrible problems in the birth mother's life."

"Yeah," Donna agreed. "What if some poor woman gets knocked up accidentally, has the baby, gives it up for adoption, marries some guy and never tells him about the child, and then *wham*, one day there comes a knock on the door. Dad answers it. Or Sonny. 'Hi, can I speak to my Mom?' Imagine how angry someone would be."

"On the other hand," Kelly said, "think of the joy of seeing your child again. Think of seeing your mother for the first time. It's got to be one of the most powerful, urgent, primitive longings human beings know."

Something in her voice caused the others at the table to fall silent.

Jason sipped his wine and leaned back in his chair. "I've always admired people who adopt."

"So have I," Kelly agreed eagerly.

"But I could never do it myself."

"Oh, really." Kelly sat up straighter in her chair.

The waitress appeared at their table, arms laden. "Who has the primavera?"

Donna had the primavera; Kelly, the scallops; Jason, the swordfish; and Eric, the veal. Veal, Kelly thought, how attractive. She glanced at Donna. Donna kept her eyes on her plate.

Eric picked up the thread of conversation. "I agree with Jason. I think adoption is a real crap shoot. You don't know what kind of kid you'll get."

"You don't know that when you give birth to your own child," Kelly pointed out.

"Ah, I disagree. You do have more information, simply because you know what sorts of things run in your family. Illnesses, personality problems, psychological tendencies."

"Or talents," Jason interjected.

"Right. Or talents. You know in general whether or not, let's say, schizophrenia or a propensity for violence runs in the family. Intelligence or retardation. Any day now they'll be able to test embryos for certain diseases. Cystic fibrosis, for example. Alzheimer's. Parkinson's. Genes are everything, we know now."

"I wouldn't say they're *everything*," Kelly responded mildly.

Jason spoke up. "The idea of genetic testing is so new it still makes everyone nervous. Forget about that, then. The point is, with your own child, you at least have some idea what to prepare for. If old Grandfather Joseph was a closet alcoholic, for example. If Sister Susie had diabetes."

Donna leaned forward, cheeks burning. "Then what do you gentlemen propose we do with all the children who are born to mothers out of wedlock, mothers who don't want their children, parents who abandon them?"

"Hey, hey, hey." Eric held up his hands as if being arrested. "I didn't say *someone* shouldn't adopt those kids. I'm just saying I couldn't do it."

"I'm with Eric," Jason began.

Kelly cut him off. "How can you be? I mean, how can you say you wouldn't adopt? You're fortunate. You're healthy. You're wealthy. Don't you feel the need to balance out your karma? Or simply just to be on the side of the good in life? If you, who have everything, who have more than your fair share, won't take on some responsibilities for the poor, the weak, the unfortunate, then who will? How can you be so—so greedy, so selfish?"

There was one beat of silence at the table. Jason had a quizzical expression on his face as he tried to decide whether this was a personal attack or an especially heated academic debate. Both, he decided apparently, for he placed his hand on Kelly's when he spoke. "I don't mean to be selfish. *You* know, at least I think you do, that I mean to do some good in life."

"Income tax law," Kelly retorted. "Your clients are all

wealthy." Had she never realized this before?

"True. But Kelly, you know I give a lot to charity. My entire family has always been committed to philanthropy. We make more of a difference with our cold, hard, anonymous cash than the hundreds of earnest souls who donate an hour a week at a day care."

"I'm not so sure about that—" Kelly began.

"Oh, for Christ's sake! Our family foundation gave an entire children's wing to a hospital." He leaned both elbows on the table, closing in. "But to go back to the original point, about adoption. I think it's a good idea. I think people should do it, and thank God there are kinder, more compassionate, stronger people than I in this world who would enjoy doing it. All I'm saying is that as a lawyer I need to *choose my battles*. Whatever I do in my life, whatever battles I fight during the day, I want to have peace in my home. Peace at home equals competency at work."

"Then I hope you don't have a child who's frail, or violent, or mentally challenged!" Kelly snapped.

Jason's smile was crooked. Pointedly, he said, "I hope *we* don't, either, my darling."

"How's your veal?" Donna asked brightly.

"I like Eric," Jason said once they were tucked inside his car and on their way through the summer night to Kelly's apartment.

Kelly didn't respond. Leaning her head against the backrest, she closed her eyes.

"Don't you?" Jason prodded.

"Yes. He seems very nice."

"The food was great."

"Mmmm."

At the long stoplight on Mass Ave and Rindge, Jason fixed Kelly with a look she could sense through her closed eyes. "I don't understand what I've done wrong." His voice was controlled, very quiet.

Kelly sighed. "You haven't done anything wrong, Jason."

"I must have. You've treated me as an adversary all night."

"That's not true. Besides, we all enjoy being adversaries. We were a quartet of lawyers, for heaven's sake, discussing difficult issues. We argue for sport. It wasn't anything personal."

The light changed. Jason gunned the engine. Putting his hand on her knee, he said, "So we're okay?"

His hand felt possessive. Restrictive. "Of course we're okay."

He moved his hand up her thigh toward her crotch.

"Don't, Jason."

"Why not?"

"We're in a convertible. People can see."

"It's never bothered you before." He didn't move his hand. "Besides, no one can see."

"Look, Jason. If I ask you to stop, you should stop."

"Fine." He pulled his hand away.

They rode in uncomfortable silence through Harvard Square. When he parked on Memorial Drive, he turned toward her. "Hey."

She didn't want to open her eyes. She was being evasive; she knew that. But she felt cranky. Backed into a corner. "I'm sorry, Jason." Opening her eyes, she forced a smile. "I know I'm being terrible tonight."

"You premenstrual?"

Relief washed over her. "As a matter of fact, I am." It was true—she was.

"Maybe you need Dr. Gray's magic massage to make you feel better." He rubbed her shoulders lightly.

She shrugged him away. "I really think I need a good night's sleep," she said. "Alone."

"You don't want me even to spend the night?"

She couldn't think how to answer this.

"You've changed, Kelly." His voice was sad.

"I know it seems that way. It's just—" Should she say it? Could she say: I'm in love with someone else?

"It's this judicial responsibility, isn't it?"

Gratefully she agreed. "Yes. Yes, Jason. I feel so overwhelmed. I have so much to *process*. My brain feels like an overheated engine."

"Maybe you need to forget about all that for a while." He pressed toward her again. "Go with your body."

"Jason, I just want to sleep. I just need to be alone. Okay?"

"What about tomorrow?"

"Here's what I'm going to do tomorrow," she announced. "I'm going to take my phone off the hook and sleep until tomorrow afternoon if I can. I'm going to organize my desk—it's a mess—and pay bills and get packed for next week."

"Where will you be then?"

"On the Cape."

"Are you staying down there?"

"I am. At the Daniel Webster Inn."

"Barnstable's only an hour and a half away."

"I know. But after these sessions, Jason, I don't have the energy to do anything but collapse in the nearest bed."

"I'll tell you what. I could come down some night. We could get Buster and Muffy to meet us for dinner."

She would have agreed to anything then, just to get the evening over with. "All right. Maybe. Let me call you." She opened the passenger door and swung her legs out.

"I'll walk you up."

"No. No, I'll be fine, Jason." Twisting around, she kissed him. He tried to prolong it, but she pulled away. "Bye."

She raced away, to the refuge of her apartment.

SEVEN

SUNDAY MORNING WHEN SHE ARRIVED at the cemetery, he was there.

He was standing outside in the terrible heat, leaning against his Jeep, his arms crossed over his chest. Even now on this day with a temperature in the nineties and the humidity sticking the heat to the skin like glue, he wore khakis, a blue-and-white-striped button-down shirt, and a blue tie, but his shirt collar was open and the tie yanked down.

At the sight of him, something deep within Kelly kicked. Something parted. Men were not called beautiful, but to her eyes he was beautiful. He took her breath away.

She parked her car next to his and stepped outside into the heat.

She walked toward him. "Hello, Ernest."

He walked toward her. "Hello, Morgan. That's quite a dress you've got on."

Flustered, she laughed. "I can't imagine what I was thinking when I bought it." She'd bought it in Pittsfield, in a fit of madness, stopped dead in her tracks by the sight of it in the shop window, this brief halter dress in red, a color she never wore, perfect for the heat, completely inappropriate for a cemetery.

"I can tell you what it makes me think." His gaze was intense.

"What does it make you think?" She stood in front of him, not quite touching him, knowing all at once what this dress was. It was an invitation.

"It makes me think we should go to my apartment. Or a hotel. Now."

"All right."

"You're sure?"

"Yes."

"Well, then."

He put his hand on her arm and ushered her quite gently around the gleaming hot green metal of his Jeep and into its steaming interior.

By the time he'd gotten in and switched on the air-conditioning, sweat was prickling along her scalp and beneath her arms and between her legs.

He turned toward her, his gaze intense. "Morgan."

"A car," she told him, nodding toward the entrance.

Without another word, he set the Jeep in motion, carefully checking the traffic before pulling out into the road. He looked over at her then and reached across the console between them to put his hand on her thigh.

She touched his hand. Wide, massive, the nails were blunt and clean, the skin near the wrist sprinkled with delicate golden hair that grew more coarsely on his arm. His shirtsleeves were rolled up, exposing the swell of muscle and cord of vein sheathed beneath his skin.

"We should talk about protection," he said.

"I'm on the pill."

"And I'll use a condom. I've had an AIDS test as well as some others done recently. I'm clean."

She swallowed. "I've only been with Jason for the past year or so, and we both were cleared before we slept together."

"That's good, then."

She studied his profile as he drove, very seriously, checking his rearview mirror, his side mirrors, flicking the turn indicator before making sharp exact turns. He was a responsible man. She saw in his profile the consequences of his generous, professional dedication: the white lines streaking out from his blue eyes, the slight pouches beneath those eyes, a looseness at the jaw that spoke of passing years and the weariness from those years. She could imagine him in a white coat, in an office, touching with infinite gentleness, with a kind of tactile listening, those patients who brought their aging bodies to him not for the purposes of growing into the future as a healthy child or making love and making babies, but for simply living out their years in the best health they could manage. She thought of her grandparents, Grandfather and Grandmother MacLeod, with their dignity, their somehow heartbreaking formality, and she wished, she hoped, that as they were dying they had had a physician as courteous and careful as the man next to her.

They came to Route 9 toward Natick and joined the stream of traffic flying westward until, through a series of complicated lefts and rights, they crossed the congested highway and drove into the parking lot of the Holiday Inn.

"I'll just be a minute."

Ernest stopped the Jeep and went through the electric doors, past a bellboy wheeling out a metal rack hung with several garment bags, into the hotel lobby.

Kelly flipped down the visor and looked in the mirror. Her eyes had gotten wide and rather idiotic-looking, like those in the ridiculous portraits painted on velvet of Victorian waifs holding kittens. And her hair, which she'd fastened in a kind of high fall, had frizzed in the humidity into something resembling a bouquet of angel's breath. Her skin was flushed—not just from the heat. She decided she looked just fine, in an insane kind of way, and then the door opened and Ernest got back into the Jeep.

"Room 304." He handed the plastic key card to her.

They drove to the side of the hotel, and she jumped out of the Jeep, too eager to wait for him to come open the door for her, and they went up the concrete sidewalk toward the brick building and out of the glare and oppression of the sun into the dim coolness.

Side by side they stood at the back of the elevator, not

speaking or touching, as a towel-draped, chlorine-smelling father and his teenage son crowded in next to them, talking and laughing and dripping water on Kelly's shoes. The elevator hummed, then dinged.

"Excuse us," Ernest said politely. "This is our floor."

Father and son squelched to one side, allowing Kelly and Ernest to step out onto the third floor, onto the ornate arabesques of the red-and-gold carpet.

"This way," Ernest said, and taking her hand, pulled her along with him down the corridor.

The doors were numbered backwards, or so it seemed, as they went past 320 and 314 and 308, past trays with half-eaten rolls waiting beneath wadded white linen napkins to be fetched by room service.

They came to 304. Kelly slid the card down into the electronic lock. A green light blinked at them. Ernest pulled down the door handle, held the door open, and together they went into the tidy anonymous room.

The mauve curtains were drawn against the sun. The room smelled of dust and air freshener. Ernest locked the door and pulled the brass chain across while Kelly stood watching him, and then he turned and looked at her with such honest, unguarded desire that her knees went weak. She sagged a bit, and put her hand out to his chest. He caught her by her elbows, braced her against the door, and brought his mouth to hers.

"I'll only be about an hour," Anne promised Tessa.

"Fine."

"Remember. Don't open—"

"—the door while you're gone. You've only told me that a billion times."

Anne's mouth tightened. "I'm trying to protect you."

"I know." Tessa stared at her mother, and with a kind of decision, changed the subject. "You look pretty, Mom. I like that dress."

Guilt and gratitude flushed Anne with an uncomfortable heat. "Thank you, sweetie." She sat down on the side of Tessa's bed. "I know this campaign business is a terrible bore."

"It's not. I think it's cool."

"Really?"

"Really."

"You are such a good girl." Anne leaned over to kiss her daughter's forehead. "I'll be home soon."

"And we don't have to go to church today, right?"

Anne sighed. "Do you hate church so much?"

Tessa squirmed. "It's summer. I just like to be lazy sometimes."

"Well, you can be lazy all morning, then." At the doorway she turned back hopefully. "You don't *have* to go out with your father today, either, if you'd rather just be a perfect slug all day. I could phone him and tell him not to come."

"No, Mom. I want to see Dad."

Anne sniffed eloquently. "All right, then. I'll be back soon."

Tessa waited until she heard the door close. She waited some more. When ten minutes had gone by, she got out of bed. The house was silent. Sometimes when it was this quiet, it spooked her, especially at night. She knew there were no such things as ghosts, but there were serial killers and rapists—her mother had warned her about them—and sometimes scenes from the movies she caught glimpses of at her friends' homes came flashing into her mind. Maybe there was a maniac hiding in the back hall.

Hunger made her bold. She slid from the bed. It was cold in the house—her mother kept the air-conditioning too high—so Tessa pulled on thick white cotton socks and a sweatshirt. Her father was taking her to the farm today, and Grandfather always had great food for her there, but her stomach was demanding food right this minute. Her socks were slick against the stairs as, hanging on to the banister, she slithered down.

It was Carmen's day off. Alone in the kitchen, Tessa filled a bowl to the top with cereal, doused it with milk, and ate in a kind of rapture, staring at nothing, thinking nothing, just shoveling the food into her mouth in a robotic way that would make her mother furious.

Almost immediately she felt better, and braver. She checked the clock: her mother had been gone only fifteen minutes.

She padded into the den and curled up on the sofa with the remote control in her hand. She was never allowed to watch television when her mother wasn't home. But it was Sunday morning—how bad could it be? She cruised through the channels: news, political commentators, talk shows, blah blah blah. Country western music. Cartoons for little kids. *Clueless*.

Clueless! Happiness jolted her. This was her favorite movie of all time, even though her mother said it was not age-appropriate. If her mother had her way, Tessa would watch nothing more sophisticated than Mary-Kate and Ashley movies. But Tessa had seen *Clueless* several times at her friends' homes. Beryl's older sister owned the video and watched it repeatedly. It was awesome fun. The clothes were so cool, the girls so totally confident. Alicia Silverstone was beautiful, and her life was so easy! Her mother had died during a liposuction operation, leaving her alone in a huge house with her father and a maid a lot like Carmen. Not to mention that cute ex-stepbrother.

"We divorce wives, not children," Cher's father said now.

Tessa was hypnotized.

The streets were wide and clear as Anne drove out to the Framingham mall. She parked in a lot near Borders and walked into the Starbucks coffee shop. Keeping her dark glasses on, she looked around. She wore her hair tucked up, completely hidden, beneath a wide-brimmed straw hat, and a loose white linen dress, and sandals. No one glanced at her twice, not even the young man at a table in the corner, engrossed in what looked very much like a comic book.

Glen Phipps was thirty years old, but looked ten years younger. Thin, nearly cadaverous, he adored costuming himself, which, combined with his sly intelligence, made him a perfect private investigator.

Today he wore combat pants, scuffed shit-kicker leather boots, and a black T-shirt with an NRA emblem on the back. He'd been completely bald the last time she met with him, a buff gay male bulging with muscles and dripping with jewelry, but now his hair was grown to about an inch in length and shorn into a bristling military brush cut. He'd taken off his earrings and removed the gold cap he sometimes wore on a front tooth. He looked tough. He looked unapproachable.

Anne crossed quickly to his table and sat down.

"Hey," Glen said, his sweet smile completely wrecking his tough image. "Good to see you. How are you? Want me to get you something? A cup of coffee?"

"Please. Black."

Off he went with a masculine stride to fetch the coffee. She surveyed the room from behind her glasses and was reassured that no one had any interest in her or him. Still, her thumb found its way to the invisible spot on her dress, just above her knee, and began its rubbing.

Glen returned, set a plastic foam cup in front of her, and sat down. "Okay. What's up?"

"We have our court date. September fifth."

"Almost exactly a month from now."

"Right. I want you to start surveilling Randall again."

"Sure, if you want me to. But I told you, ever since he filed for divorce, he's been a good boy."

"That was almost a year ago. I know Randall. He needs . . . sex."

"Most of us do, you know."

"Are you working for me or not?"

"Sorry. I just . . . Any suggestions where I should start?"

"The usual: the hospital, his office, his home."

"Is he teaching again this semester?"

"No. He wants the court to think he's got the time to take care of Tessa."

"Still living in the same apartment?"

"As far as I know. He hasn't informed me of a move, and Tessa hasn't said anything about a change. He's been taking her out to his father's farm near Concord more often than usual recently."

"Any other changes in his routine?"

Anne looked down at the spot she was rubbing on her skirt and thought. "His mother died two months ago. Tessa says he goes to visit her grave every Sunday morning."

Reaching over, Glen gently put his hand on her arm and stopped its movement. "Mrs. Madison. Anne."

Jerking her arm away, she demanded, "How dare you!"

"You need to know. That rubbing thing. It looks odd. It looks *neurotic*."

She flinched. "My idiosyncrasies are not your concern."

"You want me to help you get full custody of your daughter, don't you?"

Her eyes filled with tears.

"I'm just saying, you need to control that. At least in front of a judge."

"Yes, very well. I will."

"Have you thought about seeing someone? A doctor?"

"You mean a psychiatrist? While I'm campaigning for a public position? Oh, I don't think so." Regaining her composure, Anne reached into her purse, pulled out an envelope, and tossed it on the table. "This should take care of your fee for the next thirty days. Follow him everywhere. All the time."

"You got it."

"I'll need your report before September fifth."

"Of course."

"Thank you." She rose.

"Thank *you*." He rose, as well, courteously.

She strode from the shop, away from the pity in his eyes.

They lay together in the mauve hotel room, curled in each other's arms. From beneath the hem of the curtains, and at the slender gap where they met, sunlight slipped through, providing a slight illumination by which they could see the outline of their bodies, the gleam of their eyes.

"Morgan," he said.

"Mmm?" She was so exhausted, so satisfied, her body felt like honey.

"I can't call you Morgan any longer. I want to know your real name. I want to know everything real about you."

Lazily she considered this. "Are you sure?"

"Absolutely." With the tips of his fingers he traced her neck, shoulder, arm, waist, hip. "I want to tell you everything about me. I want us to become genuine, honest, open to one another."

She turned toward him, nuzzled her face against his chest. She could hear the firm, determined beating of his heart. "But . . . I don't want to ruin . . . this."

"You think we'll ruin it if we become real to one another?"

"I don't know. Maybe."

Gently he pushed her away from his chest so that he could look into her face. "All right. If we ruin it, what would happen? We'd stop seeing one another. You would marry your assertive Jason. I would finish the divorce and wander off into the world where I'd eventually find someone else, but no one, I'm sure, as right for me as you."

She smiled, and tried to kiss him, but he held her away.

"But what if we *don't* ruin it?" he asked. "What if we discover that we love each other, and want to be with each other, what then? Then you would have to break your engagement, for one thing. Is that what's holding you back? Do you love Jason?"

Kelly twisted around, pulled the sheet up over her shoulders. "It's cool in here."

He reached down to pull the blanket up over them and snuggled spoon-style against her, waiting without speaking.

"I do love Jason," she said at last. "In a way. I care for him, certainly. I wouldn't want to hurt him. But that's not what's holding me back."

"What, then?"

"What if I told you everything about me, and that made you stop wanting me?"

His laughter made her hair drift against her neck. "I don't see that as anywhere near possible. But let's start with some easy things. What's your name?"

Still, she hesitated.

"All right. We'll start with first names. My real name is Randall."

"Randall." She tasted it. "I never would have guessed that."

"And your name?"

"Kelly."

"And do you work, Kelly?"

Kelly chuckled. "Oh, dear, do I work? Oh, Randall"— she turned toward him, smiling—"yes, I do see you're right. I mean, I know you're a physician, and I assumed you understood I was . . . a professional person, but for all you know, I could be anything at all in the world!"

"And you are—"

She hedged. "A lawyer."

"Good God. The last thing I would have suspected!" Randall shoved his pillow behind his back and sat up.

Kelly turned onto her stomach, looking up at him. "Because you think lawyers are all sharks? Hard, manipulative, vain, incapable of moral decisions?"

"I didn't say that."

"But you're a little harsh on the subject."

"That's true."

"I'm proud of being a lawyer."

"Yes, I'm sure. What kind of law do you practice?"

"Family and probate. For three years I was with a firm specializing in divorce. Their client list was wealthy. When I felt safe financially, I moved to another law firm, also specializing in family matters but with a more varied clientele. I do a lot of *pro bono* work."

"And you work for my ex-wife. You've been hired to enchant me."

"That's not funny."

"No, I guess it's not. Oh, man. Look at the time. I promised my daughter I'd pick her up at noon." Grabbing her shoulders, Randall said, "Look, can I see you tonight? Tomorrow?"

"I have to go out of town this week, on business."

"Next Sunday, then. At the cemetery."

"Fine."

"You know, there's a lot I want to say to you. A lot I want to know about you. *Everything*."

"I know. Me, too."

"But we've got to go." He looked tortured.

Kelly smiled at him. "I know. Let's go."

Randall threw himself from the bed and rushed into the bathroom. Kelly gathered her clothes, which were mostly in a pile by the door, and when Randall had finished with his shower, she took one herself, hastily dressed, then raced with him down the long corridor to the elevator and on out to the Jeep.

The traffic was heavier than it had been, the interior of the Jeep hotter, Randall's need to hurry filling the space like a kind of pressure.

As he brought them to an abrupt stop at a red light, he asked, "Do you want children?"

"Well . . . yes."

"Because I like children. I want more children. Not dozens. Not even four or five. But at least two or three."

"Do you think a woman should stay home to care for the children?"

"To be honest, when they're infants, yes, I do. For the first year. I don't think a woman should give up her career. It's not a matter of time so much as a matter of desire. I mean, my wife is a professional woman, and always has been, and that's where her heart is. She has tried to be loving, but she doesn't have that fierce passionate joy most women have for their children, and I don't think it's because Tessa's adopted."

"Your daughter's adopted?"

"Well, in a way." He turned onto the winding road leading to the Forest Hills gates and Kelly's car. "It's a long story, and complicated. I'll tell you next week." Sliding his Jeep next to Kelly's Subaru, he said, "I'm sorry about this rush. If it were anyone else but Tessa, I'd cancel, but I can't disappoint her."

"Of course. I understand."

Randall took Kelly's face in his hands. "Next Sunday? Here?"

"Next Sunday. Here."

He kissed her, roughly, with haste. Then Kelly stepped down from his high Jeep, on legs that were weak from lovemaking and amazement, into the hot bright world that had been suddenly and entirely transformed.

"What are you doing!"

Tessa almost flew straight up into the air. She'd been so engrossed in the movie—this was the part where Cher realizes she likes her ex-stepbrother—that she hadn't heard her mother come in.

"I was just watching a movie, Mom."

"Haven't I told you I don't want you watching television without my permission?"

"Yes, but—"

Anne grabbed the remote control and pressed the OFF button. Cher vanished into obscurity.

"I'm disappointed in you, Tessa."

Tessa hung her head. "Sorry."

"I leave you alone in the house for one minute and you sneak down and watch *trash*."

"It's not trash, Mom—"

"Go to your room."

"Mom—"

"Now."

Tessa slumped out of the room and up the stairs. It was only eleven. An hour before her dad was to arrive. She fell facedown on her bed, her nose buried in the covers. She could smother like this. What if she smothered? Why not?

But without thinking, her head turned. Involuntarily she gasped for air.

She had friends whose mothers sat and watched *Clueless* with them. And laughed. Tessa wished her mother would do that. Or she wished she didn't have a mother.

If you thought about it, all the best books were about orphans. *Anne of Green Gables. The Secret Garden. Anastasia*—well, that was a movie, not a book. But her favorite fairy tales: *Cinderella, Snow White, The Little Mermaid.* Their mothers were all gone. Dead. They had mean stepmothers.

Oh, no. Tessa had a terrible thought. What if her dad remarried? What if she had a mean stepmother?

She pulled the pillow over her head.

"Tessa?"

"Yes, Mom?"

"Are you ready?"

Tessa looked at the clock. "Almost," she lied. Flinging herself from the bed, she threw herself into shorts, T-shirt, and sneakers. She brushed her teeth, washed her face, brushed her hair, and clipped it back. She galloped down the stairs.

Her mother was pacing up and down the marble hallway, her heels clicking like little bursts of gunfire.

Dread plunged through Tessa. "What's wrong, Mom?"

"Your father's late." Anne glared at her wristwatch. "He promised he'd be here at twelve on the dot. This is incredibly irresponsible of him! Typical!"

"Not typical, Mom," Tessa protested. But she was worried. Her father had always been late for everything until he moved out and filed for divorce; since then he was blamelessly punctual. Was he backsliding into old habits? Didn't he realize that her mother would use even the tiniest of sins against him in court, to prevent him from gaining even joint custody of her?

"I have an important appointment! And Randall knows this!"

Wrenching the powder room door open, Anne flew inside, turned on the hot water, and frantically scrubbed her hands.

Tessa came to the doorway to watch her. "Go to your appointment, Mom. I'll be fine here till Dad comes."

"That's not the point! The point is: your father will do anything he can to demonstrate his lack of affection and respect for me. He knows I have an appointment!" Angrily she dried her hands on a thick terry-cloth towel, and then dropped the towel into the hamper below it, took a clean one out of the cupboard above the toilet, and draped it on the rack.

"Mom," Tessa said, "hand lotion."

"What? Oh. Right. Thanks." It was important to Anne that her hands look soft and well-tended, and she did have a weekly manicure, but her constant hand-washing turned the skin on her hands red and scaly. She was trying, God knew, to cut down on the hand-washing, but at times like this, when Randall made her so *frustrated* . . .

"*Go*, Mom. Go on. I'll be fine."

Anne wiped the excess lotion on a tissue. "I suppose I have no choice if I want to be on time for my appointment."

Tessa followed her out to the front door.

"Tell your father I want you home in time for dinner."

"All right."

"And don't let him fill you up with junk food."

"All right."

"And if you ride those filthy horses, wash your hands afterward."

"All right."

"I'm serious, Tessa."

"I know you are, Mom."

"Oh, Tessa, I wish you wouldn't look at me that way. I'm only trying to protect you."

"I know."

"No, you don't. You have no idea." Anne checked her image in the mirror one last time; then she stepped out into the harsh glare of a summer day. "You'll be sure to lock the door behind you."

"I will."

"All right, then." Leaning forward, she pecked a kiss on her daughter's forehead and hurried to the shelter of her air-conditioned car.

After Tessa shut the door, she stood by the front window and stared through the leaded glass. She waited a few moments until she was sure her mother was gone. Then she hurried back to the kitchen.

She was still hungry. She hated herself for it, but she couldn't seem to subdue her stomach's cravings.

Inside the refrigerator were some watermelon, bean sprouts, baby carrots, lettuce, and radishes. She shut the door.

She knew what was in the cupboards, but she searched through them anyway, just in case Carmen had left something. Her mother's Ry-Krisp crackers stood next to the nearly empty box of Cheerios, a small jar of instant coffee, a large box of white powdered artificial sweetener (which Tessa had tried once to eat by itself; she shuddered at the memory), and some old cans of bouillon. As she stared at the food, her heart did that funny skipping-racing thing it was doing more and more, as if it had turned into a bird fluttering to escape its cage. It was a disgusting feeling, but it certainly turned her thoughts away from food.

"Tessa?" Her father's voice came booming down the hallway.

"Hi, Dad. You're late."

"I know, honey. I'm sorry. Did your mother throw a fit?"

Tessa hated it when her father dissed her mother. It made her feel sick inside, as if she'd done something really wrong.

"No. She was all right. She just had to leave for an appointment."

"Great. Ready to go?"

Tessa stared at her father. Something was different about him. His face looked . . . soft, kind of. "I'm ready."

They left the house, double-checking as Tessa's mother always reminded her to, to be sure the front door was locked, hopped into the Jeep, and headed out toward the country.

Her father steered them down Brattle toward Route 2. "Want to stop at McDonald's on the way?"

Hunger and guilt battled within her. She weighed herself all the time, secretly, on the professional scales in her mother's bathroom, and she hadn't gained any weight. In fact, she'd lost a couple of pounds. Now the thought of the plump, yielding, hamburger bun, the zest of onions and mustard, the dense dark meat obsessed her. Her stomach growled. Some girls her age dreamed of Leonardo DiCaprio. She also dreamed of hamburgers.

And the French fries . . . golden sticks of hot salty grease . . .

"Sure."

Her father bought her a hamburger and fries, and a cheeseburger for himself. Riding toward Concord, they ate while listening to the radio. Her dad liked some of the music she liked, which was kind of cool and kind of weird.

After they'd crumpled their wrappers and tossed them

into the bag, her father said, "Tessa. I've decided to make another change in our lives."

Tessa's lunch turned to stone in her stomach. What now? she thought. Not another woman in his life, not yet, it would make her mother insane. Her mother hadn't given up on the hope they might reconcile. Tessa hadn't, either.

"I've decided to move in with Grandpops. My apartment is just too small. I know you hate staying there. I know how much you love the farm. And heaven knows the house is big enough for me to have my own space, and for you to have a really nice room. Concord has excellent schools . . . if it turns out that you end up living with me. With us. I know how much you love your grandfather, and this way, if I have to go off on an emergency, you'll have him there to take care of you." He looked over at her, smiling.

So this was why he was so happy. He looked younger, and kind of glowing, as if a light had clicked on inside.

"So what do you think?" he asked.

"Cool, I guess." Tessa chewed on a fingernail. A convertible passed them, a man with a white poodle in the passenger seat, its long ears flying backwards. Her mother hated convertibles, said they were accidents waiting to happen.

"You *guess*? Anything you want to tell me?"

She'd made her father's brow furrow with concern. The light coming from him dimmed. It was so hard, being responsible for her parents' feelings. Sometimes she thought she didn't have the energy to do it anymore. Sometimes she felt like opening the door and throwing herself outside. She'd smash into a million pieces, her molecules would escape into the open air, and it would all be over. She'd never make anyone feel bad again.

"What will Mom think?"

"You mean because it's further away from her house? Or because she doesn't like the farm?"

"The farm."

"Well, Tessa, let's look at the problem rationally. Your mother's concerned about germs from the farm, right? So remember that not only did I grow up there in abundant health, but your Aunt Evangeline did, as well. If you did some research, I believe you'd discover that most people consider farms, country life, to be a bonus as far as health goes. Fresh air, that sort of thing. Besides, I'm a physician. I'm qualified to judge whether or not you're healthy and to take care of you in an emergency. Not to mention that your grandfather is also a physician and has been healthy all his life."

"Mom thinks he's getting senile."

"I know she thinks that. And not without reason. Grandmom's death really knocked the stuffing out of him. It's only natural that he's been forgetful recently. This isn't the reason I'm moving out there—I'm thinking of you, and what's best for you—but I know it will be a great joy in Grandpops' life to have you around. The best medicine in the world for grief."

I don't want to be medicine, Tessa thought crankily. She couldn't bear it that her father was so *happy*, humming along with Britney Spears and drumming his fingers on the steering wheel, happy for his father, happy for Tessa, happy for himself, and totally not caring how upset her mother was going to be about all this. She knew her father wasn't moving to the farm simply to drive her mother crazy, but he had to know that's what would happen, and he had to know that it would be Tessa who would have to try, somehow, to make things right.

When she grew up, *if* she grew up, she was never having children.

Mont Madison was out in the vegetable garden, weeding. He'd been there since six, with a break for lunch. After Madeline's death, he'd just let the garden go, unable to summon up the energy to give a damn about anything, but now that Randall and Tessa were moving out to the farm, he realized he couldn't expect them to feel comfortable with him sitting around with a long face, and besides, if he ever got to heaven, Madeline would kiss him first and slug him second, for allowing her beloved garden to go to pot.

Hearing the Jeep's tires crackle on the gravel, Mont straightened, pulled a handkerchief from his back pocket, and wiped the sweat off his forehead and neck. He never could believe how Tessa's face lit up when she saw him. The sight of his wrinkled old mug in a mirror always made him shake his head in despair.

Tessa jumped out of the Jeep. "Hi, Grandpops!"

She came toward him, all long legs and dangling arms, a scarecrow of a girl. *Why* did they let that child get so thin? He didn't want to be an interfering old pain in the ass, but it took all his willpower not to pounce on Randall about it.

"Hi, Tester," he said. Just this year, perhaps because of the divorce or perhaps because of her own inner clock, his granddaughter had become less physically affectionate. She didn't run to squeeze him in a rib-cracking hug anymore, and she seemed in general more hesitant about any kind of touching. Now he reached out and ruffled her hair.

She looked around. "How are the raspberries?"

"Not ready yet. Maybe next week. But I've got these for you." He held out a bowl of peas, which she loved to shell from the pod and spill into her mouth like tiny green candies.

"Yum." Tessa grabbed a handful and tore into them.

"Hey, Dad." Randall crossed the grass and leaned on the wire fence that kept the deer and rabbits out.

"Hello, son. Come on in the house. I've got a surprise for you."

Closing and latching the garden gate, Mont crossed the yard and led them through the cool, dark house, past all the clutter, up the stairs. He still slept in the front bedroom where he'd spent most of the adult years of his life, in the old brass double bed that had once seemed too small, and that now, without Madeline, was far too large and lonely.

Randall's old room was on the left, pretty much unchanged from his tenure as a boy.

Mont opened the door to Evangeline's room. He'd closed it on purpose, earlier that morning, so he could do this with a flourish. The room was empty of furnishings but full of light, the old wide pine floorboards glowing glossily in the sunshine.

"Wow," Tessa said.

"Where'd you put all Eva's stuff?" Randall asked.

Madeline and Mont had left it all there, like a Museum of Evangeline, the good solid oak furniture overwhelmed by its purple walls, batik bedspread, posters of Van Morrison and Joan Baez, mirrors, photographs, postcards, and great shaggy tufts of wool from a Scottish farm which once Evangeline had intended to card and spin and weave into a sweater.

"I cleared it out. Oh, don't worry, I phoned Evangeline, and got her permission. She told me it was about time. She *is* forty-five. Anyway, I moved her bed into your mother's old sewing room. That will be a guest room. This is *your* room, Tessa. I sanded and polished the floor and washed the windows, but I was waiting for you to tell me how you want it decorated. What color would you like it painted? Or would you prefer wallpaper? And what kind of furniture? I thought of buying you a canopy bed, but then I thought you might prefer something completely different."

Tessa turned in a full circle, slowly, savoring the empty space.

"Is it okay? Would you prefer that I go ahead and furnish it—"

"No, no, Grandpops, it's great. It's perfect."

"It's wonderful," her father told Mont.

"There are some good curtains in the attic, and some of your grandmother's quilts. Would you like those?"

"I don't know. I don't know what I want."

Randall took his father by the arm. "Let's go down and

have some coffee. Give Tessa some time to get used to it."

Tessa flashed her father a grateful smile. Sometimes he seemed to know exactly what she needed.

"Thanks, Grandpops," she said.

"You're more than welcome, sweetheart."

Mont nodded to his son. "What about your room?"

They went out, shutting the door, leaving Tessa alone.

Tessa sank down onto the floor, cross-legged, and just sat. She breathed so deeply her stomach swelled out like a Buddha's. Looking up, she saw that Grandpops had even taken down the glow-in-the-dark stars Evangeline had plastered all over the ceiling. What a wonderful room this was, she thought. It was all hers. Even the air was hers, without anyone else's emotions crowding in like dark clouds around her.

Randall's bedroom was still a boy's, with Red Sox pennants on the wall, and charts of the circulatory and digestive systems of the human body, and a few empty spaces where he'd hung glossy photos of sexy women: Farrah Fawcett, he remembered with a rush of embarrassment, and Bo Derek. He'd taken those posters down long ago.

"I assume you'll want to make some changes, too," Mont said.

The two double beds which could be stacked to make bunks lay side by side, covered with matching quilts. On the desk by the window sat a dusty brass telescope, a globe of the world, and the Incredible Human Male model he'd put together, with meticulous attention, in high school. On his closet shelf his old baseball sat in the palm of his old leather catcher's mitt. There had been a time when he'd dreamed of passing this and other guy treasures along to his son, but those times had passed. A pang pierced his heart, and for a moment he let himself mourn the son he'd wanted but never had. These spells of sadness possessed him a lot recently, no doubt because with his divorce he was reminded of just how old he was, just how many dreams he had and had not seen come true.

And yet—he might still have a son. He might still have a wife who loved him.

"I say we clear it all out," he announced.

"All of it?"

"Down to the last Monopoly card. Give what's worth it to the thrift shop, take the rest to the dump."

"You better think about it."

"I don't need to. Remember, Dad, I've got a ton of furniture in my apartment that I'll want to bring here. I've got the handsome old walnut bed and bureau you gave me, and a grand leather recliner."

Talking, they wandered into Mont's room.

"Speaking of clearing out . . ." Randall said.

"What do you mean?"

"Well, Dad." Randall gestured around the room. His mother's perfumes, comb and brush, and jewelry box sat expectantly on the bureau, as if any moment she would come in to use them. On her side of the bed waited a pile of books, a floral box of tissues, and the hand lotion she rubbed on just before turning off the light. "It's been over three months. This is too much, somehow. Too much like brooding."

Mont drew himself up straight. "I expect to brood every day of my life over the loss of your mother."

"Dad, I loved her, too. You know that. I'll miss her every day of my life as well. But look at you. You're only seventy-seven. You're healthy. You're handsome. You might even want to get married again."

Mont recoiled as sharply as if his son had spat at him. "How dare you."

"I'm thinking of you, Dad. But of Tessa, too. How will she feel when she sees all her grandmother's things here, just as if she were still alive?"

Mont strode angrily across the room, folded his arms over his chest, and glared out the window. He was just about ready to have a heart attack and he rather wished he would, it would serve his damned impudent son right.

"And come on, Dad. What is this?"

Mont turned. Randall was pointing to the bed. Madeline's pink slippers waited obediently, side by side, on the floor, while her pink-and-white robe draped itself in readiness over the bedpost, where Mont usually kept his plaid wool robe.

"Are you wearing her things, Dad?"

Mont felt his lip quiver.

"Dad."

Mont couldn't trust himself to speak.

Randall sucked in a deep breath, blew it out. "Well. You know, I'm longing for a good strong cup of coffee. I bought Tessa some lunch on the way out here, and I should have gotten some coffee for myself. I think I'll go on downstairs and grind some beans and brew up something strong."

Gratefully Mont cleared his throat. "The hazelnut beans are in the freezer."

"Super. I assume you want a cup, too?"

"Absolutely. I'll be right down."

"Take your time." Randall went off down the hall and down the stairs, whistling and stomping and making as much noise as he had when he was a clumsy, scatterbrained adolescent.

"Grandpops? I think I know what color I'd like my room to be."

Mont turned to see his granddaughter in the doorway, her amazing blond hair flying out around her like angel's wings. And she *was* a kind of angel to him, the angel of life, a reason to remain alive.

EIGHT

THE BARNSTABLE COUNTY COURTHOUSES WERE located on Route 6A, a two-lane road winding past historic clapboard homes which, with their carriage houses and barns, glowed in picture-postcard perfection behind stone walls or white picket fences. High on a hill, in somber majesty, sat the distinguished granite building, green lawns flowing from it like skirts from a Victorian regent.

Behind the original courthouse, up on the hill, the parking lot accepted the vehicles of the modern world. Early Monday morning Kelly parked her car and headed for the new building housing the Probate Court.

She was glad she was going to work that was compelling and absorbing. She'd tossed and turned all night, her thoughts yo-yoing between elation and despair. She was sleeping with one man while engaged to another! But, oh, what she had with Randall was so sweet! She wasn't being completely truthful to either man—but the only truth that mattered was how she felt in Randall's arms.

A fine judge you are, she chastised herself silently as she entered the judge's chambers.

"Good morning, Judge MacLeod! Ready to start the day?"

Petite and energetic, with glittering black eyes, a pointed nose, and shaggy auburn hair, Judge Parsons resembled a fox. Walking rapidly on stiletto heels that would have made Kelly lame, but which Judge Parsons undoubtedly used to provide an illusion of height, the judge clicked her way into her courtroom, shooting brief bullets of information at Kelly as she went.

"This courthouse is smaller than what you're used to up in the big city, but we've got the same kinds of problems and just as many."

Kelly settled next to Judge Parsons behind a pale elegant judge's bench, thinking that her grandparents would have loved this handsome room, with its spare, clean, sharp lines, and its glowing pale oak.

"What have you got for us today?" Judge Parsons asked her clerk, and the week began.

Reverend Christian Christopher resembled a crow with his beaky face and black suit brightened only slightly by the white collar at his neck. Monday morning he folded himself into a chair, tucked his jacket around him like wings, clasped his hands on his knees, and presented Dr. Lawrence with a look of lugubrious anticipation.

"Thank you for coming in, Reverend Christopher," Dr. Lawrence said. "May I offer you some refreshment? Coffee? Tea?"

"No, thank you. I'd like to make this brief. Although, of course, I want to do what I can to help."

"I appreciate that. Anne Madison, as you know, suggested I speak with you about the recent changes in her family, especially as it impacts her daughter."

"Ah, yes," the minister sighed. "I'm always saddened when the home of one of my parishioners is broken apart. Divorce is the scourge of our society."

"And yet a fact of life. Fifty-five percent of all marriages end in divorce. We can't change that, so we must do what we can to help those involved in a divorce, especially the children."

"True."

Dr. Lawrence consulted his notes. "You've known the Madisons for several years?"

"Indeed. I married them." A smile sliced jaggedly over

his face. "They were a exemplary young couple. Absolutely glowing with good will. I had great hopes for them."

"They both seem to have accomplished a great deal, professionally."

"True. And Anne, I'm certain, will go on to even grander accomplishments in public service."

"You know Tessa."

"But, of course. She's a lovely child. I christened her. I've watched her grow. She attends our Sunday School."

"What can you tell me about her?"

The minister spread his hands, palms up. "Not a great deal. I see her only once a week, if that often. She seems like a pleasant young girl, amiable and obedient. Intelligent."

"Does she like Sunday School?"

Reverend Christopher smiled. "It's a challenge these days, to keep young people interested in the church. We do have a Youth Club that meets on Wednesday and Sunday evenings. Tessa has come perhaps twice. It doesn't meet during the summers—too many families are off on vacation. So I haven't seen Tessa for a while, but I haven't seen a lot of children."

"Is there anything you could tell me about Tessa and her parents?"

He stroked his chin thoughtfully. "I'm trying to be fair. It's difficult not to prefer Anne simply because she is more assiduous in her church attendance, and I might add, in her financial generosity. On the other hand, Dr. Madison is not, in general, playing golf or laying about on Sunday mornings. He works very hard and does a great deal of good, especially with the elderly. His benevolence is highly praised by those in the helping professions."

Dr. Lawrence leaned back in his chair, twiddling a pencil between his fingers. "So," he mused, "we've got two fine adults, engrossed in their work, their significant work. One child, twelve years old. Two parents who both want full custody of the child. What's the answer?"

"I suppose you could always, like Solomon, threaten to cut the child in half and give half to each parent." Noting the startled expression on Dr. Lawrence's face, Reverend Christopher hurried to add, "I don't mean to be flippant. It often seems to me that this is what divorce does to a child, cleaves her in half. It would take the wisdom of a Solomon, Dr. Lawrence, to decide which parent should have custody. I do not have such wisdom."

Dr. Lawrence nodded. "I'm grateful for your honesty."

The minister rose from his chair, as thin and brittle as a magician's wand that had telescoped and now was unfolding. The two men shook hands. At the door, Reverend Christopher turned back.

"It was Anne Madison who asked me to see you. It is Anne Madison whom I know best. I admire her enormously. I must stress that. I do admire her enormously. But she is a tough taskmaster. Most severe on herself. But the standards which she seeks—close to perfection—are difficult to attain."

"Let me ask you this," Dr. Lawrence suggested. "Do you think that Tessa is happy?"

Reverend Christopher looked away. His mouth tightened. Then, reluctantly, he said, "No."

The register called the first case. Judge Parsons said, "All right, counselors, what's up?"

"I'm Tim Feldmar, Your Honor, representing the plaintiff, Georgina Weld." Tim Feldmar was a young man in a rather wrinkled suit. He'd nicked his chin in several places and had dark circles beneath his eyes. Kelly would have bet fifty dollars there was a new baby in his home.

"Georgina Weld, Your Honor." The wife spoke softly. Very plump, with lots of black hair back-combed to frightwig volume, her face was marred by a swollen eye and bruises.

"Judge, I'm George Weld. I'm representing myself." The husband was short, stocky, and muscular in the way of weight lifters. His jeans were filthy and ripped—not fashionably—and frayed at the cuff. His hooded sweatshirt bore signs of food, dirt, and something darker that might have been dried blood. His hands were cuffed behind his back.

"George and Georgina, huh," Judge Parsons said. "All right, let's swear you in. Please raise your right hands. Mr. Weld, you raise your right shoulder."

The register read the oath: "Do you solemnly swear that the testimony you shall give in the case now in hearing shall be the truth, the whole truth, and nothing but the truth, so help you God?"

"I do," said Georgina Weld.

"I do," said George Weld.

Judge Parsons looked at her folder. "Okay. I see here we've got a motion for DNA testing. What's that about?"

"Your Honor, may I speak?" George Weld said.

"Please do."

"I have reason to believe, Your Honor, that my wife committed adultery and gave birth to a son that she claims is mine but is really the son of Landon Frank."

"How old is this child?"

"One year, Your Honor."

"One year. What makes you doubt your paternity now?"

"I found letters, Your Honor."

"Go on."

"You see, we was renting one house down on Fox Lane, and it sold, so we had to move, and I was packing up all our stuff and I found this box at the back of Georgina's side of the closet, full of letters. They was love letters, Your Honor. And they was pornographic!"

"Were they dated?"

"They were, Judge. 1998 to 1999. My son—" Suddenly he turned bright red. "*Her* son, the baby, was born in July of 1999." George Weld's eyes filled with tears. His face looked as if he'd been set on fire.

Judge Parsons looked at Mrs. Weld. "What can you tell me, Georgina?"

Georgina swallowed. Her jeans strained over her corpulent thighs. Her red-and-black flannel T-shirt looked hot in the courtroom, and two sizes too small. Even without her bruises, she did not seem like a temptress, but by now Kelly had learned that temptation and desire raged in almost every heart.

"The baby's his, Your Honor," the wife said meekly. Desperately she added, "I *swear* it's his."

"Liar," George Weld sneered.

"What about the letters from Mr., uh, Frank?"

Georgina went white. She swayed. She looked as if she were about to faint. She opened her mouth, but couldn't speak.

"Okay, Mr. Weld," Judge Parsons said calmly. "I think we'll go ahead and order the DNA testing. For you, your wife, and your son." She scribbled some notes in the folder. "Now," she said, looking up, "it costs about three hundred dollars. Who's going to pay for it?"

The husband snarled. "*She* should!"

"Do you have a job, Mrs. Weld?" the judge asked.

The wife shook her head. "I did. I stopped working when the baby came."

"Do you two have a joint checking account?" When they both nodded, Judge Parsons said, "Then you're to pay the costs from your joint checking account."

"That's not fair, Your Honor—she's the whore!" the husband shouted.

"You're getting your DNA test, Mr. Weld." Judge Parsons peered at the other man, her face calm and patient, until the angry husband settled down.

"Now. Mrs. Weld. Mr. Feldmar. We've got a motion for temporary orders from you."

Georgina Weld whispered.

"Speak up."

"Your Honor." Tim Feldmar took charge. "You can see for yourself that Mrs. Weld has been assaulted. Last night she came home from buying groceries to find her husband in a rage."

"Wouldn't you be in a rage if you discovered your wife was a whore?" George Weld shouted.

The judge made a not-now gesture with her hand.

"Mr. Weld accused Mrs. Weld of infidelity. He threw the shoe box at her, hitting her in the head. Then he slapped her, spat in her face, and when she tried to leave the room, tripped her so that she fell, hitting her head on the coffee table. He would have continued had not the neighbors, hearing the noise, intervened and called the police. When the police came, Mr. Weld refused to leave the house and had to be taken forcibly."

Wearily Judge Parsons looked at the defendant. "What do you have to say, Mr. Weld?"

"In the first place, Your Honor, any man would lose their temper when he found out what I did. In the second place, a *shoe box*—you know how light those things are. I didn't throw a knife or a heavy pot. And sure I tripped her, but how was I to know she was going to fall that way and hit her head? She probably did that on purpose to get sympathy. And of course, I refused to leave the house. It's my house. She's the whore. She should leave. She can go live with—"

"All right, Mr. Weld. That's enough." Judge Parsons tapped a red fingernail against her lips. "I'm going to sign a 209A. Mr. Weld, you're to stay away from your wife and your house for a month, until the results are back on your DNA tests."

Weld's face turned purple. "That's not fair! It's her fault! Why am I being punished?"

"Mr. Weld, you have a one-year-old child living in your home. Our first priority is the welfare of that child, and it's in his best interests for the child to remain in his home, in the care of his mother. His mother won't be able to take care of him if she's disabled or in the hospital."

"Where am I supposed to live?"

"I'm sure you have friends, Mr. Weld. There are always inexpensive residential hotels. Also, you're going to have to go over to Superior Court now, to see what they want to do with you. You might not have to worry about where you're going to stay."

"That's so bogus!"

"Mr. Weld." Judge Parsons stared the man into silence. "I'll see you and Mrs. Weld again, when the DNA results are in."

"Dr. Madison? Dr. Lawrence will see you now."

Mont entered the psychiatrist's office, shook the man's hand, and looked him over.

He was not impressed. The other man wore black jeans, a white T-shirt, and a black vest. He looked like a late-night television comedian.

On the other hand, Mont reminded himself, he probably looked like an antiquated old fart. He'd lost so much weight recently that his summer-weight blazer hung from his bones like a sail on a windless day.

"It's a pleasure to meet you, Dr. Madison," Dr. Lawrence said. "And I want to thank you for coming in."

"I'm glad to come. I'd like to do anything I can to help Tessa."

"Could I offer you some lemonade? Coffee?"

"Thank you, no." *Because I piss all the time as it is,* Mont added silently. He didn't want to have to get up in the middle of the session.

"You're a physician?"

"I am. General practice."

"Not so many of those anymore."

"No. No, these days people prefer to specialize. And with good reason. We have such amazing technological assistance."

"Do you still practice?"

"No. Oh, no." Mont shook his head. "Too old. Too forgetful." Better not let him think I'm senile, Mont quickly told himself. "I'm thinking of writing a book."

"Oh, yes?"

"About my forty years as a GP. Sort of an *All People Great and Small* sort of thing, only about humans."

"Sounds good."

"Well, I've seen a lot of changes in medicine in my lifetime."

Dr. Lawrence nodded. "And, I suppose, a lot of changes in family life."

"That's true."

"What would you say is the most significant change?"

Mont considered. "Well, I don't know if I could single one out. I suppose first I'd say the general motility of people today. When I was young, people grew up, married, and lived where they were born. Near their families. About two decades ago, anyone who worked for a corporation had to go where the corporation sent them. These days people move where their interests lie: tech whizzes to California or Seattle, sun worshipers to the Southwest. Young kids move to big cities. So on. I consider myself fortunate that only one of my children has moved far away. Most of my friends' children live clear across the country."

"You and your son are close?"

"Yes, I think so." Mont felt his face sag. "Randall was closer to his mother. She died this year."

"I'm sorry."

"Thank you. It's been hard for all of us. I think Randall's making an effort to spend time with me so I don't feel lonely, and I appreciate that. He's always been a good boy. Dutiful."

"Yes. Randall seems to prize duty."

Mont peered at the shrink. "That a bad thing?"

"Not at all. It's just unusual. Duty isn't something a lot of people even talk about these days."

"Well, I don't want to make him sound like a priss. He's never been that."

"No. But he has been—he is, I believe, idealistic. As is Anne."

"That's true. I'll tell you one thing I think Anne and Randall have in common: they're too hard on themselves. They both think they have to fix the world all by themselves, and in the process, they end up doing harm to themselves and those nearest them." No sooner were the words out of his mouth than Mont slapped himself on the forehead. "Oh, Christ, what an old fool I am. I don't mean *harm*."

Dr. Lawrence smiled reassuringly. "I think I know what you mean."

"Do you?" Mont shook his head. "You've met them both, right? They both have trouble seeing the trees for the forest." He stroked his forehead. "Yes. That's what I mean."

"The individual gets lost in the larger picture?"

"Right."

Dr. Lawrence leaned back in his chair. "You're a doctor," he said. "And you seem wise."

"Well. I am a doctor," Mont acknowledged with a smile. "Better leave it at that."

"Tell me about Tessa. About Tessa and her parents."

Mont pondered this a moment. "I had a sort of speech prepared, full of sound and fury, blasting Anne and praising Randall. Because I do want Randall to be given custody of Tessa. I *do* think that's the best thing for her. But I find, now that I've gotten right down to the wire, that I have no real yearning to denigrate Anne. She's been a good mother to Tessa. Assiduous in her caretaking. While Randall has been"— Mont cleared his throat—"a less than perfect father. Especially in the early years. Of course, that's common. I mean, Anne, like many women, tended to believe she was the only person who could take proper care of Tessa when she was an infant. She was the kind of mother who hovered if someone else held the baby. When Madeline and I visited, when Madeline asked to hold Tessa,

Anne was nearly in agony. She was always saying, 'Don't let her head droop,' or 'You've got the bottle tilted too far.' I'm a doctor, and Anne was still terrified if I held Tessa. My theory—and you can bet Madeline and I discussed this a lot—was that Anne's mother, Sarah—have you met Sarah?"

"No. Anne's parents live on Nantucket, as you know, and won't be able to get off the island. They've got a house full of immigrants."

Mont grinned. "I'll bet they do."

"You were saying that Anne's mother—?"

"Sarah. She's wonderful. Full of life. And more idealistic than Randall and Anne put together and magnified to the tenth power. But she never had much time for Anne. *She* was raised by a nanny, so she never learned how to cuddle and doddle and coo. So Anne never learned how to show affection. Add that to the fact that Anne's seen a lot of disaster in her life, as a nurse, you know, and what you've got is a mother in a pretty much constant state of alarm, whose main concern is keeping her child safe. So, Tessa's safe, and she's clean, and she's fortunate, but in many ways she's deprived." Mont wrinkled his forehead. "Have I gotten off track somehow?"

"Not at all. You're being very helpful. Tell me about Randall as a father."

Mont pulled a face. "Now that Tessa's growing up, he's becoming just about the best father a man could be. When Tessa was an infant, however, and a young child, he didn't have as much to do with her as he would have liked. It was too much of a struggle for him. Anne saw Tessa as *her* child, and she guarded her jealously. For example, if he tried to toss her up in the air—I remember this happening when Tessa was about three—Anne went crazy, sure Randall would drop her. She made such a fuss about it, about everything, it was just too much of a battle for him to interact much with Tessa. As time passed, Anne's energies were focused on the child, and her house, her committees; she shut Randall out. So Randall found, how shall I say this, other outlets for his affections."

"Anne says Randall is promiscuous."

"I'm afraid she's right. Although I do believe, over the past year at least, Randall's been a model of chastity. You know he's planning to move back to the farm?"

Dr. Lawrence checked his notes. "I didn't know that."

"I believe he's just recently decided. I think it's a good idea. I'll always be there in case Randall gets called out in an emergency. Plus, Tessa's got a good girlfriend across the road, Brooke Burchardt." Mont leaned forward. "Randall is trying to do what's right by Tessa. He spends a lot of time with her now and plans to spend more. He's changing his life so he'll be able to spend more. He made a real effort—I saw him make that effort—to make a go of his marriage with Anne. Now he's going to make an effort to be a good father to Tessa."

Dr. Lawrence wrote on a pad. Scratching his forehead with the eraser end of his pencil, he looked over his notes, then up at Mont. "Is there anything else you think I should know? About Tessa, or Randall or Anne?"

"I don't think so," Mont said.

The two men rose and shook hands, and the psychiatrist thanked Mont again for coming in. As Mont made his creaking way out to his car, he searched his mind, worried: Was there something else he should have said?

Kelly hadn't been lying when she told Jason that after each day she was seriously exhausted. If one could breathe toxic fumes while working in a polluted factory or mine, then one could just as easily breathe in the toxic fumes of all the anger, bitterness, hatred, and sorrow that steamed from the people who passed through the courtroom each day. She left the court stricken with a sort of emotional flu. Many judges alleviated this, Kelly knew, with several medicinal shots of whiskey, and Kelly didn't blame them.

Her way to exorcise her body and mind was to run.

Each night she went back to the hotel, changed into running gear, and headed out. She liked running in a strange town. The unfamiliar scenery claimed her attention, and the new roads with their sudden turns compelled her to stay in the present. She ran for an hour, returning to her hotel room physically drained and moderately brain-dead. She stood under a blissfully hot thundering shower, wrapped herself up in a terry-cloth robe, and enjoyed a room service meal while watching television.

It was a pretty efficient way to avoid thinking of her own life.

Friday began with a divorcing husband and wife who couldn't agree on anything. Most terribly, they couldn't agree on custody of their two children, a boy of seven and a girl of five, who had been adopted at birth.

Judge Parsons was a compassionate woman, willing to wait patiently for each individual to be given his or her chance to express himself. This was often a crucial moment for a person, Parsons assured Kelly, their rightful moment to stand before a judge and ask for justice.

Friday afternoon the wife's lawyer was cataloguing the list of expert witnesses he'd lined up to testify to the wife's brilliance as a mother and the husband's failure as a father when the husband suddenly blew up.

"All right!" he yelled, standing up, holding his arms up as if surrendering. A slender man, a computer entrepreneur with buckets of money, his normally pale face was suddenly flushed bright crimson. "I give up. I give up completely. Give the bitch custody of the children. Total, sole, complete custody. Oh, I'll pay the child support, but I relinquish all rights to them. I won't have them on weekends or evenings, I won't call them, I won't even see them."

"Mr. Dollard," Judge Parsons said, "if you can't control yourself, I'm going to have to ask the court officer to help you control yourself."

With a sudden transformation that was somehow chilling, the husband curbed his emotions. His entire demeanor changed.

"I'm sorry, Your Honor. I apologize. But I would like to say, Judge, I do mean what I said. I surrender completely, all access to the children."

"Well, now, Mr. Dollard, I'm not sure that would be wise. Not for you, and especially not for the children."

"It's all right. They're not really my children anyway." Shooting a smug look at his wife, he said, "I'll get married and have my own with someone who's not barren."

At this, the wife burst into tears.

"It's late in the day," Judge Parsons sighed. "And the end of the week. Counselors, I'll tell you what I'm going to do. I'm going to adjourn court now and let your clients have some time to consider the way this case is going. I'm not happy with it at all, and I bet you aren't, either." Addressing the Dollards, she said, "Take the weekend. Get some rest. Think about your children. Think about these young people whose lives you hold in your hands. I'll see you Monday morning. Okay, people, court's adjourned."

Kelly followed Judge Parsons out of the courtroom into the privacy of her chambers.

"What a pair!" Judge Parsons said. "Plenty of money, good education, and a lifetime of bitterness ahead. I've seen this before. They're going to be in and out of this courthouse like boomerangs, doing everything they can think of to aggravate one another. But this relinquishing the children bit is a new one on me."

Randall's rounds at the hospital Friday morning were grueling. He'd had to deliver too much bad news. Seen too many faces tighten with fear, too many wives' and children's faces sag with sorrow. The acrid stench of dying, open wounds, vomit, and foul breath clung to him, the moans and cries of those suffering rang in his ears, and he thought of his mother in her dark grave and his father in his shortening years. He felt deluded and helpless in his attempts to ameliorate the indignities of old age. He felt heavy with his own mortality.

At his office, all day long, there was more bad news to give. From experience he knew that this happened, that sometimes things went in cycles. For days his patients' complaints would be caused by nothing more ominous than cataracts, high cholesterol, and heartburn, and then all at once everyone who walked through the door was diagnosed with cancer, Parkinson's, or Alzheimer's. And this afternoon his nurse and first lieutenant, Pam, who ran his office with brisk humor and efficiency, had had to leave early to deal with her teenage son who'd been caught with pot in his school locker during a surprise dog-drug sweep.

At six-thirty Randall found himself at his desk, through for the day but depressed and exhausted. He was so hungry his stomach cramped, but he couldn't face any more take-out or microwave dinners. He could go to a restaurant and buy himself a proper meal with a decent wine, but the thought of sitting by himself at a table was just too bleak.

Perhaps he'd call Mont, see what he was up to. As Randall reached for the phone, it rang.

"Hi, Randall." Her voice was breathy, shy.

"Lacey. Hi."

"You said we might get together for a drink—"

"I don't—"

"But I thought you might prefer to come here for dinner instead. I've made lasagna."

Lacey's lasagna was as delicious as she was; Randall could remember that so clearly he could almost smell the spicy tomato sauce and feel the plump cheese on his tongue. There'd be a freshly tossed green salad, too, and a healthy tart dessert with oranges or apples.

"Lacey—"

"Just come for dinner. No strings attached. I mean it."

"I won't be able to stay long."

"I understand."

"I'll pick up some wine on the way."
"Great."

All of a sudden, late Friday afternoon, Anne found herself without appointments. It was an unpleasant sensation, like stepping off the solid ground into open air. Like falling.

In the privacy of her study, she reviewed her calendar. Today had been exhausting, one meeting after another, beginning at seven A.M. with a Land Conservation executive board meeting, ending with a grueling course on building a computer database. The whole week, actually, had been jam-packed with engagements, and tomorrow she would begin going door-to-door, introducing herself, handing out her brochures, personally asking people for their votes.

When she'd worked on her schedule with Rebecca, she'd insisted on leaving this evening open. Now she wondered why.

Usually, on Friday as well as Saturday evenings, she had at least one cocktail or dinner party to attend. But now it was the middle of August, when most of her acquaintances were off in summer homes on the Vineyard, or in Maine, or Nantucket.

Nantucket. Her mother would fill every spare room in the Nantucket house with immigrants, leaving not even one bedroom free so that Anne and Tessa could visit. Sarah had always been generous to the most obviously distressed, completely overlooking any needs her own normal daughter might have, and Anne's father, engrossed in the eccentricities of his own life, let Sarah rule the household. When hurricanes destroyed Florida towns, Anne's father flew down to help rebuild. Whenever a task force was formed to help assuage the ravages of a drought in Tunisia or a dictator in Africa, Anne's father rushed to take part. Both Sarah and Arthur reacted to the astonishing amounts of money they'd inherited by dashing all over the globe to help other people, feeling that it was absolutely the least they could do. They were a wonderful, liberal, magnanimous couple who received the admiration and gratitude of many.

As parents, they were strangely aloof. Anne was so exceedingly healthy, pretty, intelligent, and fortunate in every way that they could hardly bring themselves to have any interest in her at all. Of course, they never would have put it quite that way, but that was the way it had always felt, and still felt, to Anne.

"Mother," she'd asked at the beginning of this summer, "why didn't you leave bedrooms for me and Tessa? Or at least one bedroom. Don't you want us to visit?"

"Of course we do," Sarah shot back. "Don't be silly. But *you* can afford to stay in a hotel. And you must admit you can't come down very often, not with the campaigning you've got to do. It would be a terrible waste to keep one room empty just in case you wanted to use it for a few days scattered over the entire summer, when the room could be put to more worthwhile use. It will make the difference in someone's life, and in their family's lives as well."

Anne agreed with her mother intellectually, but secretly she felt slighted, resentful, even angry. She'd thought Randall's desertion would arouse some kind of protective sympathy in her mother's heart, but not so. Apparently a divorce was not a grand enough tragedy. She'd imagined that her campaign for state representative would draw her parents' attention and admiration. She'd envisioned discussing strategies with her parents, and goals to work toward. But her representation of her district, healthily although not stunningly prosperous in its quiet way, was obviously not crucial enough to lure their eyes her way. Not that she was doing all this simply to gain her parents' respect. She *wanted* to do this kind of work, she *believed* in it with all her heart and soul, and she would attempt with every dram of energy in her constitution to make a difference in the world, whether her parents ever noticed or not.

It would be just a bit nicer if her parents noticed.

What made it all even worse was Randall's announcement that he was going to live with his father. How much more clearly could Randall announce that *his* father cared for Tessa, while Anne's parents scarcely remembered she existed? Now he could inform the judge that there would be, in *his* home, *two* adults to care for Tessa, and both of them physicians. Furthermore, Mont was retired. He would be at home all the time, he would be a parent available at any moment, no matter how busy Randall was. While Anne had only Carmen to act as another adult in the home, and Carmen, of course, had her own family who came first in her affections and in her priorities, no matter how much she might care for Anne and Tessa.

She had to find a way to offset the advantage Mont would provide Randall as caregiver. She had to think. *Think.*

For one thing, it couldn't be good that both Randall and Mont were men, when Tessa was female. Surely a twelve-year-old girl needed to be with a female parent more than with a male. Yes, *that* was the tack to take. And furthermore, Mont was *old*. Perhaps not senile, not yet, but perhaps not altogether capable these days, especially with the recent death of his beloved wife. She ought to investigate this. She ought to pay Mont a visit. Mont had always liked her, or at least he had seemed to, while Madeline had been, Anne felt, a bit cool. A bit judgmental. Well, more than that, really—there had been times when Anne and Madeline had argued rather fiercely over the way Madeline let Tessa play with her filthy animals in that filthy barn. Anne hadn't been at all sad when Madeline died. If anything, she'd felt relief.

But Mont liked her. Mont was a kind and reasonable man. Anne would visit him sometime, sometime when she knew Randall wouldn't be around to interrupt them. Perhaps she could even persuade Mont to be on her side about this child custody matter. It wouldn't hurt to try.

Anne adjusted and aligned the objects on her desk a final time. She stared at her empty appointment calendar and quiescent answering machine as if the sheer force of her desire would make writing appear on the page and spur the red light into furious blinks. The house was as quiet as death all around her.

Still, she felt better. She'd made some good decisions. She would shower; then she'd take Tessa to a movie. They hadn't done that, or anything, just the two of them, for a while.

She was heading down the hall toward the stairs when the front door opened and Tessa ran in.

"Hey, Mom!"

As she did every day after camp, Tessa looked, in her blue shorts, white T-shirt, and sneakers, as disheveled and filthy as a homeless person. Perhaps Anne ought to take a photograph of Tessa like this and send it to Sarah, perhaps *that* would arouse her interest in her grandchild.

"Don't say *hey,* Tessa, that's vulgar. Say hello. Or hi. You look like you've spent a lot of time in the sun today."

"I did. Tennis in the morning, swimming in the afternoon, and we got our photos back from Youssif. Mine are so cool, want to see them?"

"Why don't you shower first?"

"Mom."

"I don't want you to track dirt through the house."

"Mom, I'm not *dirty*. I'll take them into the kitchen. Anyway, Carmen will clean in there tomorrow morning."

Tessa headed down the hall, blond braids bouncing against her back, loose curls spiraling around her ears. Anne inhaled sharply. Ever since she'd turned twelve, which was pretty much parallel to the time when Randall said he wanted a divorce and moved out of the house, Tessa had become more forward. Not *antagonistic*, but *assertive*. Probably it was just part of growing up, but Anne didn't care for this new development any more than she did the approaching sexual issues they were going to have to deal with sooner or later.

Reluctantly she followed her daughter.

• • •

Tessa slid a group of photographs from a manila envelope onto the table. They were all black and white, many out of focus. Grass. Ferns. Leaves. A bunch of white poles.

"Those are legs, Mom. Can you tell? I did a study of legs. Shins. *Shins* is a funny word, isn't it? Anyway, I think it's cool. I'm going to hold a contest to see who can guess whose legs are whose and the winner gets—oh, I don't know, help me think of a prize. I mean, could you identify your own shins from a group?"

Anne plucked a photograph from the pile. Her words came out stiff, loud. "What is this, Tessa?"

Tessa looked. "Oh, I didn't take those. Chad and Tracy did."

"Tessa. These look . . . pornographic."

Tessa laughed. "Mom! What are you talking about?"

"What were you doing here? Lying on the ground. What was this boy doing to you?"

Tessa got very quiet. "I was lying on the ground because I was photographing the underside of leaves. I was trying to get a new perspective."

"And here? Where this boy is trying to push your shirt up?"

"He wasn't trying to—"

"Look at these, Tessa! Look!"

Anne fanned the photos out on the table. In one shot the boy was absolutely *straddling* Tessa, one leg on either side of her writhing body. His hands were on her waist. Tessa's legs bent toward her belly, her back curled up, thrusting her breasts forward, her neck arched toward the margin of the paper, ending with her open mouth in a grimace. She could have been laughing, but she could have been screaming.

"He was just tickling me, Mom." Tessa's voice was very small.

"How can you be so sure? You know nothing about

men. Nothing about boys and what they like to do."

"Chad's my friend."

"You think a boy his age wants friendship from a girl like you? These are very disturbing photos, Tessa. Has your camp counselor seen them?"

"Yes. He was the one who got them developed, and he commented on all of them." Tessa reached out to take the photographs. "If you hate them so much, I'll throw them away."

"Oh, I think not." Anne snatched the photos. "I think Mrs. Allison should see these. I want an explanation."

"No, Mom! I gave you an explanation! We're not doing anything wrong!"

"If you believe that, you're naïve." Anne tapped the photos into a tidy pile and slid them back into the envelope. "I'm going to take these to Mrs. Allison."

Tessa, sobbing, reduced to a child, implored, "Mom, *don't*, please. It would totally humiliate me."

Anne studied her daughter. "Either that, or you drop out of camp."

"But Mom, I love it!"

"We'll arrange for you to have private tennis lessons."

"No, Mom, come on! I have friends there! I have fun there!"

"I'm not going to change my mind, Tessa. You have to trust my judgment. I'm the adult here, and responsible for your health and welfare, and I can see things happening here that you are just too young to understand. I'm doing this for your own protection."

"Mom, *please*." Tessa was wild with crying, her entire body shaking.

"Calm down, Tessa. You're becoming overwrought. Go shower. That will relax you."

"I don't want to relax! I want you to—"

"Tessa."

"I *hate* you!" Tessa screamed suddenly. "I don't want

to live with you anymore. You're weird and crazy and mean! I want my *real* mother!"

Anne went white.

Tessa couldn't stand the way her mother looked now, her face naked with misery, so she turned and raced up the stairs, as if she could outrun the pain.

Tessa showered a long time. The noise of the water fell around her like a refuge, obliterating all other sounds in the house. She was nearly ill with sadness and self-hatred. The way she looked in the photo made her sick to her stomach.

Worst of all was the fact that, in a way, her mother had been right. When Chad tickled her, she had felt something more than a kid would feel. His hands on her had been scary and mesmerizing. "Stop!" she pleaded, but she hadn't really wanted him to stop. She'd felt like Beryl's cat who in the midst of being petted suddenly bit you hard on the hand. Tessa had wanted to bite Chad hard, or *something*.

And all that showed in the photograph. Tessa was sick at heart.

Her mother was right. Her mother had seen the truth, and was only trying to protect her.

Tessa dried off quickly, hating her body—it was so *naked*. So gross. So full of nasty hungers, for food, even for the sight of Chad—

She had to change somehow.

She pulled on jeans and her baggy sweatshirt and padded in thick white cotton socks down the stairs.

Her mother wasn't in the kitchen or in the library. Tessa walked down the hall to her mother's study, and as she drew near to the door she heard a sound that wrenched her apart.

Her mother was crying. Sobbing, really, as if her heart were broken. Guilt flooded Tessa like a black stew. She could not bear this. She had to make this right.

"Mom?" She pushed open the door and huddled just inside.

"Not now, Tessa." Anne was sitting at her desk, her place of strength and sanctuary. Her shoulders were hunched, her face buried in her hands.

"Mom, I'm sorry. I didn't mean it. I don't want to see my birth mother. I love you."

"Oh, Tessa."

Tessa went to her mother. She put her hand on her mother's arm. "I don't have to go to camp."

Anne's eyes flickered toward Tessa's. They were red and swollen, and her nose was swollen, too. Her cheeks were tear-streaked. She looked completely undone, but at Tessa's words, she sniffed and essayed a smile.

"You could help with the campaign," Anne offered.

"Sure. That would be okay."

"It might even be fun, honey. I'm going to start going door-to-door. You could go with me. It would be a pleasure to have your companionship, and people always love to see children. Would you like to do that?"

"Sure."

Anne took a crisp embroidered linen handkerchief from her purse and wiped her face. "You're such a good girl, Tessa."

"I didn't mean . . . in that photograph—"

"We won't talk about it ever again." Anne patted the bottom drawer of her desk, which was locked. "We don't need to mention this to your father."

"All right."

"It's as good as forgotten, okay?"

"Okay."

"I know you're a good girl, Tessa. I really do. And you know I love you and only want the best for you."

"I know, Mom."

Anne nodded. "Good." She looked at her watch. "We've got to leave for our meeting with Dr. Lawrence."

"Okay."

"Are you sure you want to go like that?"

Tessa was silent. Then she said, "What do you want me to wear?"

"Your blue dress would be nice."

"Okay. I'll go change."

"Thank you, darling."

Tessa turned to go to her room.

"Oh, and darling?"

Tessa stopped.

"I won't mention the photographs to Dr. Lawrence. I don't want him to get the wrong impression of you."

Tessa stood frozen, mortified.

"All right, Tessa?"

Tessa nodded.

"After our meeting, we'll do something fun, all right? How about a movie? I think there's a new Disney one at Fresh Pond Mall."

"Okay."

"Tessa?"

"*Okay.*"

Anne looked at her watch, then rose.

The August sun was still high when Kelly set out along 6A to the Sagamore Bridge and Route 3 toward home. Luckily the heaviest traffic was headed in the other direction, for the Cape and islands. With a twenty-ounce Diet Coke and a bag of Cape Cod potato chips to fortify her for the three-hour trip, Kelly punched the radio dial to a hard rock station, snuggled down into her seat, and tried to lose herself in the undeniable beat of music.

That didn't work.

The music, slow or fast, soft or loud, made her think of Randall. Or not *think*, really, so much as remember, in a kind of insistent sensual replay that had obsessed her every night this week as she tossed and turned in the unfamiliar bed, trying to fall asleep.

His mouth on hers. Warm breath.

His body on hers. Delicious weight.

His body in hers. Dense honey, dark heat. Silence and restraint as they tried to remain on the brink, eyes closed, mouth to mouth, entirely focused on the tip and sheath of extreme pleasure, greedy for it to stay. To stay. To stay.

And then the way the floodgates had opened.

All her body asked of her now was that she remember that moment over and over again, while she drove.

But she had some serious thinking to do. Some important questions to ask herself. Like, what the hell did she think she was doing?

Jason was a good man. Actually, he was a wonderful man. And he was in love with her, and she had made a contract with him—for an engagement is a kind of contract—and she knew she should honor that contract.

Randall had said he wanted them to be genuine, honest, and open to one another. *Real* to one another.

"If we are to have a future together," he had said.

His daughter was adopted, he'd said.

He loved his daughter, more than anything in the world. Having a child had changed his life. He wanted more children.

What would he think of Kelly if he knew what she'd done?

And if he still loved her, what did that mean? What about Jason?

These questions were thorny, difficult, painful. It was much easier to drift back into sensual memories of the two of them in bed.

Dr. Lawrence opened the door to his office. "Anne, Tessa, nice to see you again."

"It's nice to see you again, Dr. Lawrence," Anne replied. With a hand on Tessa's shoulder, she guided her into the office.

Tessa went to a chair at the far end of the coffee table and sat down.

Anne sat on the sofa. Patting the seat, she said, "Honey. Come sit here with me."

Tessa paused, then complied, although she sat at the opposite end of the sofa rather than close to her mother.

"Hot out there," Dr. Lawrence remarked, settling himself behind his desk.

"Very." Anne smoothed her skirt.

Tessa folded her hands in her lap and looked down at them.

"How was your week, Tessa?" Dr. Lawrence inquired.

Softly she answered: "Fine."

"Did you go to camp?"

Anne crossed and uncrossed her legs. Not looking up at him, Tessa nodded.

Dr. Lawrence tilted his head sideways. "Do anything fun?"

Tessa shrugged.

Anne spoke up. "Tessa won't be going back to camp, Dr. Lawrence."

"Really? Is there a problem?"

Tessa chewed her thumbnail.

Anne smiled. "No problem at all. It's just that I've decided to begin door-to-door campaigning, and Tessa thought it might be fun to come along with me."

"Is that right, Tessa?"

Tessa nodded.

"Surely you don't mean to imply that I'm lying," Anne said silkily.

"Not at all. But giving up camp—most kids Tessa's age prefer to do stuff with their peers rather than their mothers."

"Tessa is hardly 'most kids,'" Anne assured him.

Dr. Lawrence picked up his pencil and studied it, as if reading a message embedded in the yellow paint. "Still," he mused aloud, "Tessa is a teenager."

"She's twelve."

"All right. She's almost a teenager. It's normal for girls

her age to like to be with their peers. During my session with Tessa, we talked about some of the things she'd like to do with her friends. Or things she'd like to do that her friends do. I think it might be a good idea if we discussed some of those ideas now."

"That's perfectly acceptable to me," Anne said. She looked expectantly at Tessa.

Tessa stared at her lap.

"Tessa?" Dr. Lawrence prompted. When she didn't speak, he tried to encourage her. "Remember what we talked about last time?" He looked at his notes. "Britney Spears?"

"Britney Spears!" Anne snapped. "She's a slut."

"I'm not sure—" Dr. Lawrence glanced at Tessa.

Tessa's cheeks flamed.

"I *am* sure. The clothes she wears, the way she exposes herself—she's pornographic."

"Okay," Dr. Lawrence studied his notes. "How about something completely different, then. Let's talk about Tessa having a computer of her own. Or, at least, access to a home computer for schoolwork."

Tessa sat silently, staring at her lap.

"You know," Anne said through pinched lips, "I'm not quite comfortable with this—whatever you call this process. I feel as if I'm being blackmailed somehow: I *have* to let Tessa have a computer, or you'll tell the judge to give Randall custody of my daughter."

"I'm sorry if you feel that way," Dr. Lawrence responded. "What I hope we can do here is listen to Tessa. Hear what she has to say. Her life is changing without her active participation—you and Dr. Randall are getting divorced. That's an enormous change, and Tessa probably feels like a lot is happening beyond her control. It's a good time to find out what *Tessa* would like to change, if she could. Large and small things."

"I have always been attentive to Tessa's needs."

"I'm sure you have. But let's talk, specifically, about

a computer. It's not an unreasonable desire on Tessa's part, to want a computer."

"She can learn anything she needs to through reading books and attending school."

"Do you use a computer, Anne?"

"Of course I do! But I'm an adult!"

"Your concerns about Tessa using a computer are—"

"Pornography. Chat rooms. Deviants who lurk and hide behind seductive disguises. Violent computer games. So much of our popular culture is harmful to young people—you agreed with me about this when I was here before!"

Tessa's eyes flew to Dr. Lawrence's face.

"True," Dr. Lawrence agreed. "Still, Tessa needs to fit in with her peers. It's a common, normal need to be part of a group. And kids Tessa's age, especially in Tessa's socioeconomic class, have access to computers. They really can be amazing tools. They can provide instant information about any subject in the world. They'd be of enormous assistance to Tessa in her schoolwork. You want her to go to college?"

"Of course!"

"Kids today use computers like we used pencils."

"So you're saying I have to get Tessa a computer."

"I'm saying I'd like you to consider letting Tessa have a computer. Or access to one. Certainly you could monitor her use."

"For schoolwork."

"That and other things. There are computer games, and Web sites, that you might approve of and Tessa might enjoy. You might even find sites you and Tessa would like to visit together."

Anne raised her eyebrow. "I hadn't thought of that. I suppose you're right." She looked at Tessa. "I wouldn't want her to have it in her room. Children can become isolated, hidden away in their room, using a computer in the middle of the night."

"There's also the issue of television shows," Dr. Lawrence said.

"Really." Anne folded her arms over her chest.

"Tessa? You'd mentioned this last time. Anything you want to say?"

Tessa rubbed a spot on her skirt. She shrugged.

"What shows would you like to see?" Dr. Lawrence prompted.

"*Buffy the Vampire Slayer.*" Tessa's voice was a whisper.

"*Buffy the Vampire Slayer* has been named one of the ten most violent television shows on the air today!" Anne argued. "I can find the statistics for you!"

"Okay. What else?" When Tessa didn't respond, Dr. Lawrence remarked, "Tessa, you're pretty quiet today."

Tessa shrugged.

"Bad week?"

"It's the end of the week," Anne pointed out. "She's tired from camp."

"All right," Dr. Lawrence said. Gently he laid his pencil on the table. "I think we've done about all we can do for today." Flipping through his desk diary, he said, "Let's schedule a meeting for next week, shall we?"

"For the two of us?"

"No. No, I think I'd like to see Tessa alone, one more time."

Anne sniffed. "If you must."

"I'm going on vacation next Tuesday, for a week. I'll be back on September third, right after Labor Day. Could Tessa come here at three on Monday afternoon?"

"I'll bring her."

"Okay with you, Tessa?" Dr. Lawrence looked at Tessa.

Shrugging, Tessa stared at her skirt.

The traffic thickened as Kelly drew close to Cambridge, but it wasn't impossible. At nearly nine o'clock on this hot

August evening, the bright lights of Mass Ave illuminated strollers out for an ice cream cone or a movie. Yawning, she realized she was exhausted, from working, driving, thinking . . . When she got home, she'd turn off the air-conditioning, open all her windows, light lots of candles, and sink in a perfumed bath. Then she'd pull on her silk robe and curl up in front of the television with a pint of raspberry sorbet. Sorbet and potato chips for dinner—adolescent behavior, perfect for her mood.

She parked in the lot behind her apartment, hefted her overnight bag and briefcase with one arm, yanked her wheeled suitcase behind her with the other, clicked over the sidewalk and up the stairs and into her foyer. She sagged against the wall of the elevator as it rose—she really was tired—thinking that a hundred years ago a judge would have some kind of valet to help her with her luggage. On the other hand, a hundred years ago women couldn't be judges.

She put her key in the lock, threw the door open, and walked inside.

"Hi," Jason said.

He was stretched out on her sofa, a pile of newspapers on the floor and coffee table next to him, the remote control in his left hand, a glass of wine in his right.

"I thought I'd surprise you," he told her, grinning.

"Oh, you surprised me." Shutting the door, she sagged against it.

Unfolding himself from the sofa, Jason crossed the room and embraced her. "I've brought a bottle of excellent merlot. And I've made fettuccine Alfredo."

"Lovely." Except (a), she thought, it's too hot for pasta, and (b) I've just eaten an entire bag of potato chips. But of course, Jason couldn't know that.

"Do I have time for a bath?"

"Absolutely. But make it quick. I'm starving. You're back later than I thought you'd be."

"It was a long day."

"I want to hear all about it."

Randall had forgotten how perfect Lacey could make things. She had no hidden agenda: wanting to please a man *was* her agenda. She welcomed him at the door with no action more demanding than a smile, and settled him on the sofa with a Scotch and water and the remote control, saying she knew he'd want to see the news before they ate. She didn't chatter through the news. At the table, while they ate her substantial, hot, melting lasagna, she kept the conversation light, focused on hospital gossip rather than the more serious discussions of HMOs and death that would spoil the taste of her delicious food.

And if she wore only khaki shorts and a tight black tank top that showed more than it concealed, if she padded back and forth from the table to the kitchen on bare feet, an ankle bracelet glittering against her tanned skin, if she managed to appear undeniably sexual and completely available, why should he be surprised? He had always known from the start what Lacey wanted: marriage and children. He had always been frank with her from the start: he was married, he had a child, he desired Lacey and admired her physical beauty, but he did not love her. He had never told her he loved her.

And what in the hell was love, anyway? Randall wondered. He knew what it was, clear as a bell, bright as a bead, definite as a bump in his chest, when it came to Tessa and his parents. He knew now that when he married Anne, he'd confused respect, affection, and idealism for love— he'd been so young then, so eager to save the world, so— *earnest*.

Ernest. The woman he'd called Morgan had touched him more deeply than she knew when she named him that. It was as if she saw instantly, instinctively, to the true core of his being. And was that love? Could love really arrive so easily, so abruptly, a shaft of unexpected sunlight, a door opening in his heart to rooms he'd never known were there? What was it he found so absolutely alluring in Morgan? She was beautiful, but many women were physically beautiful. She was intelligent, and that always had been something that attracted him even more than physical traits. He knew so little about her, and yet within him ran a certainty that he did know all the truly important things. It was a mysterious gift, the way he knew she belonged to him. It was like seeing, out of a crowd of dogs at a shelter, the face of the one dog you know belongs to you, or like hearing on the radio, during a long drive, a concerto you know you must buy and play over and over again, because it speaks to you, carries you where you want to go, or like walking into a house and knowing, at once, that you're home.

"Penny for your thoughts."

Lacey's voice made Randall jerk guiltily. "No thoughts," he said. "I'm just relaxing."

"Want to go into the living room for coffee?"

He would drink his coffee while sitting on the sofa, Randall knew, and this time she would sit next to him. Her lovely plump thigh would press against his.

"No thanks. I've reached the perfect state of equilibrium," he told her. "Coffee would startle me out of this wonderful lazy stupor I've achieved." Yawning, he stretched his arms high above his head. "I should go home. I'm beat."

"You could sleep over."

He smiled at her. "No, honey. No."

She came to him then, while he sat in his dining room chair. She stood next to him, pulling his head against her bosom, leaning her head down so that her breath stirred his hair. He put his arms around her for a moment and held her sweet warm body.

Then he pushed her away. He rose. "I'm sorry, Lacey. I've got to go home."

She was so young, and still innocent. She was uncomplicated and without guile. Her disappointment shone from her face.

"It was a great dinner. Thank you."

"Any time, Randall. You know I mean that. Any time."

Kelly came out of the bath, barefoot and wrapped in her silk robe, to find candles lighted on the table. Jason was tossing a salad, but when he saw her, he stopped and stared.

"Nice robe." He walked over to pull her against him, running his hands down her back, murmuring with pleasure when he realized she was wearing no underwear. "Why don't we eat later?"

She drew away from him gently. She could avoid it no longer. "Jason. I have to tell you something."

He cuffed her neck with his hands, something he found sexy and she found vaguely frightening. "Oh, yes?"

"I'd like a glass of wine." Breaking free of his embrace, she found her glass, poured her wine, and crossed the room to curl up in an armchair.

Jason frowned. "You look very serious."

"I *am* very serious. I've done a lot of thinking this week . . ." It was hard to continue.

Jason relaxed into the corner of the sofa facing Kelly. Behind him the windows gleamed with the wonderful peculiar blue of summer twilight. "And?"

Kelly held up her hand. "Look. This is hard for me. Let me just get it all out, okay?"

Jason arched one elegant black eyebrow. She could see how he was just on the verge of moving into the protection of sarcasm.

"Jason." She forced it all out at once, an explosion. "I had a baby. On purpose. I needed money for college. When one of my professors came to me with a proposal, I agreed to be a surrogate mother so that another couple could have a child."

He rocked back from her words. "Jesus."

"Shall I go on?"

"Of course."

"I was twenty-two years old. My mother had just married René Lambrousco, and my father's parents had just died. They'd drawn up their wills when I was a child, so of course they named my mother as beneficiary, and they never got around to changing it, but they always made it clear that their estate should go to me. Of course, they couldn't foresee that René would enter my mother's life or that he would have the power to persuade her to give all the money to him."

"She did that?"

"She did."

"Wow. You should have taken them to court."

"Perhaps. But it really wasn't that simple. It never is, I suppose. Love and money do get so mixed up together, don't they? I mean, we see it in court over and over again."

"Seems clear-cut to me. They stole your inheritance."

"Exactly. But it was more than that. It always is. My mother had never been passionately in love, and all at once she was. The next moment my grandparents were dead, and I was knocked over with grief, and before I could turn around, mother told me she was going to marry René and move to New York with him, using my grandparents' money to invest in his acting career. And they were gone. I had to find an apartment, I had to find a job, I had to get a student loan to finish college, and I had no one to help me."

"That sounds rough."

"You bet it was rough. I was lost, Jason. Absolutely lost. Perhaps I could have found some legal recourse, but I was so young and ignorant then. I had no one to turn to."

"What did you do?"

"I had one professor who cared for me. George Hammond. He was a funny little man. Dapper. He wore tweeds and bow ties. He taught a course in law and society. My junior year, he called me in to tell me I should consider a career in law. I had, he told me, a quick and incisive mind."

Kelly smiled at the memory. "He suggested books I should read. Told me what courses I should take my senior year. Told me he'd write a brilliant recommendation for me." Her smile faded. "That summer my mother married René."

"And everything changed."

"Yes." She was surprised at the power the old memory still had to wound her. "The fall of my senior year he called me into his office to ask me why I hadn't applied to law school. I told him I couldn't afford it. As if everything else weren't enough, that year all my wisdom teeth came in. I had a thousand-dollar oral surgeon bill to pay off."

Jason cringed slightly, as he often did whenever people spoke about their lack of money.

"In February, Professor Hammond came to me with a proposal. He knew a couple who weren't able to have children. They wanted to find a woman willing to be a surrogate mother, a woman who would be fertilized with the husband's sperm, who would carry the baby through the nine months of pregnancy, give birth, and legally give the child up for adoption. They wanted to find a woman who was healthy, attractive, and intelligent, and—especially—capable of doing it all in secrecy. Their need for privacy in this was paramount. Professor Hammond said he would act as intermediary and handle all legal matters."

"And in return?"

"The couple were willing to pay fifty thousand dollars."

Jason was quiet, looking down into his glass.

"Back then that was three years of law school tuition, and then some."

"So you did it."

"It's not uncommon, Jason. Many couples go this route rather than adopting. This way they have some sense of being involved in the creation of the child."

"Did you meet them?"

"No. They didn't want to meet me. The woman, understandably, was very sensitive about this matter." Kelly paused. "So I agreed."

Jason cleared his throat. "How did you . . . become pregnant?"

"How much do you want to know?"

"Everything, I guess."

"All right. First, I had to have a complete medical examination by a fertility expert in Brookline to ascertain whether or not I was healthy and a good risk for pregnancy. I had to track my reproductive cycle, which until then I'd thought of as my menstrual cycle, carefully, taking my temperature every morning and noting it on a chart. I was very regular, spiking clearly during the fifteenth day, which pleased the gynecologist. For three months I was inseminated with the husband's semen—"

"How?"

"Artificially. A gynecologist did it. With a kind of long syringe. It wasn't romantic, Jason. It wasn't painful. It wasn't *anything*. Dr. Radison chatted the whole time about the chances of the Red Sox winning the pennant that year. There was a nurse in attendance the entire time. She held my hand."

Jason looked bleak.

"After three tries, I got pregnant. I felt proud of myself, rather as if I'd made a good grade on a difficult test." She looked down into her wineglass, remembering. "Later on, though, I was terribly lonely. I didn't even have my mother's address at that point. Professor Hammond arranged for me to live in Williamstown for the tenure of my pregnancy. He had friends there with a vacation home where I stayed. It was nice, really. I had a TV, VCR, CD player, microwave. I had a queen-size bed with a down comforter and a guest bedroom which I used as a study. I read a ton of books on the law. That was really all I had to do: read and wait. Oh, I was expected to eat well and healthily, get lots of protein and vegetables, and forsake alcohol. I was to take sufficient exercise and to be certain

I got plenty of sleep. Each month I was thoroughly examined by Dr. Roberts, an obstetrician in Pittsfield who assisted me at the birth. I'd signed a series of legal agreements that Professor Hammond had drawn up, which covered every contingency, or so it seemed. I knew what would happen if I miscarried. I knew what would happen if the child were stillborn. I knew that the child would be taken from me immediately upon being born.

"And that was all right. I had no desire to see the child. I tried to think of the child as the child of Mr. and Mrs. X, whom I was only tending. Like someone watering the plants or caring for the animals of a couple off on vacation. It was a kind of job, one I could do without thinking, without even working, really. After the morning sickness had stopped, it seemed like the easiest job I'd ever had."

Kelly shifted in her chair. "Jason, listen to me. I was *glad* about it all. I was *glad* to help people. I've always had this thing about wanting to make things right, and God knows nature is hair-pullingly arbitrary. I felt I was balancing some kind of universal scale."

Jason watched her face carefully. "Go on."

Kelly realized her hands were pressed against her belly. She forced herself to rest them on the arms of the chair. "Lots of women do this, Jason. It's a wonderful thing to do. It's a gift."

"But?" Jason whispered.

"But nothing. I gave birth to a child, and she was healthy, and the nurse took her away, and I had the money for law school. That's it."

"I don't think so." Jason's voice was soft but firm.

Kelly looked away. "I don't know what you mean."

"Do me the favor of believing that I do know you a little bit, Kelly."

She stared at him, then looked away. "Jason, she was so—beautiful! She was so new, and yet so much herself. And yet, so much *mine*. They said they'd take her right away, but it was busy in the hospital, and her birth was so—so amazing! It was like sailing a boat through the heart of a storm and living to tell the tale. It was like being snatched off the earth by a tornado, and spinning out of control and then suddenly being set down safe, and all at once everything that before in life was gray now is in brilliant Technicolor!"

Jason poured them each another glass of wine, emptying the bottle.

"Go on."

Kelly lifted her eyes to him. The words seemed torn right out of her heart. "She was so beautiful, Jason. *My daughter* was so beautiful. She was as pale as frost, with funny silver fuzz all over her head, and a rosebud mouth, and the most wide, searching eyes. I held her, they let me hold her, and when our eyes met, it was like falling into the most wonderful love. It was like meeting someone I'd been looking for all my life."

They sat in silence, the kind of silence that fills the air in a sacred place, in a church or concert hall, after the music has ended.

Her voice was tight with self-hatred. "I was so stupid. So *arrogant*. Thinking I could carry a child around with no more connection to her than to a bag of groceries. I thought I could conquer nature. Well. Nature surely did bring me to my knees."

"You never saw her again?"

"Never."

Jason reached out his hand. "Come sit next to me."

She moved over onto the sofa, and he pulled her against him with one arm, and stroked her hair with his hand.

"I think you were brave and resourceful."

She sniffed. "You do?"

"Absolutely. You have nothing to be ashamed of."

She pulled away. "I'm not *ashamed*! I never said I was *ashamed*!"

"Hey, cool down! I'm at sea here."

"I didn't tell you so you could *forgive* me."

"Did I say anything about forgiveness?"

"To tell me I don't have to be ashamed means you think I *should* feel ashamed."

"Well, if you didn't feel something like shame, why didn't you tell me all this sooner?"

She glared at him. Then she nodded. "Good question." Rising, she began to pace the room, as she often did when thinking hard about her cases. "Because." Steepling her hands, she brought them to her mouth. "Because I thought it was all over." She nodded, as if agreeing with her own words would spur her thinking process. "Because I thought it—*she*—was irrelevant to my life."

"And now?"

"I want to see her. I want to be sure she's happy. Healthy. In a good home. I want to see what she looks like, know what she likes to do."

Jason shook his head. "Kelly, you know that's entering very complicated territory."

"God, don't you think I *understand* that? But that doesn't change the way I *feel*."

He asked, very quietly, "What about the way I feel?"

"What do you mean?"

"What if I told you that I have a child somewhere out there. A daughter I wanted to bring into my life."

"Then I'd support you. I'd help you."

"I don't think so. I think first of all you'd make me spend some time contemplating the consequences of such actions. There are other people to consider, after all. Not only your birth daughter, but her parents, with whom you made a legal and personal pact. You're thinking of dishonoring that agreement. You're thinking of bringing chaos and confusion into the lives of three people you've never met."

"Oh, I've *met* my daughter!"

"All right, *technically*—"

"There was nothing *technical* about it!"

"Look. You haven't seen her for twelve years. She's seen you once, if babies can even see when they're born. She won't remember you. She may not even know about you. Her parents might not even have told her she's adopted yet."

"They should have."

"Perhaps. Perhaps not. It's not your decision. They might be waiting for a special moment. You have no idea. And no right to interfere with their lives."

"Why are you so contentious?"

"I'm not—"

"Yes, you are."

"Kelly, I don't know what you want from me. I'm trying to respond to you as honestly as possible, and quite frankly, this is a hell of a lot to take in."

"You want me to pretend it all never happened?"

Jason buried his head in his hands. "I don't know what you want me to say right now, Kelly."

She sank into a chair. "I don't, either, actually."

"You seem angry with me."

"I know I do," she agreed ruefully. "And I know it doesn't make sense."

"What brings this all up now?"

She was silent.

He answered for her: "This is all stirred up because of your new duties as a judge."

"Yes. Yes, I suppose. I'm seeing things I never saw before."

"So this is what's been bugging you the past week or so."

"—Yes."

"How can I help you?"

"I don't think you can. I'm sorry."

"I'm sorry, too, Kelly. I'd like to help you. I'd like to think you want my help."

"Jason, I can't handle your emotions right now. I can barely handle my own."

"Maybe I'd better go home."

"Yes. Maybe you'd better."

They stared at one another, tired and wary. Jason rose, crossed the room, bent toward her to kiss her good-bye. She turned her head away so that his lips found only her cheek.

"Kelly."

"I'm sorry, Jason. I'm behaving strangely now. I know it. I just—we both just need some space, I think."

"Fine." Jason touched her shoulder gently, with consolation and affection, then went out the door.

NINE

SUNDAY MORNING KELLY WOKE BEFORE the alarm. Snuggling down deep into the bed, she turned onto her side, pulled the blanket up over her ear, and tried to recapture the blurry pleasure of her dream.

In her dream she'd also been in bed—with Randall. They were making love. He was inside her, and on top of her, and she had her legs and arms wrapped around him, clutching him to her. He was saying her name.

Gradually the dream faded, but as Kelly padded into the kitchen to make coffee, the warmth of the dream remained. Leaning against the kitchen counter, cradling the cup in her hands, she realized she was smiling, and smiled at herself for it.

Something amazing happened when she was with Randall. He had said so; she had felt it. Sometimes miracles did happen. The French have a word for it: *coup de foudre*. Thunderbolt. Already he was talking to her about a future together, a future with children, their own children . . . the thought nearly made her dizzy.

But they had to talk. Well, *she* had to talk. She'd lied to him, telling him she was a lawyer, or rather, she'd told a half-truth, afraid he'd back off if he knew she was a judge.

Did she want their relationship to remain in secrecy and shadows? Certainly there was a kind of deliciousness about it, a sense of risk and mystery. And a kind of abandon, as well: she could be anyone, free from all the liabilities of her past. Free from reality.

She had seen how love, or lust, or whatever her mother had fallen into with René Lambrousco, had beguiled her mother, wrecking her judgment and ruining Kelly's life. She'd seen countless divorces over the past few years, she'd heard numberless stories of people who had once experienced that magic, that sense of communion, that longing to be together for all eternity . . . and who ended up in divorce court, bitter enemies.

How could she think it would be any different for her?

She couldn't know that. She couldn't know the future.

She only knew that she wanted to be with Randall. Somehow she belonged to him, and he to her. She would tell him everything and let real life fall upon them, and then she'd find out if this magic was real.

She had to hurry if she wasn't going to be late. Fortunately she knew what she would wear . . . a brief elegant slip of white linen that fit her like a kidskin glove. Too hot if she were going to be outside for long, but she didn't intend to be outside for long, or, for that matter, inside the dress.

She drove quickly along the Jamaica Way and finally beneath the stone arch into the cemetery.

The big green Jeep was there, idling, windows closed against the heat.

She parked next to it, jumped out, opened the passenger door.

"Hey," Randall said.

He stopped the world right in its tracks. Everything else fell away—all rules, laws, logic, continents, mountain ranges, seas. Nothing existed but this moment, this man, with his Viking blue eyes, his shaggy hair, his body, as present and undeniable as truth.

Climbing into the passenger seat, she said, "Hey yourself." Suddenly she was flushed with shyness.

"I can't stay."

"Oh. Well. Oh."

He put his hands on her shoulders. "Don't think I don't want to. I want nothing more than to drive you to the nearest bed and spend all morning in it with you. But my daughter called last night. She has to spend this afternoon with her mother. Door-to-door campaigning, and it can't be done in the morning when people are in church. So I promised Tessa I'd take her to breakfast this morning. What about this afternoon? I'm supposed to go visit my father, but I can postpone that."

Desire drenched her. Shameless, she said, "This afternoon is all right—"

"Good. I'll call you, okay?"

"Yes. Okay."

"I'll come to your apartment."

"All right. But Randall, we have to talk. I have things to tell you."

"And I, you. We *will* talk. We'll have our whole lives to talk."

"Do you mean that?"

"Of course I do. Look, Kelly. I was expecting to be with you this morning like we were last Sunday, in a room shut away from all the rest of the world. And we will be that way again, but we can't be that way now."

"I understand—"

"No. Listen to me. Today I've got to be with my

daughter. She will always be my first priority. If you and I are very lucky, someday you'll meet her. Someday you'll become part of our lives. If we're very good and very lucky, someday my daughter will be your stepdaughter and a half sister to a child of our own, of yours and mine. That's what I want, Kelly. I want to make love to you here and now . . . but more than that, I want a future, with you and me and all of ours in it together."

"You sound so sure."

"I am sure. I married the first time because of my head. This time I'm following my heart." With an abashed smile, he added, "And, I must admit, certain other parts of my anatomy." He kissed her fiercely. "Let me come to your apartment this afternoon. I'll spend the night."

"I have to go out of town tonight, for a week. I won't be back until next Friday night."

"All right. We still have this afternoon."

"Yes."

"Give me your number. I'll call you after I've returned Tessa to her mother. And I'll give you my numbers, home and pager, and cell phone."

Randall took a small leather notebook from his hip pocket. Opening it, he took out a narrow silver pen.

Next to the notepad was a photograph of a girl with blond braids, blue eyes, and a leaf-shaped birthmark on her neck.

Her heart kicked at the sight.

"Kelly? What's your phone number?"

She told him.

"Here's my card. All my numbers are there." He frowned. "Are you all right?"

The notebook was still open in his hands. The little blond girl gleamed from the glossy paper.

"Is that your daughter?"

"Tessa. Yes."

"She's beautiful."

"She is. Kelly, I want to see you today—"

"Is that a birthmark?" Kelly touched the photograph with the tip of her finger.

"Yes. She's very self-conscious about it. Usually wears her shirt collar up. Wants to have it removed. I've convinced her to wait until she's a little older. I like it, myself."

"Do you remember the story by Hawthorne, about the woman who was perfect except for a birthmark on her face, and when she had it removed, she died, because nothing perfect can exist on this earth?"

"No, I don't know that one." Reaching over, he took Kelly's hands in his. "You've gotten icy cold. What's wrong?"

"I—Nothing." She slipped his card into her purse. "I'll let you go now."

"Just for the morning. We'll see each other this afternoon, right?"

"Right."

"Are you okay?"

"Yes. I'm fine."

"You know I'll see you this afternoon."

"Yes. I know."

She stumbled from his Jeep. Leaning against her own car, she watched Randall drive off, beneath the stone gates, down the winding road.

"Dear God," she moaned, rubbing her hands over her face. She could still feel his kiss on her mouth, the imprint of his hands on her shoulders.

She could still see the picture of his daughter. The image was burned into her mind.

Blindly, she walked up the avenue toward her mother's grave.

This time she didn't see the trees, lush with summer, heavy with shadows. She didn't feel the pressing heat.

She saw white hospital walls, hot lights, the doctor in a white gown and mask, a nurse in green scrubs.

She saw her knees bent, covered with white sheets, and another nurse coming toward her with an oxygen mask.

She was in a strange town on the other side of the state, a town Professor Hammond had found for her, a place where she could finish her pregnancy in anonymity. She had no friends, and she'd told no one about this child she was carrying for another couple.

She knew that labor would be painful. She'd read accounts of birth in novels, seen women grimacing on television shows. She had discussed everything with the obstetrician, who recommended that she have an epidural when the time came.

And then the time came.

Two weeks earlier than expected.

She took a cab to the hospital. It was ten o'clock at night, in February, in the middle of an ice storm. The roads were glassy, and ice fell from the sky, breaking on the windshield of the cab with an almost musical clinking, like crystal beads.

The hospital was in chaos. The ice had caused a bus of schoolchildren returning from a play in Albany to slide off the road. Ambulances screamed and glittered at the entrance to the hospital, cars came sliding into the parking lot, terrified parents spilling out the doors.

The emergency entrance was congested, the nurses pressed upon by frantic fathers and mothers, and if the cabdriver had not taken pity on Kelly and half carried her into the admitting room, she might not have made it inside.

But the cabdriver was loud and persistent. Somehow in the midst of the screaming children and frightened parents, Kelly was wheeled to a room and left to undress. She was told the doctor was on his way. She was helped onto a high bed. A nurse checked her dilation, told her she was coming along nicely, not to worry, nothing was going to happen for a few hours at least.

She lay on the high bed, hearing the cries of children in the corridors. Then she was aware of nothing but her own pain. She wished her mother were with her, or a friend, or a lover. It occurred to her that she could not do this. She could not endure this. She'd been a fool to think she could.

Perhaps they forgot about her. It felt like it. She ached with pain. She was afraid. She cried for her mother. She was alone for a very long time, until her screams—she could not hold them back—brought a nurse and doctor running toward her.

"I can't do this!" she wept. "Help me, please!"

"The baby's crowning," the doctor told her. "Push."

She pushed, not because the doctor told her to, but because her body *insisted*, and then she heard a wail, high, triumphant, indignant.

"It's a girl," the doctor said.

The nurse took the baby to the side of the room while the doctor coached the placenta from Kelly's body. Perhaps because the nurse hadn't been informed, or perhaps in the chaos she'd forgotten: the nurse brought the baby to Kelly. She put the baby in Kelly's arms. She went away, and Kelly looked down at her child.

The baby was pale, with dark blue eyes that fastened on Kelly's and would not look away. She was very calm, and she seemed to be listening. Certainly she was alert, aware, and *waiting*.

Kelly said, "Hello, baby." The baby squirmed and puckered her perfect mouth in reply.

Kelly touched the baby's head—it was small, and very hot, and it fit exactly into the curve of Kelly's palm.

She was so perfect, so new, so fragile. She gazed at Kelly with such trust, and when she rooted toward Kelly's breast, Kelly was flooded with helpless, overpowering love.

I have a daughter, she thought.

"Oh, my darling girl," Kelly whispered. She loosened the blanket wrapped around the baby and studied her child. Her stomach and chest seemed enormous, her limbs long and thin. She was as pale as the ice outside the windows, and with a similar glitter to her skin.

On the left side of her neck was a dark brown mark, like a leaf.

"Is something wrong with her?" Kelly asked the nurse.

The nurse peered down. "Oh, no. That's just a birth-mark. Distinctive, isn't it?"

"Will she always have it?"

"Well, yes. She won't feel it. It doesn't hurt or any-thing. When she's a young woman she might consider it unattractive. Then a plastic surgeon can remove it, but that would be years and years away."

"Nurse." The doctor's voice was brusque.

The nurse went off. Kelly stared and stared at the baby in her arms. Her eyes were so large and full of something like wisdom, and she made funny little squeaks, as if she were trying to speak. Kelly had never seen anything so endearing, so beautiful, so *perfect*.

The nurse came back. "All right, dearie, off we go." She lifted the baby from Kelly's arms.

The baby turned scarlet and wailed at the separation. I must protect her! Kelly thought.

"No," she said, shoving back her sheets.

"*Nurse*," the doctor said.

The nurse rushed out the door.

An arrow of anger shot through Kelly. She struggled to sit up. She wanted to throw herself from the hospital bed, grab the baby, and run.

The doctor moved to stand with his body between Kelly and the door. "Well done." He patted her on the shoulder. "You did a fine job, Ms. MacLeod. I'm sure the parents will be thrilled to have such a nice healthy baby girl. And you're looking good yourself. Nice blood pres-sure, good steady vital signs. We'll wheel you into a re-covery room as soon as we get one free. That might be a while, with all those poor people out there. You just take it easy now, and rest."

"Where are they taking my baby?"

"Now, now, that's not your concern. The baby's in good hands. You've done your job. Now you get to rest."

But when the doctor strode out through the swinging

doors, Kelly did not rest. She sobbed. She shook with sobs. She thought her heart would break.

Kelly sat at her mother's grave, remembering her daughter's birth.

She hadn't wanted children, until she'd held her own daughter in her arms.

She hadn't wanted marriage or "love," whatever that was.

She'd wanted justice. She'd *burned* with the need to make *something* right. Being powerless, she'd wanted power. And she'd wanted to be an advocate for others who were powerless, especially for children.

She could not make her mother give her back the money that was meant for her. She could not make her mother choose her daughter's rights over her husband's desires. She couldn't change the world. But she could change some things in it.

Over the past twelve years she'd worked hard. The more she worked, the more she saw needing to be done. She'd represented clients no one else had wanted, people desperately in need of baths, and toothbrushes, and AA meetings, and therapy. She'd fought with all her might for what she believed in, working in a system that was flawed, confusing, sometimes maddening. She'd seen terrible miscarriages of justice due to the incompetency of a battered woman's lawyer up against the expensive expertise of a lawyer hired by an abusive husband. She'd seen exhausted judges make stupid mistakes that wrecked lives. She'd seen greedy lawyers lie. She'd given her heart to clients who didn't know how to speak the truth, and she'd given her heart to clients who could speak eloquently yet lied, lied to her, their own advocate. She learned that the law was imperfect, impeded, arbitrary, exhausted. She'd learned that lawyers were manipulative, exploitative, egomaniacal, and deceitful.

She'd learned that what her mother had done, giving away Kelly's legacy to a new husband in the name of love was *nothing* compared to what "love" made some people do.

But she'd also seen judges making rulings so wise it took Kelly's breath away. She'd seen judges who understood how each couple standing before them was new, special, each time, and each time deserving of their fresh, careful attention and profound wisdom. She'd seen judges who were exhausted, sneezing into handkerchiefs, popping throat lozenges, eyes drooping like a basset hound's, still sitting into the cold depths of a bleak winter afternoon, patiently working with an estranged couple, handling the moment that blossomed around them with the delicacy of a master artisan shaping fragile glass, not closing court no matter how tired they were, because that frail moment would not tolerate interruption and would never come again . . . and she'd seen some couples reconcile and go forward with their lives together, and she'd seen more couples, sagging with sadness, divorce.

She'd begun by wanting justice in all its theoretical purity.

She'd arrived, desiring to be a judge, impure, imperfect, learned, exhausted, compassionate, and wise.

But she hadn't counted on *this* happening. She hadn't dreamed that one day she'd fall in love with the man who had fathered her own child.

TEN

TESSA LAY, FULLY DRESSED, ON top of her bed. Her father was coming to take her to breakfast, but somehow she couldn't get excited about it. Since her mother had said those things about the photograph of her with Chad, Tessa felt numb. Within her chest her heart ached, as cold as the tips of her fingers.

Through her window came the crackling sound of tires over gravel. Her father was here. She had to get up. With enormous effort, she forced herself from bed and out into the hall. She could say she didn't feel well enough to go out—that was true—but she didn't want to hurt her father's feelings, especially since he knew she was going out this afternoon with her mother, campaigning door-to-door. She had no choice about that.

She heard the clicking of her mother's heels over the hall floor.

"Good morning, Anne." Her father sounded happy. "Where's Tessa?"

"In her room. I'll call her in a moment. I want to speak with you privately first."

"Anne—"

"I'll be brief." The heels clicked away down the hall to Anne's study.

Tessa's stomach heaved. Her mother had *promised* not to tell her father about the photograph with Chad. She'd *promised* not to show it to him. Tessa would *die* if her father knew she'd been doing anything so gross.

She raced down the stairs, tripping over her own feet, nearly falling, wrenching her arm as she caught herself on the banister. *Calm down!* she ordered herself. She'd look *really* guilty if she showed up out of breath, out of control.

Her mother hadn't shut the door to her study. Halfway down the hall, Tessa could hear her parents clearly. Tessa froze in the hall, listening hard.

"—help me with my campaign, so she won't be attending camp any longer."

"Anne, I don't think that's a very good idea."

"I'm sure you don't. But it's what Tessa wants. You can ask her yourself."

"Anne—"

"But something has come up that I think you'll like.

Sarah called this week. She invited me and Tessa to come to Nantucket for the weekend. I think *you* should go. You and Tessa."

"Sarah's *your* mother, Anne."

"That doesn't alter the fact that she prefers your company. Besides, you like the island more than I do. Look, I'm trying to be positive. I'm trying to offer you something you and Tessa would both enjoy. *You're* the one who's always insisting that Tessa should be outdoors more. Here's a chance for you to spend some time with Tessa. Swimming. Sailing. Playing tennis. Whatever."

"Next weekend?" Her father sounded reluctant.

"Randall, you've taken Tessa to your father's every weekend for months now. The least you can do is give equal time to my parents."

"I would think that's the least *you* can do."

"You know damned well every moment of my life is booked right up to the night of the election."

Tessa's father sighed. "Why did Sarah specify next weekend?"

"Lord, Randall, why does my mother do *anything*? She's got all sorts of immigrants living there, working, and she said something about putting up some visiting musicians who'll be performing for the art society at the end of the month. You can ask her when you see her. If next weekend's not convenient, phone her about it. I would have thought you would jump at the chance to take Tessa off for a weekend. I guess you're going to balk at any suggestion I make."

"That's not it at all, Anne. I just had some plans for next weekend."

"Oh?"

Tessa strained her ears. Silence.

"I suppose it's a woman." Anne's voice was bitter. "I should have realized you'd put your own desires before Tessa's needs."

Her father sighed again. "Look, Anne . . . Oh, hell. I'll take Tessa to Nantucket next weekend."

"Not if it's going to be a hardship for you."

"Anne, it's never a *hardship* for me to be with my daughter. I'm just going to have to rearrange some plans, that's all. I'll phone Sarah tonight and tell her we'll come. I'll see if I can reschedule my Friday afternoon appointments, and perhaps we can leave before the rush."

"Let me know so I can have Tessa ready."

"Of course."

"Good. That's settled."

"Anything else?"

"No. Only have Tessa back by noon today."

"All right."

Tessa tiptoed back up the hall toward the front stairs, but she could still hear their voices.

"And Randall, do me a favor, would you? When you take her for breakfast, see that she eats fruit. Don't fill her up on pancakes and sweet junk, please? Every weekend you undo all the good I've done during the week."

"Anne, I'll say it again. Tessa's too thin. I'm a doctor, and—"

"And I'm a nurse, and a woman. Oh, I don't know why I even try. Go on. She's up in her room."

Tessa sped up the stairs and into her room so they wouldn't know she'd been spying on them. That would make both of them angry.

Back at her apartment, Kelly forced herself to focus on her packing. Her fourth and final judicial training session would take place in Nantucket, where the judge often had only two or three days a month in court. But because there were two acrimonious and complicated divorces on the docket, Judge Calloway had told her to plan on staying the entire week. Still, Kelly tossed in a bathing suit, on the chance that court might adjourn early, allowing her time to get to the beach.

At her desk, she double-checked her Palm Pilot: she had a reservation on the fast ferry for seven o'clock this evening, which meant she had to leave for the drive down to Hyannis no later than five.

If Randall came to her apartment around one, that would leave them a good four hours to be alone together. Long enough for her to share her conjecture about Tessa with him. Long enough to begin a difficult discussion.

A knock sounded on the door. Heading down the hall, she pondered: Jason? No. He was angry with her. He'd told her he was going sailing with friends on the Vineyard today. Randall? Not yet. Donna was in Maine with her parents.

She looked through the peephole.

A Gothic angel stood there, slouching. Thick black hair clouded over a pale face. Black jeans, black turtleneck. In this heat, a black turtleneck. Who the hell—?

Felicity.

René Lambrousco's daughter.

Her mother's other daughter.

Her half sister.

Kelly opened the door. "Felicity?"

Felicity's eyes were hidden behind dark glasses. Her lipstick was black. In one hand she held a scuffed duffel bag, in the other a suitcase tied with rope.

"Can I come in?"

"Well . . . yes, of course. Are you all right?"

"I've got to live with you."

Kelly stared at the girl, dumbfounded. The girl stood there, blackly implacable as the thirteenth fairy.

"I really have to pee." Felicity dumped her bags on the floor just inside the door. "Which way's your bathroom?"

"Second door. On the left."

Felicity glanced around. "God, did you just move in?"

"No."

"Then why don't you have anything pretty in here? It

looks like, I don't know, the home of a serial killer or something. It's way too clean."

Kelly put her hands on her hips. "I thought you had to use the bathroom."

"I'm *going*." Felicity took her stormy self off.

Kelly's mind raced. She'd seen Felicity only twice in her life, once at their mother's bedside and again at their mother's funeral. Where had the girl found the nerve to just show up like this with her impossible announcement?

What a dumb question . . . Nature had no doubt bequeathed René's daughter René's arrogance, while René's example had taught her audacity as a way of life.

Felicity came out of the bathroom. "I'm starving. What do you have to eat?"

"Not much, I'm afraid . . . I'm going to be gone all this week, I hadn't stocked up . . ."

Felicity peered into Kelly's cupboards. "You've got to have peanut butter."

Kelly folded her arms and leaned against the folding door separating the tiny efficiency kitchen from the rest of the living space. "Actually, no."

"Jeez." Felicity opened the freezer. "I'll just have ice cream."

"Look," Kelly said, deciding it was time she reclaimed her territory, "you can't eat only ice cream. Sit down. I'll heat up some soup for you—"

"I'm a vegetarian."

"It's tomato soup. And I've got a nice bit of cheddar left. I'll make you a grilled cheese sandwich. Okay?"

Felicity plopped down on a chair. "Great."

Kelly blinked. How had this happened? The girl had been in Felicity's apartment five minutes, and already Kelly had become Felicity's servant.

Moving aside a small jar of caviar and a tin of sardines, Kelly took out the can of soup, opened it, poured it into a bowl, and set the bowl in the microwave.

"So. What's going on?" she asked as she melted butter in a skillet.

Felicity shrugged. Her dark glasses obscured all emotion. "René's moving to L.A. I can't go with him."

"Why is he moving to L.A.?"

"Because," Felicity said in the patient tone necessary for an imbecile, "Elizabeth thinks he should try to make it in the movies."

"Elizabeth?"

"His girlfriend."

Kelly turned from the stove. "His girlfriend? That was fast. He certainly didn't spend much time mourning."

"*Duh*. He was with Elizabeth the whole time Mom was in the hospital."

"I had no idea." Asshole, she thought, flipping the sandwich over to brown the other side. "Is he going to marry this Elizabeth?"

"I doubt it. I think René's decided that marriage kind of cramps his style."

Kelly punched the microwave on. "Milk?"

"I'm not a kid! Don't you have some Coke?"

"Did no one teach you the word *please*?"

Felicity glared "*Please*."

"Fine." Kelly filled a glass with ice and set it, along with a can of Coke, in front of the girl. The timer on the microwave dinged, and she slid the bowl of steaming soup onto a plate and put it next to the sandwich. Fishing a knife, fork, and spoon from the drawer, she arranged them at Felicity's place with a paper napkin beneath the fork. She lifted the grilled cheese sandwich, nicely toasted, onto a plate and set it in front of Felicity.

Her fingers had scarcely left the utensils when Felicity grabbed the sandwich up and bit off a savage bite. Kelly filled a glass with ice and water for herself and sat down at the table across from the girl, studying her as she ate. Felicity's hands were trembling, and her hair, Kelly now realized, was lank and oily. Her skin was specked with red

zits and black dots of acne. She was too thin. A terrible
and uncomfortable pity moved through Kelly.

"Are you living in the same apartment you were this
spring?"

Around the final bite of sandwich, Felicity answered,
"Until the end of the month we are. Then Dad says they're
moving to L.A."

"And you don't want to go."

The girl snorted. "*No.* They don't want me to go, either."

"Your father doesn't want you to go with them?"

"Why are you so surprised?"

Kelly blinked. "Well, Felicity, you are his daughter—"

"Big fucking deal."

"Please don't use that language. And let me finish.
René is your father. He's legally responsible for you until
you're eighteen."

"So what am I supposed to do? Sue him?" Her sandwich finished, Felicity slurped a spoonful of soup.

Resting her elbows on the table, Kelly steepled her
fingers and leaned on them. "Let's try a different approach.
How much money did Mother leave you?"

"Please. You must be kidding."

"There has to be some money. When my mother married your father, she had quite a hefty bank balance, thanks
to my father's parents. It was money, just for your information, that my grandparents intended to go to me."

"Well, if it makes you feel any better, they never spent
any of that money on me." Felicity picked up her bowl
with both hands and drank the rest of the soup. She set the
bowl back down.

"That can't be true. And you have a soup mustache."

Felicity swiped at her mouth with the napkin. "We
have always been poor. *Always.*"

"Even when you were a baby? Even when you were
all living in New York?"

Felicity shrugged. "Maybe not then. Maybe not *poor*. I was too young to remember. Sometimes we were better off than others. For a few years, while I was in elementary school, Dad was artistic director of an actors' troupe in Ohio. I liked it there. We lived in a real house. Rented, but it was like what I thought home should be. But Dad hated it there. He wanted to go back to New York. Thought he'd never be 'discovered' in the boondocks. So we went back."

"And you've lived in Boston how long?"

"We came here last October. Now can I have ice cream?"

Kelly brought her the pint of Cherry Garcia and another bowl and spoon. "Help yourself."

"Can I have it all?"

"Sure."

"Good. Then I don't need a bowl." Felicity stabbed her spoon into the container.

"If René doesn't want you going with him to L.A., what does he propose you do?"

"Move in with you, of course."

"He might have had the courtesy of asking me how I felt about the proposition."

"He did try. He says you threw him out of the office."

Kelly nodded. "He wasn't clear about what he wanted." Kelly gave a bitter laugh. "He's got brass balls. First he takes my inheritance; then he thinks he can just dump responsibility for *his* daughter on me."

Felicity stopped eating. Very carefully she set the spoon on the table. The girl's nails, Kelly noticed, were bitten to the quick.

"Look," Kelly snapped, "for God's sake, take your sunglasses off, Felicity."

"I know René's my father, and I know he's awful," Felicity said quietly. "But I *am* your half sister. Your mother was my mother, too."

Kelly stared at the teenager, whose hair was as black

as her father's, whose face and figure carried her father's lines.

Then Felicity removed her glasses, and Kelly looked into her mother's eyes.

Mont Madison was up on a ladder, painting Evangeline's room for Tessa. The girl had chosen a deep green, nearly black, and she'd asked for a carpet in the same deep shade.

"Kind of a strange color for a young girl's room," Mont had observed.

"That's probably exactly why she chose it," Randall had answered.

Tessa wanted her father's bunk beds moved into her room.

Randall had protested. "Honey, they're ugly. Scarred, beaten up."

"I like them." Tessa was firm. "They'll make the room feel like a kind of tree house, and I can have a friend sleep over."

It was humid today in the room. In order to keep the paint fumes from the rest of the house, Mont had shut the bedroom door, which had sealed the room off from the air-conditioning. The two windows were open, but probably they did more harm than good, for the air outside was tropical.

Mont had always enjoyed painting. It delivered results so immediately, and with such power. He found the act itself soothing, the repetition of dipping and stroking a kind of calming exercise lending itself to meditation.

Randall was hopeful that sometime this fall Tessa would start attending the public school in Concord. Randall seemed optimistic that if Anne won the election in September, which she probably would, she might be feeling happy enough, and busy enough, to allow Tessa to live with Randall and Mont. Their divorce trial was set for next week; too bad they didn't wait. As far as legal custody, who knew what the judge would decide? Randall's lawyer had said that for a very young child, there was a "tender years presumption," that the child would be better off living with her mother. But Tessa was twelve. Also there was a movement in Massachusetts, fathers joining to fight for more equality in custody matters, an issue of which the judges were well aware.

Mont was just sorry that Tessa had to go through all this mess. It had to be confusing for her, never mind the fact that she was adopted in the first place. Randall and Anne had agreed that very early in her life they'd tell her she was adopted. Much fine and helpful literature had been published on the subject, and Tessa always seemed at peace with the knowledge. They had not told her she had been conceived through artificial insemination, using Randall's semen and an unknown, unseen woman's ovum and body for the pregnancy and birth; they had agreed not to tell her this until she was an adult.

Mont and Madeline had understood the wisdom of this. The tragedy of two ectopic pregnancies had been enough cruelty for Anne to live with, and as a child Tessa needed only so much information. There was a limit to what a little girl could comprehend.

How easy it would be, Mont thought, for Randall, now in the heat and throes of a bitter divorce, to let the information slip: Tessa was genetically Randall's daughter, and not Anne's. But Randall would never do that. He'd promised Anne that—and in general, as much as possible, Randall was a man who kept his promises. Besides, Randall felt much more pity for Anne than anger, and it was anger that spurred people to commit vengeful deeds.

The humidity was making the paint sticky and the fumes hung in the room like a thick chemical mist. Mont was just a bit dizzy. He was an idiot to be up on the ladder, as if no one had ever informed him that heat rose. But he'd begun in the morning, when the air had been fresher, and now, nearly noon, he had three walls done and was eager to finish the fourth.

Brooke Burchardt from the farm across the street had already phoned this morning, asking when Tessa was coming out, telling Mont she wanted to invite Tessa over to her house this afternoon to go for a swim in their backyard pool. Tessa should go, Mont thought, it was too hot to ride; besides, he had a feeling he'd want to rest after he'd finished painting.

There was just a small patch left unpainted, high in the corner where two walls met. He ought to climb down, move the ladder, and climb back up again, but Mont thought that if he stretched, he could reach it.

He dipped the brush into the gallon can, drew it out carefully, slowly wiping the excess off each side on the inner lip of the container so the paint wouldn't drip. The paint was the thick deep green of a Norway spruce. The color made him think of Christmas.

Firmly gripping the side of the ladder with his left hand, slowly he extended his right, holding the brush out like a fencer brandishing a sword. The sweep of paint across the pale patch of wall was always so satisfying, the whisper of the bristles, the neat, obedient lines left by the brush. Just one more spot . . .

His left hand, slick with sweat from the humidity and his exertions, slipped. He overbalanced. With infinite surprise he felt his torso wobble and slant. He tried to turn, tried to grab the metal rung, and succeeded only in hitting his hand against the aluminum.

He fell.

With a crash he landed on the floor.

He did not lose consciousness, but he could not breathe. His chest caved in. He did not seem to be a person anymore, but a kind of skin around an explosion of pain.

He was piercingly afraid.

Then he could breathe, although it hurt like fire. His body returned to him, a section at a time. His chest, a conflagration. His head turned sideways. He could see. That was good. He was on his stomach, both arms flung forward in a parody of Superman's position for flight. The paintbrush had bounced somehow, landing on the other side of the room. He was glad he'd covered the entire floor with old sheets.

His head hurt.

He couldn't move his legs.

You stupid old man, he told himself. What if he died? What if he had to be hospitalized? That would be a great housewarming gift for Tessa and Randall.

And *damn it*! They were coming out today. Mont didn't want them to find him lying helpless like this.

Indignity upon indignity.

He couldn't even paint a room anymore.

Tears stung his eyes. If he could have moved, he would have slapped himself for being so pathetic.

A fly flew in the open window, buzzing like a tiny lawn mower through the air. It circled Mont and landed on his cheek. The delicate touch tickled, but Mont found the creature more comforting than annoying. Then his cheek twitched, and the fly sped away, leaving Mont much cheered, for a twitching cheek was surely a good sign.

A fierce urge to urinate possessed him. He'd be damned if he'd lie here and wet himself.

After a while he decided he was glad Randall and Tessa were coming today. If he just had someone to help him stand, someone he could lean on while he shook his limbs back into life . . .

The phone rang. Mont tried to heave himself up, but at the moment not every part of his body was responding. He did not feel *hurt* so much as absent.

"Sorry we can't come to the phone right now. Please leave a message, and we'll call you right back." It was Madeline's voice on the tape. Mont hadn't found the heart to tape over her voice and wasn't sure that he ever would. It was always a pleasure to hear her speak. For a moment it made her alive to him again, as if she were just in the other room.

"Hi, Dad." Randall's clear voice spilled from the answering machine. "There's been a change of plans. Anne wants Tessa to go with her today, campaigning door-to-door, so I've agreed to take Tessa out for breakfast and let Anne have her the rest of the day. So we won't be coming out this afternoon. Hope this doesn't foul up any of your plans. Give me a call."

Well, then, Mont thought. Relaxing, he closed his eyes.

Kelly felt as if a bomb had gone off inside her life, leaving, in the midst of the wreckage, this teenage girl with the sullen face sitting in her kitchen.

Yet no one knew better than Kelly what Felicity was going through just now.

"All right," Kelly conceded. "I'll consider having you live with me. But I've got to have some time to think about it—"

"Our lease is up at the end of the month. This Thursday."

"Felicity—"

"We have to be out of the apartment by then. Dad and Elizabeth are planning to pack up the car and start driving on Thursday."

"Look," Kelly said. "This is crazy. Even if I could and would take responsibility for you, you couldn't just move in all of a sudden, today."

"Why not?"

"Why not? Well, Felicity, look around. Where would you sleep? I don't even have a spare bedroom."

"You've got tons of empty space!"

"Felicity—"

"Besides, you're a judge. You ought to be able to afford a larger apartment."

"What I can afford is not the point."

"I've got a lot of my mother's furniture I could use. It's sort of cool stuff, you'd like it. Honey-colored teak, really plain. A double bed with a slatted headboard, although the mattress isn't much anymore. A bureau and a desk—"

"My grandparents' furniture!"

"I don't think so. My mother never received anything from her father. Not even a letter."

"I don't mean Mother's parents. I mean my father's parents. I mean the MacLeods." Suddenly Kelly was excited. She stood up, then sat back down again. "I thought it had all been sold. It happened so fast, when I was away at college. René and Mother didn't tell me they'd kept some of the furniture."

"And you never came to visit."

"Indeed, I did not. Felicity, your father stole my inheritance. Why would I want anything to do with him? And I never even knew you were in Boston until René called to tell me Mother was in the hospital."

"Okay, don't get all upset."

"It sounds as if some of their furniture is in your apartment."

"Well, you can have it, if you want it."

"Oh, I want it."

"Okay. Let's go get it."

"Wait a moment." Kelly shook her head. "I've got things to do today. And I have to go to Nantucket tonight. I've got to be in court in the morning."

"Dad's planning to have some guys from a secondhand shop come in and price the stuff and buy it. He and Elizabeth want to start fresh."

"Well, he can just wait till next weekend."

"No, Kelly, he can't. He won't. They're packing up. They're selling everything tomorrow. They're leaving Thursday."

"I can't believe this. I really can't." Kelly rubbed her hands over her face.

"It's not like you don't have some spare room," Felicity pointed out.

"I haven't had the time to think about decorating! Besides, I like a spare, uncluttered room."

"We could put your desk in the bedroom," Felicity said. "I could put my bed in that space over by the window. You could move that bookcase, and the bureau could go at the end, and the cobbler's bench—"

"They still have the cobbler's bench?"

"Yup."

Kelly rose. "All right. Let's go get your furniture." She halted dead in her tracks. "Wait a minute. We won't be able to fit furniture in my car. And the truck rental agencies probably aren't open on Sunday."

"I know a guy who has a truck," Felicity said.

Kelly looked at Felicity. "Why," she said wryly, "am I not surprised?" She ran her hands through her hair. "All right. Just a moment. I have to make a phone call."

Sliding Randall's card from her purse, she found his number and dialed it. No answer. He was still, no doubt, with his daughter. *His daughter.* Tessa. The phone came alive as his recorded tape informed her he was out. Just the sound of his voice made Kelly go weak. She thought she could just dial his number over and over and over again, until she could see him.

And it was something concrete, something real, that she had his number.

"Randall," she said to the machine, "something's come up. I've got to help move my half sister into my apartment this afternoon. It's all a bit complicated. I'll tell you when I see you. I should be back here by three. But I've got to head for the Cape at about five. I hope . . . I hope I see you before I go."

Randall took Tessa for breakfast at Carla's Café on Mass Ave, a favored haunt they frequented so often that the waitresses and Carla the cook knew their names.

Even on this beautiful hot August morning, when most people were either gearing up for a day at the beach or sipping iced tea behind closed drapes in their air-conditioned homes, the café was packed. Tessa and Randall waited patiently in line outside in the heat, and then inside where they had to stand crushed against others waiting to be seated, but at least it was cool. Right in front of Tessa was a boy not much older than she was, with a man who was undoubtedly his father.

"So!" The father wore a Hawaiian shirt and white shorts. He had what Beryl called a "toilet head," completely bald on top with a strip of hair circling his scalp. "Your mom tells me you've been making a lot of money this summer."

The boy shrugged. He wasn't much taller than Tessa. He wore baggy jean shorts and a white T-shirt, and he had a thick thatch of dark hair falling nearly to his shoulders. Tessa wondered if he ever had nightmares about going bald like his dad.

"Mowing lawns," the boy said. "Baby-sitting."

"Baby-sitting?" The father frowned. "Isn't that kind of a girl thing? I mean, do *guys* baby-sit?"

"*I* do," the boy shot back.

"I don't know if that's a good idea," the father said.

"It's a little boy, Dad. He's nine years old. I play ball with him."

"The responsibility is what I'm talking about. What if—"

Monica, a waitress in pink shorts and a matching top bobbed up on her air-foam sneakers and led the father and son away. Tessa hoped she and her father would get seated in an adjoining booth. She wanted to hear the rest of the conversation.

A quartet of little old orange-haired ladies wearing enough makeup for Halloween squeezed past Tessa and Randall and out the door, all talking at once, snipping and snapping their pocketbooks open and shut, asking one another if they'd remembered their glasses.

Monica rushed up. "Hi, Randall! Hi, Tessa, honey.

Give me a minute to clear the table, and I'll seat you."

A few moments later, Tessa and Randall slid into a booth. Monica poured Randall a mug of hot coffee. "I know what you want," she said to Tessa. "Pancakes and bacon, right?"

"Um, no," Tessa said, ducking her head. "I think I'll look at the menu."

"Sure thing, baby doll."

"I'll have the pancakes and bacon," Randall announced.

Tessa scoured the menu. "I'd like a fruit cup."

"A fruit cup!" Randall said. "Honey. What kind of breakfast is that?"

"I'm not very hungry, Dad." Tessa felt her face burning. She hated arguing with her parents in front of people.

"It's this heat," Monica said placatingly. "Everyone loses their appetite."

"Tessa. You have to have more than a fruit cup."

Tessa shrugged. "Okay. And a glass of orange juice."

Randall snorted. "Give her pancakes, too."

"Dad, I don't want pancakes."

"I'll be back in just a minute." Monica took herself diplomatically off.

Randall spoke quietly. "Tessa. Look at me. Is something wrong?"

"No, Dad. Why does it have to be a federal case if I don't want pancakes?"

"All right. That's fine. But you need something substantial to start your day. You know that. How about—?" He scanned the menu. "Waffles with strawberries."

Tessa shook her head.

"French toast?"

"Dad."

Randall looked at Tessa. Then he smiled. "Mushroom omelet?" He knew she hated mushrooms.

"Maybe just a soft-boiled egg."

"That's good."

But when Monica returned and Tessa told her, "A fruit cup and a soft-boiled egg," Randall added, "And toast."

"So," Randall said when Monica went off. "I hear you don't want to go to camp any longer."

Tessa shrugged. "There's only one more week, anyway."

"So there is. Fall is fast approaching. And school."

Tessa traced the raised designs on her place mat.

"You know Grandpops and I are hoping you'll be able to live with us and attend the public school."

Tessa chewed her lip.

"And you know, of course, your mother wants you to stay with her. Remain in private school."

Monica returned with their juice.

"We don't want to create an impossible situation for you, Tessa. We both love you and want what's best for you. I know it's hard, being your age, having your life in such turbulence. But I really do believe it's the best for all of us."

"I know, Dad."

Randall studied her as he drank his coffee in silence. After a while, he said, "Your mother tells me that Sarah has invited you to visit next weekend. Since your mother's got so much campaigning to do, she thought it might be a good idea if you and *I* go. What do you think of that?"

"Okay."

"Of course," her father said casually, "you could go by yourself, but then you'd have no buffer person."

Tessa grinned in spite of herself. Her grandparents were truly generous, good-hearted people, but also disorganized and eccentric. Capable of making complicated arrangements to provide jobs and housing for Russian immigrants—they seemed to want to take on the problems of the entire Russian population single-handed—they had trouble making a grocery list. When Tessa was ten, and invited to stay with them for a week in July, they'd driven her to the beach and dropped her off for the day without providing her with a lunch, beach blanket, sun block, or money, and then they'd forgotten to pick her up. She'd trudged home, feeling hot, pathetic, and sunburned, and later insisted that she'd never go visit them all by herself until she had her own car.

"Remember the time we all went there for Thanksgiving, and Sarah had forgotten to buy a turkey?" Randall asked.

"We just had tons of vegetables and pie."

Their meals came, and Tessa was glad for the diversion of Sarah stories. Her father tucked into his food like a starving man. Tessa ate her fruit cup very slowly; then she decapitated the egg in its little white cup with great deliberation. She tore up the toast in little bits, hoping her father wouldn't notice that she wasn't actually eating it. The truth was, the fruit cup and egg made her feel stuffed.

It was just before twelve when Randall dropped his daughter back at her mother's house.

"I'll phone you, Tessa. We'll leave sometime Friday afternoon, but I'll let you know exactly when after I rearrange my schedule."

"Okay, Dad."

"If you feel like it, and your mom can spare you, I'd love to take you out to see Grandpops some evening this week, since he didn't get to see you today."

"I'll ask Mom."

Randall gave his daughter a hug. "I love you, Tessa."

"Love you, too, Dad."

He sat in his car until she was safely inside. He was tremendously concerned about how little she was eating, how thin she was. Clearly her appetite had diminished, and her hands were cold. He was glad the divorce trial would be held in just ten days. He felt comfortable with Dr. Lawrence, who seemed like an observant, even-minded man. Surely the GAL would, if nothing else, speak to the matter of Tessa's thinness. Until then, there was no point arguing with Anne; it only escalated the anger between them and tore Tessa apart.

So, he thought, driving away from the trim French provincial. Now: Kelly. He was looking forward to seeing her apartment. A home told so much about a person. Well, he amended his own thought, sometimes it did. He would hate to be judged by the anonymous transitional apartment he slept in these days.

Perhaps he was behaving impetuously, thinking he wanted to marry this woman Kelly MacLeod when he scarcely knew her. Yet he had lived his life until now with great forethought and caution, and he had to say it had not brought him much joy. Well, Tessa had brought him joy, of course. He did believe that some power somewhere in the mysterious tangle of life forces had caused him and Anne to come together not for the purpose of a long happy marriage but for the needs, actions, and decisions that had eventuated in the breathtakingly lovable person that was Tessa. Her welfare and happiness would always be his first consideration.

But now he might find happiness for himself, as well.

His cell phone rang. Kelly, he thought, wondering how soon I'll be there.

But at first he couldn't hear the caller. "Hello?" he asked again.

"Randall."

An arrow of ice spliced his spine. "Dad? I can't hear you."

The old man's voice was quavery and dim. "I fell. Can you come?"

"Of course, I'll come. I'm in the car, I'll head out your way right now." Checking his rearview mirror he made a U-turn that led him toward Route 2. "How did you fall?"

"Painting. Ladder."

"Dad, do you need an ambulance?"

"No!" His father's voice gained strength. More quietly he added, "No need for any fuss."

"Did you break any bones?" Now he was on a ramp leading to the eight-lane highway.

"No. Just knocked the wind out. Gave myself a scare."

"Did you pass out?" Randall gunned the engine, cut into the fast lane, and kept his foot on the pedal.

"No. Hurt my pride more than anything." After a moment, Mont Madison said, a note of satisfaction in his voice, "Got most of Tessa's room painted, though."

"Listen, Dad. I need to make a call. I'll phone you right back."

"No need. I'll see you when you get here. Thanks for coming. Sorry to be such a pain in the neck."

"You're not a pain in the neck, Dad."

Randall clicked off, waited until he'd turned off Route 2 on the two-lane road to his father's farm, and punched in Kelly's number. To his surprise and disappointment, he got her answering machine.

"Kelly, I'm terribly sorry, but my father just phoned. He's had a fall, from a ladder, while painting a room in our house. He says he's okay, and he's a physician himself, so I'm sure he knows, but he wouldn't call me and ask me to come out if it wasn't necessary. I don't know how long I'll be with him. I'll call you as soon as I can. I'm sorry. I'm—I'm sorry."

Felicity lived in a two-family house in Everett. Kelly parked the car at the curb, and they stepped out into the heat, a wild storm of barking assaulting their ears.

Felicity led the way, calling over her shoulder, "That's Gargoyle. The upstairs neighbor's dog. He's harmless. Anyway, he's locked in the back yard. He can't get out."

The Lambrouscos' apartment was on the second floor. Living room, dining room, two bedrooms, kitchen and bath, all painted in muted greens and blues with clean white trim woodwork—no doubt Ingrid's touch. An ancient tweedish sofa worn shiny at the arms and back stood alone in the living room. Indentations in the carpet, dark rectangles on the wall, proved that once this place had looked like a home. Bits of paper, cardboard boxes from a liquor store, now filled with glasses, and bundles of fabric lay scattered over the floors. They went down a hall.

"My room," Felicity said, throwing open a door.

Kelly stepped inside.

This room had been painted indigo. Dark blue fabric printed with stars and moons had been tossed over the rod to serve as a curtain over the one window. Leftover bits of tape glittered from the walls and the closet door where once posters had hung. In the open closet three lonely dresses hung deserted.

The furniture made Kelly gasp. It was all so familiar—the bed, the cobbler's bench, the bureau, the desk—for a moment she was a child again, with her grandparents just in the other room.

"Anybody home? Felicity?"

A young man bounded into the room. He wore a Red Sox T-shirt and baggy red shorts drooped from his hip-bones, exposing the white band of his Fruit of the Loom undershorts.

"Hi, Sly. Kelly, this is my friend Sly."

Kelly shook his hand. The young man did resemble Stallone; he had the same dark good looks. No wonder Felicity was adamant about not moving to California.

"Thanks for coming on such short notice," Kelly said.

"No problem." He had a strong Boston accent. "So, you want all this stuff moved?"

"Yes," Felicity told him. "And those boxes of books."

Kelly knelt by the boxes. Eight of them, packed with hard- and softbacks. "You've got quite a library here."

"Secondhand stores. My treasures. Can't part with them, but idiot me, I filled the boxes all so full I couldn't pick them up."

"No problem," Sly said again. "Let's start with the furniture."

Kelly ran her hands over the bureau. Still a work of beauty, its surface was pitted, gouged, and scratched. She looked around. "What did you do to this furniture, go after it with a bat?"

"No, we just moved a lot. And did most of the moving ourselves." Felicity lifted the mattress off the bed and leaned it against the wall. "I think I've lived in at least twenty different places in fifteen years."

"You're lucky," Sly said. "I've never been anywhere."

Together they lifted the bed slats out and separated the headboard from the side pieces.

"I've got the headboard," Felicity said.

"I'll take one of the sides," Kelly said.

"Nah, I'll get them both," Sly told her. "You can be in charge of the doors."

Slightly amused, Kelly obeyed. Sly probably thought she'd strain herself, injure herself. She could remember when anyone over thirty might as well be over fifty. She propped the apartment door open, and while Felicity and Sly moved the furniture down the stairs and into the open bed of Sly's pickup truck, she walked through the apartment, her mother's last home.

The shades were down in René's bedroom, which, Kelly decided, was a blessing. The room was a sty. The bed had no headboard, the bureau screamed *tag sale*, and clothes were piled everywhere. The air was fragrant, though, and Kelly found a bottle of Poison on the bureau, next to a tangle of jewelry that even in this light gleamed its authenticity: heavy gold, real diamonds. No doubt the charming Elizabeth. This time René had, literally, struck gold. She felt no sense of her mother in this room, and she left, pulling the door closed behind her.

The kitchen was her mother's, she could tell. Or had been. Crusted dishes towered in the sink, and wineglasses with lipstick stains lined the counters along with mugs of cold coffee. But copper-bottomed pans once belonging to her grandparents hung in neat lines behind the stove, their bottoms, after all these years, still gleaming. African violets sat on the windowsills. Her mother had loved African violets, docile, patient creatures like herself. Now the leaves hung limp, desperate for water if not already dead. Kelly found a box and set them inside.

The dining room table was buried beneath piles of magazines, newspapers, mail, and a stack of black-and-white glamour shots of René. A glint of silver caught her eye. From beneath phone books, calendars, and *TV Guide*s, Kelly unearthed a double frame: Felicity, about seven years old, in a *Lion King* sweatshirt, her black hair gathered in a scrunchie, clutching a stuffed lion, laughing. And Kelly, also about seven, her blond hair in neat braids tied with tartan ribbons that matched her smocked cotton school-dress.

Her mother's daughters. Together in this frame, which might have sat at the end of the table where Ingrid could see them while she paid the household bills.

She tucked the frame into her purse.

Off the kitchen, in a kind of mud room/pantry, Kelly found a pillowcase stuffed with discarded clothing, too old and out of style to belong to Felicity. Quickly she sorted through it: stained, torn underwear; a terry-cloth robe with a ripped pocket; jeans worn at the knees, sweaters stretched out of shape and shabby. Sadness and a terrible guilt filled Kelly at the thought that her lovely mother had had to resort to wearing clothes like these. Perhaps Felicity had already taken the good things to the thrift shop. Perhaps these were meant to be thrown out.

At the bottom, a treasure. A sweater hand-knit from fine strong wool, dark blue with red hearts and white flowers across the bodice and around the hem of the sleeves. She could remember her mother knitting this, so many years ago. Bringing the sweater to her face, she inhaled its scent and thought she could detect her mother's fragrance, as faint and pale as a rose in November.

"Kelly? We're ready!"

Felicity's voice snapped her back to the present. Sweater in hand, Kelly rose, leaving the other abandoned garments behind.

Randall braked his Jeep to a halt, threw himself out, and raced into the house.

"Dad?"

His father wasn't in the kitchen or the living room. Randall took the steps to the second floor two at a time.

He found Mont lying on the bedroom floor. He'd crawled into the room and pulled the phone down next to him. He'd dragged Madeline's old pink robe dōwn on top of him as a covering. He lay curled and still and gray.

"Dad." Randall's heart was galloping.

Mont opened his eyes. "I'm all right. Don't fuss. Just help me up, will you? I need to go to the bathroom."

Randall moved behind his father, bent, and put his arms under his father's arms, lacing his fingers together across the old man's chest. He heaved. Mont grunted and, staggeringly, rose.

"Does anything hurt?"

"*Everything* hurts," Mont groused. "I ache all over. And I'm cold. It's just the shock of the fall. I need a pee and a shot of whiskey and a hot bath and a long nap, and then I'll be as good as new."

"You're sure you don't want me to drive you over to the hospital? Have a doctor look at you?"

"You're a doctor. You're looking at me right now, for God's sake. Now get me into the bathroom before I embarrass myself."

Randall half carried him into the bathroom. "Want some help with your clothes?"

Mont growled a negative. The right side of his face was bruised and swollen.

"I'll get your whiskey."

In the dining room Randall found the Dewar's and two heavy cut-glass tumblers. He poured a stiff drink for his father and one for himself as well: preventive medicine. He tossed back a swallow before heading back up the stairs. It had given him quite a scare, seeing his father like that. He just wasn't ready for the man to be feeble. Not yet.

Upstairs, he knocked on the bathroom door.

"Just a minute." The toilet flushed. "Come on in."

Mont leaned against the bathroom wall. He took a tumbler from Randall and drank. "Good." He shook his head. "Don't look so terrified, Randall. I'm all right."

"You've got a contusion along the left side of your face."

"I imagine I've got bruises all up and down my entire body," Mont told him. "I've got some Epsom salts in the cupboard. If you'd be good enough to run me a hot bath and fill it with salts, I think I'll be just fine."

"You're sure? The hot water might make you woozy."

"If it does, I'll go to bed. I want to go to bed, anyway. I need a good rest. But a bath and a drink and a nap are all I need, Randall, so relax. I'm just an old man who fell off a ladder and feels a little discomposed. That's all."

Randall scrutinized his father. His eyes were clear, and the gray was slowly seeping out of his face, replaced by a healthy pink.

"Okay." Turning, he fitted the rubber plug into the drain of the old claw-foot bathtub, then turned on the taps full blast, adjusting it to make it hot but not scalding. He took the Epsom salts from the cabinet and dumped in a good dose. "I took Tessa for breakfast this morning," he said. "Sarah phoned and asked Anne and Tessa to visit next weekend, and Anne can't because of the campaign, so I'm going to go and take Tessa." When the water was almost at the top of the tub, he turned it off. "There."

Mont shook his head. "I didn't hear a word you just said. The water drowned you out."

Randall grinned back. "Sorry. I'll tell you later. Want me to help you undress?"

"No, thanks. I'm okay now."

"Tell you what. I'll wait outside the door. You give a call if you need help getting in or out of the tub." At his father's expression he hurried to add, "The hot water might make you dizzy."

"All right," Mont said. "Go on. I'll call you if I need you."

While his father bathed, Randall used the bedroom phone to pick up messages from his answering machine. Kelly's half sister was moving into her apartment today? So much for time alone with Kelly. He'd known that real life with all its complications would have to intrude on their idyllic relationship. He just hadn't thought it would happen so soon.

"Toss me my pajamas, would you?" Mont called.

Randall found his father's blue-and-white-striped cotton pajamas from beneath his pillow, opened the bathroom door, and laid them on the closed toilet. "Okay?"

"Fine."

"More Scotch?"

"That would be good." Mont's scrawny arm appeared, an empty glass in his hand.

Randall went back downstairs, filled the glass half-full, and brought it back up.

Mont was propped up in bed, waiting. Wearing his pajamas, and over them, Madeline's old pink robe.

"For God's sake, Dad. You look like an idiot."

Mont grabbed the glass of Scotch, swigged a hearty swallow, and set the glass on the bedside table. "Look. I've fallen. I'm tired. I ache all over. The air-conditioning makes me feel chilled. Madeline's robe comforts me. If the Governor and his wife pay a call, I'll take the robe off, but just for the next hour or so, I'm going to wear the damned thing. All right?"

Randall smiled. "The fall doesn't seem to have affected your mind." He went out of the room. "Call me if you need anything. I'm going to clean up Tessa's room. It looks great, by the way."

Mont slid down in the bed, pulling the soft old cotton sheet and the light quilt Madeline had made by hand fifty years ago up to his shoulders. "You'll be here till I wake up?"

"I will. And you *will* wake up, Dad."

ELEVEN

KELLY REALIZED THAT MOST PEOPLE who came to Nantucket at the end of August wanted the time to pass slowly.

But then, most people who came to Nantucket were not there for work, and were with the people they knew and loved—husband, parent, friend—rather than their volatile, emotional, newly discovered, hyper-intense half sister.

There were moments when Kelly was glad Felicity was around, moments when she thought she could get to like the girl. Certainly moments when she felt a kinship with her.

But there were also moments when whatever was the most aggravating about René—his dramatic self-interest, his inability to see another point of view—seemed to flare up inside Felicity, making her irrational and intractable.

After much negotiation, the hotel clerk managed to give Kelly a small room with two twin beds rather than the larger room with one queen-size bed that Kelly had reserved. It wasn't exactly cheap to add another person to a hotel bill at the end of August. The least Felicity could do,

Kelly thought, was to enjoy the sunshine and sparkling water, the fresh air and golden beaches.

But every morning Felicity dressed and accompanied Kelly to the courthouse. The first day they argued all the way there.

"You should go swimming," Kelly insisted.

"I want to see the courtroom," Felicity replied. "I want to see you at work."

"You're on Nantucket, for heaven's sake. People come here for fun."

"So, watching you in court is my idea of fun." At Kelly's indignant sidelong glance, she added, "I don't mean *amusing*. I mean *interesting*. How many people have a judge for a sister?"

"You can watch me any other time, on the mainland."

"No, I can't. I'll have to start school."

"But Felicity, it's the end of summer! Your last chance to be at the beach! You could meet people your own age."

"I already know all the people my own age I want to know."

As they went up the sidewalk to the small brick town building, Kelly sighed. "I just don't understand you."

"You don't?" Felicity held the door open for her. "Well, where would you rather be? On the beach or in the courtroom?"

And what could Kelly do then but smile?

The Nantucket court was the smallest one Kelly had yet entered. The probate court didn't have its own building—it didn't even have its own courtroom, but shared with the superior and district courts the courtroom on the second floor of the town building, a modest two-story brick building next to the police station, across from the Whaling Museum.

It was an easy walk from the hotel, fortunately, since Kelly hadn't been able to get a reservation to bring her car over on one of the ferries. Each morning as she set off, stepping carefully over the cobblestones and bricks in her suit and heels, she was aware that everyone else on the island wore shorts or wispy summer dresses. Women congregated on Main Street to buy fresh vegetables from the farm trucks. Families rolled past with helmeted children on tandem bikes. Men in Nantucket red trousers and polo shirts carried bags of wine and imported cheeses down to their boats. Laughter filled the air as friends greeted one another. Truly this was a holiday world.

Inside the town building, on the second floor, the mood changed. The long narrow hall was crowded with lawyers and clients in suits clustering together, whispering. The air was a sense-storm of aftershave, perfume, deodorant, and nerves. The hall wasn't air-conditioned, but the offices, the judge's lobby, and the courtroom were.

Kelly had met the Nantucket County probate judge, Felix Mann, before, because when he was not on Nantucket, he sat at whatever court in the commonwealth needed him. In his forties, blond, with the lean body of a serious runner, he was an ambitious, driven, impatient man with his staff, a demanding husband and father—he had five children—and a formidable legal intellect, determined to make the law more responsive to the needs of the people.

Kelly introduced Felicity to Judge Mann, then sent her out to sit in the courtroom. She had only enough time to meet the register and her clerks, when Judge Mann said, "Let's get going."

First they dealt with a number of motions and contempts that needed clearing up. That took most of the morning. Judge Mann sent the assistant register and the court officer off to buy sandwiches, gave them less than fifteen minutes to gobble them down and then returned to the courtroom where they settled in for the long haul, a complicated and gruelingly emotional divorce, involving young children, their wealthy parents, their stepsiblings and stepparents, grandparents, baby-sitters, therapists, guardians *ad litem*, and ministers. The mother wept. The father groaned and buried his head in his hands. The lawyers nearly spat at each other. From opposing sides of the courtroom, grandmothers glared hatefully at each other.

By the end of each afternoon, Kelly couldn't wait to rush back to the hotel, grab her bathing suit, and dash to the Jetties Beach for a long, bracing swim. She was not a natural swimmer, and so the full attention the waves called from her was therapeutic. Her mind rested while her body worked. Felicity wasn't interested in swimming, so she spent the time wading at the water's edge, dreamily drawing designs in the sand with her toes.

In the evenings, after showering and pulling on sundresses, the sisters strolled around town, listening to the street musicians, enjoying the fresh warm air. They ate leisurely meals at restaurants with outdoor patios, happy to be outside watching the sky turn periwinkle, listening to the music of other people's laughter.

It was good to hear people laugh.

The only time Kelly could think of Randall was when she finally said good night to Felicity, switched off her light, and snuggled down into the bliss of her cool, crisp sheets. The air conditioner hummed. In the bed next to hers, Felicity's breathing deepened, embellished with a tiny wheeze. *Randall,* Kelly would think, and then fall helplessly, exhaustedly, asleep.

Sometimes, Randall thought, the world seemed populated with fools.

Last night he'd driven out to visit his father.

"Hey, Dad!" he'd yelled, entering the kitchen.

No one answered.

"Dad?" he'd called again.

No answer. Heart pounding, Randall tore through the downstairs. He found Mont teetering at the top of a ladder in the library.

Fear had made him burst out: "Jesus Christ, Dad! What do you think you're doing?"

"What the hell does it look like I'm doing? I'm getting a book."

"Didn't you hear me call you?"

"Obviously not. No reason to get in such a lather."

Randall held his tongue while his father made his slow, faltering descent, both hands on the rungs, the thick book tucked under his arm.

Once Mont was safely on the floor, Randall said, with gritted teeth, "I suggest that you wait until I'm out here to get you anything you want from the top shelves."

"Oh, and why do you suggest that?" Mont demanded. "Because I'm a doddering incompetent old nincompoop who can't be trusted to do anything himself?"

With flushed face and trembling hands, Mont crossed the room to his chair and carefully, still sore from his fall, lowered himself into it. He clamped his mouth tight, staring straight ahead, fighting for dignity. Randall felt sick with guilt.

"I'm sorry, Dad. I didn't mean to imply that you're incompetent. I just worry about you, that's all." When his father still looked unappeased, he added, "Would I bring Tessa out here to live if I thought you weren't in apple pie order?"

That had soothed his father and smoothed things between them for the evening, but this morning Randall woke with his head full of doubts. *Should* he bring Tessa out to live with his father? Would she feel—would she *have to be*, at times—responsible for her grandfather? If Mont's hearing was going—would it be the blind leading the blind? How could Randall take care of them both and still work?

Now, the Tuesday before Labor Day weekend, his schedule was crowded with patients as old, stubborn, and foolhardy as his father, coming in with sunburns, sprains, and fractures from trying to do too many things with their grandchildren in the last hot days of summer. One of them, an elderly gentleman with a history of heart problems, was in the hospital now, recovering from a mild coronary infarction and a broken leg from *skateboarding*, for God's sake, with his visiting grandson.

Randall looked at his schedule for the day. No time for lunch unless his sent Pat out for a deli sandwich. His stomach sent up a warning flare of acid at the thought. Was he getting an ulcer? Probably. God knew he deserved one.

The private line on his phone lit up; he answered.

"Randall?" It was Lacey's voice, breathy and sweet. "I wondered if you'd like to come over for a Labor Day picnic this weekend."

"Sorry. I'm taking Tessa to visit her grandparents on Nantucket."

And I'm dreading it, he thought. Oh, he appreciated the eccentric charm of his in-laws, but they were not restful company, and right now, only a few days before his divorce hearing, with everything around him in chaos, he found himself craving tranquillity.

"Well, then, how about coming over for dinner tonight?" Lacey asked.

Randall closed his eyes and rubbed the bridge of his nose. Everything was too hard right now. Every decision he made, every word he spoke, seemed to carry the weight of injuring someone.

He would like to be with Kelly, but that wasn't possible. She wasn't in town.

The least he could do, he thought, was buy Lacey a nice meal to repay her for the one she'd prepared for him.

He said, "Let me take you out. We'll go to the Ritz."

Her voice buoyed with delight. "Oh, how lovely. What time?"

So he was making someone happy. "Eight? I'll phone you back if I can't get reservations."

"Perfect. Do you want to pick me up?"

The question seemed so innocent, so natural. Randall paused. "Sure," he said. "I'll pick you up." Which meant, he knew, that he'd be driving her back to her apartment.

• • •

As Randall followed Lacey across the dining room of the
Ritz to their table by the window, he knew every man who
watched her walk past would find himself fantasizing about
being alone with this woman whose full figure and sweet
face somehow combined Madonna and whore in one
knockout combination.

They settled at the table, ordered drinks. The hushed
elegance of the room, the discreet, ceremonious presence
of the waiters who appeared at his shoulder exactly when
he wished and retreated like smoke, soothed his psyche.
Here, he was off duty, free of the fears, pain, and foolish-
ness of his patients—and free of responsibility (for a while,
at least) for his father and his daughter, as well.

He was very tired.

"You look tired," Lacey said at that moment.

He focused on her. "I am."

Lacey wore an amazing garment seemingly made of
black Cling Wrap, cut very low in front. Last year, when
they were lovers, her long girly-girl curls had made her
look even younger than she was and rather insipid. Now
her severe new hair style gave her a sense of mystery, even
worldliness, and she had shadows beneath her eyes that
were oddly alluring. She looked like a woman who could
understand a complicated man.

They ordered. Oysters, salmon, crème brûlée. Excellent
wine. They kept the conversation light and impersonal, discussing hospital matters, movies, politics. He was aware
that Lacey asked him questions about topics he cared about
and read up on, so that he could hold forth, appearing wise.
She always had done this, and he knew why. Last year he'd
discovered a book hidden beneath her bedside table, a
woman's guide, promising that this sort of romantic strategy would help a woman lure and catch a man, as if he
were some kind of trout.

A man was what Lacey wanted. A man to whom she
could dedicate her life. Randall was not unaware of the

charms marriage to such a woman might hold. He'd been married to one professional, intelligent, career-dedicated woman. Now he considered: why would he want to be married to another? As his senses were lulled by the delicious food and the rich red wine, he admitted to himself that he'd been thrown when Kelly announced that she was a lawyer. A lawyer—that meant she was as ambitious and driven as Anne.

Lacey's laughter rippled around him like satin. She glowed. She was happy, here, now. She didn't want to save the world. She wanted simply to love a man and raise his children, to keep a happy home, as his mother had. Nutritious meals ready when he needed them, clothes tended to, house shining, friends entertained, children bathed, dressed, read to. True, his mother had had her painting, but her husband and children had always held first place in her life.

And what about Tessa? What kind of woman would be best for Tessa? The question gleamed like a vein of gold in Randall's thoughts. Tessa already had a mother who provided a role model of a highly active, successful, professional woman. Kelly would be more of the same, wouldn't she? All the traveling she was doing, for example, gone for a week at a time—what kind of stepmother would she make?

Lacey would be a storybook mother. Always home, cooking nutritious meals, making sure everyone's clothes were clean and organized, eager—truly *fulfilled*—to hear about the accomplishments of her husband and children. Tessa and Randall would be the center of her world, and that, Randall knew, from being the center of his mother's world, built up a child's sense of self like nothing else could.

Certainly, Randall thought, Lacey's example would encourage Tessa to eat.

The meal was over. The bill in its leather folder was presented; Randall brought out his credit card. Lacey leaned forward, her bell of hair slipping against her cheeks. Eating had worn away her lipstick, and her lips gleamed with oil and moisture, as pale and denuded as if from kissing. Her breasts swelled toward him.

"Let's have coffee at my place," she suggested.

He nodded, far too relaxed to disagree.

They seemed to move seamlessly from dining room to car to Lacey's apartment, where he found himself sobering up slightly at the sight of all her dolls and stuffed animals.

But Tessa would like the dolls, the stuffed animals.

"Come stretch out on my bed," Lacey invited. "I'll rub your back."

A back rub: irresistible. Nearly in a stupor he went into the bedroom and let himself be divested of his clothing slowly, tenderly, by Lacey. Her touch was gentle but firm. She unbuckled his belt and slid his trousers down. Somewhere in the distance it seemed a warning bell rang, but all he had to do was turn his head against the pillow and that sound faded, as he was lost to Lacey's ministrations.

When they first arrived on Sunday night, Kelly phoned Randall to tell him where she was staying, but managed to reach only his answering machine. She left a message, and when she returned to her room on Monday, found a message from him. They kept missing each other, and with Felicity hanging around, it was impossible to find a moment of privacy to have a real conversation.

Finally, on Thursday evening, while Felicity was in the shower, Kelly dialed his number and Randall himself answered.

"Kelly. Thank God. What a week. I thought we'd never make contact."

The sound of his voice smoothed and soothed the tips of every frazzled nerve end.

She asked, "How's your father?"

"Physically, fine. Emotionally, he's pretty battered. The fall frightened him. Embarrassed him, really. He's always been so strong and capable. Now he feels old, weak, foolish. He's being pretty tough on himself. How are you?"

"I'm good. Tired, but good. There's so much I'd like to tell you about. I can't wait to see you Sunday."

"That's a problem. I've promised Tessa I'd take her to Nantucket to visit her mother's parents. They're rather eccentric and don't often issue invitations, so we've got to go while we can."

"When are you coming?"

"Sometime Friday."

Kelly's heart leapt with hope, then crashed. "You'll be *here* . . . but we're leaving the island Friday night!" She thought aloud: "I could stay, perhaps, but I've got to get Felicity organized for school. Besides, it's Labor Day weekend. All the hotels are full."

"It's probably just as well. I'll have to devote all my attention to Tessa and her grandparents. They're not exactly *neglectful,* just rather daffy. And it will be a good opportunity for me to spend a substantial hunk of time with Tessa."

"That will be nice for you. And for her."

"And what about you and your half sister? What's happening there? She's moving in with you?"

"Yes. She's with me now, actually. Taking a shower in the other room. Her father and his new honey are moving to Los Angeles, with great dreams of René finally, at the age of sixty, becoming a movie star. Felicity didn't want to go with them, and I don't blame her. So—"

The bathroom door opened. A cloud of steam billowed out into the room and with it Felicity, swathed in a cluster of towels. If Kelly wanted a shower, she thought bemusedly, she'd have only a washcloth left to dry off with.

"I'll tell you more when I see you."

"When do you think that will be?" Randall asked.

"When do you get back from Nantucket?"

"Monday night. Monday's Labor Day."

"Ah. Right." Kelly tried to concentrate while Felicity moved around their small room, dropping damp towels, digging through clothes piled haphazardly in a drawer, looking for her pajamas with one hand while flicking the remote control with the other. "Felicity. Could you keep the volume down, please? I'm on the phone." The girl complied, still pawing through her rumpled clothing like a dog after a bone. "Your pajamas," Kelly reminded her, "are probably under your pillow where you left them this morning."

"Oh. Thanks." Felicity snagged them from the bed and took them with her into the bathroom. She left the door open.

"What were we talking about?"

"Our schedules."

"Right. Felicity's school starts this Tuesday."

"Tessa's in a private school. It doesn't begin for another week."

"Tuesday morning I start—"

"Just a minute," Randall interrupted. "I'll be right there, Dad!" he called. "Kelly. I'm sorry. Dad needs me. Look. I'll call you Monday night, and we'll make arrangements, okay?"

"Okay, but—I have a lot to tell you, Randall."

"And I, you. I'm sorry this is all so complicated—*I'm coming*!" In a rush, Randall said, "Kelly, trust me. We'll work this all out. We have to. I think I love you."

He hung up, and Kelly was left, astonished, looking at the phone buzzing in her hand.

"Wanna watch television?" Felicity asked, and without waiting for an answer, she grabbed the remote and clicked the volume up.

"Hello, Tessa," Dr. Lawrence said. "Thanks for coming in."

"You're welcome, Dr. Lawrence." Tessa was the very model of politeness as she crossed the room to settle in the chair across from the psychiatrist's desk. With the flat of her hands, she smoothed her pink linen sundress over her legs. Her blond hair, brushed to a sheen, lay neatly, held back by a silk headband that matched her dress.

"How are you today, Tessa?"

Meekly, she replied, "Fine."

He held two pencils today, one in each hand. He tapped them on the edge of his desk, seven quick beats: *Do me a fa-vor: Drop dead.* "Just fine?"

Worriedly, she asked, "What's wrong with *fine*?"

"Not a thing, if that's the truth. But I'd think you might have a few other feelings going on. Your parents are getting divorced. It's the end of the summer. School's going to start pretty soon, and you don't know where you'll be living."

She looked back down at her lap and said nothing.

"I've met with quite a few of the people in your life, Tessa. Your parents, of course, and your grandfather, and Carmen, and your minister. They are all good, caring people, and they all love you."

"I know," Tessa replied quietly. "I know I'm very fortunate."

"Fortunate." Dr. Lawrence beat another riff on his desk. "Yes. That's true. Your family is financially well off, your parents are educated, they both love you. Still, Tessa, you're allowed to admit that things aren't perfect. You're allowed to be angry—or sad. And it might be helpful to you if you told me about some of those feelings. I might be able to help you in ways those closer to you can't."

Tessa didn't reply.

"Okay." He sighed, leaned back in his chair, and slowly swiveled in a complete circle. When he'd settled back in place, he said, "You seem sad today, Tessa."

"I'm just tired."

"Tired. Didn't you sleep well last night?"

She shrugged.

"Sometimes our emotions make us tired. Anger or sadness, if we try to hide it or stuff it down inside us, that can make us exhausted."

She didn't respond.

"You might, for example, feel angry at your parents for getting a divorce. Or you might feel sad about that."

Tessa pleated her skirt with her fingers. "Not really."

"You're not sad? Not angry?"

She shook her head.

"Okay, then." He beat the pencils against the desk and then laid them carefully on either side of his blotter. "Tell me how you do feel."

"I told you. Tired."

"Tired and *worried*?" When she didn't reply he said, "Tired, but *happy*? Like someone who's just won a race?"

She glanced at him. "No."

He squinted his eyes, considering. "Tired but *determined*? Like someone starting a race?"

Her head lifted. Tears welled up in her eyes. "I wish—"

"Yes?"

"I wish, I wish I *could* feel like I was starting a race. I wish I could feel *strong*. Tough."

"Aren't you strong?"

"Not really. Not like I want to be."

"How strong would you like to be?"

Tessa chewed her nail. "Like Jodie Foster in *Candleshoe*? Did you see that movie?"

"I think so. Refresh my memory."

"She was an orphan in New York. She was tough. She played basketball with guys. She was my age, twelve. And she got taken to this castle in England to find a sea captain's treasure that was hidden there, and she and her friends— they were kids, too—they found the fortune and beat up the bad guys and saved the castle for the good grandmother." Leaning forward, she continued, "And did you see *Fly Away Home*?"

"The one about the girl who raises the Canadian geese?"

"Yes, that's the one. Remember, when the police officer tried to clip a baby goose's wing, she hit him on the head with a pan? And *she* learned to fly an airplane so she could teach her geese to fly."

"That's true, Tessa, but—"

"They all fix things!" Tessa cried. "Even in cartoons, like *The Little Mermaid Two*—Melody is just my age, and she doesn't think her mother understands her either, and Melody is the one who saves everyone! She grabs the trident from the evil Morgana! She saves her grandfather; she saves her friends!"

"All right. I get the idea." Dr. Lawrence frowned. "But those are movies, Tessa. The Little Mermaid is a cartoon character, and a fictional one. Those aren't real girls."

"I *know* that!" she snapped. "I'm not *crazy*." She put her hand to her mouth. "I'm sorry. I didn't mean to sound rude." She shrank back into her chair. All animation left her face. She smoothed her skirt.

Dr. Lawrence cocked his head and blew a breathy little whistle. "You know what I think? I think you *are* determined. I think you have a plan to fix things."

She looked at him.

"Have you thought of a way to get your parents back together?"

Tessa pulled a face. "I told you I'm not crazy."

"Well then, what *are* you plotting?"

"I'm not *plotting* anything."

He sat quietly, letting the silence build.

Tessa sighed. "I just—I've just decided that I'm going to help my mom."

"Okay. Good. How are you going to do that?"

"Well, she's really sad that Dad's leaving. Dad's happy, plus he's going to live with Grandpops, so *he* already has someone on his side. My mother needs me. She's really happy that I'm going to go door-to-door campaigning with her. She really likes it when I wear dorky dresses like this. It will really help her if I'm good, so I'm going to be good. Really good."

Dr. Lawrence frowned. "What about you, Tessa? Will 'being good' make you happy?"

She wriggled in her chair. "I think so."

"I'm not so sure. It sounds to me like an awful burden you're taking upon yourself. It's not the best thing, at times like this, to hide your emotions, Tessa. It's all right to be angry, and scared, and worried. And you're a child, remember, not an adult. You're not responsible for your parents. They're responsible for you."

Tessa dropped her eyes. "I'm really tired," she said meekly. "And my stomach hurts."

"Are you going to throw up?"

"No. No, it just aches."

"Does it ache a lot these days?"

"I guess."

"Have you told your mother you'd like to meet your birth parents?"

Tessa stared at her lap. In a small voice, she said, "No."

"Are you planning to tell her?"

Shrugging: "I don't need to anymore."

Dr. Lawrence leaned back in his chair. After a while he said, "Tessa, I'm going on vacation tomorrow. I'll be back next week, after Labor Day, and I'll be speaking to the judge during your parents' divorce, but I probably won't see you again. I'd like to suggest something, and I'd like you to think about this seriously. I think you should try to persuade your parents, both parents, to arrange counseling for you."

Tessa looked up, alarmed.

"I don't think you're crazy. I think you're a smart, good, interesting girl. And I think you've got a lot of pressures weighing in on you from all sides. Too much pressure for one twelve-year-old girl to handle alone. I think it would help you a lot to see a counselor during the next few months, to help you sort out your emotions. Whatever happens in court, you've got a lot of changes coming your way. And this idea of yours of being good—well, frankly, it bothers me."

"Why?"

"Well, let's see. For example, you've told me you like

to ride horses. Your mother's afraid of horses. Does being good mean you won't ride horses anymore? Not even your grandfather's old nags?"

Tessa put her hands to her stomach.

"Tessa, no one can be perfect. No one can be totally responsible for someone else's happiness." He leaned forward. "And you are just a kid. A smart, clever, fortunate kid, but still just a kid. Your parents are pretty engrossed in their own life changes right now. You need someone impartial to talk things over with. You really do."

"Are you going to tell my mother that?"

"Yes. Your father, too."

"Can it be you?"

"No, honey. But I can recommend someone. There are lots of great counselors around." He looked at his clock. "Time's up. I'll walk out and say hi to your mom."

Tessa rose and walked toward the door.

"Tessa," Dr. Lawrence said.

She looked at him over her shoulder.

"Tessa, you don't have to go through this alone."

"All right, Dr. Lawrence," she responded dutifully.

Friday evening was calm and clear as the fast ferry sped over the deep water to Hyannis. Kelly sat out on deck, eyes closed, head tipped back to receive as many of the sun's rays as possible this late in the day. Inside, like Dracula, Felicity hulked away from the sun, reading a paperback novel by Scott Turow.

The boat was crowded, which seemed odd to Kelly—who would leave Nantucket on a lovely summer's eve? Bits of conversation drifted her way, answering her question: people who had to get back to work after a month or a week in paradise.

Kelly had not come to the conclusion that Nantucket was paradise. It seemed, in fact, as subject to stresses and flaws as any other place of habitation. This week she'd seen two bitter divorces, the first of a family of amazing wealth and stature in the community, the other involving a nearly destitute family. All the people involved were as angry and vengeful as anyone living in what Nantucketers called "the real world." It was not simply location that made a place idyllic.

Or was it?

She and Randall had met in a cemetery, away from the troubles, pressures, and eyes of the people they knew. Was their relationship no more than that of a hothouse orchid, coming to life only under ideal conditions? If so, it was about to be brought out into the full heat, glare, and vicissitudes of real weather, and then what would happen? Within a month of their meeting she had acquired, without foreknowledge or desire, a half sister who needed a home and a strong hand. Randall's father had fallen; who knew what consequences that fall would have for the father's life and those around him?

And what did it mean, really, that she and Randall had met at all? They had met at their mothers' graves. She was certain that his adopted child was the daughter she had carried in her own body and given up for adoption. The workings of the universe were mysterious and complex: perhaps they had been moving toward one another all along.

The ferry dropped speed as it entered the long Hyannis harbor. All around her, people prepared to disembark, gathering up duffel bags, backpacks, shopping bags with Nantucket logos. Like a giant creature stirring all its tentacles, they congregated in long lines streaming toward the exit. Kelly's suitcase was on one of the luggage racks that would be wheeled off only after all the passengers were off; it made no sense to hurry. Instead of joining the crush shoving toward the stairs and the ramp, Kelly went to the side of the boat, leaned on the railing, and looked down.

Rumbling, the ferry slid neatly into its slip. The crew, handsome young men in maroon polo shirts, fastened ropes, fixed the ramp in place. Couples hurried out of the ticket office, other couples raced in, taxis pulled into the parking lot, their doors flying wide to disgorge more passengers. Dogs barked, children cried, college kids erupted with laughter. From behind a rope a line of people waiting to board the ferry snaked along the edge of the dock. From Kelly's vantage point, they seemed like a pointillist painting, dots and blurs of color.

Suddenly, one person drew her eye.

Randall.

His silver-blond hair blazed like a fire, catching the sun's light. His clothing was less casual than the other travelers'; while everyone else wore shorts or jeans or khakis, Randall wore light gray trousers, a yellow-and-white-striped button-down shirt, a blue tie loosened around his neck. With one finger he'd hooked his suit jacket over his shoulder. No doubt he'd worked until the very last minute.

Next to him stood a girl in black jeans and an oversize navy cotton shirt that hung nearly to her knees. Against the dark fabric, the girl's hair shone like sunlight. She was thin, tall, gawky, a baby giraffe of a girl.

The sight of the child slammed her square in her belly. *This was her child.*

Randall bent to speak to his daughter. Tessa nodded her head. Now passengers were coming off the Hy-Line, tromping single file down the ramp onto the shore. Passengers waiting to embark shuffled and dipped, hefting their bags, pushing, eager.

The girl tipped her head back, looking up at the boat. A beautiful girl with a level brow and a patient expression, she scanned the decks idly, her gaze moving past Kelly's without hesitation.

"Kelly? What are you doing? Come on!"

Kelly jumped, startled.

"Kelly?"

She caught her breath. Of course. Felicity.

"Are you seasick?" Felicity asked. "You've gone all white."

"No, I'm fine. I'm coming." Hoisting her shoulderbag, she followed her half sister down the stairs and across the stern of the boat to the small metal ramp leading to the walkways. They stepped onto shore amid a crush of people hugging one another, searching for their luggage, chasing after errant toddlers.

Kelly turned, trying to catch sight of Randall and Tessa, and found their shining bright heads in the advancing line. He was bending to her, giving her a ticket.

Kelly started to call out his name, then suddenly changed her mind. All at once she didn't want Randall to see her. She wanted to be free to stare shamelessly, avidly, without interruption, at Tessa.

The girl *was* thin. She looked tall for her age; perhaps she'd be as tall as Kelly. Other kids her age fidgeted and squirmed, unable to stand still, but Tessa was very still, shoulders squared, chin high, very self-contained. She seemed older than her age. Kelly yearned to protect the girl, to encircle her in the safety of her arms so that Tessa could drop her vigilance and *relax*. And be a child.

"Kelly?" Felicity tugged on her sleeve. "Let's go."

The boarding line began to move. Randall's bright head and Tessa's pale one were absorbed in the crowd filing up the ramp.

Tessa *was* her child. Kelly had no doubts. In her heart, longing blazed, stronger than logic or law.

TWELVE

ON SUNDAY, A HURRICANE OFF the shores of North Carolina drove high winds laden with flooding rain through all of New England. Summer vanished in the great storm's power. The temperature plummeted. Windows banged. Wind screamed around the corners of houses and roared down chimneys. Petals and leaves were ripped from flowers and trees, and carried sideways through the churning air.

Dutifully Anne dressed warmly and took herself off to church, even though she disliked going by herself and knew the attendance would be sparse on this miserable Sunday in the middle of Labor Day weekend.

Afterward, she met Rebecca and Eleanor and a few other hard-core party supporters for lunch in their favorite Cambridge bar and grill. They sat around a circular table tucked off in a corner, discussing strategy and plans and flaws and assets, making lists on napkins (Anne made lists in her Palm Pilot), plotting, laughing, while rain thundered on the roof. It was cozy. It was, Anne felt, very much like a kind of home for her, and her political allies a kind of family. Certainly a more trustworthy family than the one into which she'd been born or had married into.

Finally they adjourned, forcing themselves out into the dark afternoon. She couldn't help but be aware, as she walked through the crowded room, of the admiring glances that followed her. Strangers nodded to her, said hello, gave her the thumbs-up. It was early yet, of course, but all signs were positive. It looked very much like Anne would be elected, and then she'd really be able to dig in and accomplish something.

At the door, Anne tied the belt of her raincoat around her slender waist, flipped the hood up over her sleek hair, bade farewell to her companions, and ran, avoiding puddles as best she could, to the shelter of her BMW. It was so dark that when she clicked her key holder to unlock the door, the lights blinked on automatically.

She loved her luxurious automobile, and she relaxed on the leather seat for a moment, catching her breath, turning the windshield wipers and defogger on. She was energized by the war talk at lunch, by her run through the rain. She felt confident, attractive, ready to take on the world. Randall and Tessa were still in Nantucket and wouldn't be coming back until tomorrow. What could she do with the rest of the day?

Now, she realized, was the perfect time to drop in on Mont. Have a little chat with him. See if she could win him over to her side. Certainly it was worth a try. Anne had never felt comfortable with Madeline—the two women just didn't like one another, although they both had tried to hide this—but Mont had always been kind to Anne, and complimentary.

She should take him something. Chocolates? No, it was Madeline who had liked chocolates. Madeline, the pig, had had a real sweet tooth. Mont liked cheese, and pâté, salty things. She stopped at Dean & DeLuca and bought a rich Stilton in a pot, a wrapped cloth bundle of goose liver pâté, and crackers.

She drove to Route 2 through the flooding rain, her wipers flicking rapidly as passing trucks drenched her with their spray. When was the last time she'd seen Mont? Hard to believe, but it had been at least three months ago—at Madeline's funeral.

What a grim time that had been. Randall had asked Anne to allow him to take Tessa to the funeral; it was, he'd pointed out, *his* mother who had died. But Anne had refused. Death was a serious matter, the kind of traumatic

event that necessitated delicacy and restraint, especially
when dealing with a girl of Tessa's tender years. Mont and
Randall were both just too emotional right now, Anne had
argued. Look at the way Randall had broken down and
wept when he came to tell Tessa her grandmother had died.
Really, he should have shown more self-restraint. He could
have frightened Tessa. As it was, the girl had been nearly
savage in her grief, dissolving in an orgy of sobs and collapsing in her room like some Victorian waif, pale, listless,
lying on her bed with her face turned to the wall. For God's
sake! Anne had wanted to yell, Madeline was old. Old people die!

Anne had held her tongue, ministering dutifully to
Tessa's dramatic misery. She'd sent a lavish bouquet from
herself and Tessa to the mortuary. She'd bought Tessa a
nice black skirt and blouse for the funeral; she'd taken
Tessa to the funeral, the mawkish graveside service and the
reception at the farm, comporting herself with the necessary
attitude of sorrow.

It had been an awkward time. She and Randall had
separated, were living apart, but were not yet divorced, and
so she was both part of the family and detached, so, not
certain of the etiquette, she'd written Mont a note of con-
dolence on her finest, stiffest stationery, and insisted that
Tessa write one, as well.

So Mont should have no reason to behave without ci-
vility to her, Anne decided. It was a rainy day. His son and
grandchild were visiting her parents. He was probably
alone, probably lonely. He'd welcome Anne in, make a pot
of tea, or even, perhaps, offer her a bit of Scotch. It was
cool enough today for a small fire. They'd sit in the living
room, talk about old times, and she would be charming, for
she could be, when she set her mind to it, very charming.

She could see the scene quite clearly in her mind. She
could almost hear the old man say, why, yes, when she put
it *that* way, it *would* be better for a young girl to live with
her mother than with two men.

Right now, Anne realized, Randall and Tessa were

with *her* parents on Nantucket. It was nicely *symmetrical*, that Anne should visit Mont.

The farm looked rather bleak in the rain. The horses stood still as statues on the field, resigned to the downpour. All Madeline's beloved perennials, her mums and morning glories and climbing roses, were drained of color by the lightless sky, and even the trees drooped with the weight of water on their leaves, bending defeated on either side of the lane.

The house itself was drenched in darkness, except for one light burning on the second floor. Mont and Madeline's bedroom, Anne remembered, with those hideous rag rugs that Madeline's mother had made, which Madeline still used and treasured. Why people who had plenty of money chose to live like peasants, Anne could not understand.

At least those vile dogs weren't here to jump on her, muddying her coat, making runs in her hose. She parked as close as she could get to the door; then she jumped out of the car and raced to the house.

She hammered on the door and tried the knob. It would be open—they never locked their doors, ever. Hurriedly she stepped into the shelter of the mudroom, thinking, as always, how bizarre it was that people who had money and not inconsiderable taste—Madeline had been an artist, after all, and a decent one at that—would allow the world to achieve its first vision of their residence in a grubby hall with ancient coats hanging off wooden pegs and abandoned boots covered with mud and manure scattered willy-nilly over the cement floor.

Hurriedly she went into the kitchen.

"Mont?" Stripping off her raincoat, she draped it over a chair. She didn't especially want it touching any of those old garments in the mudroom; they were still undoubtedly covered with dog hair or horse hair.

"Mont?" she called again. "It's Anne."

The kitchen was cluttered but clean. Clean enough. Not up to Anne's standards, of course, but not filthy, either. Odd things in odd places—shoes on the table—but it had always been so in this house. Anne touched her hand to the kettle on the stove. It was just barely warm to the touch.

"Mont?"

"Anne? Is that you?"

Turning, she saw Randall's father coming toward her from the gloom of the hall. Behind him, the door to the library stood open and light fell in a lozenge onto the hall floor. Mont limped as he came toward her. He *shuffled*.

Something about Mont made all the small hairs on Anne's arms stand on end. Something about Mont was creepy.

He stepped into the watery half-light of the kitchen. "Anne. What a surprise. I was reading—"

He was wearing a woman's robe. A pink terry-cloth robe with white piping. White flowers on the chest pocket. His bristly neck, with the Adam's apple shuddering inside its tunnel, rose from his naked chest, a few sparse crinkled gray hairs curling upward.

"Oh." Mont stopped, looking down at himself. "I was outside, fastening up the tomatoes against the wind, and I got completely soaked. I just grabbed this . . ."

Anne looked down. His feet were tucked into a woman's pink slippers.

Mont tried to smile, but only managed an apologetic grimace. "Anne . . . you caught me by surprise . . ."

"Why, you're *sick*," Anne gasped. Horror flared up inside her like a bonfire. "You're . . . you're wearing *women's* clothing!"

"It's just Madeline's—"

"You filthy, perverted old man!" She backed away from him, snatching her raincoat off the back of the chair.

"No—for God's sake, Anne—" He clutched the neck of the robe tightly in his gnarled bony hands.

"And to think I had actually considered letting Tessa live with you!"

"Anne, *please*—"

Her lip curled in contempt. "I'll tell my lawyer about this. I'll tell the judge. I'll see that you're never allowed near Tessa again."

Burning with indignation, she turned on her heel, slammed the door to the mudroom back against the wall, and ran out into the rain, where she threw herself into her car, stabbed the key into the ignition, gunned the motor, and spun away from the house. Her body shuddered in a rush of euphoria—the fear, consternation, the righteous fury felt glorious.

And now, Anne thought triumphantly, Randall wouldn't have a chance in hell of gaining custody of Tessa.

Even though rain poured down Sunday morning, Kelly took Felicity with her to visit their mother's grave. The night before they'd bought a sheaf of fresh lilies, which they laid in front of their mother's stone. Now they stood in the soft grass at the side of the grave, sheltered slightly by the trees. Kelly wore a raincoat; Felicity, an old yellow slicker of Kelly's. Kelly held an umbrella over their heads. There was something oddly comforting about the rain, its companionable tappings on the leaves and umbrella, the way it cooled the heated world, making it green.

"It's nice here," Felicity said. She'd come without her Goth makeup, and her bare face made her seem innocent and young.

Kelly smiled. "Yes. It is."

"Peaceful. Safe."

Kelly nodded.

"Kelly?"

"Yes?"

"What do you think happens when you die?"

"I don't know, honey. No one knows."

"But what do you *think*?" When Kelly didn't respond immediately, Felicity said, "I think your spirit is set free. I think you get to keep *you* but you don't have to remain trapped in your body. You don't have to worry about get-

ting too fat or being too uncoordinated to swing on the
parallel bars in gym. You don't have to brush your teeth
and you can't get yeast infections. But you can fly if you
want to, all over the sky, looking down on everything, and
you can swim, too, under the ocean with all the fish. Or
you can sit on a mountain in the Himalayas and look at the
snow but not be cold. And you can curl up anywhere and
feel safe, and you're never lonely, because spirits are all
around you."

"Sounds very nice," Kelly said.

"And there won't be any sex, because sex makes people act like morons."

Kelly laughed.

"And you can see God whenever you want to, and God
will look just like you, a woman in a judge's robe."

Startled, Kelly demurred. "I'm hardly godlike, Felicity."

"But you are! You're wise, and you're tough, but
you're kind. And generous." Tears came to her eyes, and
all of a sudden her face crumbled. "Kelly, I was so *scared*.
Mom's dead, and Dad's an idiot. I didn't have anybody to
take care of me. It took so much courage to knock on your
door. What would have happened if you hadn't been there
or if you'd told me to go away?"

Kelly put her arms around the girl and pulled her close.
"It's okay. I *was* there. I didn't tell you to go away. I'll
always be there for you. I'll take care of you."

Felicity said, "I hope Mom can hear us."

Kelly looked at the quartz rock, then up at the sky. "I
hope so, too."

They went to a mall afterward, for a gigantic breakfast
that provided them with the energy to shop for school
clothes for Felicity. The girl was ebullient, nearly giddy
with the pleasure of buying new clothes, whatever she
wanted, from wherever she wanted, and Kelly realized that
one of life's greatest pleasures, even richer than that of

getting what you want in life, was being able, quite simply, to give someone you love what they want.

Afterward they brought home huge sub sandwiches, which they devoured in front of a video.

The Weather Channel said it was raining in Boston, but on Nantucket the sun shone down vigorously, making it a perfect day for the beach. Late that afternoon, Sarah, Herbert, Randall, and Tessa spilled out of the Range Rover, lugging picnic baskets, beach towels, blankets, umbrellas. Everything was covered with sand.

"Toss it all in the garage," Herbert directed. "We'll sort it out later."

They entered the house by the breezeway. Brownie sat up in her expensive doggie bed, wagging his tail and barking.

"Oh, my darling boobieboo," Sarah squealed, rushing to hug the animal. "People are so unkind, not wanting a sweetie-pie pumpkin like you at the beach."

"She is a pit bull," Herbert reminded her. "If you had a small child, you wouldn't want Brownie around, either."

"That is so generalist of you," Sarah said.

"You can have the first shower," Randall told his daughter.

"Thanks, Dad." She raced from the room, up the back stairs.

"I'll use the outdoor shower," Herbert announced. "Got enough sand in my suit to start my own beach."

"I'll make drinkies," Sarah chimed. "Randall, go on and use our bathroom. There's enough hot water. I don't need a shower right away." She hadn't removed her brilliant turquoise shift at the beach, or her pink rubber-and-sequin sand shoes.

"Thanks, Sarah." Randall headed up the stairs.

Sarah ambled contentedly around the kitchen, filling the silver ice bucket, setting out cheese and crackers, spreading anchovy paste on toast points, giving one to

Brownie for every one she set on the silver tray. She hummed. Life was good. It had been a perfect Sunday. That her own daughter was not there did not diminish the perfection.

At that very moment, the phone rang. Sarah glared at it. She knew without a doubt who it was, as if her thoughts had wafted over the distance to trigger Anne's dialing finger.

Sighing, she answered.

"Mother."

"Hello, Anne."

"How's Tessa?"

"*I'm* fine, dear, and how are you?" Sarah bent to let Brownie lick anchovy paste off her finger.

"Mother, I don't have time for games."

"Common courtesy—"

"Mother, may I please speak to Randall?"

"I think he's just gotten in the shower, dear, but I'll check. Actually, I've got the portable phone with me, so we can have a little chat while I go upstairs. Brownie, you come with me. I don't want you eating the cheese. How's your campaign going?"

"Very well. I only wish my home life were as pleasant."

"Remember the yin/yang thingy, Anne. Nothing's ever perfect."

"I wish you would take me seriously sometimes, Mother."

"I do, darling. Brownie, not now! Randall?" Huffing and puffing, Sarah reached the second floor. She peeked into the master bedroom, not wanting to startle Randall in his birthday suit.

"Did you call me?" Randall stepped out of the dressing room that had been converted long ago to a guest bedroom. His thick hair was wet from the shower, slicked back and gleaming. He'd pulled on a pair of Nantucket red shorts and a striped rugby shirt.

"My, you're a beautiful man," Sarah told him. She handed him the phone. "Anne. For you." She rolled her eyes at him and walked away, Brownie waddling in her wake.

"Randall!"

Anne's voice was sharp yet exuberant, the way it always was when she was on one of her holy crusades. Randall wanted to moan. "Hello, Anne."

"Randall, we have to talk."

"All right."

"Why didn't you tell me about your father?"

His chest tightened. "Dad? What's wrong? Is he okay?"

"No, he's not *okay!*"

"Anne—"

"He's lost his mind. I can't believe you've let Tessa see him."

"What are you talking about?"

"Don't be coy with me."

"I'm not being coy, Anne. Honest to God, I don't know what you're referring to."

"I'm referring to the fact that your father wears women's clothing."

Randall collapsed in the chair by the fireplace. "When did you see him?"

"This morning. I dropped by without phoning first, and I'm glad I did! It was raining, I didn't have any meetings, and I wanted to talk with him about Tessa. About your idea of living out there and having Tessa live with you. As if living with two men isn't bad enough, I found Mont in a woman's robe and slippers."

"Anne. They're Madeline's. Have some compassion. He's having a hard time dealing with Mother's death."

"So you did know he's wearing women's clothing."

"He isn't *wearing women's clothing.* For God's sake."

"Don't swear at me, Randall."

"Look, Anne. Dad is perfectly sane. It's just the robe he wears, and only when he's feeling low. He had a fall from a ladder last week, and it shook him up. He's old, he's got lots of aches and pains."

"That doesn't excuse him wearing a woman's robe."

"No. I realize that. And he's never worn it around Tessa. But if he did, Tessa wouldn't mind."

"That shows how little you know about young women!"

Sarah sailed into the room, carrying a gin and tonic. "Thought you might need this," she whispered.

"Thanks," Randall told her.

"What?" Anne snapped.

"Your mother gave me a drink. I was thanking her."

"Oh, you're all so very chummy there, aren't you? Well, enjoy yourself, because Tuesday morning in court I'm going to present the judge with an irrefutable argument. I'm sure even the most liberal judge will agree that a twelve-year-old girl shouldn't be around an old man who wears women's clothing!" Anne slammed the phone down.

Late Sunday evening, Kelly opened her apartment door to Jason's knock. She wore an old baggy shirt, ripped jeans, battered sneakers, and no makeup. She was trying to look unattractive, and she felt pretty sure she'd succeeded.

"Jason, hi. Thanks for coming." Her voice sounded high and pinched; she reminded herself to slow down. Take deep breaths.

"You don't have to thank me, Kelly." Leaning forward, he kissed her cheek. He smelled like salt, sunshine, and soap, the scents of a healthy male who's spent the weekend on the water.

She moved away. "Drink?"

"Sure. Vodka tonic?"

"I'll make two."

Jason looked around. The apartment was crowded with furniture from Felicity's house, as the far end of the room had been transformed into Felicity's space. Kelly's grandparents' bed stood against the wall, surrounded by boxes of Felicity's belongings, everything covered with flamboyant silk scarves and spreads from thrift shops.

"Where's Felicity?"

"In my room. Sleeping."

"Asleep at this time of the day?"

"Teenagers seem to have an infinite capacity for sleeping. Besides, she's had a rough time recently. Her mother died, her father dumped her, she's had to squeeze into my space, and Tuesday she starts at a new school."

Kelly brought the tall glasses, tinkling with ice, fragrant with slices of lime, to the sofa, which had been moved closer to the kitchen.

"Thanks." Taking his glass, Jason settled in the middle of the sofa.

"To your health," Kelly toasted, sitting in the armchair at right angles to the sofa. She took a long drink. She was so nervous, she felt like grabbing the bottle and pouring it all straight down her throat.

Jason said, "What's up? You sounded very serious when you phoned yesterday. I had to give up a day of sailing to drive up from the Cape."

"I'm sorry I inconvenienced you. But I felt I had to talk with you immediately."

"How formal you are."

Kelly nodded. "Yes. Well, I suppose, in a way, this is a formal occasion." She set her glass on the coffee table. She took a deep breath. Here it was, she thought: the moment of truth. Right up to this moment she could still change her mind. In just a second, it would be too late. Tears sprang to her eyes, surprising her. He did not deserve to be hurt. But he did deserve someone who truly loved him.

"Jason, I can't marry you."

He frowned. "You're kidding."

"I'm not kidding." She had not realized it would be so painful. "I'm so sorry."

An angry flush rose up his neck. "You're breaking off with me?"

"Yes." Working the diamond ring off her finger, she held it between her thumb and finger, toward Jason.

His face burned crimson. Hoarsely he demanded, "Can you give me one good reason why?"

"I'm so sorry," she told him, and as gently as she could, whispered, "I don't love you." She set the ring on the coffee table.

"Jesus!" Jason flinched, as if she'd hit him. He glared at her, and seeing something close to pity in her eyes, slammed his glass onto the table, rose, and strode across the room. There was little room to pace in, however, and frustrated, he turned back. "Jesus Christ, Kelly!"

She felt like someone who had kicked an animal. "Listen to me, Jason. I admire you. I like you. I think you're absolutely brilliant and wonderful fun, but I don't love you, not like whoever marries you should love you."

Collapsing on the sofa, he rubbed his hands over his face. "Then why in God's name did you accept my proposal?"

"Mostly, because I thought it would make my mother happy."

Jason groaned.

"And I was so flattered by the way you pursued me. It was terribly seductive. And I do think we've been good friends. And I do feel fond of you."

"Fond!"

"Jason, listen to me. I've been afraid of love all my life because of what it made my mother do. I thought marrying you would be the right thing to do, because with you I don't feel swept away, overwhelmed with passion, all of that. But now I know I do want that, and I want you to have someone who feels that, too—madly, insanely, *painfully* in love."

"How kind of you."

"I'm so sorry. I feel rotten. I'll miss you. I'll miss your mother—"

"She won't miss you," Jason snarled.

Kelly sat back in her chair. "What?"

"She's *never* liked you, Kelly. She's always thought you were beneath me. And she's been quite amused that you're so dim you haven't even suspected this."

"Oh," she whispered. "Wow." She shook her head. How could she be a judge when she couldn't even see the truth in the people closest to her?

Jason reached out and took her hand. "Sorry, Kelly. That was nasty of me. I guess I just wanted to hurt you back."

Stunned, she said, "It's all right, Jason. It doesn't matter."

He winced. "*Touché.*" He dropped her hand, stood, and walked across the room. Slowly, thinking it through aloud, he said, "I think you're confused, Kelly. I think your appointment to the judiciary, and your mother dying, and your half sister showing up, all this family stuff, wanting to find your daughter—I think it's all confused you. I think you're lost, and you don't know it, and I think you're going to wake up some morning and realize you need me."

"That's probably true," she told him.

She'd spoken too quickly, too effortlessly, just wanting to appease him. He squinted his eyes at her, alert and curious, a creature of the hunt sniffing out a lie.

"Is there someone else?" he demanded.

She shook her head, unable to meet his eyes.

Jason reached down, picked up the ring, and, holding it in his palm, studied its glitter. He waited for her to speak. When she didn't, he shoved the ring in his pocket. "If you ever do need me, Kelly, don't bother to call, because I won't come back."

Opening the apartment door, he stormed off.

• • •

Monday morning Randall and Tessa flew from Nantucket to Hyannis. Randall retrieved his car from a parking lot, tossed their bags in the trunk, and joined the line of cars heading for Boston. He'd assumed that Tessa would sit in the front, torturing him as she always did by pushing the SEEK button on the radio every thirty seconds, but today Tessa crawled into the backseat. She wanted to nap, she said.

This concerned him. They'd just awakened, really, and had a large if eccentric breakfast of cheese and crackers and chocolate cake—Sarah said it was European. Tessa hadn't eaten much, although at her father's bidding she'd finished a small glass of juice.

No doubt Tessa was worried about tomorrow, when her parents would go to court to fight for custody. Any child would be worried. Randall was worried. The odds were stacked in the mother's favor, always, and this thing with his father in Madeline's robe, no matter how innocent, could prove just the right straw to break the camel's back.

Mont had phoned Randall last evening, terribly distressed. Don't give it a second thought, Randall had told his father. It had been an unsettling conversation. More and more Randall found himself in the role of the caregiver, the nurturer, the wise one, as the man he'd once considered indomitable weakened, almost daily, before Randall's very eyes.

Anne did have a point, didn't she? It could be detrimental to Tessa—frightening, even—to see her grandfather in her grandmother's robe.

Yet Randall believed strongly that the process of aging should be given the same value as any other stage of life in our society, that it should be seen as a part of human life equal to infancy and adolescence, with all the mental and physical vicissitudes. The elderly deserved respect, and love, and generosity—Jesus God, Anne believed that,

Randall knew she did! She believed it *in principle*. Why could she not act on her beliefs?

Just thinking of Anne made him weary. As he steered his car up and over the Sagamore Bridge, he let his thoughts wander to Kelly. It was so long since he'd seen her. She was almost a fantasy more than a memory—that stolen morning in bed together.

Kelly had accepted him into her body with such willingness, such eager pleasure that it had been spiritual as much as physical for him. A kind of redemption. His greedy body, with all its hungers and needs, suddenly in Kelly's arms became whole, and good, and competent. The excess of his sexual desires were all at once not disgusting, but valuable, because they were matched by an equal need, and responded to with gladness.

It had been different with Lacey, and a bitter taste filled his mouth at the thought of the whole sorry, sordid liaison and its aftermath, when he lay collapsed on Lacey's double bed, staring out at her shelves of dolls, hating himself, and not much fonder of the woman next to him, who had only pretended to enjoy the sex.

"Was that all right?" she'd asked, worried. "Did you like it? Want me to do something else?"

There had been no love in the intercourse, no respect. No honesty. She wasn't wild with ardor for him; she never had been. She'd always focused on pleasing him, making it clear that she'd be glad to earn marriage to a doctor in this way, or in any way he wished. They did have some affection for one another, and yet as they lay together on the bed, Randall had felt cold and lonely and hollow and shamed.

Lacey had made a sniffling noise.

"Lacey," he'd begun, not knowing how to let her down gently, wishing he'd never started this all up again in the first place.

"It's all right, Randall," she'd replied. "You don't have to say anything."

He'd sat up, swung his legs over the side of the bed,

looked at his clothes lying rumpled on the floor. He'd dressed.

Lacey lay on the bed. She'd pulled the sheet up over her naked body and covered her eyes with one arm.

"You're a beautiful woman, Lacey," Randall had said.

"Just go," she'd whispered. "Please. Just go."

On Nantucket he'd chewed on his thoughts, indulging in a quiet feast of self-hatred that made his stomach rumble with acid. He was ashamed of himself for sleeping with Lacey, and yet he could not deny that it had clarified something for him. He was not just a lecherous cad who wanted to sleep with every female he saw. Or if he had been that way, he was no longer so. He wanted something real when he made love. He wanted a woman who wanted him back. Even though briefly, he'd experienced with Kelly a genuine emotional and physical reciprocity. He wanted nothing less ever again.

He was in his early forties. He had given a lot to his community—this was true, he knew. He had worked hard, behaved with skill, compassion, and integrity. But he wasn't a young man any longer, and he was not a happy man. Had not been a happy man for many years. Somehow fate had brought this new woman to him, this tall blonde with a ready smile who took pleasure in his presence. He had met her in the cemetery where his mother lay, where, he could believe, his mother's spirit hovered—and didn't that mean something?

There was something earthy about Kelly. She was intelligent, but she found pleasure in the physical—he'd liked the way she ate her pancakes that morning in the diner. He liked the way she threw her head back when she laughed. He liked the way she made love. He relished the way he felt after they made love, like the very best of friends.

Mont would like her, and she would like Mont. Tessa would like her, and she would like Tessa. And if Kelly was a career woman, well then, somehow they would make that work, too.

• • •

Monday evening Randall and his father sat on the porch, drinking whiskey, looking out at the pasture where the horses ambled with their noses in the grass.

"At first I considered suicide," Mont said.

"Oh, Dad."

"Now, now, hear me out." Mont tossed some of the warm amber liquid down his throat, appreciating the fire it lit inside him. "I'm not afraid of death, you know. Especially now that your mother's gone. I'm kind of looking forward to seeing her again. Or being with her, some way. So suicide was my first thought. Here I am, a worthless old man. A pervert, Anne called me."

"I'm so sorry, Dad."

"Don't be. It's not your fault. It's my fault, for looking like an old fool. For giving Anne ammunition against us in court. 'Randall's father's senile, he wears women's clothing, he could be dangerous to a young girl—' "

"Dad, I don't—"

"Let me finish. I played it out in my mind. I commit suicide, and *I'm* okay. But that would really tie the package up in a pretty bow for Anne. You'd have a dead father. A father so nuts he killed himself. Certainly not the best timing to take on the full custody of a twelve-year-old girl. Plus your whole plan to have two adults in the house to take care of Tessa, someone here when you're at work and she's out of school, all that gets lost if I top myself."

"Would you *stop*—"

"I made myself think of Tessa. What's best for Tessa. I don't want her ever to think that suicide's an option, no matter how crushed a person feels."

"Good."

"I think I made a fairly good impression talking with Dr. Lawrence the other day. I think I appeared to be a rational man. So that's good."

"Yes. That's good."

"Randall, I intend to come to court every day you're there. I'll wear my best suit and do my damnedest to look like a respectable, optimistic, reliable member of your family."

Randall swallowed. "Thanks, Dad."

"And by the way. Just so you'll know: I packed up the robe."

"Mom's robe?"

"Along with all her other clothes. I let Dorothy take them to the church for their fair."

"Well, Dad. Good for you."

"Yes, I suppose it's good for me. Good for Tessa, that's what I'm hoping for."

They stood like conspirators, whispering together in the front hall.

"It's all here," Glen Phipps promised, handing Anne a manila envelope. "Exactly what you need."

It was almost eleven, but Anne had insisted that the investigator come late, when she could be sure Tessa was asleep and she wouldn't be interrupted by telephone calls.

"Here's your payment." She handed a white envelope to him.

Glen Phipps tore it open, pulled out the check, and looked at it. "Thanks," he said, tucking it into his shirt pocket. "Anything else?"

"Not at this time." She wanted him to go, *now*. She burned to read the material he'd given her.

"Okay, then. Thanks." He reached out for a handshake.

She shook his hand. Pretended to smile. God knew she could summon up that much, a polite smile, these days.

Finally he went out the door.

She waited until she saw the car pull out of her drive, and lights winking, disappear into the darkness.

She went into her study, sat down behind her desk, pulled out the two neatly typewritten pages, and began to read.

GP Investigations
1474 Massachusetts Avenue
Arlington, Massachusetts 01742

September 1, 2000
TO: Mrs. Anne Madison
FROM: Glen Phipps
RE: Dr. Randall Madison

Monday, August 21 to Thursday, August 24
    Dr. Madison followed routine schedule, going to apartment, Mt. Auburn Hospital, private office on Mass Ave., father's farm.

Friday, August 25
    Dr. Madison's schedule was as usual for the day.
    At six-forty-five Friday evening, he left office, made one stop at Al's Liquor Store, then drove to the apartment complex on 441 Adams Avenue, the home of Lacey Corriea, with whom, you may remember from my earlier reports, Dr. Madison had a liaison last year before your separation.
    Dr. Madison left Ms. Corriea's apartment at eleven-thirty, drove to his apartment, and spent the night there alone.

Saturday, August 26 to Monday, August 28
    Dr. Madison followed routine schedule, going to apartment, Mt. Auburn Hospital, his father's farm, his own office. Sunday, briefly entered Forest Hills Cemetery, then went to your home to take Tessa to breakfast at Carla's Café. Sunday afternoon at father's farm.

Tuesday, August 29
    Dr. Madison's routine schedule for day. He left his office at five-thirty, drove to his apartment. At

seven-thirty, he left apartment, drove to 441 Adams Avenue, and picked up Lacey Corriea. From there he proceeded to the Ritz-Carlton on Boylston. Dr. Madison and Ms. Corriea were in the dining room from eight o'clock until ten-thirty.

At ten-thirty Dr. Madison drove Ms. Corriea to her apartment. Parked his car on Adams. Escorted Ms. Corriea into apartment complex. Remained there until one-thirty on Wednesday morning, when he left the apartment complex to drive to his own apartment.

Wednesday, August 30 to Thursday, August 31
Dr. Madison's routine schedule. Stayed at his apartment all evening and night.

Friday, September 1
Dr. Madison left his office at noon to pick up Tessa at your home.

Respectfully submitted,
Glen Phipps, Investigator

Anne folded the paper, returned it to the envelope, and locked it in her desk. She pinched the bridge of her nose as hard as she could. She looked at the cold, clean objects on her desk—blotter, calendar, trays—and tried to remember the comfort they had always provided.

THIRTEEN

September 5, 2000

TUESDAY MORNING KELLY DROPPED OFF Felicity, clad in a mixture of gothic and Gap, on Cambridge Street.

"Have fun," Kelly said.

Felicity snorted. "Right." She sauntered away toward the high school, her face a perfect mask of boredom.

Come on, God, Kelly implored, *let her like her school.*

What a day this was. Her first day in her own courtroom. Felicity's first day at school. The first day of Randall's divorce trial. She wondered where Tessa was right now.

She put her car in gear and continued on down Cambridge Street, toward the courthouse.

She'd phoned earlier this morning, to tell her secretary she had to get Felicity to school and might be a few minutes late. She looked at the clock on her dashboard—she was right on time. Not surprising, since she'd been awake, tossing and turning, since dawn.

She turned off Cambridge Street onto Thorndike Street and drove into the lot behind the building. She amused herself with the fancy that her car actually purred as she pulled it into the parking space marked: RESERVED FOR JUDGE MACLEOD. She sat a moment, soaking in satisfaction; then she checked her lipstick in the mirror, took a deep breath, and stepped outside.

She locked her car. Striding toward the century-old, stately, redbrick courthouse, she found the newest key on her ring and let herself in through the back entrance. Nodding at the security guard and smiling at a pair of lawyers she recognized, she briskly wove through the crowd milling around the large lobby. Just last spring she had been one of the attorneys like the group huddled together next to the men's rest room, engaged in a last-minute conference.

Most cases settled out of court. Often this exact moment, the magnificent reality of the courthouse, the thrilling, overwhelming buzz of confrontations and consultations, the sharp shine and scent of expensive leather briefcases, caused a client to physically, *viscerally* appreciate the significance of a courtroom trial in a way he or she hadn't before. The sight of the judge in her black robe made them understand that they were about to put their lives in someone else's power.

Too impatient for the ancient elevator, Kelly hurried up the smooth, wide steps, their marble worn into silky troughs. Her courtroom was on the fourth floor. She was glad for the exercise, knowing that she might be sitting for the rest of the day.

At the end of the hall were her chambers.

Her chambers!

Printed in gold on the glass door were the words:

JUDGE KELLY MACLEOD

PRIVATE

DO NOT ENTER

She took a deep breath. She entered.

"Good morning, Judge." Her secretary, an Asian woman in a plaid suit, was already at her desk, up to her elbows in cases and folders.

"Good morning, Luanne."

"Good morning, Judge," said the court officer, Ed Harris, a tall, bald, stately African-American, in his navy blue uniform.

Kelly smiled. "Good morning, Ed."

"Good morning, Judge." Dignified in her beige silk suit

and pearls, Sally Beale, Kelly's clerk, was the key to a smooth transition into this court. Sally had been here for a dozen years. Sally knew everything.

"Hi, Sally. Great suit."

"Thank you, Judge."

"What have we got today?" Kelly asked, looking toward the door to the courtroom. That door was all that stood between this place of quiet and the storm of human lives.

Sally handed her the trial list. "First, a quick and easy divorce. Then a child custody case. That won't be short, and it won't be sweet."

"Then we'd better begin."

"Right. See you out there." Sally slid through the door into the churning whispers of the courtroom.

Kelly took her black robe off the hanger, pulled it on over her gray pantsuit, adjusted the shoulders and collar. Quickly she scanned her reflection in the mirror hanging on the closet door. She'd subdued her blond hair in a twist at the back of her head, and not a hair had dared escape. Fine. She looked fine. No reason to hesitate. She nodded to Officer Harris.

He asked, "Ready, Judge?"

"Ready."

He opened the door.

Kelly walked into the courtroom.

Her courtroom.

She'd been in this room before, many times, as a lawyer representing one side or another in a divorce or child custody case. The enormous room was brightened by many windows, its walls painted a peaceful pale blue trimmed with cream. The ceilings were perhaps twenty feet high. The wood of the railings, witness stand, conference tables, clerk's and judge's bar, officer of the court's station, was golden oak, darkened by the years, glowing with the patina from the touch of generations of petitioners, lawyers, registers, and judges.

It was a lovely room.

Behind her, his voice rich and solemn, Officer Harris announced, "Hear ye, Hear ye, Hear ye. Court, all rise. The Middlesex Probate and Family Court is now in session, the Honorable Judge Kelly MacLeod presiding. God save the Commonwealth of Massachusetts. Turn off all cell phones and pagers."

The Honorable Judge Kelly MacLeod settled in her chair behind the high bench, her black robe resting at her ankles. She nodded good morning to the court stenographer and then looked out, with confidence, at the courtroom.

She saw, as she knew she would, clusters of people seated in the gallery. She saw a young couple, well-dressed, elegant, and miserable, sulking next to their attorneys at the lawyers' table. Their divorce. Her first case.

Beyond the railing, she saw a lovely, slender, blond woman, the female plaintiff in the child custody case, with her lawyer.

She saw another lawyer speaking to the male defendant in the child custody case.

And she saw, with a terrible thrill, that the man was Randall Madison.

She felt unmasked before him. She felt more exposed now than she had been when they made love. This is who I am, she thought: Randall, this is who I am. A judge. If that's too much, if that makes it impossible for me to be a wife and mother, then so be it. Here I am.

Sally Beale called the first case, consisting of the name of the parties, the docket number, and the cause of actions before the court. Kelly forced herself to concentrate. She scanned the file in front of her. This was an easy, uncontested divorce, with no children involved. It would be over in minutes. She waved the group up to the bench. She was piercingly aware of her every move with Randall as an audience. She glanced at Anne Madison, curious and shamed by her curiosity. She had to send them to another courtroom, but not yet. Not just yet.

Four people gathered around the witness stand: a man, a woman, two lawyers, all clad in dark, expensive suits. The register swore them in.

"Good morning," Kelly said. Her voice was level, assured.

"Good morning, Your Honor," both lawyers chimed.

"I'm Bartholomew Towers, Your Honor, representing Mrs. Baker."

"I'm Daniel Sanders, Your Honor, representing Mr. Baker."

Kelly nodded. "Counselors," she instructed, "please make your *prima facie* case."

The wife's lawyer turned to her: "Please state your name."

"Bobby Baker." Glossy and precisely groomed to the last hair on her perfectly arched eyebrows, Mrs. Baker trembled inside her Chanel suit like a racehorse at the starting gate. Her earrings, heavy gold and diamonds, splintered the light around her.

"Are you married to the co-petitioner William Baker?"

She cleared her throat. "I am."

"Please state your address."

As the wife reeled off the information, Kelly glanced out at the Madisons, seated behind the bar. Anne Madison was petite, as pale and as delicate as a glass flower, and, Kelly sensed, as strong as a diamond.

Now the husband's lawyer led him through the necessary information: his name, address, when he last lived with his wife, whether or not there were any minor children. The husband's suit, beautifully cut from light gray flannel, looked infinitely soft, but the man himself, muscular and taut, looked carved from granite. *Body language,* Judge Parsons's voice flashed through her mind, and Kelly glanced down once more at the divorce papers. This couple was wealthy; the assets were being divided fifty-fifty. She saw no sign of hostility between the couple. The wife was asking for no alimony.

"All right," Kelly said. "Mr. Baker, Mrs. Baker, I need to ask you some questions. Do you believe your marriage is irretrievably broken?"

"I do," they both responded.

"Did you sign this separation agreement of your own free will?"

"I did," they answered.

"Do you believe that it is fair and reasonable?"

Mrs. Baker swayed slightly. "I do."

Mr. Baker's jaw clenched. Through gritted teeth, he replied in the affirmative.

Kelly looked at the wife. "Do you believe your spouse gave you complete and accurate information on his financial statement?"

"I do."

Kelly repeated the question to the husband and received the same response.

Something here bothered Kelly. She glanced down at the divorce papers once more. Everything was in order. No doubt it was only her own emotional turbulence plaguing her.

"Mrs. Baker," Kelly said, "are you satisfied with your attorney and his advice?"

"I am."

"Is this a final settlement of all issues between you and Mr. Baker?"

"Yes." The woman's hands were clasped so tightly her fingers were white.

Kelly asked the husband the same questions and received the same answers.

"Very well, then, I find this marriage to be irretrievably broken and a judgment will render in thirty days. Mrs. Baker, do you wish to resume the use of your maiden name?"

"No."

"Your counselors have explained to you that you must wait one hundred and twenty days for the divorce to be-

come absolute. You both understand that?" When they nodded, she added, "All right, then. Good luck to you both."

The divorced couple and their lawyers turned, heading
toward the back of the courtroom. Kelly leaned toward her
clerk, who passed her a thick red divorce folder marked
MADISON. Randall and Anne and their lawyers rose, gathering together the piles of materials necessary for a contested divorce, in preparation for coming around the bar to
the lawyers' table.

She felt Randall's eyes on her.

She signed the Bakers' divorce decree. She handed it
back to her clerk. Out of the corner of her eye, she saw the
Bakers and their lawyers walking, single file, toward the
wide mahogany-and-glass doors.

Suddenly, in a flash of movement, Mr. Baker charged
forward and, swinging his arm, brought his laptop computer
up and smashed it hard into his ex-wife's face.

There was a sickening noise, the crunch of snapping
bone. The woman screamed and staggered backward. Blood
spurted. The lawyers yelled. Bobby Baker went down, falling like a stone. Her lawyer lunged forward, catching her
in time to save her from hitting her head on the floor.

The courtroom exploded with noise. The woman
shrieked. Her lawyer bellowed for help.

"Bitch!" The husband roared. "I hope you're satisfied
now, you greedy slut!"

"Court officer!" Kelly yelled.

Ed Harris was already on his way, shoving into the
chaos. Shouldering the dumbfounded, gaping Sanders
aside, he wrestled the furious husband away from his wife.

"Call for an ambulance," Kelly ordered her clerk.

Randall, Anne, and their lawyers had risen, as had the
other members of the courtroom. The ex-wife's lawyer sat
on the floor, holding the injured woman to his chest, pressing his white handkerchief to her bloody face. Mrs. Baker
screamed and screamed. Mr. Baker continued to shout
abuse at the court officer, his ex-wife, his ex-wife's lawyer,

and Kelly, as Officer Harris, struggling, subdued the man, yanking his arms behind his back and securing them in handcuffs.

"I'm a doctor," Randall announced, trying to get past the horrified crowd of onlookers.

Mrs. Baker screamed. Blood poured down her suit jacket and darkened the lawyer's white shirt. Then she stopped screaming. She went limp in her lawyer's arms. The sudden silence was shocking.

"Jesus," Bartholomew Towers cried, "I think she's dead."

The husband roared triumphantly. Ed manhandled him into a chair. The courtroom doors flew open, and three EMTs rushed into the room.

"Register Beale," Kelly said. "Get the Cambridge police. Officer Harris, bring Mr. Baker to me."

The EMTs strapped the wounded woman onto a stretcher.

"How is she?" Kelly called.

"Alive," one of the medics called back.

"Keep us apprised of her condition," Kelly instructed. "Register Beale, give the EMTs our number."

Register Beale left her desk, crossed the courtroom, and handed a slip of paper to the medic. Officer Harris ushered William Baker before Kelly's bench. The ex-husband stood there, flushed and trembling.

Kelly gestured toward the two lawyers standing flabbergasted at the back of the courtroom. "Mr. Sanders, you're this man's lawyer, I want you to get up here now. Mr. Tower, you, too."

The lawyers hustled up. Tower's shirt and suit were damp and matted with blood.

Kelly glared down at the handcuffed man. "Mr. Baker," she said. "You've chosen the wrong courtroom in which to assault your wife. I'm sentencing you to forty-five days in jail for assault and a ten-thousand-dollar fine for disturbing the order of my courtroom. In addition, you are to pay for all Mrs. Baker's medical costs, down to the last penny, including mental and physical therapy. I'm imposing a restraining order on you: You are not to be within twenty-five feet of Mrs. Baker for the next six months. You are not to telephone her. You are not to send her a letter or a fax or an e-mail or have any communication with her. If you do, you will be in contempt of court, and I'll sentence you to more jail time. Is that clear?"

"Yes," William Baker replied. His lawyer nudged him. "Yes, Your Honor."

"Mr. Tower. I want you to keep this court apprised of Mrs. Baker's condition. Do you have someone in your firm who does criminal law?"

The lawyer nodded.

"Good. I want charges brought against Mr. Baker for premeditated murder."

"Hey! You can't do that!" William Baker yelled.

"That's ten more days you're going to serve," Kelly snapped. "Take him to the back to wait for the police," she told Officer Harris. She turned to Register Beale. "Do you have all this, Register?"

"I do, Your Honor."

"I've been to a fund-raiser for Mrs. Madison. Tell the Madisons' lawyers they'll have to take their divorce to another courtroom."

"Yes, Your Honor."

"Call the other courtrooms. See if Judge Parsons can take the Madison case. Tell her we'll take everything she's got in return. Call the other courtrooms, too; tell them we're open for business and can take any overflow."

"Yes, Your Honor."

"Court's in recess for fifteen minutes," Kelly said.

"All rise," the court officer bellowed.

She felt Randall's eyes on her as she walked away from the bench into the privacy of her chambers.

The day flew past, jammed with cases, lawyers, motions, and paperwork. Not until Kelly was in her car, headed home, did she find time to catch her breath and reflect on the events of the morning. She was wondering how the day had gone for Randall, when her cell phone rang. She answered it as she stopped for a red light on Cambridge Street.

"I need to see you," Randall said.

"I'd love that."

"Now. Anywhere you say."

"Meet me at the cemetery."

Once more she drove through the gates of Forest Hills into this mysterious world where the questions of life mattered no longer and the people were composed of spirit and stone. Exhilarated from her day, she decided she preferred the living, imperfect world.

She parked her car and stepped out into the heat. Stripping off her suit jacket, she laid it on the car seat. As she shut the door, Randall's Jeep pulled in beside her. Her heart leaped when she saw him, flushing her entire body with love. She moved toward him, but he stood still next to his Jeep, as if keeping his distance.

"Hello," she said, suddenly shy.

"Hello, Judge MacLeod."

"Oh, Randall. I didn't mean—"

"Why didn't you tell me?"

"For many reasons—there wasn't enough time. It didn't seem real when I met you. *We* didn't seem real, here. I'd just been appointed. I was beginning a month of training, at different courts all over the commonwealth."

"That's why you were out of town so often."

"Right. Believe it or not, today was my first day on the bench by myself." She paused. "Also, you haven't had many kind things to say about the judicial system."

"True."

Hearing the tension in his voice, she looked up at him. "How did it go today?"

He hesitated, then sighed. "Let's walk."

They went slowly along Mulberry Path, unconsciously heading for the stone where Kelly had fallen and they had met. After the noise of the rushing traffic, the air of the cemetery was as still as a held breath, the air moist and scented with flowers.

"Which judge did you have?" she asked.

"Judge Spriggs. The GAL testified."

"Who?"

"Dr. Lawrence. Martin Lawrence."

"I know him. He's fair."

"Yes. Yes, I think he is."

"What did he recommend?"

"Joint physical and legal custody."

"And?"

"And we're continuing the trial tomorrow."

"What does your lawyer say?"

"What he's always said, that in most cases the mother gets custody."

"Randall, tell me the truth, please. Is the divorce why you approached me here? Why you 'courted' me? So that I could give you custody—"

"No!" Randall stopped dead on the pavement. "Of course not. Is that what you think?"

She stopped, too, and turned to face him. "I don't know what to think."

Angrily he protested, "I had no idea you were a judge!"

"And if I had told you?"

"Well, you didn't, did you?" He ran his hands through his hair and tossed himself down onto the grass, staring out at the serene green waters of Lake Hibiscus.

Kelly settled down in the grass next to him. For a while they just sat in silence.

Then Randall put his hand on Kelly's as it lay in the grass. "Kelly, I love you."

Kelly closed her eyes. His warmth moved through her, a current of golden pulses. She said, "I love you, too."

Randall lifted his hand away. "But our lives are complicated. I've got to think of my daughter—her real name's Tessa. And Anne. And my father, who wears his wife's robe and slippers and may be getting a bit batty."

Kelly looked at Randall, concerned. "Alzheimer's?"

"I don't think so. We had a good talk recently, and he's given the robe away. He's going to try to pull himself up out of his depression, because he wants to help me and Tessa."

"That's good, then."

"Yes. Although Anne can still use that in court as proof that his home might not be the best environment for a young girl." He paused. "There's something else."

Kelly waited.

"I've seen another woman."

"Seen?"

"I've slept with another woman. Her name is Lacey Corriea. She's a nurse. I worked with her last year at Mt. Auburn. We had an affair. I ended it. Then I saw her again. Twice. About two weeks ago and again just last week. For one night."

Kelly couldn't find her breath. She couldn't turn to look at the man next to her. From a tree behind her, a leaf drifted down, landing on her arm, and she could not move to brush it away.

Quietly, Randall continued. "I don't love Lacey. I never told her I did. In my defense I never promised her anything. I'm sorry I hurt her, if I did." He cleared his throat. "But you see, Lacey would make an excellent mother. And I need to be with a woman who will be a good stepmother for Tessa. And the truth is, as much as I love you, I don't know if you could be that woman."

Kelly looked at him. She let herself perch on the edge of the moment, as if on a diving board over a fathomless ocean. There could be no coming back. She decided. She said, "Would it help if I told you that I'm your daughter's birth mother?"

He stared at her as if she'd just gone mad. As if she'd just spoken in tongues. As if she were a stone angel who'd fallen off her pedestal and come to life.

"What are you saying?"

"I'm saying that I told you the truth, but not the whole truth. I didn't tell you that after René took my inheritance, a professor came to me with a proposition. He told me that if I would be a surrogate mother, and do it in complete privacy, he would arrange to see that I received fifty thousand dollars, enough for law school."

"George Hammond," Randall said.

The name jolted through her. So it really was true. "Yes. Professor Hammond."

They stared at one another, dumbstruck. Kelly whispered, "I held my daughter when she was born. She had a birthmark like a leaf on the left side of her neck."

"Tessa's birthmark."

"Of course we could do DNA testing to be sure."

"This is too wild." Randall rose. "I've got to walk." Reaching down, he took Kelly's hand and pulled her up.

They set off up the hill, striding toward Fountain Avenue and Tulip Path, toward their mothers' graves.

"This changes everything," Randall said.

"Yes." Kelly couldn't stop smiling. "It does."

"It means we have to go at this slowly. *Carefully.* Very carefully."

Kelly frowned. "I don't understand—"

"Tessa has been wanting to meet her birth mother. I can't just say, okay, here's the woman I'm going to marry, and by the way, she's your birth mother. We have to go about it the other way around. For her sake. That's too fast. If it's confusing for us, think how it will be for her. We have to let her meet you, and get to know you, and feel comfortable with you, and come to like you."

"You know, in Massachusetts the birth mother and

both adoptee parents have to give their written permission before the identifying information can be released."

"God." Randall ran his hand through his hair. "Anne won't give her permission. Perhaps, if I'm awarded custody, I could speak to Anne about this from a position of strength."

"Perhaps." Long shadows fell across their path. "Let's see what Judge Spriggs decides. Then we'll go from there."

"All right. Look," Randall said, taking her by the arm. "I want to promise you—there'll be no more women for me. No matter how tired or depressed or confused I get. I've learned who I want, and I'm certain about that now. So you can trust me. Okay?"

She searched his face. She could not help herself: she loved this man. She had to trust him. They had to trust one another. "Want to seal your vow?" she asked lightly.

And, not lightly, he kissed her.

Wednesday afternoon in Courtroom 1, Kelly was at work again, sitting at her bench in her black robe, listening to a case between grandparents and father fighting for custody of a five-year-old boy. His parents had divorced when he was two, and his father had moved to another state. His mother had been ill for three years. During that time, the mother and the little boy had lived with his maternal grandparents. Now the mother had died and the father wanted to take his son with him to another state. But the little boy had seldom seen his father for five years. He knew his grandparents' house and neighborhood as his home. He loved his grandparents, who were young and healthy.

They were grief-stricken at the thought of losing him. Yet the father had legal rights of custody. It was another heartbreaking case.

That afternoon, in Courtroom 5, Randall Madison and Anne Madison stood in rigid attention before Judge Spriggs.

"Look, Mrs. Madison, Dr. Madison," Judge Spriggs

said. "You are both good parents. You're both civilized, capable, and loving. I don't know why you're here in the first place. Seems to me you should have been able to figure this out yourselves. But you're here, and I've heard all your witnesses and read all your documents and I'm not going to take up anybody's time with this. Your daughter, Tessa, is a twelve-year-old girl. She's on the verge of puberty. She's been living in one house all her life, and that's home to her, that's where she's safe. Now, Dr. Madison, you're a fine parent, too"—she waved an admonishing finger at Anne—"and I don't care how many women you sleep with, it seems to me you're not letting that interfere with your parenting of Tessa. Still. Still, I think it's in the best interest of this child to remain with her mother in the house where she's been raised. I'm granting joint legal custody to the parents, and sole physical custody to the mother."

Judge Spriggs continued speaking, talking about the mother's responsibility to discuss health and educational matters with the father, but Anne didn't really hear her. She was so relieved, so exhilarated, so *triumphant*, that blood rushed through her ears like the applause of thousands. She had *won*, she thought. *She had won.*

For the kids who attended the public schools, classes had begun, but Tessa's private school didn't start until next week. She was glad. It was an enormous relief to be allowed to stay at home with Carmen while her mother and father were in court. While she waited to see who would be awarded custody of her.

Awarded. As if she were some kind of prize.

Actually, she felt like that's what she was to her mother, like a kind of badge, or one of those fancy medallions that royalty wore hanging from a scarlet sash over a satin gown. She was an accomplishment of Anne's, an ornament Anne could display to the public as one more bit of evidence that she was a magnificent woman.

Tessa lay in her room on her bed, reading and trying not to mess up the comforter too much. She was deep into a book called *Misty Midnight*, about an ill-tempered orphan girl sent to live on a farm where she develops a relationship with a tempestuous colt no one could break. It was one of Tessa's favorite books, and for a while during the day she'd been able to lose herself in it, she'd been *there*, in the barn, smelling the sweet hay, hearing the huff of the colt's breath on her neck, feeling the danger of the large, unhappy, unpredictable animal so near to her own cranky and fragile self.

But now it was after five, and she was trapped in the Ice Palace waiting for the Ice Queen, who would be home soon.

Then she heard the sound of tires against gravel. And a different engine humming. Two doors slammed. Two cars. Her mother and father.

Tessa smoothed her shirt and brushed her hair. She heard voices downstairs, her mother talking with Carmen. The front door shut: Carmen had left.

"Tessa?" her mother called up the stairs. "Could you come down, please?"

And Tessa knew.

Her mother's voice in all its variations was as familiar to Tessa as her own weather system of moods. Her mother didn't even have to say words, she could call out the Declaration of Independence and Tessa would know how to translate it. Her mother's voice could be as light as a butterfly dipping through flowers when she was happy, and that was the way it sounded now.

Tessa trudged down the stairs.

Her parents were in the living room. Her mother was at the drinks cart, fixing a pair of vodka tonics over ice in cut-crystal glasses. Her father sat on a sofa, elbows on knees, hands hanging down, shoulders slumped. When he saw Tessa, he sat up straight and smiled.

"Hey, Tessa," he said. "How's it going?"

She shrugged and gave him a black look. *What did you do wrong?* she wanted to demand. *Why didn't you win?*

Didn't you try hard enough? Didn't you want to bad enough?

Her mother was squeezing a slice of lemon into each glass. "Would you like some juice, Tessa?" her mother asked sweetly.

"No."

"No?"

"No, thank you."

"Sit down for a moment, dear. We want to talk to you."

Tessa perched on the end of a chair next to her father. Her mother handed him his drink, then sat across the coffee table from him on the smaller sofa her mother called a loveseat. *Loveseat*, hah.

"It's official, Tessa," her mother announced. "Your father and I have been granted a divorce." Her cheeks were flushed as she looked over at Randall and raised her glass in a toast. "Cheers."

"Cheers," Randall replied, raising his glass as well.

Her mother sipped her drink and smiled at Tessa. "And the judge has awarded full physical custody to me."

Tessa sat still. Nothing she could say or do would make a difference.

"But joint legal custody to both of us," her father hastened to add. "Which means that on any important decision, about where you go to school, or trips, or religion, or should you want rhinoplasty—"

Anne cut him short. "This is not a joke, Randall!"

"No. No, I know it's not. I was just—" Randall looked down at his drink, then up at Tessa. "Honey, I'm still going to be as much a part of your life as before. Maybe more so."

"But I won't live on the farm? I won't have my room there?"

"Of course you'll have your room there. And you'll live there sometimes. I've got liberal visitation rights—that means I can have you stay with me a lot, Tessa. At least two weekends a month, maybe more."

"The judge left it to us to decide," Anne added. "Sometimes in cases like this, the child spends one school night with the noncustodial parent, but it's such a long drive for you from Concord in to your school that Randall and I have agreed it would be best for you to spend all school nights here, and most weekends with your father and grandfather."

"But I'll come in to take you out to dinner during the week. Or drive you to school events, that sort of thing—whatever you want. And I'll be allowed to have you with me for entire months in the summer," Randall hastened to add. "And for holidays."

"Some holidays," Anne corrected. "We'll decide as we go along."

"Are you going to keep your apartment?" Tessa asked her father.

"I don't think so, honey. I want to move out to the farm. I'm cutting back on all my hours. I might even close my practice here and open up a smaller one in Concord."

"Basically, your life won't change much at all, darling," Anne said. "Except that you'll probably see more of your father than you used to."

"Do you have any questions?" Tessa's father asked.

Tessa shook her head.

"You know we both love you, Tessa," Anne assured her. "And we'll try very hard to see that you're happy. I know it will be hard, at first, having divorced parents, but many of your friends have parents who are divorced, don't they?"

Tessa nodded her head obediently.

Randall drained his glass, put it on the coffee table, and rose. "Well, then, I guess I'll go."

"Have a date?" Anne asked archly.

"Yes. With my father." Randall knelt in front of Tessa and hugged her to him. "I'll see you this weekend, kid. I'll call you tomorrow night. And you call me whenever you want, right?"

She nodded.

"Okay, then."

"I'll walk you to the door." Anne rose.

They left the room. Tessa sat alone. Anne's perfume lingered in the air, and a kind of shadow form of Tessa's father remained as well. She'd always liked having him in the house. He was like a live, hungry animal rambling around in a museum. He was like a steady throb of rock music after the polite fussiness of Mozart. He was like a great big McDonald's meal with a hot fudge sundae from Friendly's instead of a tossed salad and a chicken breast. It was irrational, Tessa knew that much, but when she heard the door shut and then the engine start up in the driveway, she felt abandoned by her father. She felt angry, and lonely, and cold.

"Well!" her mother said, returning to the living room. "Let's go out to dinner and celebrate!" She smiled at Tessa—then suddenly swooped down and hugged her. "I'm so glad I'll have you with me." Taking Tessa's face between her hands, she asked, "You're glad, too, aren't you, darling?"

Sick at heart, Tessa nodded.

"Lovely. Well, run up and put on a dress, why don't you, and we'll be off to dinner."

FOURTEEN

SUNDAY MORNING, AT THE CEMETERY, Randall said, "We've got to stop meeting like this."

Laughing, Kelly stepped out of her car and walked over the Jeep. "Sorry I'm late. I had to drop Felicity at the mall."

Randall kissed her firmly. "I'm serious. We do have to stop meeting like this."

"And do what instead?"

Randall took his hand in hers as they strolled along the winding cemetery paths. "Meet in public. Meet at your apartment. I want to get to know Felicity—how does she like school?"

"She loves it. She's making friends, and at the parent-teacher conference the other night, her teachers told me she's exceptionally bright. She's just got to learn to concentrate, and it looks like I've got to be the one to make her turn off the TV and apply herself."

"Well, I want to meet her. I want her to know I'm more than a voice on the telephone."

"Oh, she knows that. I've told her I've got a new man in my life."

"Good. And I want you to come out to the farm and meet Mont. I've told him about you."

"Oooh, scary, meeting your dad," Kelly said, only half joking.

"More scary than meeting my child?"

Kelly shook her head. "Even the thought of that takes my breath away. Look." Kelly pointed to an ancient spreading maple. "The leaves are already beginning to turn." They stood together looking up at the beauty change had wrought, the yellow and gold gilding the green. "How is Tessa?"

"I'm not sure. Anne's had her with her pretty much full-time for the final leg of the campaign."

"I saw them both on television. Anne's a brilliant speaker, and I must say I like her ideas."

"The primary's this Tuesday. Anne agreed that if I let her have Tessa with her for these past two weeks, I'd get Tessa for the full week of Thanksgiving holiday."

"So you two are negotiating and working things out. That's good."

"Spoken like a judge."

Kelly looked up at him. "And like a—relative. One who knows the best environment for a child is one in which the parents cooperate rather than fight."

"If Anne wins, I think she'll be more receptive to our news."

"I've been thinking, Randall, what if I spoke with Anne?"

"Wow." Randall shook his head. "I don't know."

"As one mother to another."

"But do you honestly feel like a mother?" Randall asked.

Kelly hesitated, then asked, "Do you honestly feel like a man who can be faithful to one woman for the rest of his life?"

By five o'clock Tuesday afternoon, Anne Madison knew she'd won the primary. No matter how many more votes came in, she'd already received such a landslide over the incumbent that Marshall O'Leary had just called her to congratulate her on her win.

At her campaign headquarters on Mass Ave, a celebration was already in full swing. Rebecca Prentiss was there, and Lillian Doolittle, and Eleanor Marks, and Adelaide Stein, and thirty or so others, men and women who had helped her in her campaign. Mick Aitkins, the videographer, helped Rebecca bring in the iced case of champagne and the rented flutes Anne had waiting in her car. Now the air was full of the sound of popping corks.

"You can have a sip," Anne told her daughter. "Just a little celebratory sip."

"Okay, Mother," Tessa replied.

Anne smiled down at Tessa, a picture-book child with her long hair and her pink dress. Anne was letting her stay up late tonight even though tomorrow was a school day. Tonight was her mother's victory celebration, after all. Besides, Anne could do pretty much whatever she wanted with Tessa's schedule.

Rebecca approached, a silver tray in her hand.

"Have a canapé, darling," Anne urged her daughter.

Very quietly, Tessa said, "I don't like caviar."

"Oh, but of course you do! Or if you don't, you should. It is a bit of an acquired taste, I admit, but you're old enough to begin acquiring it." Plucking a caviar-covered cracker off the tray, Anne handed it to her daughter. "Come on, darling. Eat it."

Tessa obeyed. She choked. Her face went white.

Don't you dare vomit out here in public, Anne thought. Leaning down, she whispered, "Go to the bathroom." She gave her daughter a little shove in the right direction. Tessa went off just in time.

"Kevin! Darling! How good of you to stop by! Have some champagne."

Anne leaned forward, accepting an air kiss from one of the local Democratic honchos, a handsome older man with exquisite taste in clothing.

Friday evening, when the doorbell rang, Anne was on the Internet, gathering information about the Millennium Democracy Institute, an international assemblage of informed politicians who would gather in Washington, D.C., one weekend a month to write a handbook for emerging democracies across the world. From this group, delegates would be chosen to represent the MDI, traveling to fledgling capitalist nations across the world. MDI could be of stunning international significance, and Anne had been asked to become one of the members.

Behind the scenes, those in power were already discussing the possibility of Anne running for the U.S. Senate in 2002.

And from there—with her ambition, wealth, intelligence, and good looks, not to mention her sterling character and her genuine desire for reform—who knew what Anne could achieve? She was only in her early forties. She might even be one of the first female vice presidents. She might even—

With a sigh of regret, she pulled her attention away from the computer screen and flicked it off. She glanced at her calendar—yes, she did have an appointment now, at three o'clock. The afternoon had slipped past so quickly. Thank God Randall took Tessa with him during the weekends. That way she could work without interruption.

She surveyed the items so neatly arranged on her desk and, cramped from sitting, rose and stretched her arms high over her head. From the hall she heard Carmen's polite voice and the equally polite tones of the woman Carmen was leading down the hall toward Anne's office.

Anne looked down at her calendar again. *"Judge MacLeod,"* she'd written there in red ink. Who, the woman had said, when she telephoned, wanted to meet in private, about a personal matter.

Judge Kelly MacLeod entered the room. In her thirties, she was tall, with a chignon of blond hair and pale blue eyes. She could be my younger sister, Anne realized, holding out her hand.

"Judge MacLeod. Nice to meet you. Won't you sit down?" Coming around the side of her desk, she settled opposite the judge in a wing chair by the fireplace. "Would you like something to drink?"

"Thank you, no." The woman seemed oddly nervous.

"All right, then." Anne turned to Carmen. "That will be all, Carmen. Shut the door, will you?"

Carmen went out, closing the door with a whisper of wood on wood.

Anne tilted her head, waiting.

"First of all, Mrs. Madison—"

"Anne, please."

"Anne." Kelly MacLeod licked her lips. "First of all, Anne, I'd like to congratulate you on winning the election. I've followed your career, and I voted for you. I know you'll do a great deal of significant good work in the future."

"Thank you." Anne crossed her legs. Something was making the other woman apprehensive, Anne could feel it like the rumbling of distant thunder.

"I'm here, as I said on the phone, on a personal matter." The judge took a deep breath. "Twelve years ago I gave birth to a baby girl. She had a small birthmark on her neck—" Her voice caught. She cleared her throat and began again. "I was a surrogate mother to the baby. I was artificially inseminated by a couple who wanted a child they weren't able to have by themselves."

Anne put her hand to her throat. "You've saying that you are Tessa's birth mother."

Judge MacLeod nodded.

Anne stared at the other woman and saw that what she said was true. The pale hue of Tessa's skin, the long line of her bones, the shape of her eyes and ears, the way she sat, with such ramrod dignity—it was all Tessa.

"We paid you fifty thousand dollars," Anne reminded the woman.

Judge MacLeod put out a hand, as if to stop her words. "I'm not here about money."

"Then what—?" Suddenly fear ignited within her. All at once she knew what this woman wanted, and adrenaline sped through her body, filling her with alarm. *"No."* She half rose from her chair. You can't have her. She's my daughter. You're a judge. You know the laws—"

"Please. I'm not trying to take her away from you." The judge put her hands together in supplication. "Listen to me, please. It's very complicated. I'm here to ask for your help. For your advice."

"My advice?"

"Yes."

Anne looked down at her skirt. A wave of nausea from the adrenaline rush blackened her vision; then it passed.

She took a deep breath. "Go on, then." Anne rubbed at the spot on her skirt.

"I need to tell you a story. A true story."

"I'm listening."

"This summer," the judge said, "I fell in love. With a man I met in a cemetery."

"Dear God," Anne moaned. She closed her eyes and leaned her head back against the chair.

"My mother had just died. His mother had recently died. We talked. We talked, and we fell in love."

Anne opened her eyes and looked wearily at Kelly. "Of course you fell in love with Randall," she said. "Every woman does."

Judge MacLeod said quietly, "And Randall fell in love with me."

Anne snorted. She felt stronger now, on safer ground. She clasped her hands together. "This summer? Randall fell in love with you this summer? Randall was having an affair with Lacey Corriea this summer. I have proof if you'd like—"

"I know about Lacey Corriea. Randall told me. That doesn't matter. He's asked me to marry him."

Anne stared at the other woman. She was very pale and trembling. Anne thought perhaps she really had not come here out of triumph or vengefulness. "What do you want?"

"I told Randall I believe I'm Tessa's mother."

And Anne suddenly understood it all. The knowledge burned through her like a conflagration, leaving her soul in ashes.

"And you and Randall are going to get married and live happily ever after with *your* daughter?" Anne asked. Hideously, tears were pushing at the defenses of her eyes. How could she feel so empty and yet so full, nearly explosive, at the same time?

Very softly Judge MacLeod said, "She's *your* daughter, Anne. I know that. I don't want to take her away from you. I don't have the right. That's why I'm here. Because I know that she's your daughter, and I'm asking you to help me."

"To help you do *what*?"

"I don't know, precisely. Maybe simply to let me into the equation. I love Randall. I want to marry him. I want to be part of Tessa's life, and his life, which means being part of your life. I need your help. For one thing, I need your help in deciding when to tell Tessa I'm her birth mother."

Anne couldn't keep her voice steady. "If you marry Randall, if you tell Tessa *you're* her mother—she won't need me. She won't want me."

"I don't think that's true," Judge MacLeod disagreed, her voice low and respectful. "I really don't. You are the mother she knows, Anne. You are the one who held her and rocked her and cared for her when she was a baby." Tears came to her eyes. "You're the one whose smell she knows by instinct, whose voice is as familiar as her own. You're the one whose praise she needs, and the one she runs to when she's hurt. She knows you. You are her mother. You've been her mother for twelve years. I am a stranger to her."

Surprised and oddly comforted by the other woman's tears, unable to sit still any longer, Anne rose and paced the room. It was too much, too powerful, this strong blond woman who could be her sister, who was her daughter's birth mother, here in the room, saying these things.

"But Tessa will *like* you," Anne said bitterly. All at once her heart seemed to break. Turning to look at the other woman, she whispered, "Tessa hates me."

"Oh, I'm sure she doesn't—"

"She does. She disagrees with me all the time." Astonished at her confession, Anne put her cold fingertips on her cheeks and felt her own tears there.

Kelly MacLeod rose and went to Anne, standing near her but not touching her. "*Of course* she hates you. *Of course* she disagrees with you. She's twelve years old. You're her *mother*. You're the person she has to rebel against. Didn't you ever hate your mother? Didn't you ever rebel against her?"

Anne choked a laugh out at the thought of Sarah, frustrating, infuriating, hopeless Sarah. Her mother. She was a better mother to Tessa than Sarah had been to her—wasn't she?

"If Tessa didn't love you as completely as she does, she couldn't rebel against you. If you weren't so important to her, she wouldn't hate you!"

Anne turned her back on the other woman. She put her hands to her face, but they did not hold back the words. "Tessa isn't rebelling," she whispered. "She's stopped rebelling. She's being very good. She's being perfect."

"Oh, Anne—"

"She fainted in school yesterday." Anne wiped her cheeks with her hands. Bleakly she turned to stare at Kelly MacLeod. "The nurse told me she's not getting enough to eat. She's malnourished. My own child."

Kelly drew in a deep breath, looking shocked and sad.

"I've tried *so hard* to do what's right. You know how cruel children can be, teasing one another for the slightest flaw! You know how easy it is to gain weight. And Randall is such a big man, and he's her biological father—I was afraid she would be *big*. Fat. And children would tease her."

"I know," Kelly agreed.

"But I never meant for this to happen." Anne shuddered with revulsion. "Sometimes I think that nature knew what it was doing when it prevented me from having my own children."

"That's nonsense!" Kelly exclaimed. "Don't even *think* that way. No mother does everything perfectly. No father does, either. We're all only human, we all have to just feel our way along, trying to do our best."

Anne looked at Kelly. She felt infinitely tired. "That's kind of you to say."

Kelly said, "It's true."

"You think I haven't ruined Tessa?"

"You know you haven't."

Anne walked to her desk, opened a drawer, and took out a box of tissue. She held it out to Kelly, who took one and blew her nose and wiped her face while Anne did the same thing. Anne straightened her dress. Then she sat down at her desk. Immediately she felt better, stronger, in control. Having the large, ornate, majestic piece of furniture between her and this other woman was exactly what she needed. She took a deep breath.

"All right, then, tell me again what you want."

Kelly MacLeod sank into a chair facing the desk. She looked at Anne with a level stare and said, "I want you to be my friend. I want to marry Randall someday. I want to be Tessa's stepmother, and someday I want to tell her that I'm her birth mother. But not right away. Not until the three of us agree the time is right."

Anne passed her hand over her forehead. "It's all so peculiar. So abnormal."

"What? That she'll have three adults to love her? As well as Mont and your parents? Oh, yes, there's also my half sister, Felicity. She's fifteen, and living with me now. God only knows how those two will get along." Kelly leaned forward. "Anne. There's no one right kind of family. No normal family. No perfect family. I've seen children living happily with their grandparents. With stepparents. With uncles and aunts and cousins. I've seen two women, living together, adopt a baby and raise a happy child, and I've seen two men, living together, do the same thing. I've seen a single man adopt his nephew and niece when their parents died in a car accident. I've seen a single woman adopt a little girl who was orphaned." She pressed her case. "You've read about all this. This isn't new to you. And it's only going to get more complicated with developing technology. And who is to say what's right or wrong? Certainly it took the three of us to bring Tessa into this world, and you must agree that was the right thing to do. What would be wrong, if the three of us who created her, loved her and cared about her, worked together in her best interests?"

Anne stared back. This woman wanted to share her daughter's life. That was terrifying. And yet, this young woman was a judge. She was intelligent, well educated, and reasonable. God knew she was articulate.

"But we won't agree on everything," Anne protested. "We'll *fight*."

"I'm sure we will," Kelly replied honestly. "But if you and I have learned anything in our careers, it's how to compromise. And we'll be doing it for Tessa."

Anne rose. "This is a lot to throw at me all at once. I need some time to think."

Kelly stood. "Of course. Here are my phone numbers, in case you want to call and talk to me about anything." Taking a card from her purse, she laid it on Anne's desk.

Anne stared at the white piece of paper marring the serene perfection of her desk. Picking it up, she slipped it into the middle drawer without looking at it. "It's Randall I need to speak with."

"Of course."

They walked down the hall in silence. Anne opened the door and stood back to let the other woman pass.

Instead, Kelly stopped and looked around her, at the gleaming, orderly entrance hall with its polished table and the stern oil portraits of Anne's grandparents. "This is a beautiful house," she said.

"Yes, it is." Anne's tone was cool.

"Thank you for seeing me."

Anne didn't reply.

Anne watched the other woman walk across the drive and settle in her car. So that, she thought, was what Tessa would look like when she was grown.

Something moved in Anne's heart. It was painful. It

was strangely exciting. It was like a terrible fear, and the oddest kind of hope. It was, she imagined, how a woman felt on the delivery table, clutching a nurse's hand for support. Perhaps this was how one of the women Anne worked for would feel, a single mother living on welfare, needing help feeding or educating or protecting her child, when one of the programs that Anne was fighting for was passed and implemented. When that woman knew with relief that someone out there was on her side. When she realized she would no longer have to do this alone, this challenging, chartless, heartbreaking job of *being a mother*.

FIFTEEN

SATURDAY MORNING FELICITY, WITH A face like a storm cloud, flung herself into the front seat of Kelly's Subaru.

"Felicity," Kelly said. "Please. I'm asking you as nicely as I know how. Be pleasant."

"I am pleasant," Felicity growled. Reaching forward, she snapped on the radio and hit the dial until she found a hard rock station.

Kelly sighed. Was this how it was going to be for the next few years? "I just don't understand why you object so strenuously to spending one day outside in the sunshine."

"Because," Felicity said through gritted teeth. "I'd rather be with my friends."

"You were with Sly last night. You've been with your new friends in school. You're having Jamie over to spend the night tonight. I don't think one afternoon is so tragic. Come on, Fel. Give it a chance. You might even like these people."

"Why, because you do?"

"As a matter of fact, yes. I mean, my judgment isn't completely terrible, is it? After all, I like *you*."

Felicity moaned and threw her head back so hard Kelly was surprised the headrest didn't fly out the back window.

"Look," Kelly persisted, keeping her voice as rational as possible, "you've met Randall. You think he's nice enough, don't you?"

Felicity shrugged.

"And I've met his father, Mont, who is as sweet an old dear as ever walked the planet."

"Yeah, I am so dying to meet some dried-up old geezer."

"Don't be ageist," Kelly snapped. "Mont Madison's a doctor. He has a farm. He's working on a book. He's not a dried-up old geezer."

"Whatever."

"And Randall's daughter, Tessa, will be there." Kelly swallowed. "I haven't met her, but I'll bet she's really nice."

"Oh, goodie. A twelve-year-old. Gee, maybe we'll play dollies."

Kelly snapped. "Felicity Lambrousco! What the hell has gotten into you? I've been as nice to you as humanly possible over the past few weeks. And in return you act like one of Satan's spawn."

"So fine. Send me back to René."

"What?" Kelly looked over at the adolescent huddling inside her storm cloud of emotion. Felicity's face was blotchy and sullen.

"Oh, Fel." Kelly reached over to touch Felicity's hand. Felicity snatched it away. "What is going on in your convoluted little brain?"

Felicity's black mascaraed lashes glittered with tears. "You're going to marry this Randall guy."

"Maybe. Yes, it's possible that I am going to marry this Randall guy. It's very possible that sometime within the next year or so I'll marry him and move out to live on his farm. And if I do, Felicity, you're moving with me. You're living with me, wherever I go, whether you like it or not."

"You can't make me," Felicity growled.

"Hey, you know what? I'm a *judge*. I know quite a few people in high places. I bet I *can* make you stay with me, at least until you're an adult."

"You wouldn't do that."

"Of course I would. I've lived too long without you, Fel. I'm not letting you get away. Ever." Reaching over, she took Felicity's hand. This time, Felicity let her keep it.

"Do you think she'll want to ride, Dad?"

Tessa was wired, a spinning mass of nervous energy. She didn't care about meeting Dad's woman friend. It was the girl she was bringing with her. A fifteen-year-old. Tessa was nearly puking with nervousness. *Felicity*—such a cool name. Tessa's dad had met her, said she was nice, in a Goth sort of way. Tessa thought she'd die with excitement. She'd never known anyone who was Goth.

"I don't know if she's ever ridden before, Tessa," her father said. The Burchardts had brought over a trailer-load of hay. Randall and Tessa's grandfather were in the barn with pitchforks, lifting the bales off the trailer, stacking them in the loft for winter. The air smelled as sweet as spring.

Tessa groaned and twisted her hands. Would Felicity think Tessa was cool if she arrived to find her on a horse, or would she think she was dinky? Neither one of the horses was exactly Black Beauty.

"Tessa?" Mont called down. "Would you do me a favor and bring me a glass of water?"

"Sure, Grandpops."

Tessa raced into the kitchen, glad for something to do. The kitchen smelled even better than the outside. Mont had made coffeecake this morning, one of Madeline's recipes, with walnuts and brown sugar and tons of butter. He'd made two, actually, and good thing, because Tessa had already eaten almost half of one.

She got a glass down from the cupboard, then another one. Dad was probably thirsty, too. As she stood, holding them under the tap, she looked at the postcard held to the refrigerator with magnets. Two different shots of Washington, D.C. One at day, one at night.

Tessa's mother *rocked*. She was doing so much cool stuff. Her picture was in the *Globe* like all the time. People thought she might be a senator someday, or even a vice president of the entire United States. Everyone at school wanted to be Tessa's friend because of her mother. And the weird thing was that now when Anne took Tessa with her to do her political stuff, Tessa actually enjoyed it. She didn't even mind wearing those dorky dresses. And her mom was happy, so happy she hadn't even criticized Tessa for gaining weight.

As Tessa carried the glasses of water out to the barn, she saw a silver Subaru come down the road. She looked down at her tummy. What if this Felicity was, like, *thin*? Would she think Tessa was fat? Would she think that Tessa, in her jeans and T-shirt and riding boots, was geeky? Would she even talk to Tessa? Maybe she'd just snort and roll her eyes and go in the house and watch television. What would Tessa do then? She was kind of terrified.

Kelly steered her car down the gravel lane, bringing it neatly to a stop next to Randall's Jeep.

"Look. Horses," Felicity said. "Cool."

"Ummm," Kelly agreed. Her voice wasn't working. Her face felt hot. She hadn't been this excited, and hopeful, and terrified since—well, since her swearing-in ceremony.

Felicity got out of the car, slamming the door. Kelly got out and went to the trunk. She'd brought cider doughnuts she and Felicity had made the night before. She lifted the basket out, glad to have something to do.

"Hey!" Randall came out of the barn. He wore jeans, boots, and a blue denim shirt with bits of straw stuck to it here and there. His hair was as golden as the sun, and over the past few days he'd acquired a sunburn across his nose and cheeks. "Hi, Felicity." Without any self-consciousness at all, he enveloped the girl in a hug. "Good to see you."

"You, too," Felicity muttered.

"Hey, beauty," Randall said to Kelly. He hugged her and kissed the top of her head.

"We made doughnuts," Kelly said.

He looked down at the basket in her arms. "Great."

"Kelly!" Mont strode toward them, a handsome man, tall and distinguished-looking. "Good to see you again, Kelly. And you must be Felicity."

Felicity stood paralyzed.

Mont didn't try to shake Felicity's hand, but gave her a great big smile, then went right up to Kelly and gave her a hug. "How's business, Judge?"

"Frantic," Kelly said. "It was an exhausting week. I can't tell you how glad I am to be out here in the fresh air."

"Well, as a doctor, can I advise some physical therapy? There's nothing like good hard labor to take your mind off your work."

"Pay no attention to him, Kelly," Randall said, laughing. "He's just trying to get out of lifting all those bales of hay."

"Actually," Mont said, "I was thinking that if Kelly could help you, I could take Felicity and Tessa with me over to the Meyers'. They've got some six-week-old pups. Lab-and-husky mix. I was thinking we ought to get one for the farm. Maybe two." He looked at Felicity. "Do you like dogs, Felicity?"

"I don't know," Felicity replied. "I've never had one."

"Ever ridden a horse?"

"No."

"City girl, huh. Well, come on over and meet our

horses. Don't be afraid. They're big, but pet their noses and give them an apple, and they'll follow you anywhere."

"Where did Tessa go?" Randall asked.

"I don't know. Tessa?"

Mont led them across the yard to the pasture. They leaned on the white boards, looking at the two horses who grazed idly nearby, their ears pricked in expectation.

"The gray one's Blue Boy," Mont said. "The chestnut's Frisk."

At their names, the horses snickered softly and ambled over to the fence, sniffing the air.

Behind them, the screen door slammed. They all turned to see Tessa coming toward them, a bunch of carrots in her hands.

Her blond hair was braided and fastened with colored rubber bands. She wore a baggy T-shirt, blue jeans, and boots. Her cheeks were pink, her nose sprinkled with freckles. She was tall for her age, and slender.

"Hi," she said, approaching the group.

"Tessa," Randall said. "This is my friend, Kelly. And her sister, Felicity."

"Hi," Tessa said to Kelly, flashing a careless smile. Her attention was drawn to Felicity, lounging against a fence-post. "Do you like to ride horses?"

"I don't know," Felicity said. "I've never tried."

"Want to try?"

Felicity shrugged. "I don't know. I guess."

"Here," Tessa said, holding out a carrot. "You give one to Frisk, and I'll give one to Blue Boy. Then they'll be our slaves for life."

Felicity took a carrot.

"Like this," Tessa said, holding the carrot flat on the palm of her hand.

Tessa stretched out her hand. Felicity stretched out hers. The horses leaned out their powerful necks, drew back their rubbery lips, and picked the carrots up in their long yellow teeth.

"Good boys," Mont said.

"Their breath tickles!" Felicity whispered.

"Want another?" Tessa asked.

"Yeah." Felicity reached out and took another carrot from Tessa. "Here, Frisk," she said.

Randall looked over at Kelly and smiled.

Some days, Kelly thought, are more important than others. Some days you wake with your heart pounding and your hopes higher than the sky. Some days you know you are exactly where you are meant to be.